Praise for Susan Wiggs and *Summer by the Sea*

"Susan Wiggs paints the details of human relationships with the finesse of a master."

—Jodi Picoult

"This is the perfect beach read."

—Debbie Macomber

"Susan Wiggs writes with bright assurance, humor and compassion."

—Luanne Rice

"[Wiggs's] keen awareness of sensory detail ensures that the scents and sounds of Rosa's kitchen are just as palpable as the heady attraction between the protagonists."

—*Publishers Weekly*

"Wiggs is one of our best observers of stories of the heart… She knows how to capture emotion on virtually every page of every book."

—*Salem Statesman Journal*

Also by #1 *New York Times* bestselling author Susan Wiggs

For a complete list of all titles by Susan Wiggs,
visit www.susanwiggs.com.

SUSAN WIGGS

Summer
by the Sea

mira

ISBN-13: 978-0-7783-1205-5

Summer by the Sea

First published in 2004. This edition published in 2022.

For questions and comments about the quality of this book, please contact us at CustomerService@Harlequin.com.

Mira
22 Adelaide St. West, 41st Floor
Toronto, Ontario M5H 4E3, Canada
BookClubbish.com

Printed in U.S.A.

Recycling programs
for this product may
not exist in your area.

Dear Reader,

They say you never, ever forget your first time. It's one of those "aha" moments when the world shifts, and afterward, nothing is quite the same.

And for me, that moment happened in a bookstore in Texas, circa early 1980s. That was where I discovered romance novels. I always knew I would write; that was clear from the time I learned to talk. But as an emerging novelist, I hadn't found my "voice" as a writer. Fresh out of graduate school, I had been trying to figure out what sort of book I longed to write—a literary masterpiece, a dark thriller, a shoot-'em-up Western?

To be honest, the reader in me was ready for a fabulous sweep-you-away novel to give my brain a vacation. A book called *Shanna* by Kathleen Woodiwiss, with a tangerine cover and lush, sexy illustration, jumped off the shelf and into my cart. I dove right in and didn't come up for air until I'd savored every thrilling word.

But by the end of the first chapter, I had an epiphany. *This* was the sort of book I was yearning to write. I wanted to take the reader on a fabulous journey filled with love, adventure, danger, heartfelt emotion and pulse-pounding passion. Not long afterward, my first novel was published, and it was filled with—you guessed it—all of the above.

Summer by the Sea has everything I was looking for that day so long ago. There's a lonely young woman who still dreams of the boy who stole her heart, a nostalgic beach restaurant offering delicious shore dinners (recipes included), and an emotional ride filled with laughter and tears. I'm thrilled that it's available again, because it's one of those books that has been sprinkled with fairy dust from the very start, thanks to readers. It's been a national bestseller and a winner of the RITA® Award for Best Contemporary Romance. It's been translated around the globe, and now it's heading right back where it belongs… into the hands of my favorite people in the world—readers like you.

Happy reading,

Susan Wiggs

www.SusanWiggs.com

In memory of Trixie, beloved companion, faithful friend.

Summer
by the Sea

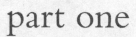

part one

ANTIPASTO

Antipasto: The Italian word for a snack served before a meal. These are dishes to pique the appetite, not quench it. Antipasto literally means "before the meal." Mamma used to say it was the anti-noise course because my brothers, Robert and Sal, would be so busy stuffing their faces that they'd forget to complain about being hungry.

Caponata

This has an excellent flavor and makes a very nice presentation on a perfect leaf of lettuce, not that Robert and Sal ever gave a hoot about presentation. And it's even quite low in calories, not that guys care about that, either. Serve this as a traditional antipasto with a good crusty Italian bread and a glass of chilled Pinot Grigio.

Peel and dice an eggplant, toss with salt, put in a colander and drain for at least a half hour. Then heat up a heavy skillet and add 1/4 cup olive oil, a small onion, chopped, and a stick of celery, also chopped. Add the eggplant and sauté. Finally, add three chopped tomatoes, three minced anchovies, a pinch of sugar, 1/4 cup wine vinegar and a spoonful of capers (the best ones come from Pantelleria Island). If your family likes olives, add some of those, too, along with a pinch of red pepper flakes. Simmer for ten minutes. Cool, then store overnight in a glass container. For a smoother spreading consistency, you can whirl the mixture in the food processor, but don't overdo it. Things that are too smooth lose their character.

one

Rosa Capoletti knew that tonight was the night. Jason Aspoll was going to pop the question. The setting was perfect—a starlit summer evening, an elegant seaside restaurant, the sounds of crystal and silver gently clinking over quiet murmurs of conversation. At Jason's request, the Friday night trio was playing "Lovetown," and a few dreamy couples swayed to the nostalgic melody.

Candlelight flickered over their half-empty champagne flutes, illuminating Jason's endearingly nervous face. He was sweating a little, and his eyes darted with barely suppressed trepidation. Rosa could tell he wanted to get this right.

She knew he was wondering, *Should I reach across the table? Go down on one knee, or is that too hokey?*

Go for it, Jason, she wanted to urge him. Nothing's too hokey when it's true love.

She also knew the ring lay nestled in a black velvet box, concealed in the inner pocket of his dinner jacket, right next to his racing heart.

Come on, Jason, she thought. *Don't be afraid.*

And then, just as she was starting to worry that he'd chickened out, he did it. He went down on one knee.

A few nearby diners shifted in their chairs to look on fondly. Rosa held her breath while his hand stole inside his jacket.

The music swelled. He took the box from his pocket and she saw his mouth form the words: *Will you marry me?*

He held out the ring box, opening the hinged lid to reveal the precious offering. His hand shook a little. He still didn't know for sure if she would have him.

Silly man, thought Rosa. Didn't he know the answer would be—

"Table seven sent back the risotto," said Leo, the headwaiter, holding a thick china bowl in front of Rosa.

"Leo, for crying out loud," she said, craning her neck to see past him. "Can't you tell I'm busy here?" She pushed him aside in time to watch her best friend, Linda Lipschitz, stand up from the table and fling her arms around Jason.

"Yes," Linda said, although from across the dining room Rosa had to read her lips. "Yes, *absolutely.*"

Atta girl, thought Rosa, her eyes misting.

Leo followed her gaze to the embracing couple. "Sweet," he said. "Now what about my risotto?"

"Take it back to the kitchen," Rosa said. "I knew the mango chutney was a bad idea, anyway, and you can tell Butch I said so." She let Leo deal with it as she walked across the dining room. Linda was wreathed in smiles and tears. Jason looked positively blissful and, perhaps, weak with relief.

"Rosa, you won't believe what just happened," Linda said.

Rosa dabbed at her eyes. "I think I can guess."

Linda held out her hand, showing off a glittering marquise-cut diamond in a gold cathedral setting.

"Oh, honey." Rosa hugged Linda and gave Jason a kiss

on the cheek. "Congratulations, you two," she said. "I'm so happy for you."

She'd helped Jason pick out the ring, told him Linda's size, selected the music and menu, ordered Linda's favorite flowers for the table. They'd set the scene in every possible way. Rosa was good at things like this—creating events around the most special moments in people's lives.

Other people's lives.

Linda was babbling, already making plans. "We'll drive over to see Jason's folks on Sunday, and then get everyone together to set a date—"

"Slow down, my friend," Rosa said with a laugh. "How about you dance with your fiancé?"

Linda turned to Jason, her eyes shining. "My fiancé. God, I love the sound of that."

Rosa gave the couple a gentle shove toward the dance floor. As he pulled Linda into his arms, Jason looked over her shoulder and mouthed a thank-you to Rosa. She waved, dabbed at her eyes again and headed for the kitchen. Back to work.

She was smiling as she crossed the nonskid mat and entered the kitchen through the swinging doors. Quiet elegance gave way to controlled chaos. Glaring lights and flaming grills illuminated the crush of prep workers, line cooks and the sous-chef hurrying back and forth between stainless steel counters. Waiters tapped their feet, checking orders before stepping through the soundproofed doors that protected the serenity of the dining room from male shouts and clattering dishes.

The revved-up energy of the kitchen was fueled by testosterone, but Rosa knew how to hold her own here. She walked through a gauntlet of aproned men with huge knives or vats of boiling water, pivoting around each other in their nightly ballet. A stream from a hose roared against the dishwashing sink, and hot drafts from the Imperial grill licked like dragon's breath at precisely 1010°F.

"Wait," she said as a prep worker passed by with a plated steak that had been liberally sprinkled with tripepper confetti.

"What?" The worker, a recent hire from Newport, paused at the counter.

"We don't garnish the steaks here."

"Come again?"

"This is premium meat, our signature cut. Serve it without the garnish."

"I'll remember that," he said, and set the plate on the counter for a server to pick up.

She planted herself in front of him. "Go back and replate the steak, please. No garnish."

"But—"

Rosa glared at him with fire in her eyes. *Don't back down,* she cautioned herself. *Don't blink.*

"You got it," he said, scowling as he returned to the prep area.

"Well?" asked Lorenzo "Butch" Buchello, whose fresh Italian cuisine was drawing in patrons from as far away as New York and Boston.

"Yep." Rosa grinned and selected a serrated knife from the array affixed to a steel grid on the wall. "Went down on one knee and everything."

Neither of them stopped working as they chatted. He was coordinating dessert while she arranged fluffy white peasant bread in a basket.

"Good for them," said Butch.

"They're really in love," Rosa said. "I got all choked up watching them."

"Ever the incurable romantic," Butch said, piping chocolate ganache around the profiteroles.

"Ha, there's a cure for it," Shelly Warren cut in, whisking behind them to pick up her order.

"It's called marriage," Rosa said.

Shelly gave her a high-five. She had been married for ten years and claimed that her night job waiting tables was an escape from endless hours of watching the Golf Channel until her eyes glazed over.

"Hey, don't knock it till you've tried it, Rosa," said Butch. "In fact, what about that guy you were dating—Dean what's his name?"

"Oh, actually, he did want to get married," she explained.

Butch's eyes lit up. "Hey! Well, there you go—"

"Just not to me."

His face fell. "I'm sorry. I didn't know."

"It's all right. He joins a long and venerable line of suitors who didn't suit."

"I'm starting to see a pattern here," Butch said. He took a wire whisk to a bowl of custard and Marsala, creating an order of his famous zabaglione. "You run them off and then say they didn't suit."

She finished up with the bread baskets. "Not tonight, Butch. This is Linda's moment. Send them a tiramisu and your congratulations, okay?"

She headed back to the dining room and went over to the podium, which faced the main entrance. It was a perfect Friday night at Celesta's-by-the-Sea. All the tables in the multi-level dining room were oriented toward the view of the endless sea, and were set with fresh flowers, crisp linens, good china and flatware.

This was the sort of scene she used to dream about back when the place was a run-down pizza joint. Couples danced to the smooth beat of a soft blues number, the drummer's muted cymbals shimmering with a sensual resonance. Out on the deck, people stood listening to the waves and looking at the stars. For the past three years running, Celesta's had been voted "Best Place to Propose" by *Coast* magazine, and tonight was a perfect example of the reason for its charm—sea breezes, sand and surf, a natural backdrop for the award-winning dining room.

"Did you cry?" asked Vince, the host, stepping up beside her. They'd known each other since childhood—she, Vince and Linda. They'd gone through school together, inseparable. Now he was the best-looking maître d' in South County. He was tall and slender, flawlessly groomed in an Armani suit and Gucci shoes. Rimless glasses highlighted his darkly lashed eyes.

"Of course I cried," Rosa said. "Didn't you?"

"Maybe," he admitted with a fond smile in Linda's direction. "A little. I love seeing her so happy."

"Yeah. Me, too."

"So that's two of us down, one to go," he said.

She rolled her eyes. "Not you, too."

"Butch has already been at you?"

"What do you two do, lie awake at night discussing my love life?"

"No, sweetie. Your lack of one."

"Give me a break, okay?" She spoke through a smile as a party of four left the restaurant. She and Vince had perfected the art of bickering while appearing utterly congenial.

"Please come again," Vince said, his expression so warm that the two women did a double-take. Glancing down at the computer screen discreetly set beneath the surface of the podium, he checked the status of their tab. "Three bottles of Antinori."

Rosa gave a blissful sigh. "Sometimes I love this job."

"You always love this job. Too much, if you ask me."

"You're not my analyst, Vince."

"Ringrazi il cielo," he muttered. "You couldn't pay me enough."

"Hey."

"Kidding," he assured her. "Good night, folks," he said to a departing threesome. "Thanks so much for coming."

Rosa surveyed her domain with a powerful but weary pride. Celesta's-by-the-Sea was the place people came to fall in love. It was also Rosa's own emotional landscape; it structured her days and weeks and years. She had poured all her energy into the restaurant, creating a place where people marked the most important events of their lives—engagements, graduations, bar mitzvahs, anniversaries, promotions. They came to escape the rush and rigors of everyday life, never knowing that each subtle detail of the place, from the custom alabaster lampshades to the imported chenille chair covers, had been contrived to create an air of luxury and comfort, just for them.

Rosa knew such attention to detail, along with Butch's incomparable cuisine, had elevated her restaurant to one of the best in the county, perhaps in the entire state. The focal point of the place was a hammered steel bar, its edges fluted like waves. The bar, which she'd commissioned from a local artisan, was backed by a sheet of blue glass lit from below. At its center was a nautilus seashell, the light flickering over and through the whorls and chambers. People seemed drawn to its mysterious iridescence, and often asked where it came from, and if it was real. Rosa knew the answer, but she never told.

She checked the time on the screen without being obvious. None of the servers wore watches and there was no clock in sight. People relaxing here shouldn't notice the passing of time. But the small computer screen indicated 10:00 p.m. She didn't expect too much more business, except perhaps in the bar.

She could tell, with a sweep of her gaze, that tonight's till

would be sky-high. "I'm so glad summer's here," she said to
Vince.

"You know, for normal people, summer means vacation
time. For us, it means our lives belong to Celesta's."

"This is normal." Hard work had never bothered Rosa. Outside the restaurant there was not much to her life, and she had
convinced herself that she liked it that way. She had Pop, of
course, who at sixty-five was as independent as ever, accusing
her of fussing over him. Her brother Robert was in the navy,
currently stationed with his family overseas. Her other brother,
Sal, was also in the navy, a Catholic priest serving as chaplain.
Her father and brothers, nieces and nephews, were her family.

But Celesta's was her life.

She stole a glance at Jason and Linda, and fancied she could
actually see stars in their eyes. Sometimes, when Rosa looked
at the happy couples holding hands across the tables in her restaurant, she felt a bittersweet ache. And then she always pretended, even to herself, that it didn't matter.

"I give you two months off every year," she pointed out
to Vince.

"Yeah, January and February."

"Best time of year in Miami," she reminded him. "Or are
you and Butch ready to give up your condo there?"

"All right, all right. I get your point. I wouldn't have it any
other—"

The sound of car doors slamming interrupted them. Rosa
sent another discreet look at the slanted computer screen under
the podium. Ten-fifteen.

She stepped back while Vince put on his trademark smile.
"So much for making an early night of it." The comment
slipped between his teeth, while his expression indicated he'd
been waiting all his life for the next group of patrons.

Rosa recognized them instantly. Not by name, of course.

The summer crowds at the shore were too huge for that. No, she recognized them because they were a "type." Summer people. The women exuded patrician poise and beauty. The tallest one wore her perfectly straight golden-blond hair caught, seemingly without artifice, in a thin band. Her couture clothes—a slim black skirt, silk blouse and narrow kid leather flats—had a subtle elegance. Her two friends were stylish clones of her, with uniformly sleek hair, pale makeup, sleeves artfully rolled back just so. They pulled off the look as only those to the manor born could.

Rosa and Vince had grown up sharing their summers with people like this. To the seasonal visitors, the locals existed for the sole purpose of serving those who belonged to the venerable old houses along the pristine, unspoiled shore just as their forebears had done a century before. They were the ones whose charity galas were covered by *Town & Country* magazine, whose weddings were announced in the *New York Times*. They were the ones who never thought about what life was like for the maid who changed their sheets, the fisherman who brought in the day's catch, the cleaners who ironed their Sea Isle cotton shirts.

Vince nudged her behind the podium. "Yachty. They practically scream Bailey's Beach."

Rosa had to admit, the women would not look out of place at the exclusive private beach at the end of Newport's cliff walk. "Be nice," she cautioned him.

"I was born nice."

The door opened and three men joined the women. Rosa offered the usual smile of greeting. Then her heart skipped a beat as her gaze fell upon a tall, sandy-haired man. No, it couldn't be, she told herself. She hoped—prayed—it was a trick of the light. But it wasn't, and her expression froze as recognition chilled her to the bone.

Big deal, she thought, trying not to hyperventilate. She was bound to run into him sooner or later.

"Uh-oh," Vince muttered, assuming a stance that was now more protective than welcoming. "Here come the Montagues."

Rosa struggled against panic, but she was losing the battle. *You're a grown woman,* she reminded herself. *You're totally in control.*

That was a lie. In the blink of an eye, she was eighteen again, aching and desperate over the boy who'd broken her heart.

"I'll tell them we're closed," Vince said.

"You'll do nothing of the sort," Rosa hissed at him.

"I'll beat the crap out of him."

"You'll offer them a table, and make it a good one." Straightening her shoulders, Rosa looked across the room and locked eyes with a man she hadn't seen in ten years, a man she hoped she would never see again.

two

"You asked for it." As though flipping a switch, Vince turned on the charm, stepping forward to greet the latest arrivals. "Welcome to Celesta's," he said. "Do you have a reservation?"

"No, we just want to drink," said one of the men, and the women snickered at his devastating wit.

"Of course," said Vince, stepping back to gesture them toward the bar. "Please seat yourself."

The men and their dates headed to the bar. Rosa thought about the nautilus shell, displayed like a museum artifact. Would he recognize it? Did she care?

Just when she thought she'd survived the moment, she realized one man held back from the group. He was just standing there, watching her intently, with a look that made her shiver.

Her task, of course, was simple. She had to pretend he had no effect on her. This was easier said than done, though, because she had trouble keeping her feelings in. Long ago, she'd resigned herself to the fact that she was a walking cliché—a curly-haired, big-breasted, emotional Italian American.

However, cool disregard was the only message she wanted to send at the moment. She knew with painful certainty that the opposite of love was not hate, but indifference.

"Hello, Alex," she said.

"Rosa." He lifted the corner of his mouth in a half smile.

He'd been drinking. She wasn't sure how she knew. But her practiced eye took in the tousled sandy hair, the boyish face now etched with character, the sea-blue eyes settling a gaze on her that, even now, made her shiver. He looked fashionably rumpled in an Oxford shirt, chinos and Top-Siders.

She couldn't bear to see him again. And oh, she hated that about herself. She wasn't supposed to be this way. She was supposed to be the indomitable Rosa Capoletti, named last year's Restaurateur of the Year by Condé Nast. Self-made Rosa Capoletti, the woman who had it all—a successful business, wonderful friends, a loving family. She was strong and independent, liked and admired. Influential, even. She headed the merchants' committee for the Winslow Chamber of Commerce.

But Rosa had a secret, a terrible secret she prayed no one would discover. She had never gotten over Alexander Montgomery.

"'Of all the gin joints in all the towns in all the world, he walks into mine,'" she said. She pulled it off, too, with jaunty good humor.

"You know each other?" The woman with the Marcia Brady hair had come back to claim him.

He didn't take his eyes off Rosa. She refused to allow herself to look away.

"We did," he said. "A long time ago."

Rosa couldn't stand the tension, although she struggled to appear perfectly relaxed as she offered an impersonal smile. "Enjoy your evening," she said, every bit the hostess.

He looked at her a moment longer. Then he said, "Thanks. I will," and he stepped into the bar.

She held her smile in place as he and the others settled into an upholstered banquette. The women looked around the bar with surprised appreciation. The norm in these parts consisted of beach shacks, fried food, dated seaside kitsch. Celesta's one-of-a-kind bar, the understated handsomeness of the furnishings and the unparalleled view created an ambience of rare luxury.

Alex took a seat at the end of the table. The tall woman flirted hard with him, leaning toward him and tossing her hair.

Over the years, Rosa had kept up with his life without really meaning to. It was hard to ignore him when she spotted his face smiling out from the pages of a newspaper or magazine. "The thinking woman's hunk," one society columnist dubbed him. "Drives Formula One race cars and speaks fluent Japanese…" He kept company with billionaires and politicians. He did good works—funding a children's hospital, underwriting loan programs for low-income people. Getting engaged.

Pharmaceutical heiress Portia van Deusen was the perfect match for him, according to the people-watchers. With a slight feeling of voyeuristic shame, Rosa had read the breathless raves of society columnists. Portia was always described as "stunning" and Alex as "impeccable." Both of them had the social equivalent of champion bloodlines. Their wedding, of course, was going to be the event of the season.

Except that it never happened. The papers ceased to mention them as a couple. The engagement was "off." Ordinary people were left to speculate about what had happened. There was a whisper that she had left him. And she appeared so quickly on the arm of a different man—older, perhaps even wealthier—that rumor had it she'd found greener pastures.

"Vince said he offered to beat the crap out of him," said Shelly, holding aloft a tray of desserts and espresso.

So much for privacy. In a place like Celesta's, rumors zinged around like rubber bullets.

"As if he could stand to have one hair out of place." In spite of herself, Rosa smiled, picturing Vince in a fight. The sentiment was touching, though. Like everyone who had seen the wreckage Alex had left in his wake, Vince was protective of Rosa.

"Are you all right?" Shelly asked.

"I'm fine. You can tell that to anyone who's wondering."

"That would be everybody," Shelly said.

"For Pete's sake, we broke up eons ago," Rosa said. "I'm a big girl now. I can handle seeing a former boyfriend."

"Good," Shelly said, "because he just ordered a bottle of Cristal."

From the corner of her eye, Rosa saw the sommelier pop the cork of the bottle, listed at $300 on the menu. One of the women at Alex's table—the flirt—giggled and leaned against him as he took a taste and nodded to Felix to pour. The six of them lifted their glasses, clinking them together.

Rosa turned away to say good-night to a departing couple. "I hope you enjoyed your evening," she said.

"We did," the woman assured her. "I read about this place in the *New York Times* 'Escape' section, and have always wanted to come here. It's even nicer than I expected."

"Thank you," Rosa said, silently blessing the *Times*. Travel writers and food critics were a picky lot, as a whole. But her kitchen had proven itself, again and again.

"Are you Celesta, then?" the woman asked as she drew on a light cotton wrap.

"No," Rosa said, her heart stumbling almost imperceptibly as she gestured at the lighted portrait that hung behind the podium next to the numerous awards. Celesta, in all her soft, hand-tinted beauty, gazed benevolently from the gilt frame. "She was my mother."

The woman smiled gently. "It's a wonderful place. I'm sure we'll be back."

"We'd love to have you."

When Rosa turned from the door, she used every bit of her willpower to keep from spying on Alex Montgomery. She knew he was watching her. She just knew it. She could feel his gaze like a phantom touch, finding her most vulnerable places.

They had said goodbye many years ago, and it was the sort of goodbye that was supposed to be permanent. She wondered what he was thinking, barging in on her like this.

"May I have this dance?" Jason Aspoll held out his hand to Rosa.

She smiled at him. It was a well-known fact that on most nights, near closing time, Rosa enjoyed getting out on the dance floor. It was good marketing. Show the public you like your place just as much as they do. Besides, Rosa did love dancing.

And she didn't like going home. There was nothing wrong with her place, except that it simply wasn't…lived in enough.

"I'd love to," she said to Jason, and slipped easily into his arms. The ensemble played "La Danza," and they swayed, grinning at each other like idiots.

"So you finally did it, you big goof," she said.

"I couldn't have done it without you."

"I know," she said breezily, then patted his arm. "Seriously, Jason, I'm honored that you asked for my help. It was fun."

"Well, I'm in awe. You managed everything perfectly, down to the last detail. Her favorite food was tonight's special, the ensemble kept playing songs she loves… You even had special flowers on all the tables. I didn't know Lily of the Valley was her favorite."

"In the future, knowing her favorites is your job." Rosa was always mystified that people simply didn't notice things about other people. She had once dated an airline pilot for five months, and he never learned how she took her coffee. Come to think of it, no man had ever bothered to learn that about her, except—

"How does Linda take her coffee?" she asked Jason suddenly.

"Hot?"

"Very funny. How does she like her coffee?"

"Linda drinks tea. She takes it with honey and lemon."

Rosa collapsed against him in exaggerated relief. "Thank God. You passed the test." She didn't mean to dart one tiny glance at Alex. It just happened. He was looking straight at her. Fine, then, she thought. Let him look.

"I didn't know there was a test," Jason whispered to her.

"There's always a test," she said. "Remember that."

The music wound down and then stopped. During the polite patter of applause, Linda joined them.

"I've come to claim my man," she said, slipping her hand into his.

"He's all yours." Rosa gave her a quick hug. "And that's for you. Congratulations, my friends. I wish you all the happiness in the world."

Linda jerked her head in the direction of Alex's table. "What the hell is he doing here?"

"Drinking a $300 bottle of champagne." Rosa held up a hand. "And that's all I have to say on the subject. Tonight is your night. You and Jason."

"You're meeting me for coffee tomorrow, though," Linda insisted. "And then you'll spill."

"Fine. I'll see you at Pegasus tomorrow. Now, take your man and go home."

"All right. Rosa, I know how much you did to make this

night special," said Linda. "I'll never be able to thank you enough."

Rosa beamed. The look on Linda's face was reward enough, but she said, "You can name your first child after me."

"Only if it's a girl."

She and Linda hugged one more time, and the happy couple left. The music started up again, Rosa went back to work and pretended not to see Alex ask the tall woman at his table to dance.

This was absurd, she thought. She was an adult now, not a wide-eyed kid fresh out of high school. She had every right to go over to him this minute and demand to know what he was doing here. Or for that matter, what he'd been doing since he'd said, "Have a nice life" and strolled off into the sunset.

Did he have a nice life? she wondered.

He certainly looked as though he did. He seemed relaxed with his friends—or maybe that was the champagne kicking in. He had an air of casual elegance that was not in the least affected. Even when she first met him, as a little boy, he'd had a certain aura about him. That in-born poise was a family trait, one she'd observed not just in Alex, but in his parents and sister, as well.

The quality was nothing so uncomplicated as mere snobbery. Rosa had encountered her share of that. No, the Montgomerys simply had an innate sense of their place in the world, and that place was at the top of the heap.

Except when it came to loving someone. He pretty much sucked at that.

Maybe he'd changed. His date certainly appeared hopeful as she undulated her *Sex and the City* body against his on the dance floor.

"You want I should break his kneecaps?" inquired a deep voice behind her.

Rosa smiled. "Not tonight, Teddy."

Teddy was in charge of security at the restaurant. In another sort of establishment, he'd be called a bouncer. The job required a thorough knowledge of digital alarms and surveillance, but he lived for the day he could wield those ham-sized fists on her behalf. "I got lots of footage of him on the security cameras," he informed her. "You can watch that if you want."

"No, I don't want," Rosa snapped, yet she could picture herself obsessively playing the tape, over and over again. "So does everybody in the place know the guy who once dumped me is here tonight?"

"Oh, yeah," he said unapologetically. "We had a meeting about it. We don't care how long ago it happened. He was harsh, Rosa. Damned harsh. What a dickwad."

"We were just kids—"

"Headed to college. That's pretty grown-up."

She'd never made it to college. Her staff probably had a meeting about that, too.

"He's a paying customer," she said. "That's all he is, so I wish everyone would quit trying to make such a big deal out of it. I don't like people discussing my personal affairs."

Teddy gently touched her shoulder. "It's okay, Rosa. We're talking about this because we care about you. Nobody wants to see you hurt."

"Then you've got nothing to worry about," she assured him. "I'm fine. I'm perfectly fine."

It became her mantra for the remainder of the evening, which was nearly over at last. The bartender's final call circulated, and the ensemble bade everyone good-night by playing their signature farewell number, a sweet and wistful arrangement of "As Time Goes By."

The last few customers circled the dance floor and then dispersed, heading off into the night, couples lost in each other and oblivious to the world. Rosa couldn't keep count of the times she had stood in the shadows and watched people fall in love right here on the premises. Celesta's was just that kind of place.

How'm I doing, Mamma?

Celesta, twenty years gone, would undoubtedly approve. The restaurant smelled like the kitchen of Rosa's childhood; the menu featured many of the dishes Celesta had once prepared with warmth, intense flavors and a certain uncomplicated contentment Rosa constantly tried to recapture. She wanted the restaurant to serve Italian comfort food, the kind that fed hidden hungers and left people full of fond remembrances.

She pretended to be busy as Alex and his friends left. Finally she let out the breath she hadn't known she was holding. When the last patron departed, so did the magic. The lights came up, revealing crumbs and smudges on the floors and tables, soot on the candle chimneys, dropped napkins and flatware. In the absence of music and with the kitchen doors propped open, the clank and crash of dishes rang through the building.

"Ka-*ching*," Vince said as he printed out a spreadsheet summarizing the night's receipts. "Biggest till of the year so far." He hesitated, then added, "Your dumbshit ex-boyfriend left a whopper tip."

"He's not my ex-anything," she insisted. "He's ancient history."

"Yeah, but I bet he's still a dumbshit."

"I wouldn't know. He's a complete stranger to me. I wish everyone would get that through their heads."

"We won't," he assured her. "Can't you see we're dying here, Rosa? We're starved for gossip."

"Find someone else to gossip about."

"We were all watching him with the new security cameras," Vince said.

"I can't believe you guys."

"Teddy can zoom in on anything."

"Good for him." Her head pounded, and she rubbed her temples.

"I got this, honey," Vince said. "I'll close tonight."

She offered a thin smile. "Thanks." She started to remind him about the seal on the walk-in fridge, the raccoons in the Dumpster, but stopped herself. She'd been working on her control-freak impulses.

As she left through the back entrance, she wished she'd thought to grab a sweater before rushing out today. The afternoon had been hot; now the chill air raised goose bumps on her bare arms.

Debris from last week's windstorm had been cleared away, but broken trees and fallen branches still lay along the periphery of the parking lot. The power had been knocked out for hours, but the cameras had come through unscathed.

Her heels rang on the pavement as she headed for her car, a red Alfa Romeo Spider equipped with an extravagant stereo system. As she used the remote on her key chain to unlock the driver's side door, a shadow overtook her.

She stopped walking and looked up to see Alex, somehow not surprised to find him standing in the dull glow of the parking lot lights. "What, you're stalking me now?"

"Do you feel stalked?"

"Yeah, I generally do when a man approaches me in a deserted parking lot at midnight. Creeps me out."

"I can see how that could happen."

"You should hear what they're saying about you inside."

"What's that?"

"Oh, all sorts of things. Dumbshit, dickwad. Stuff like that. Two different guys offered to break your kneecaps. They liked your tip, though."

He offered that crooked smile again, the one that used to practically stop her heart. "It's good to know you surrounded yourself with quality people."

She gestured at the security camera mounted on a light pole.

"What are you doing?" Alex asked.

"Trying to let my quality people know I don't need rescuing." It was late. She couldn't keep batting this pointless conversation back and forth. She just wanted to go home. Besides, it was taking every bit of energy she possessed to pretend he had no effect on her. "What are you doing here, Alex?" she asked.

He showed her his hand, which held a palm-sized cell phone. "I was calling a taxi. Is the local service as bad now as it used to be?"

"A taxi? You'd be better off hitchhiking."

"That's supposed to be dangerous. And I know you wouldn't want to put a customer in danger."

"Where are your friends, anyway?"

"Went back to Newport."

"And you're headed...?"

"To the house on Ocean Road."

No one in his family had visited the place in twelve years. It was like a haunted mansion, perched there at the edge of the ocean, an abandoned, empty shell. Wondering what had brought him back after all this time, she shivered. Before she realized what he was doing, he slipped his jacket around her shoulders. She pulled away. "I don't—"

"Just take it."

She tried not to be aware of his body heat, clinging to the lining of the jacket. "Your friends couldn't give you a ride?"

"I didn't want one. I was waiting for you... Rosa."

"What, so I can give you a lift?" Her voice rose with incredulity.

"Thanks," he said. "Don't mind if I do." He headed for the Alfa Spider.

Rosa stood in the amber glow of the floodlights, trying to figure out what to do. She was tempted to peel out without another word to him, but that seemed a bit juvenile and petty. She could always get someone from the restaurant to give him a ride, but they weren't feeling too friendly toward him. Besides, in spite of herself, she was curious.

She didn't say another word as she released the lock on the passenger side door. She waved goodbye to the security camera; then they got in and took off.

"Thanks, Rosa," he said.

Like he'd given her a choice. She exceeded the speed limit, but she didn't care. There wasn't a soul in sight, not even a possum or a deer. This area was lightly patrolled by the sheriff's department, and given her association with Sean Costello, sheriff of South County, she didn't have much concern that she'd get a ticket.

At the roadside, beach rose hedges fanned out toward the dunes and black water. On the other side lay marshes and protected land, an area mercifully untouched for generations.

"So I guess you're wondering why I'm back," Alex said.

She was dying to know. "Not at all," she said.

"I knew Celesta's was your place," he explained. "I wanted to see you."

His directness took her aback. But then, he used to be the most honest person she knew. Right up until he left, never looking back.

"What for?" she asked.

"I still think about you, Rosa."

"Ancient history," she assured him, reminding herself he'd been drinking.

"It doesn't feel that way. Feels like only yesterday."

"Not to me," she lied.

"You were dating that deputy. Costa," Alex said, referring to the day he'd briefly returned, about ten years ago, and she'd sent him away. He would remember that, along with the fact that she didn't need or want him.

"Costello," she corrected him. "Sean Costello. He's the sheriff now."

"And you're still single."

"That's none of your business."

"I'm making it my business."

Rosa drove even faster. "It was awkward, you showing up like that."

"I figured it would be. At least we're talking. That's a start."

"I don't want to start anything with you, Alex."

"Have I asked you to?"

She pulled into the crushed gravel and oyster shell drive of the Montgomery house. Over the years, the grounds had been kept neat, the place painted every five years. It was a handsome Victorian masterpiece in the Carpenter Gothic style, complete with engraved brass plaque from the South County Historical Preservation Society.

"No," she admitted, throwing the gear in Neutral. "You haven't asked me for anything but a ride. So here's your ride. Good night, Alex." She thought about tossing off a remark—*Say hi to your mother from me*—but couldn't bring herself to do that.

He turned to her on the seat. "Rosa, I have a lot to say to you."

"I don't want to hear it."

"Then you won't. Not right now. See, I'm drunk. And when I say what I want to say to you, I need to be stone-cold sober."

three

The next morning Rosa went to Pegasus, a coffeehouse furnished with overstuffed sofas and chairs, low tables and a luxurious selection of biscotti. The café offered the *New York Times* and *Boston Globe,* along with the *Providence Journal Bulletin* and local papers. Rosa was friendly with the proprietor, Millie, a genuine barista imported from Seattle, complete with baggy dress, Birkenstocks and a God-given talent for making perfect espresso.

While she fixed a double tall skinny vanilla latte, Millie eyed the stack of notebooks and textbooks Rosa had set on the table.

"So what are we studying now?" She tilted her head to the side to read the spines of the books. "*Neurolinguistic Programming and its Practical Application to Creative Growth.* A little light reading?"

"It's actually an amazing topic," Rosa said over the *whoosh* of the milk steamer. "Did you know there's a way to recover creative joy simply by finding pleasurable past associations?"

Millie set the latte on the counter. "Too advanced for me, Einstein. What school?"

"Berkeley. The professor even offered to read my final paper if I email it to him."

Millie eyed her admiringly. "I swear, you have the best education money can't buy."

"Keeps me out of trouble, anyway." Rosa had never left home, but over the years she'd managed to sample the finest places of higher learning in the world—genetics at MIT, rococo architecture at the University of Milan, medieval law at Oxford and chaos theory at Harvard. She used to contact professors by phone in order to finagle a syllabus and reading list. Now the internet made it even easier. With a few clicks of the mouse, she could find course outlines, study sheets, practice tests. The only cost to her was the price of books.

"You're nuts," Millie said with a grin. "We all think so."

"But I'm a very educated nut."

"True. Do you ever wish you could sit down and take an actual class?"

Long ago, that had been all Rosa had dreamed of. Then she'd found herself in the midst of an unspeakable tragedy, and the entire course of her life had shifted. "Sure I do," she said with deliberate lightness. "I still might, one of these days, when I find the time."

"You could start by hiring a general manager for your restaurant."

"I can barely afford my own salary." Rosa had a seat and opened one of the books to an article on Noam Chomsky's Transformational Grammar.

Linda showed up wearing a T-shirt that read What if the Hokey Pokey *is* what it's all about? and went to the counter to order her usual—a pot of Lady Grey with honey and a lemon wedge on the side. "Sorry I'm late," she said over her shoulder.

"I tried to get off the phone with my mom, but she couldn't stop crying."

"That's sweet."

"I guess, but it might be a little insulting, tóo. She was just so…relieved. She's been worried that I'd never get married. A major tragedy in the Lipschitz family. So the fact that Jason's Catholic didn't even faze her." She held out her hand, letting the sunlight glitter through the facets of the diamond in her new engagement ring. "It looks even better in broad daylight, doesn't it?"

"It's gorgeous."

Linda beamed at her. "I can't wait to change my name to Aspoll."

"You're taking his name?"

"Hey, for me it's an upgrade. We can't all be born with names like Puccini opera characters, Miss Rosina Angelica Capoletti." Linda drizzled honey into her tea. "Oh, and I have news. The wedding has to be in August. Jason's company transferred him to Boise, and we're moving right after Labor Day."

Rosa smiled at her friend, though when Jason had told her that, she'd wanted to hit him. "So we have less than twelve weeks to plan and execute this wedding," she said. "Maybe that's why your mom was crying."

"She's loving it. She'll be flying up from Florida next week. There's nothing quite like my mom in event-planning mode. It's going to be fine, you'll see."

She seemed remarkably calm, Rosa thought. The reality of getting married and leaving Winslow forever probably hadn't hit her yet.

Linda lifted her cup. "How you doing, Ms. Rosa? Still recovering from the shock of seeing Mr. Love-'em-and-leave-'em?"

Rosa concentrated on sprinkling sugar in her latte. "There's nothing to recover from. So he showed up at the restaurant, so what? His family still owns that property out on Ocean Road. I was bound to run into him sooner or later. I'm just surprised it took so long. But it's no big—"

"You just put four packets of sugar in that coffee," Linda pointed out.

"I did not..." Rosa stared in surprise at the little ripped packets littering the table. She pushed the mug away. "Shoot."

"Ah, Rosa." Linda patted her hand. "I'm sorry."

"It was just weird, okay? Weird to see that someone who was once my whole world is a stranger now. And I guess it's weird because I had to imagine him having a life. I didn't do that when we were little, you know? He'd go away at the end of summer, and I never thought about him in the city. Then when he came back the next year, we picked up where we left off. I thought he only existed for the three months he was with me. And now he's existed for twelve years without me, which is completely no big deal."

"Oh, come on, Rosa. It's a big deal. Maybe it shouldn't be, but it is."

"We were kids, just out of school."

"You loved him."

Rosa tried her coffee and winced. Too sweet. "Everybody's in love when they're eighteen. And everybody gets dumped."

"And moves on," Linda said. "Except you."

"Linda—"

"It's true. You've never had anyone really special since Alex," Linda stated.

"I go out with guys all the time."

"You know what I mean."

Rosa pushed the coffee mug away. "I went out with Greg Fortner for six months."

"He was in the navy. He was gone for five of those six months."

"Maybe that's why we got along so well." Rosa looked at her friend. Clearly, Linda wasn't buying it. "All right, what about Derek Gunn? Eight months, at least."

"I'd hardly call that a lifelong commitment. I wish you'd stuck with him. He was great, Rosa."

"He had a fatal flaw," Rosa muttered.

"Yeah? What's that?"

"You'll say I'm petty."

"Try me. I'm not letting you out of my sight until you 'fess up."

"He was boring." The admission burst from Rosa on a sigh.

"He drives a Lexus."

"I rest my case."

Linda got an extra mug and shared her tea with Rosa. "He's got a house on the water in Newport."

"Boring house. Boring water. Even worse, he has a boring family. Hanging out with them was like watching paint dry. And I'll probably burn in hell for saying that."

"It's best to know what your issues are before going ahead with a relationship."

"You been watching too much Dr. Phil. I have no issues."

Linda coughed. "Stop that. You'll make me snort tea out my nose."

"Okay, so what are my issues?"

Linda waved a hand. "Uh-uh, I'm not touching that one. I need you to be my maid of honor, and it won't happen if we're not speaking. That's what this meeting's about, by the way. Me. My wedding. Not that it's anywhere near as interesting as you and Alex Montgomery."

"There is no me and Alex Montgomery," Rosa insisted.

"And—not to change the subject—did I just hear you ask me to be your maid of honor?"

Linda took a deep breath and beamed at her. "I did. You're my oldest and dearest friend, Rosa. I want you to stand up with me at my wedding. So, will you?"

"Are you kidding?" Rosa gave her friend's hand a squeeze. "I'd be honored."

She loved weddings and had been a bridesmaid six times. She knew it was six because, deep in the farthest reaches of her closet, she had six of the ugliest dresses ever designed, in colors no one had ever seen before. But Rosa had worn each one with a keen sense of duty and pride. She danced and toasted at the weddings; she caught a bouquet or two in her time. After each wedding, she returned home, carrying her dyed-to-match shoes in one hand and her wilting bouquet in the other.

"...as soon as we set a date," Linda was saying.

Rosa realized her thoughts had drifted. "Sorry. What?"

"Hello? I said, keep August 21 and 28 open for me, okay?"

"Yes, of course."

Linda finished her tea. "I'd better let you go. You need to deal with Alex Montgomery."

"I don't need to deal with Alex Montgomery. There's simply no dealing to be done."

"I don't think you have a choice," Linda said.

"That's ridiculous. Of course I have a choice. Just because he came back to town doesn't mean it's my job to deal with him."

"It's your shot, Rosa. Your golden opportunity. Don't let it pass you by."

Rosa spread her hands, genuinely baffled. "What shot? What opportunity? I have no idea what you're talking about."

"To get unstuck."

"I beg your pardon."

"You've been stuck in the same place since Alex left you."

"Bullshit. I'm not stuck. I have a fabulous life here. I never wanted to be anywhere else."

"I don't mean that kind of stuck. I mean emotionally stuck. You never got over the hurt and distrust of what happened with Alex, and you can't move on. Now that he's back, you've got a chance to clear the air with him and get him out of your heart and out of your head once and for all."

"He's not in my heart," Rosa insisted. "He's not in my head."

"Right." Linda patted her arm. "Deal with him, Rosa. You'll thank me one day. He can't be having an easy time, you know, since his mother—"

"What about his mother?" Rosa hadn't heard talk of Emily Montgomery in ages, but that was not unusual. She never came to the shore anymore.

"God, you didn't hear?"

"Hear what?"

"I just assumed you knew." Linda jumped up and rifled through the stack of daily papers. She returned with a *Journal Bulletin,* folded back to show Rosa.

She stared at the photo of the haughtily beautiful Emily Montgomery, portrait-posed and gazing serenely at the camera.

"Oh, God." Her hands rattled the paper as she pushed it away from her on the table. Then, in the same movement, she gathered the paper close and started to read. "Society matron Emily Wright Montgomery, wife of financier Alexander Montgomery III, died on Wednesday at her home in Providence…"

Rosa laid down the paper and looked across the table at her friend. "She was only fifty-five."

"That's what it says. Doesn't seem so old now that we're nearly thirty."

"I wonder what happened." Rosa thought about the way Alex had been last night—slightly drunk, coming on to her.

Now his recklessness took on a different meaning. He'd just lost his mother. Last night, she had dropped him off at an empty house.

Linda leveled her gaze at Rosa. "You should ask him."

four

Rosa drove along Prospect Street to the house where she'd grown up. Little had changed here, only the names of the residents and the gumball colors of their clapboard houses. Buckling concrete driveways led to crammed garages with sagging rooflines. Maple and elm trees arched over the roadway, their stately grace a foil for the homely houses.

It was nice here, she reflected. Safe and comfortable. People still tended their peonies and hydrangeas, their roses and snapdragons. Women pegged out laundry on clotheslines stretched across sunny backyards. Kids rode bikes from house to house and climbed the overgrown apple tree in the Lipschitzes' yard. She still thought of it as the Lipschitzes' yard even though Linda's parents had retired to Vero Beach, Florida, years ago.

She pulled up to the curb in front of number 115, a boxy house with a garden so neat that people sometimes slowed down to admire it. A pruned hedge guarded the profusion of roses that bloomed from spring to winter. Each of the roses had a name. Not the proper name of its variety, but Salvatore, Roberto, Rosina—each one planted in honor of their first communion. There were also roses that honored relatives in Italy whom Rosa had never met, and a few for people she didn't know—La Donna, a scarlet beauty, and a coral floribunda whose name she couldn't remember.

The sturdy bush by the front step, covered in creamy-white blooms, was the Celesta, of course. A few feet away was the one Rosa, a six-year-old with a passion for Pepto-Bismol pink, had chosen for herself. Mamma had been so proud of her that day, beaming down like an angel from heaven. It was one of those memories Rosa cherished, because it was so clear in her heart and mind. She wished all the past could be remembered this way, with clarity and affection, no tinge of regret. But that was naive, and by now, she had figured that out.

She used her ancient key to let herself in. Pop had given it to her when she was nine years old, and she had never once lost it. In the front hall, she blinked the lights a few times. Out of habit she called his name, though it had been some years since he'd been able to hear her.

An acrid odor wafted from the kitchen, along with a buzzing sound.

"Shit," she muttered under her breath, clutching the strap of her purse to her shoulder as she ran to the back of the house. On the counter, a blender stood unattended, its seized motor humming its last, rubber-scented smoke streaming from the base. She grabbed the cord—it felt hot to the touch—and jerked it from the wall. Inside the blender, the lukewarm juice sloshed. The kitchen smoke alarm blinked—what good was that if Pop wasn't looking?

"Jesus, Mary and Joseph, you're going to kill yourself one of these days," Rosa said, waving the smoke away from her face. She peered through the window and saw him out in the backyard, puttering around, oblivious.

On the kitchen table, a newspaper lay open to the Emily Montgomery obituary. Rosa pictured her father starting his breakfast, paging through the paper, stopping in shock as he read the news. He'd probably wandered outside to think about it.

She opened the windows and turned on the exhaust fan over the range, then emptied the blender carafe into the sink. As she cleaned up the mess, Rosa felt a wave of nostalgia. In the scrubbed and gleaming kitchen, her mother's rolled-out pasta dough used to cover the entire top of the chrome and Formica table. Rosa could still picture the long sleek muscles in her mother's arms as she wielded the red-handled rolling pin, drawing it in smooth, rhythmic strokes over the butter-yellow dough.

The reek of the burnt-out motor was a corruption here, in Mamma's world. The smell of her baking ciambellone used to be so powerful it drew the neighbors in, and Rosa could remember the women in their aprons and scuffs, sitting on the back stoop, sharing coffee and Mamma's citrusy ciambellone, fresh from the oven.

To this day, the sweet, dense bread was one of the signature brunch items at Celesta's-by-the-Sea. Butch prepared the dough directly on the countertop with his bare hands, no bowls or spoons, just like Mamma had. Rosa appreciated Butch's skill at cooking and his exquisite palate, but some subtle essence was missing; she could only put it down as magic. No one could capture that, though Rosa knew in some part of her heart that she would never stop trying.

She went out back to talk to her father. The yard had a long rectangular garden that had been laid out and planted by her mother before Rosa was born. Nowadays, her father tended the heirloom tomatoes, peppers, beans and herbs, happy to spend his silent hours in a place his young wife had loved.

He was seated on a wooden folding chair beneath a plum tree, smoking a pipe. A few branches lay around, casualties of the recent windstorm. He looked up when her shadow fell over him.

"Hi, Pop," she said.

"Rosa." He set aside the pipe, stood and held out his arms.

She smiled and hugged him, then gave him a kiss on the cheek, inhaling his familiar scent of shaving soap and pipe tobacco. When she stepped back, she made sure he was looking directly at her, and told him about the blender.

"I guess I forgot and left it on," he said.

"The house could have burned down, Pop."

"I'll be careful from now on, okay?"

It was what he always said when Rosa worried about him. It didn't help, but neither did arguing with him. She studied his face, noticing troubled shadows in his eyes, and knew it had nothing to do with the blender. "You heard about Mrs. Montgomery."

"Yes. Of course. It was in all the papers."

Pop had always been addicted to reading the newspapers, usually two a day. In fact, Rosa had learned to read while sitting in his lap, deciphering the funny pages.

He took her hand in his. He had wonderful hands, blunt and strong, callused from the work he did. His touch was always gentle, as though he feared she might break. "Let's sit. Want some coffee?"

"No, thanks." She joined him in the shade of the plum tree. He seemed…different today. Distracted and maybe diminished, somehow. "Are you all right, Pop?"

"I'm fine, fine." He waved off her concern like batting at a fly.

This wouldn't be the first time he'd lost a client. In the forty years since he had emigrated from Italy, he'd worked for scores of families in the area. But today he seemed to be particularly melancholy.

"She was still so young," Rosa commented.

"Yes." A faraway look came into his eyes. "She was a bride when I first saw her, just a girl, younger than you."

Rosa tried to picture Alex's mother as a young bride, but the image eluded her. She realized Mrs. Montgomery must have been just thirty the first time Rosa had seen her. It seemed inconceivable. Emily Montgomery had always been ageless in her crisp tennis whites, her silky hair looped into a ponytail. She wore almost no jewelry, which Rosa later learned was characteristic of women from the oldest and wealthiest families. Ostentation was for the nouveau riche.

Mrs. Montgomery had lived in terror for her fragile son and had regarded Rosa as a danger to his health.

"I wonder how she died," Rosa said to her father. "Did any of the obituaries say?"

"No. There was nothing."

She watched a ladybug lumber over a blade of grass. "Are you going to the service, or—"

"No, of course not. It is not expected. She doesn't need the gardener. And if I sent flowers, well, they would just get lost."

Rosa got up, pacing in agitation. She walked over to the tomato bushes, the centerpiece of the spectacular garden plot. In her mind's eye, she could see her mother in a house dress that somehow looked pretty on her, a green-sprigged apron, bleached Keds with no socks, a straw hat to keep the sun from her eyes. Mamma never hurried in the garden, and she used all her senses while tending it. She would hold a tomato in the palm of her hand, determining its ripeness by its softness and heft. Or she would inhale the fragrance of pepperoncini or bell peppers, test a pinch of flat leaf parsley or mint between her teeth. Everything had to be at its peak before Mamma brought it to the kitchen.

Rosa bent and plucked a stalk of dockweed from the soil. She straightened, turned to find her father watching her, and she smiled. His hearing loss broke her heart, but it had also brought them closer. Of necessity, he had become incredibly attentive, watching her, reading every nuance of movement and expression with uncanny accuracy. His skill at reading lips was remarkable.

And he knew her so well, she thought, her smile wobbling. "Alex came by the restaurant last night."

Pop's eyebrows lowered, but he didn't comment. He didn't have to. Years ago, he had thought Alex a poor match for her, and his opinion probably hadn't changed.

"He didn't say a word about his mother," she continued. That was when she felt a twist of pain. He'd been drinking last night because he was hurting. Surely his friends must've realized that. Why had they simply left him? Why didn't he have better friends? Why did it matter to her?

"Well." Pop slapped his thighs and stood up. "I must go to work. The Camdens are having a croquet party and they need their hedges trimmed."

Rosa removed his flat black cap and kissed his balding head. "You come up to the restaurant tonight. Butch is fixing blue-fish for the special."

"I'm gonna get fat, I keep eating at your place all the time."

She gave his arm a playful punch. "See you, Pop."

"Yeah, okay."

She stepped through the gate and turned to wave. The expression on his face startled her. "Pop, you sure you're doing all right?"

Instead of replying to her question, he said, "You shouldn't mess with that guy, just because he came back."

"Who says I'm messing with him?"

"Tell me I'm wrong, Rosa."

"Don't worry about me, Pop. I'm a big girl now."

"I always worry about you. Why else am I still here on this earth?"

She touched her hand to her heart and then raised it to sign *I love you.*

He'd learned American Sign Language after losing his hearing in the accident, but rarely used it. Signing in public still made him feel self-conscious. But they weren't in public now, so he signed back. *I love you more.*

As she pulled away from the curb, she let her father's warning play over and over in her head. *You shouldn't mess with that guy, just because he came back.*

"Right, Pop," she said, then turned onto Ocean Road, heading toward the Montgomery place.

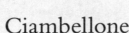

Ciambellone

Ciambellone is a cross between a cake and a bread, with a nice texture well suited to be served at breakfast or with coffee. The smell of a baking ciambellone is said to turn a scowl into a smile.

4 cups flour
3 eggs
1 teaspoon vanilla
1 cup sugar
1 cup milk
1 teaspoon cinnamon
1/2 cup oil
1 teaspoon baking powder
zest from 1 lemon, finely chopped
garnish: milk, coarsely granulated sugar

Make a mound with the flour on a board, creating a well in the center. Using your fingers, begin alternating the liquid and other dry ingredients into the well, mixing until all the ingredients are combined, adding additional flour as needed and kneading to make a smooth dough. Divide into 2 parts and shape into fat rings. Brush the tops with milk and sprinkle with sugar. Place the coils on a buttered baking sheet and bake at 350° F for about 40 minutes or until golden brown.

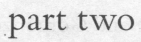

part two

INSALATA

When she made a salad, Mamma used only the most tender hearts and cores of the lettuce. She tossed everything in a bowl so big and wide, a small child could sit in it. That's the secret of a great salad. Give yourself plenty of space to toss. You always need more room than you think you need.

Romaine and Gorgonzola Salad

Wash two heads of romaine lettuce in cold water, discarding the tough outer leaves. Shake dry and tear into bite-sized pieces. Add basil sprigs and cherry tomatoes, cut in half. Right before serving, toss the lettuce with Gorgonzola vinaigrette.

Gorgonzola Vinaigrette

1/4 cup white wine vinegar + 1/4 cup apple juice
1 Tablespoon minced shallots
2 Tablespoons mustard
2 teaspoons chopped basil
2 Tablespoons toasted pine nuts (pinones)
1/4 cup walnut oil + 3 Tablespoons olive oil
2 Tablespoons crumbled Gorgonzola—preferably the aged variety from Monferrato
freshly ground black pepper

Put everything in a jar and shake well. Makes about 1 cup. Store in the fridge for up to 5 days.

five

When Rosa Capoletti was nine years old, she learned two important lessons. One: after your mother dies, you should still remember to talk to her every day. And two: never put up a rope swing in a tree containing a beehive.

Of course, she wasn't aware of the hive when she coiled a stout rope around her shoulder and shinned up the trunk of a venerable elm tree by the pond in the Montgomerys' garden. The pond was stocked with rare fish from Japan and water lilies from Costa Rica, and had a burbling fountain. Pop had told Rosa she should never bother the fish. The pond was Mrs. Montgomery's pride and joy, and under no circumstances must it be disturbed.

Pop had told her to stay out of trouble. He was going to the plant nursery with Mrs. Montgomery and Rosa was not to leave the yard. That was fine with her, because it was a perfect summer day, third grade was behind her and she had nothing but lazy days ahead. When Mamma was alive, Rosa used to help her in the kitchen garden at home. Mamma's tomatoes and basil were so good they won prizes, and she always made Rosa wear a straw hat with a brim, tied on with a polka dot scarf. She said too much sun was bad for the skin.

Since Mamma died and the boys went into the navy, there was no one to look after Rosa once school let out for summer, so she went to work with Pop each day. The nuns from school urged Rosa's father to send her to a Catholic summer camp. Rosa had begged to stay home, promising Pop she'd stay out of the way.

Going to work with her father turned out to be the only thing that kept Rosa from shriveling up with sadness over Mamma. He used to be a familiar sight around the area, going from place to place on his sturdy yellow bicycle. Now they drove together in the old Dodge Power Wagon, with all his gardening tools in the back. During the summer, he worked from dawn to dusk at six places—one for each day of the week—mowing, pruning, digging and clipping the yards and gardens of the vast seaside estates that fringed the shoreline.

This was Rosa's first visit to the Montgomery place, a giant barge of a house with a railed porch on three sides and tall, narrow windows with glass so old it was wavy. She found all sorts of things to explore in the huge, lush yard that extended out to touch an isolated stretch of beach. Still, she was bored. She wanted to go to the beach, to take the little dinghy out, to go on adventures with her friends. But she was stuck here.

Spending the afternoon alone would be a lot more fun now that she had a rope swing, she thought, sticking one bare foot in the bottom loop and pushing off. She laughed aloud and started singing "Stray Cat Strut," which played on the radio at least once a day. She didn't really know what a "feline Ca-

sanova" was, but it was a good tune, and her big brother Sal
had taught her all the words before he left.

He and her other brother, Rob, took the train early this
morning. They were going to something called Basic Training, and who knew when she'd see them again?

She soared high enough to see the empty beach beyond the
lavish gardens and then low enough to skim the soft, perfectly
groomed carpet of grass. The sky was bluer than heaven, like
Mamma used to say. In the garden below, the button-eyed
daisies and fancy purple lobelias were reflected in the surface
of the pond. Seagulls flew like flashing white kites over the
breakers on the beach, and Rosa felt all the fluttery excitement of freedom.

Summer was here. Finally, endless days out from under the
glare of Sister Baptista, whose stare was so sharp she could
make you squirm like a bug on a pin.

The little seaside town of Winslow changed in the summer.
The pace picked up, and people drove along the coast road in
convertibles with the tops down. Pop would comment that
the price of gas and groceries went sky-high and that it was
impossible to get a table at Mario's Flying Pizza on a Friday
night, even though Rosa and Pop always got a table, because
Mario was Mamma's cousin.

Rosa came in for a landing, aiming her bare foot for the
crotch of the tree. Her foot struck something dry and papery
that collapsed when she touched it. A humming noise mingled
with the rustle of the breeze through the leaves. Then Rosa's
foot burst into flame.

A second later, she saw a black cloud rise from the tree, and
the faint humming sound changed to a roar. A truly angry roar.

She didn't remember getting down from the tree, but later
she would discover livid rope burns on the insides of her knees,
along with a colorful variety of scratches and bruises. She hit

the ground running, howling at the tops of her lungs, then stabbing the air with a separate shriek each time she felt another sting.

She headed straight for the pond with its burbling fountain.

Rosa took a flying leap for the clear, calm water. She couldn't help herself. She was on fire. It was an emergency.

The cool water brought relief as she submerged herself. The places she'd been stung were instantly soothed by the silky mud on the bottom. She broke the surface and saw a few bees still hovering around, so she sat in the shallow water, waving her arms and legs, stirring up brown clouds. She didn't know how long she sat there, letting the mud cool the stings. She could detect six of them, maybe more, mostly on her legs.

"What in heaven's holy name is going on?" demanded a sharp voice. A woman rushed out of the house and down the back stairs.

Rosa almost didn't recognize Mrs. Carmichael in her starched housekeeper's uniform. The Carmichaels lived down the street from the Capolettis, and usually Rosa only saw her in her housedress and slippers, standing on the porch and calling her boys in to dinner. Everything was different in this neighborhood of big houses overlooking the sea. Everything was cleaner and neater, even the people.

Except Rosa herself. As she slogged to the edge of the pond, feeling the smooth mud squish between her toes, she knew with every cell in her body that she didn't belong here. Muddy and barefoot, soaked to the skin, bee-stung and bruised, she belonged anywhere but here.

She waited, dripping on the lawn as Mrs. Carmichael bustled toward her. "I can explain—"

"What are we going to do with you, Rosa Capoletti?" Mrs. Carmichael demanded. She was on the verge of being mad, but she was holding her temper back. Rosa could tell. People tried to be extra patient with her, on account of her mother had died on Valentine's Day. Even Sister Baptista tried to be a little nicer.

"I can get cleaned off in the garden hose," Rosa suggested.

"Good idea. I hope you didn't do in any of the koi."

"The what?"

"The fish."

"I didn't mean to."

Mrs. Carmichael shook her head. "Let's go."

As she followed Mrs. Carmichael across the lawn, Rosa glanced at the house and saw a ghost in the window. A small, pale person with a round Charlie Brown head stood staring out at her, veiled by lace curtains. She looked again and saw that the ghost was gone, shy as a hummingbird zipping out of sight.

"Holy moly," she muttered.

"What's that?" Mrs. Carmichael cranked opened the spigot.

"Oh, nothing." It was kind of interesting, seeing a ghost. Sometimes she saw Mamma, but she didn't tell anyone. People would think she was lying, but she wasn't.

"Stand right there." Mrs. Carmichael indicated a sunny spot. The grass was as soft as brand-new shag carpet. "Hold out your arms."

Rosa's shadow fell over the grass, a skinny cruciform with stringy hair. An arc of fresh water from the hose drenched her. "Yikes, that's cold," she said.

"Hold still and I'll be quick."

She couldn't hold still. The water was too cold, which felt good on the beestings but chilled the rest of her. She jumped up and down as though stomping grapes, like Pop said they used to do in the Old Country.

The ghost came to the window again.

"Who is that?" Rosa asked through chattering teeth.

"He's Mrs. Montgomery's boy."

"Is he all alone in there?"

"He is. Put your head back," Mrs. Carmichael instructed. "His sister went away to summer camp."

"I bet he's lonely. Maybe I could play with him."

Mrs. Carmichael gave a dry laugh. "I don't think so, dear."

"Is he shy?" Rosa persisted.

"No. He's a Montgomery. Now, turn around and I'll finish up."

Rosa squirmed under the impact of the cold stream of water. When the torture stopped, Mrs. Carmichael told her to wait on the back porch. She disappeared into the house, carefully closing the door behind her. She returned with a stack of towels and a white terry-cloth bathrobe. "Put this on, and I'll throw your clothes in the dryer."

As Rosa peeled off her wet clothes, Mrs. Carmichael stared at her legs. "Mother of God, what happened to you?"

Rosa surveyed the welts on her feet and legs. "Bee-stings," she said. "I kicked a hive. It was an accident, I swear—"

"Why didn't you tell me?"

Rosa thought it would be rude to point out that she had already tried to explain.

"Heavenly days," said Mrs. Carmichael, wrapping a towel around her. "You must be made of steel, child. Doesn't it hurt like hellfire?"

"Yes, ma'am."

"It's all right to cry, you know."

"Yes, ma'am, but it won't make me feel any better. The mud helped, though. And the cold water."

"Let me find the tweezers and get those stingers out. We might need to call a doctor."

"No. I mean, no, thank you." Rosa hoped she sounded firm, not impolite. While Mamma was sick, the whole family had had their fill of doctors. "I don't need a doctor."

"You sit tight, then. I'll get the tweezers."

A few minutes later, she returned with a blue-and-white first-aid kit and used the tweezers to pluck out at least seven stingers. "Hmm," Mrs. Carmichael mused, "maybe it wasn't such a bad idea, jumping in the pond. I think it'll keep the swelling down." She gently pressed the palm of her hand to Rosa's forehead, and then to her cheek.

Rosa closed her eyes. She had forgotten how good it felt when someone checked you for fever. It had to be done by a woman. A mother had a way of touching you just so. It was one of the zillion things she missed about Mamma.

"No fever," Mrs. Carmichael declared. "You're lucky. You're not allergic to beestings."

"I'm not allergic to anything."

Mrs. Carmichael treated the stings with baking soda and gave Rosa a grape Popsicle. "You're very brave," she said.

"Thank you." Rosa didn't feel brave. The beestings hurt plenty, like little licks of fire all over, but after what happened with Mamma, Rosa had a different idea about what was worth crying about.

Mrs. Carmichael got a comb and tugged it through Rosa's long, thick, curly hair. Rosa endured it in silence, biting her lip to keep from crying out. "This is a mass of tangles," Mrs. Carmichael said. "Honestly, doesn't your father—"

"I do it myself," Rosa said, forcing bright pride into her tone. "Pop doesn't know how to do hair."

"I see."

Rosa pressed her lips together hard and stared at the painted planks on the porch floor. "Mamma taught me how to make a braid. When she was sick, she used to let me get in bed with her, and she'd do my hair." Rosa didn't tell Mrs. Carmichael that by the end, Mamma was too weak to do anything; she couldn't even hold a brush. She didn't tell her that the sickness that had taken Mamma took some of Rosa, too, the part that was easy laughter and feeling safe in the dark at night, the security of living in a house that smelled of baking bread and simmering sauce.

"Dear? Are you all right?"

Rosa tucked the memories away. "Mamma said every girl should know how to make a braid. But it's hard to do on your own head."

Mrs. Carmichael surprised her by holding her close, stroking her damp head. "I guess it is hard, kiddo."

"I'll keep practicing."

"You do that." Like all grown-up women, Mrs. Carmichael was a champ at braiding hair. She made a fat, perfect braid down Rosa's back. "I'll put these things in the dryer. Wait here, and try to stay out of mischief."

six

The housekeeper disappeared again and Rosa tried to be patient. Waiting was the pits. It was totally boring, and you never knew when it would end. She fiddled with the long tie that cinched in the waist of the thick terry robe. It was way too big for her, the sleeves and hem practically dragging.

Somewhere far away, the phone rang three times. Mrs. Carmichael's voice drifted through the house. Rosa couldn't hear the conversation, but Mrs. Carmichael laughed and talked on and on. She probably forgot all about Rosa.

The door to the kitchen was slightly ajar. Rosa pushed it with her foot and, almost all by itself, it swung open. She gasped softly at what she saw. Everything was white and steel, polished until it shone. There were miles of countertops, and Rosa figured the Montgomerys owned every tool and utensil that had ever been invented—strainers and oddly shaped spoons, gleaming pots hanging from a rack, a huge collection of knives, baking pans in several shapes, timers and stacks of snow-white tea towels.

Boy, thought Rosa, Mamma would love this. She was the world's best cook. Every night, she used to sing "Funiculi" while she fixed supper—puttanesca sauce, homemade bread, pasta she made every Wednesday. Rosa had loved nothing better than working side by side with her in the bright scrubbed kitchen in the house on Prospect Street, turning out fresh pasta, baking a calzone on a winter afternoon, adding a pinch of basil or fennel to the sauce. Most of all, Rosa could picture, like an indelible snapshot in her mind, Mamma standing at the sink and looking out the window, a soft, slightly mysterious smile on her face. Her "Mona Lisa smile," Pop used to call it. Rosa didn't know about that. She had seen a postcard of the Mona Lisa and thought Mamma was way prettier.

Rosa walked through the strange high-ceilinged kitchen, running her finger along the edge of the counter. She stood on tiptoe to peer out the window over the sink. It framed a view of the sea. Her mother would've gone nuts for this kitchen.

But it didn't smell like anything, just faintly of cleanser. Mamma's kitchen always smelled like roasting chicken or baking pizza or freshly squeezed lemons.

Rosa finished her Popsicle and put the stick in a shiny, bullet-shaped trash can. She tried to keep still, she really did, but curiosity poked at her. She knew it was wrong, but she was going to snoop. She had always wondered about these great big houses. She'd seen them from the outside, painted giants with white scrollwork trim, shiny cars in the circular drives and yards where people in summer hats and starched white shirts held garden parties.

She walked down a hallway, her bare feet soundless on the polished wood floor, the hem of the robe dragging. Her hand stole inside the bathrobe to clutch at the shiny new key Pop had given her. She was old enough to have a house key now, and he told her never to lose it.

She could hear snatches of Mrs. Carmichael's phone conversation, and when she realized it was about her, she froze right under a big painting of a sailboat in a rustic frame.

"...know what to do with that poor little girl all summer. Pete wasn't gone five minutes and she got in trouble."

Pete was Pop. It seemed like every woman who knew him was waiting for him to mess up now that he didn't have a wife anymore.

"Oh...no idea," Mrs. Carmichael was saying. "The kindest thing he can do for that child is remarry. She needs a mother."

No, thank you. Rosa buried her face in the overly long sleeves of the bathrobe to stifle a snort. She absolutely did not need a mother. She had the best mother in the world, and just because she wasn't around anymore didn't mean she was gone. She belonged to Rosa in a special way. That's what Father Dominic said, and everyone knew priests didn't lie.

I still talk to you, don't I, Mamma? She thought the words as hard as she could.

"At least Pete's got his work," Mrs. Carmichael went on. "He's happy when he works. He's like a different person." She gave a gentle laugh. "Hmm. I know. And with those looks of his..."

Rosa got bored with eavesdropping. Everyone was always saying how Pop was still young and good-looking, and that he ought to find another wife. Why did people think you could replace someone, like she was a lost schoolbook and all you had to do was bring a check to the office and they'd give you another?

She continued her silent exploration of the house, feeling as though she had stepped into an enchanted castle. The front room was all white and lemony-yellow, with white furniture and a seashell collection in a jar. Photographs in silver frames pictured people in white clothes without wrinkles, just like in a magazine ad. There was a huge bouquet of cut flowers, probably from the garden Pop took care of. The glass-topped coffee table displayed an important-looking scrimshaw collection. The mantel had a crystal candelabrum with long white tapers that had never been lit.

This wasn't like going over to Linda's house to play. Everything was so big and so incredibly quiet. The flowers made it smell like the funeral home where they took Rosa's mother.

She backed out of the room and tiptoed down the hall. Tall double doors with glass panes framed a room that had more books than the Redwood Library in Newport.

Rosa loved books. When Mamma got too sick to do anything else, and couldn't even braid hair anymore, Rosa used to get in bed with her and read and read and read—*The Indian in the Cupboard, Tales of a Fourth Grade Nothing, Charlotte's Web* and poems from *A Light in the Attic.* And of course, *Goodnight Moon,* which Mamma used to read to Rosa every night when she was tiny.

She stepped into the room and inhaled the musty sunshine smell of books. She walked over to the lace-paneled windows and discovered a view of the garden and pond. Rosa caught her breath. The ghostly boy had stood right there, at the window, watching her run from attacking bees.

She wanted to browse through the books on the shelves, but she became aware of a hissing-gurgling-sucking sound. A creepy chill slipped over her skin. This was a haunted library.

She spun away from the window and saw the ghost on the couch.

Rosa had to push both fists against her mouth to keep from screaming. He was doing a terrible thing, sucking steam from a snaky plastic tube into his mouth. The tube was attached to a box, which emitted the hissing sounds.

Finally she found her voice. "What are you doing?"

He pulled the tube away from his mouth. "This helps me breathe," he said. "It's a portable bronchodilator."

She edged a little closer, but still felt wary. He was very skinny, lying on a leather sofa with a sailboat quilt covering him up. He wore wire-rimmed glasses and had a nice face, nicer than you'd expect for a ghost boy. Pale yellow hair, pale blue eyes, pale white skin.

"You need help breathing?" she asked.

"Sometimes." He set aside the tube, hooking it into a holder on the side of the machine. A wisp of steam coughed from the mouthpiece. "I have asthma."

"Can you get rid of it?" Rosa tensed up, wishing she hadn't asked. Sometimes a person got sick and there was no way to get better.

"No one can tell," he said. "It can be controlled, and maybe it'll improve when I get bigger and my lungs grow. What's your name?"

"Rosina Angelica Capoletti, and everyone calls me Rosa. What's yours?"

"Alexander Montgomery."

"Does everyone call you Alex?"

He offered a mild, sweet smile. "No one calls me that."

"Then I think I will."

They verified that they were just a year apart in age, but in the same grade. Alex had started kindergarten a year late on account of having trouble with his asthma. He admitted that he disliked school, and she got the impression that he got bullied a lot. She declared that she, too, despised school.

"I know I have to go," she lamented. "It's the only way to get ahead."

"Ahead of what?" he asked.

She laughed. "I don't know. My brothers were in ROTC and joined the U.S. Navy for their education."

"You go to college to get an education," he said with a frown.

"If you go in the navy first, then the navy pays for it," she explained patiently. "I thought everybody knew that." She indicated the book that lay open across his lap. "What are you reading?"

He picked it up and showed her the spine. "*Bulfinch's Mythology*. It's a collection of Greek myths. This one is about Icarus. There's a picture."

Rosa sat beside him on the sofa and scooted over to see. Alex thoughtfully put half the book on her lap. "He's flying," she said.

"Yes."

"He doesn't look like he's having much fun."

"Well, he's in pain."

"Why would he fly if it hurts him?"

"Because he's flying," Alex said as if that explained everything.

Rosa stuck out her bare foot. The beestings formed red dots on her ankle and shin. "I tried flying, and trust me, it's not worth the pain."

"I saw you," he said. "I was watching from the window."

"I know. I saw you watching me."

"I was going to come and help, but I didn't know what to do."

"That's all right. Mrs. Carmichael came straightaway when she heard me yelling."

He nodded gravely, studying her with such total absorption that she felt like the only person on the planet. "Do the beestings hurt?"

"Not anymore. Mrs. Carmichael put baking soda on them. She said I'm lucky I'm not allergic."

"You are lucky," he said with a funny, dreamy look on his face. "You get to be outside and do whatever you want."

She thought about telling him just how unlucky she was. She was a girl without a mother. But she didn't want to say anything. Not just yet. It might be too scary for him, this sick boy, to hear about a sick person who had died.

"You mean you're not allowed outside?"

He pushed his glasses up the bridge of his nose. "Not without supervision. I might have an asthma attack."

"Going outside causes an attack?"

"Sometimes."

She'd heard of a heart attack. An attack of nerves. But not an asthma attack. "What's it feel like?"

"It's like...drowning. But in air instead of water."

Rosa had some knowledge of the sensation. More than once, while swimming, she'd gone out too far and under too deep, and she'd experienced the momentary panic of needing air. The feeling was horrifying. "Then you'd better not go outside."

He stared down at Icarus, whose mouth was twisted in agony as he flew too close to the sun. Then he looked up at Rosa, and there was a new light in his blue eyes. "Let's go anyway."

"Really?"

"My lungs were twitchy this morning, but I'm better now. I'll be okay."

She looked at him very closely. There were no lies in that face of his. She could just tell. "I have to get my clothes. Mrs. Carmichael put them in the dryer."

"I think that might be in the utility room."

As she followed him through the house, she marveled that he didn't know for sure where the dryer was. At her house, everyone knew, because laundry was everyone's business. He

opened a painted door in the kitchen to reveal a dim, cavern-
ous room dusty with dryer lint. "It's in there."

"You wait here."

"Are you sure?"

"I have to change. I sure don't need any help doing that."
The room smelled of must and dryer lint, and a hissing sound
came from the water heater. Her clothes were still damp, but
she put them on anyway—undies, cutoffs and a T-shirt from
Mario's Flying Pizza. The sun would finish the job of drying
them. She left the bathrobe on top of the dryer and hurried
back to the kitchen.

There, she found Alex and Mrs. Carmichael locked in a
staredown. "I'm going," he said to the housekeeper.

She sniffed. "You're not to leave the house."

"That was this morning. I'm better now. I have my inhaler
and my EpiPen, see?" He took a plastic thing in a yellow tube
from the pocket of his shorts.

"I'll watch him," Rosa blurted out. "I will, Mrs. Carmichael. If he starts looking sick, I'll make him come right back
inside."

The housekeeper kept her hands planted on her hips, though
her eyes softened and there was a barely perceptible easing of
her shoulders. Mothers were like that. They gave in with their
eyes and their posture before saying okay out loud. "You will,
will you?" she asked.

"Yes, ma'am. I got my things from the dryer. Thank you,
Mrs. Carmichael."

"You're very welcome." She looked from Alex to Rosa.
"Try to keep your noses clean, all right?"

"Yes, Mrs. Carmichael," they said together, trying not to
look too gleeful.

Out in the sunlight, Rosa noticed that Alex's eyes were
ocean-blue, and they crinkled when he grinned at her. She

vowed to be on her best behavior, just like Mrs. C had admonished them. If she got in trouble, Pop wouldn't let her come to work with him anymore. He'd make her stay with that dreadful Mrs. Schmidt, the widow with the mustache, whom Rosa likened to a circling buzzard. Even before Mamma died, Mrs. Schmidt had started coming around the house, bringing covered dishes and making eyes at Pop, which of course he never even noticed.

"Here. Have a cookie." As they headed for the door, Mrs. Carmichael held out a white jar in the shape of a sandcastle.

"Thank you." They each took one and stepped out into the sunshine. Rosa nibbled on the cookie as she grinned at Alex.

It was a store-bought sugar cookie. Not as good as Mamma's, of course. Mamma made hers with a secret ingredient—ricotta cheese—and thick, sweet icing. Now *that* was a cookie.

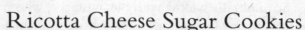

Ricotta Cheese Sugar Cookies

1 cup softened butter
2 cups sugar
1 carton full-fat ricotta cheese
2 eggs
3 teaspoons vanilla (the kind from Mexico is best)
1/2 teaspoon salt
1 teaspoon baking soda
1 teaspoon grated lemon zest
4 cups flour

For the glaze:

1 cup powdered sugar
2-4 Tablespoons milk
2 drops almond extract (optional)
sprinkles

Preheat oven to 350° F. Mix cookie ingredients to form a sticky dough. Drop by teaspoonfuls on an ungreased cookie sheet. Bake 10 minutes or until the bottoms turn golden brown (the tops will stay white). Transfer to wire racks to cool. To make the glaze, stir milk a few drops at a time, along with the almond extract if desired, into the powdered sugar in a saucepan. Stir over low heat to create a glaze. Drizzle over cooled cookies and top with colored sprinkles. Makes 3–4 dozen cookies.

seven

"Too bad about the rope swing," Alex said, eyeing the rope that still hung from the tree branch.

"I took it from that shed behind the—what is that building, anyway? It's too big to be a garage," Rosa said, stopping to put on her flip-flops. The tall building was painted and trimmed to match the house. It had old-fashioned sliding wooden doors like a barn, an upper story at one end with a row of dormer windows facing the sea and a cupola with a wind vane on top.

"My mother parks her car there. She calls it the carriage house even though there's no carriage in it."

Sunlight glinted off the windows at the top of the house. "I knew it was way too fancy to be called a garage. Does somebody live there?"

"No, but somebody used to. In the olden days, a caretaker lived upstairs."

"What did he take care of?"

"The horses. And carriages, I guess, but that was a long time ago. My grandfather used it as an observatory. He showed me how to spot the Copernicus Crater with a telescope."

He sure did seem smart. Rosa nodded appreciatively, as though she knew what the Copernicus Crater was.

"My grandfather was teaching me about the stars, but he died when I was in first grade."

Rosa didn't quite know what to say about that, so she followed him across the property to the carriage house. The front doors were stuck, but they struggled together to push them along the rusted runners. Inside was a maze of spiderwebs, old tools and some sort of car under a fitted cover. "My mother's car," Alex said. "She calls it her beach car. It's a Ford Galaxy. She hardly ever drives it, though."

"My mother didn't like driving, either."

He shot her a quick look, and Rosa realized that now was her chance to tell him, because she'd said "didn't" instead of "doesn't." But she decided not to say anything. Not yet. She might later, though. She'd already decided he was that kind of friend.

Before he could question her, she ran up the stairs. Sure enough, there was a whole house up there, flooded with dusty sunshine. Alex sneezed, and she turned to him. "Is this going to cause an as—" She couldn't remember the word. "An attack?"

"Asthma attack. I don't think so." He stuck his hand into his pocket and she could see him feeling for the inhaler. Still, he seemed fine. So far, so good.

The furniture was stacked in a broken heap, like old bones on Halloween. The most interesting item was a spinning wheel. Rosa stepped on the pedal, and when the large wheel spun, she jumped back with a yell of fright.

Alex laughed at her, but not in a mean way.

"What are you going to do with all this stuff?" Rosa asked.

"I don't know. My mother says she keeps meaning to clean

it out, but she never gets around to it. I get to keep the telescope, though." It was on a table in front of the biggest window. He opened the long black case to reveal the instrument
broken down in parts.

"Can you see the man in the moon with that?" Rosa asked.

"There's no such thing as the man in the moon."

"I know. It's just an expression."

He shut the case, and a cloud of dust rose. When he breathed,
he made a scary wheezing sound, and his face turned red.

"Hey, what's wrong?" Rosa asked.

He waved his hand and headed for the stairs, gasping all
the way like a cartoon character pretending to die. Rosa followed him in terror. When they got outside, she headed for
the house to tell Mrs. Carmichael, but Alex grabbed her arm
and pulled her back.

His touch felt desperate but not angry. "I'm okay," he said,
though his voice was only a whisper.

"Are you sure?"

He nodded. "Cross my heart and hope to— I'm sure." His
eyes looked brighter, somehow, than they had before. Magni-
fied by the lenses of his glasses, they appeared huge.

"Was that an asthma attack?"

He grinned. "No way. That was just a little wheezing."

"I'd hate to see an attack, then."

"I'm all right. Let's go to the beach."

She hesitated, but only for a second. You just didn't say
no to a kid who spent half his life cooped up like Alex did.
"Okay," she said.

The Montgomery house overlooked a part of the shore almost no one visited, an area known as North Beach. It was
a long, isolated curve of the coastline, a good hike from the
nearest public beach. It was also a bird sanctuary, safe from
development and a good distance from town. A path, over-

grown by runners from wild roses and greenbrier, led through the sanctuary to the shore. The summer crowds had never discovered the marsh-rimmed beach, or if they had, it was too rocky to be popular.

"Too cold for swimming yet," Rosa said, running down to the water's edge. "But soon. Ever seen a tide pool?"

"In a book," he said, following more slowly, breathing hard.

"I can take you to see some real ones."

"All right."

His breathing worried her. "Can you make it?"

"Sure, I'm okay."

It was impossible to walk in a straight line on the beach; Rosa had never been able to do it. They darted back and forth, examining shells, overturning rocks to watch the tiny crabs run for cover, picking out a perfectly round, flat stone to skip.

Alex turned out to be a big talker. In fact, he was a funny, clever boy who took delight in everything she said and did, everything she showed him. And he knew things, too. He knew a dolphin swims at thirty-five miles per hour, and a baby gray whale drinks the equivalent of two thousand bottles of milk each day. So all that reading was good for something, after all.

He had a sister who was away at horseback riding camp. "Her name's Madison. She's fifteen. I'm not allowed to go to camp on account of my asthma."

"It's just as nice here," Rosa declared, though she had no idea whether or not that was true.

"My family's firm has offices in the city, and my father comes to the beach house only on weekends and holidays," he said.

She didn't really get what a firm was, but it seemed to keep his father plenty busy. "Which city?"

"New York City. And Providence, too. Where do you live?"

"In Winslow."

"You're lucky. I wish I could live here all year around."

"I don't know. It gets pretty cold in the winter. Summers are the best. Do you like swimming or hiking, going out in boats?"

"I don't do things like that," he said. "I'm not allowed."

"That's too bad." What an odd boy, she thought. "Pop says when I'm twelve, I can go parasailing."

"See what I mean? Lucky."

"I guess. Maybe we could go down to the docks at Galilee and catch a ride on a fishing boat that's heading out for the day. Mrs. Carmichael's husband is a lobsterman. Did you know that?"

"No."

She had a feeling he didn't do much talking to the housekeeper. "My brothers' names are Roberto and Salvatore. We call him Sal but never Sally." She pointed out a firepit with the charred remains of a few logs. "My brothers used to build bonfires that would shoot sparks a mile high." Just saying it made her miss Rob and Sal, who were so much older than her. Her parents used to call her their last blessing. After the boys, they weren't really expecting to have a daughter, too, nine years later. Her parents had been older than the parents of her friends, but Rosa never cared about that. She was surrounded by love, she was the last blessing and she used to think she was the luckiest girl in the world.

"Maybe we could build a bonfire," Alex said.

It was nice, the way he seemed to feel her turning sad, and spoke right up. "Maybe," she said, and took him past the public beaches and parking lots to the rocky tip of Point Judith. "You have to be careful here," she warned him. "The rocks are slippery. Sharp, too."

He took a step and wobbled a little on his skinny white legs, then regained his balance. He looked very small, standing on the sharp-edged black rock with the waves exploding high into the sky.

Rosa put out her hand. "Hang on and watch where you step."

He grabbed on, and his strong grip surprised her. He studied each move with deliberation, but they made steady progress. When a fount of white foam erupted between the rocks he was straddling, Alex jumped, but not in time to avoid getting his shorts soaked.

"Are you all right?" asked Rosa.

"Yes." With his free hand, he straightened his glasses. "It's steep."

"Don't worry." She stepped down to the next rock. "I'll catch you if you fall."

"What if *you* fall?" he asked.

"I won't," she declared. "I never fall." Step by unsteady step, she led him down to the placid clear pools that stayed filled at low tide. They studied hand-sized starfish and sea cucumbers, neon-colored algae and clusters of black mussels clinging to the rock. Alex knew what everything was from his reading, but he didn't know how to make sunburst anemones squirt. Rosa showed him that. Splat, right on his eyeglasses.

Alex laughed aloud as he wiped his face, and the sound made her smile bigger than she'd smiled in weeks. Months, maybe. Crouched by the pool, she felt a slight change, like the wind shifting. They weren't just two kids anymore. They were friends.

She sat back on her heels and tilted her face up to the clear blue sky. A trio of seagulls swooped over them, and Rosa looked away. Mamma used to have a lot of superstitions. *Three seagulls flying together, directly overhead, are a warning of death soon to come.*

Until Mamma, Rosa had never known a person who died.

She used to think she knew what death was: a bird fallen from the nest. A possum at the side of the road, buzzing with flies. She had grandparents who had died, but since she'd never met them, that didn't count. They were from a place in Italy called Calabria, which her parents called the Old Country.

One time, she asked Pop why he never went to Italy to see his parents while they were alive. You can't go back, he'd said dismissively. It's too much bother.

Rosa didn't really care. She didn't want to go to Italy. She liked it right here.

"What school do you go to?" asked Alex.

"St. Mary's." She wrinkled her nose. "I think classes are boring, and the cafeteria food makes me gag." When they had to say the blessing right after Second Bell, she used to give extra thanks for her mother's sack lunches—chicken salad with capers or provolone with olive loaf, sometimes a slice of cake and a bunch of grapes. There was always a funny little message on the napkin: "Smile!" Or "Only 12 more days to summer!"

"I like sports," she told Alex, not wanting him to think she was a total loser. "I can run really fast and I like to win. My big brothers taught me everything they know, which is a lot. I play soccer in the fall, swimming in the winter, softball in the spring. Do you play sports?"

"Not allowed," he said, trailing his hand in the crystal clear water. "Makes me wheeze." Then he was quiet for several minutes. Rosa watched the way the breeze tossed his shiny white-blond hair. He looked like a picture in a book of fairy tales, maybe Hansel, lost in the woods.

He turned those ocean-blue eyes on her. "Your mom died, didn't she?"

Rosa felt a quick hitch in her chest. She couldn't speak, but she nodded her head.

"Mrs. Carmichael told me this morning."

Rosa drew her knees up to her chest, and as she watched the waves exploding on the rocks, she felt something break apart inside her. "I miss her so much."

"I was scared to say anything, but…it's okay if you want to talk about it."

She started to shake her head, to find a way to change the subject, but this time the subject refused to be changed. Alex had brought it up and now it was like the incoming tide; it wouldn't go away. And to her surprise, she kind of felt like talking. "Well," she said. "Well, it's a long story."

"The days are long in the summer," he reminded her. "The sun sets at 8:14 tonight."

She rested her chin on her knees and gazed out at the blue distance. Usually she tried not to bring up the subject of her mother's death. It made her brothers all awkward, and Pop sometimes cried, which was scary to Rosa. Now she could feel Alex staring right at her, and it didn't scare her at all.

"When Mamma first got sick," she said, "I didn't worry because she didn't really act sick. She went for her treatments, and came back and took naps. But after a while, it got hard for her to act like she was okay." Rosa thought about the day her mother came home from the hospital for the last time. When she took off her bright blue kerchief, she looked as gray and bald as a newborn baby bird. That was when Rosa finally felt afraid. "The nuns came—"

"Like Catholic nuns?" Alex asked.

"I don't think there's any other kind."

"Are you Catholic, then?" he asked.

"Yep. Are you?"

"No. I don't think I'm anything. I want to hear about the nuns."

"They used to sit and pray in the bedroom with my mother. My father got really quiet, and his temper was short." Rosa wasn't going to say any more about that. Not today, anyway. "My brothers had no idea what to do. Rob went to Mamma's garden, which she didn't plant last year because she was too sick, and he mowed down a whole field of brambles using only a machete." Rosa pictured her brother, sweat mingling with the tears on his face even though it was the middle of winter. "Sal lit so many candles at St. Mary's that Father Dominic had to tell him to put some of them out to avoid starting a fire."

None of it helped, of course. Nothing helped.

"Mamma said it was a lucky thing, to be able to say goodbye, but it didn't feel...lucky." Rosa pressed the heel of her hand into the rock hard enough to hurt. Her mother had been too weak to prop up a book, so Rosa got on the bed and lay down beside her and read *Grandfather Twilight,* and it felt strange to be the one reading it.

"She died on Valentine's Day," Rosa told Alex. "A week after my ninth birthday. All kinds of people came, and the neighbors brought food, but mostly it just spoiled in the refrigerator and then we threw it out because nobody was hungry. Some of the women got right to work on my father. They wanted him to marry again immediately." She shuddered.

"Mrs. Carmichael thinks he looks like Syvester Stallone. I heard her talking to somebody about it on the phone."

Rosa made a face. "He just looks like Pop."

The chill water sluiced in, breaking over Rosa's feet and Alex's checkered Vans sneakers.

"Tide's coming in. We'd better go back," he said.

"All right." She stood up and offered her hand.

"I can make it," he said.

As they headed back along the public beach, she glanced at the sky. It wasn't that late yet. "Do you think we should hurry?"

"No, but my mother doesn't like me to be late for dinner.

At least when we're at the shore, we don't have to dress for dinner like we do in the city."

"You mean you eat naked?" Rosa fell down laughing, landing in the sun-warmed sand.

"Ha-ha, very funny," he said, trying to act serious. But he fell down next to her, clearly not in a hurry anymore. They watched windsurfers skimming along, and families having picnics and feeding the seagulls. Alex found a piece of driftwood and dug a deep moat while Rosa formed the mound into a castle. It wasn't a very good one, so they weren't sorry when a wave sneaked up and swamped it. Rosa jumped up in time to avoid getting wet, but Alex got soaked to the skin.

"Yikes, that's cold," he said, but he was grinning. When he stood up, he had something in his hand. He bent and washed it in the surf. "A nautilus shell. I've never found one before."

It was a nice big one, a rare find, not too damaged by the battering waves. Alex couldn't know it, but it was Mamma's favorite kind of shell. The nautilus is a symbol of harmony and peace, she used to say.

"You can have it if you want," he said, holding the shell out to her.

"No. You found it." Rosa kept her hands at her sides even though she wanted it desperately.

"I'm not good at keeping things." He wound up as if to throw it back into the surf.

"Don't! If you're not going to keep it, I will," Rosa said, grabbing it from him.

"I wasn't really going to throw it away," he said. "I just wanted you to have it."

When they got back to Alex's yard and Rosa saw what awaited them, she closed her hand around the seashell. "I hope this thing brings me good luck. I'm going to be needing it," she said.

Mrs. Montgomery and Pop stood waiting for them, both their faces taut with worry and anger. Before either of them spoke, Rosa could already hear them. *Where have you been? Do you know how worried we've been?*

"Where on earth have you been?" demanded Mrs. Montgomery. Rosa was speechless at the sight of her. She had flame-red hair and wore a straight white summer dress and white sandals. Her long, thin fingers held a long, thin cigarette. Mrs. Montgomery herself looked like a cigarette. A giant human cigarette.

"What are you thinking, eh? I told you to stay out of trouble," said Pop.

"And you're soaking wet," Mrs. Montgomery declared as though being wet was the crime of the century. From her shiny white handbag, she took out a bunch of what appeared to be first-aid gear. "Honestly, Alexander, I can't imagine what you were thinking. Come over here and let me take your temperature."

He dragged his feet, but submitted to her with the resignation of long habit. Mrs. Montgomery didn't check for fever like a regular mother, by feeling with her hands. She stuck a cone-shaped thing in his ear and then took it out and read the number.

"All right for you," Pop said, marching Rosa toward the truck. "We're gonna get you home, talk some sense into you."

As their parents separated them, Rosa and Alex caught each other's eye. Neither of them could keep from grinning. They both knew this wasn't the end of their adventure.

eight

Summer 1984

During the second summer Rosa and Alex spent together, she saw him suffer a full-blown asthma attack, and it made her weep with terror. She had never seen anything like it before. She had stopped thinking of him as being sick at all, because the medications and breathing apparatus kept his condition under control.

But not always. On a bright August day, they convinced his mother to allow them to fly kites on the beach, something that—incredibly—Alex had never done before. Rosa showed up with a kite her brother Sal had sent from Hong Kong, where the destroyer he was serving on had made port. She and Alex spent an entire morning putting the kite together, then headed for the beach.

At the long shoreline, isolated from the public beaches by a dense salt marsh, the wind was perfect for kite-flying. It blew strong and steady, a warm current up from the south. Rosa held the kite for Alex to launch. He got so excited and ran so fast along the beach that at first she had no clue there was anything wrong.

"Go, Alex, go!" she called, waiting to feel the wind fill the kite so she could launch it. "Faster!"

But he didn't go faster. He stumbled as though tripping over a log, yet there was nothing but sand beneath his feet.

"Hurry up," she urged.

He collapsed like a bird shot from the sky. His glasses flew off and landed in the sand.

"Alex!" she said, dropping the kite. She plunged to her knees beside him and touched his shoulder.

His face was turning blue and gray, like a ghost's. The rattle and wheeze of his struggling lungs terrified her, and she burst into tears. "Oh, Alex, I don't know what to do," she said, feeling helpless and horrible all at once. She looked around wildly, but there was nothing in sight except a pair of blue herons wading in the shallows. "Tell me what to do."

He shook his head and groped in the pocket of his khaki shorts. He took out his inhaler and inhaled three quick puffs. His eyes looked bright and desperate, but his coloring didn't improve and his wheezing grew worse. He couldn't seem to get his lungs working right.

Then he took something from another pocket. A black-and-yellow tube. He ripped open the plastic packaging and then, with his teeth, removed the gray cap from the end. Finally, in one smooth movement, he stabbed the black tip of the tube at his thigh and held it there for several seconds. He wheezed hard four times—in a panic, Rosa counted them—but then his breathing seemed to start working better.

He slowly removed the tube and inspected the black tip. Rosa was horrified to see a rather large needle sticking out of it. The whole business had taken only a few seconds. In the strange aftermath, Alex lay weak upon the sand, and Rosa was still crying.

"It's okay," he said, his voice soft and raspy. "I'm all right. Cross my heart and hope—"

"Are you going to be able to make it back home?"

"I need a minute."

Rosa started to scramble to her feet, but stopped when his cold hand touched hers. "No, wait," he said. "The kite—"

"You're not flying the kite."

"I know. But...how about you fly it for me? I need to rest." His voice was thin and pleading. "Come on, Rosa. She's going to take me straight to the hospital. That's the rule."

"Then I should go right now and get help."

"A few minutes won't make any difference one way or another. I'll be able to walk back if I can rest a little. The shot lasts twenty minutes, and I'm over the wheezing anyway. Fly the kite. *Please.*"

"I can do that. But only for a minute." She looked down at their hands—hers dark, his pale—and felt a wave of emotion moving through her. Then she gave him his glasses. Spying a mermaid's purse in the sand, she gave him that, too. "For luck," she explained, closing his hand around the small shell.

It felt particularly important to get it right. Like if she didn't, if she messed up, she would be letting him down along with the kite. It was a beautiful, one-of-a-kind kite, yellow with red streamers, and Pop had given her a brand-new spool of string to use. She refused to let Alex launch the kite, because he needed to rest. Instead, she planted it in the sand to catch the wind, and ran with the string shortened until the kite spiked up. Then she put on a full burst of speed and paid out the string.

She could hear Alex saying, "Go, Rosa," and that only made her run faster. *Don't let him down,* she thought. *Don't let him down.*

She managed to hoist the kite upward until it took off as though it had a will of its own, and would stay up no matter what she did on the ground. Breathless from running, she brought the string spool to Alex.

"It's up," she said.

"It's up," he echoed, taking hold and watching with shining eyes.

The moment they got back, there was a big fuss, just as Alex had warned her. They tried to act as though nothing had happened, but Alex's mother had an uncanny eye, and the minute she saw him, she said, "You were running on the beach, weren't you?"

"No, we just—"

"You were running, and you started wheezing."

He stared at the floor as he held out the autoinjection tube for her to inspect. Her face turned hard as alabaster marble. "I need to get my purse," she said. She brushed past Rosa as though she didn't see her at all.

Rosa and Pop stood on the porch and watched them go. Mrs. Montgomery hardly ever drove the car that was parked in the old carriage house, and when she gunned the engine, it coughed and wheezed worse than Alex. She didn't seem to be a very good driver, either, Rosa observed. The blue Ford Galaxy lurched and shuddered backward out of the driveway, and the engine banged and backfired all the way down Ocean Road.

"It's so sad that he's sick," Rosa said to her father. "When he couldn't breathe, I got really scared, like—" She stopped, not wanting to upset her father by mentioning Mamma. "Do you think Mrs. Montgomery is really mad at me?"

"She is afraid for her boy." Pop grabbed his pruning shears, ready to get back to work. "I think next week, you will stay with one of the neighbors."

"Pop, no." Rosa panicked. The neighbor ladies—those who stayed home instead of going to work—were old and smelled funny and some even had chin whiskers. Worse, the widowed ones all wanted to marry her father. "Please, Pop, I'll be good, I swear I will. Just give me a chance, okay, Pop. *Okay?*"

Returning from the doctor's a couple of hours later, Alex seemed to be having a similar argument with his mother. "It's no big deal, you know it's not," he said, banging the car door shut.

Rosa came running from the yard, where she had been watching the koi fish feed on hapless bugs. "Are you all right, Alex?" she asked. "Hello, Mrs. Montgomery."

Mrs. Montgomery was inspecting Alex fiercely; she didn't even seem to hear Rosa. "You're not to do anything but rest," she scolded. "You heard the doctor."

"Fine," Alex said. "I'll teach Rosa to play chess."

"I don't think Rosa—"

"I already know how to play chess," Rosa declared. "We could have a tournament."

"Then that's what we'll do," Alex said. "We'll have a chess tournament."

Rosa was aware of Mrs. Montgomery's stern disapproval, but she chose to ignore it.

So did Alex. He had the key to his mother. She would rather put up with Rosa than say no to Alex. He showed her that he had kept the mermaid's purse she'd given him. "I think it did bring me luck," he said.

He was good at chess, way better than she was. She was impulsive, he was deliberate. She moved by intuition while he applied his knowledge and intelligence. She didn't bother looking ahead at things; he studied the board as though it held the meaning of life.

Despite her poor skills, she managed to win a few victories. She improved quickly, and before long, she was asking about all the other interesting games stashed in a tall cabinet in the library.

"Canasta and backgammon," he said, then took down a long, narrow pegboard. "Cribbage."

She chuckled. "Sounds like something to eat."

"It's a good game. I'll show you."

nine

By their fourth summer together, Rosa and Alex had fallen into a routine. From mid-June until Labor Day, they were best friends. Mrs. Montgomery objected, but as usual, Alex knew how to handle her. He had all these long arguments about how being with someone his own age helped him manage his illness, because being alone was stressful and made his lungs twitchy.

Rosa couldn't believe his mother bought that. Maybe a mother's love made her putty in his hands. She was a severe woman but she adored Alex. She used to try to get him to invite other boys over, "other" meaning boys like him, summer people. Alex pitched such a fit that eventually his mother stopped trying. Rosa was just as glad about that. With the exception of Alex, summer people were snooty, and they seemed to have nothing better to do than work on their tans or shop.

Pop said they were his bread and butter so she'd better be polite to them.

Each year at summer's end, Alex went away, and Rosa felt bereft after he was gone. They always said they'd write to stay in touch, but somehow, neither of them got around to it. Rosa got busy with school and sports, and the year would speed past. When the next summer rolled around, they fell effortlessly back into their friendship. Getting together with Alex was like putting on a comfortable old sweater you'd forgotten you had.

That fourth summer, they were both going into the seventh grade, and they didn't ease back into the friendship as effortlessly as before. For some strange reason, she felt a little bashful around him that year. He was just plain old Alex, skinny and fair-skinned and funny. And she was just Rosa, loud and bossy. Yet there was a subtle difference between them that hadn't been there before. It was that stupid boy-girl thing, Rosa knew, because even the nuns were required to show kids those dumb videos, *Girl into Woman* and *Boy into Man*.

According to the videos, Rosa was still at least ninety percent girl, and Alex was definitely a boy. He had the same scrawny chest and piping boyish voice. She was pretty scrawny herself, and even though she sometimes yearned for boobs like Linda Lipschitz's, she also dreaded the transformation. Maybe if her mother was still alive, she'd feel differently, but on her own, she was more than happy for nature to take its time.

Mrs. Montgomery hadn't changed one bit, either. The whole first week of summer, Alex was confined to the house because his mother said he had a head cold. Fine, thought Rosa, trying not to feel frustrated about missing out on perfect weather. They'd find indoor things to do.

One day in June she showed up with an idea. She found Alex in the library, reading one of his zillions of books. Before she could lose her nerve, she took out a folded flyer and handed it to him.

"What's this?" he asked, adjusting his glasses.

With great solemnity, she indicated the flyer. "Just read it."

"'Locks for Love,'" he read. "'A non-profit organization that provides hairpieces at no charge to patients across the U.S. suffering from long-term medical hair loss.' And there's a donation form." He touched his pale hair. "Who would want this?"

She sniffed. "Very funny. Get the scissors."

He eyed her thick, curly hair, which swung clear down to her waist. "Are you sure?"

She nodded, thinking of her mother, the baby-bird baldness that had afflicted her after the chemo kicked in. She'd worn scarves and hats, and someone at the hospital gave her a wig, but she said it didn't look like real hair and never wore it. If only Rosa had known about Locks for Love then, she could have given Mamma her hair.

"Do it, Alex." She blew upward at the springy curls that fell down over her forehead. Her hair was always a mess. There was never a hair tie or barrette to be found in the house. Pop never thought to buy them, and she never remembered to tell him.

She looked up to see Alex watching her. "What?"

"You really want me to cut off your hair?"

"I need a haircut, anyway."

He grew solemn. "There are salons. My mother takes me to Ritchie's in the city."

"I don't think I would like a salon. Mamma used to cut my hair when I was little." Suddenly it was there again in her throat, that hurtful feeling of wanting. She blinked fast and tried to swallow, but it wouldn't go away. That was another thing about this girl-into-woman business. Sometimes she cried like a baby. Her emotions were as unpredictable as the weather.

Alex watched her for a moment longer. He pushed his glasses

up the bridge of his nose—a nervous habit. She looked him straight in the eye and conquered her tears. "Go get the scissors. And a hair tie."

"A what?"

She rolled her eyes. "You know, like a rubber band with cloth on it for making a ponytail. Or just a rubber band will do. The instructions say I have to send my hair in a ponytail. Do it, Alex."

"Can't we maybe get Mrs. Carmichael to—"

"*Alex.*"

Like a condemned man walking to the gallows, he went upstairs, where she could hear him rummaging around. Then he returned with a rubber band and a pair of scissors. That was the thing about Alex. As her best friend, he did what she wanted him to do, even when he didn't agree with her.

It felt like another adventure. She grabbed a towel and they went outside, Alex grumbling the whole way.

"Wait a minute," she said. "I have to brush my hair and make a ponytail."

He shook his head. "Have at it."

Her thick, coarse hair was hopelessly tangled. She'd washed it that morning in anticipation of the shearing, but during the bike ride over, the wind had whipped it into a snarled mass. Alex watched her struggle for a few minutes. Finally he said, "Give me the brush."

She felt that funny wave of bashfulness again as she handed it over. "Have at it," she said, echoing him.

"Turn around." His strokes were tentative at first, barely touching. "Jeez, you've got a lot of hair."

"So sue me."

"I'm just saying— Hold still. And be quiet for once."

She decided to cooperate, since he hadn't wanted to do this in the first place. She stood very still, and all on his own Alex figured out how to brush through the tangles without tugging or hurting. He started at the bottom and worked upward until the brush glided easily through her hair. His patience and the gentleness of his touch did something to her. Something strange and wonderful. When his fingers brushed her nape, she shut her eyes and bit her lip to stifle a startled gasp.

She could hear him breathing, and he sounded all right. She was always leery of setting off an asthma attack. But he was on some new medication that controlled his condition better than ever.

"Okay," he said softly. "I think that's got it pretty good." He smoothed both hands down the length of her hair, gathering it into a ponytail. Then he stepped out from behind her. "Rosa."

Her eyes flew open. "What?"

"You look weird. Are you sure you want me to do this?"

"Absolutely."

"Your funeral." A moment later he stood behind her, snipping away. It was nothing like the way Mamma used to do this, but she didn't care. She was happy to get rid of all the long, thick hair. It took a mother to look after hair like this, and without one she might as well get rid of it. Besides, there was someone out there who needed it more than Rosa did.

She felt lighter with each decisive snip. The fat ponytail fell to the ground and Alex stared down at it. "I'm not too good at this," he said.

She fluffed her hand at her bare neck. Her head felt absolutely weightless. "How does it look?"

He regarded her with solemn contemplation. "I don't know."

"Of course you know. You're looking right at me."

"You just look...like Rosa. But with less hair."

What did a boy know, anyway? With the exception of her friend Vince, no boy ever had a clue about hair and clothes. She'd have to get Vince and Linda to tell her.

She picked up the long ponytail and held it out at arm's length. Alex stepped back, as though it were roadkill.

"Well," she said. "They ought to be able to make a wig out of this."

"A really good wig," he said, edging closer. "Maybe two."

She put the hair into a large Ziploc bag, like the instructions said to do. At that moment, Pop rolled a wheelbarrow around the corner from the front yard. He was whistling a tune, but it turned to a strangled gasp when he saw Rosa.

"Che cosa nel nome del dio stai facendo?" he yelled, dropping the handles of the barrow and rushing to her side. Then he rounded on Alex, spotted the scissors in his hand and raised a fist in the air. "You. *Raggazzo stupid.* What in the name of God have you done?"

Alex turned even paler than usual and dropped the scissors into the grass. "I... I... I..."

"I made him do it," Rosa piped up.

"Do what?" Mrs. Montgomery came out to see what all the ruckus was about. She took one look at Rosa and said, "Dear God."

"It is the boy's fault," Pop sputtered. "He—he—"

"I said, I made him do it," Rosa repeated, more loudly. She held out the clear plastic bag. "I'm donating my hair to..." Suddenly it was all too much—Alex's sheepish expression, the horror on Pop's face, Mrs. Montgomery's disapproval, the bag of roadkill hair. The explanation that had made such perfect sense a few minutes ago suddenly stuck in her throat.

And then she did the unthinkable. Right in front of them all, she burst into tears. Her only thought was to get away as fast as possible, so she dropped the bag and ran, all but blinded by tears. She raced as though they were chasing her, but of course they weren't. They were probably standing around shaking their heads saying, *Poor Rosa* and *What would her mother think.*

She ran instinctively toward the ocean, where she could be alone on the empty beach. Breathless, she flopped down and leaned against the weatherbeaten sand fence and hugged her knees up to her chest. Then she lost it for good, the sobs ripping from a place deep inside her she had foolishly thought had healed over. It would never heal, she knew that now. She would always be broken inside, a motherless daughter, a girl forced to raise herself all on her own, with no one to stop her from doing stupid things, or to tell her everything was going to be okay after she did them.

Her chest hurt with violent sobs, yet once she started, she couldn't stop. It was as if she had to get out all the sadness she usually kept bottled up inside. The crashing surf eclipsed her voice, which was a good thing, because she was gasping and hiccupping like a drowning victim. After a few minutes of this, she felt weak and drained. The wind blew her chopped-off hair, and she brushed at it impatiently.

"Are…you okay?" asked a voice nearby.

Startled, Rosa crabwalked backward, mortified that he'd seen her lose it. "What are you doing here, Alex?"

He offered a half smile—half friendly, half scared she might explode. And he held up a manila-colored padded envelope. On the front, he'd carefully printed the address. "I told our parents about your project and they understood. It's okay, Rosa. It's perfectly fine. Your dad got all proud of you and my mom said you did the right thing. You don't need to worry about getting in trouble."

She used her shirttail to wipe her face. She should probably feel mortified, but she didn't. She just felt…emptied out. Sitting back on her heels, she looked up at Alex. "I didn't think things through, and I'm so embarrassed," she confessed. "I look like a freak."

He dropped to his knees beside her. "Naw. You look good. Honest."

And then somehow everything shifted and changed in the blink of an eye. He set down the thick envelope and put his arms around her, awkwardly but with absolutely no hesitation. Rosa had no idea how to react, she was so surprised, and so...something. She didn't know what. She didn't even feel like herself, but like a different person, sitting here with his arms around her and his face so close she could hear every breath he took.

"It'll be okay, Rosa," he said. "I swear."

And then it happened. He kissed her. His lips touched down, first lightly and then pressing a little harder. She kissed him back, knowing she had never felt anything quite like this. She was engulfed, and for the first time she understood that a kiss wasn't something you did with your lips but with your whole self. It was a kind of surrender, a promise, and she couldn't believe how wonderful it made her feel.

They came apart slowly. He was red to the tips of his ears, and Rosa figured she probably was, too.

"Well," he said, adjusting his glasses, "I guess you're my girlfriend now."

"You?" She burst out laughing and jumped to her feet, grabbing the envelope. "Dream on, Alex Montgomery."

"You know you want to be," he said. His eyes crinkled when he grinned at her. He chased her halfway down the beach before she started to worry about his breathing and slowed down. And then they sort of fell together, shoulders touching, their hands caught, and they walked slowly back toward the house, talking like they always did, the best of friends. The coolness of the breeze on Rosa's neck made her smile.

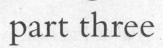

part three

MINESTRA

We never tired of being asked, "What makes Joe Louis
win all his fights?" because we loved to shout the answer:
"He eats pasta fazool, morning and night."
This simple dish is almost too hearty to be termed a
"minestra" (soup), but it's served in thick bowls rather
than on plates, and eaten with a spoon. During Lent,
this meatless dish is always on the menu.

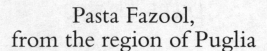

Pasta Fazool,
from the region of Puglia

Warm 4 Tablespoons of fruity extra-virgin olive oil in a large saucepan and gently sauté 1/2 onion, chopped, a peeled and chopped carrot, a rib of chopped celery and some minced garlic. Open a can of cannelini or Jackson Wonder beans and drain, then add to the vegetables along with 4 chopped plum tomatoes, a pinch of fresh rosemary and 2 cups boiling water. Bring back to a boil, then reduce heat and simmer for thirty minutes. Transfer about half of the beans and their liquid to a food processor and process to a thick purée.

Stir the purée back into the beans. Add 1/4 pound of ziti (or other pasta) and another 1-2 cups of boiling water to the beans in the pot. Cook, stirring constantly, until the pasta is tender, about 10-15 minutes. Remove from heat. Add salt and lots of black pepper to taste.

Serve in warm bowls, garnished with a drizzle of olive oil, a sprinkle of chopped flat-leaf parsley and some parmigiana.

ten

Alex Montgomery awoke with the rumble of an eighteen-wheeler pounding through his head. His eyelids felt glued shut, and his mouth was so dry that for a moment he panicked, fighting for breath. Then, slowly, bit by bit, he peeled his eyes open to a painful squint and propped himself up on his elbows.

It wasn't a rumbling eighteen-wheeler he heard, but the roar of the surf outside his bedroom window. And he wasn't sick, but hung over.

Same difference.

With a groan, he pushed the covers away and sat up. In college, he used to consider head-banging debauchery liberating. Amusing, even.

Not anymore.

He groped for his glasses, found a pair of frayed, cutoff blue jeans and put them on, then staggered to the bathroom to brush his teeth before his mouth was declared a biohazard.

The picture in the mirror of the medicine cabinet made him groan. Beard stubble, bloodshot eyes, a mouth that had forgotten how to smile. He shuddered and opened the cabinet to make the reflection go away.

Brick-red water sputtered from the choking faucet. He turned the spigot another notch, and the spurt turned to a stream, and the stream turned—well, not quite clear but good enough for brushing his teeth. He studied the contents of the cabinet. Baby aspirin, its expiration date marked 1992. A bottle of iodine, its cap fused by rust. And of course, one of the ever-present syringes of his youth. He scooped it all up and threw it into the trash can.

Having second thoughts, he took out the baby aspirin and stuffed the bottle in his pocket.

Then he splashed water on his face and hair, scrubbed the towel over his head and put his glasses back on. He couldn't face shaving yet, and refused to think about putting in his contact lenses. "Coffee," he murmured, slinging the towel around his neck and shuffling down the stairs to the kitchen.

Here in this house, his mother was everywhere, as he'd known she would be, even though she had stopped coming here a dozen years ago. The house and grounds had been kept up, because God forbid it should look shabby.

As he passed the master bedroom, he imagined catching a whiff of her trademark scent—Chanel No. 5 and Dunhill cigarettes. He recognized her tasteful eye in the white painted frames of the photos on the wall of the stairwell, in the careful arrangements of dishes in the kitchen cupboards. He opened the pantry to find a few rusting cans of tuna and anchovies, baked beans, Campbell's soup and, of course, a lifetime's supply of martini olives—but no coffee.

The fridge held only the six-pack of Narragansett he'd stashed there yesterday when he arrived. He looked at the beer for a long time. Then he looked at the clock on the stove—

10:30 a.m. The refrigerator motor kicked on as if prodding him to make up his mind.

"Screw it," Alex muttered. He grabbed a can of beer, opened it and took a slug. It was clean and cold—good enough.

Scratching his bare chest, he walked out to the veranda facing the ocean and sat in a half-rotten wicker chair. The cushions hadn't been put out in years. Maybe now they never would be again. In the past, before Memorial Day, his mother had ordered the house to be opened, the pantry stocked and the furniture uncovered.

Not this year. Not next. Never again.

Yesterday he'd sought solace from his friends, people who had known him for years, people who were supposed to care about him. The liquid sympathy they'd offered had barely scratched the surface of his grief. Numbness, that was all he felt. That, and annoyance because Natalie Jacobson had chosen last night to come on to him.

Mindless sex was always welcome, he conceded, even right after your mother dies. But when he looked into Natalie's hungry eyes, even the wine he'd drunk couldn't keep him from feeling a faint self-loathing.

Besides, by that point, his thoughts had been consumed by Rosa Capoletti. He'd actually believed the sight of her would make the old feelings go away. Fuzzy logic at best, but it had made perfect sense after partying with his friends all evening.

He should have known it wouldn't work like that. Rosa was special to him in ways he didn't even understand, and seeing her again only confirmed it. The moment he'd laid eyes on her, he'd known. The sight of the nautilus shell, in a place of honor and with its own special lighting behind the bar, underscored his certainty. The shell was the first gift he'd ever given her, and discovering she'd kept it gave him food for thought.

He took another swig of beer and peeled the towel from

around his neck. The day was already hot, but here on the shady veranda, the temperature felt perfect. Through stinging eyes, he surveyed the ancient property, once a place of family gatherings and elegant parties, a place where he used to run free with the best person he knew.

Even though the grass was cut and the hedges pruned, the garden had a neglected air. Lilypads choked the pond, probably fertilized by carcasses of koi.

On the far edge of the property was a huge stump, freshly cut and partially uprooted like a giant compound fracture. In a recent windstorm, the fallen tree had crushed the front section of the carriage house, crashing through the single-story garage while leaving the living quarters intact. Live electrical wires were involved, so the local authorities had ordered the tree removed. Power company workers had sectioned and stacked the logs and fed the branches to the chipper.

Other than structural damage to the building, which would be covered by insurance, the only casualty was his mother's old car, a blue Ford that hadn't been driven in twelve years or more. Each year his mother claimed she'd send someone to clean out the shed and have the old furniture, tools and car hauled away, and each year, she never got around to it.

Mother Nature put an end to the procrastination, and the local sheriff took care of having the car towed to the junkyard.

It was strange, being here at the beach house, a place haunted by cobwebs and memories. As he sat drinking and looking out over the yard toward the sea, he could hear echoes of his mother's voice as she talked on the phone to this designer or that decorator, to his doctors and women she called "school chums" no matter how old they got. He could feel her hand stroking his forehead at night when he was sick, which was pretty much every night.

And there, where the property sloped down toward the

beach, was the place he'd first seen Rosa Capoletti. The friendship they'd started that day had been touched by the bright, ephemeral magic of summer. In time their friendship had flared briefly, painfully, to passion and then finally disintegrated in an eruption of tears and recriminations.

He hadn't thought it would hurt so much to see her again. He wasn't prepared for that. He should have realized that what was between them had never died. It just lay dormant until the sunshine of Rosa's smile and the moisture of old tears brought it back to life.

The beer imparted a faint buzz in his head. The need to sort out everything that had happened pulsed hard inside him, insistent, unexpected.

Unfortunately, if last night was any indication, she didn't feel the same way at all. She'd regarded him like an uninvited wedding guest. Too damn bad. He was back, this was a small town and it was long past time that they figured things out between them. Of course, he could and maybe should simply deal with the property and take off again, but that didn't feel right. His mother's passing had shaken him in ways he hadn't expected. There was something so achingly tragic about her death, because she'd never really lived.

It was probably a mistake to move back here, Alex reflected, yet it didn't seem wrong. He'd made the decision impulsively, walking away from an apartment, friends, a whole life in New York City. In addition to leaving the city, he had committed to taking the summer off for the first time in his professional career. His assistant, Gina Colombo, would manage things for a few months. He only hoped he could do so without going stir-crazy.

His decision was fast morphing into something crazy and real. He'd come to a point in his life where he didn't much like himself. He'd neglected the invisible, essential things, favoring a lifestyle over a life. He needed to figure out who he was when he wasn't in the company of air-kissing friends and the strangers he called family. He needed the vibrance and fulfillment he'd found only once before—with Rosa.

A seagull circled and then hung suspended above the shallows as though tethered by an invisible kite string. The first time he'd ever flown a kite, he had been with Rosa. She was there for a lot of firsts: the first time he caught a striped bass, fishing in the surf. The first time he'd sailed a Laser all by himself, skimming like a guillemot over the waves at a speed that stole his breath away. She was the first girl he'd ever kissed.

He could only wish she'd been the first woman he'd made love to, that he'd come to her as pure and full of joy and apprehension as she'd come to him, but it wasn't so. Even then, when he was gathering her into the deepest reaches of his heart, another part of him was running from her.

After leaving Rosa, he'd spent a few years trying to forget her. He did a good job of it, drinking and partying his way through college and business school, pretending he didn't notice when a small, dark-haired woman walked past or when he heard a certain kind of laugh or a distinctive Rhode Island accent. Now, seeing her again, he understood that even after all these years, she still lived inside him the way no other person ever had. She was part of his blood and bone. From the first day they met, it had been that way for him.

Leaving her, when all his heart wanted him to do was love her, was the hardest thing he'd ever done—harder than understanding the mysteries of his family, harder than growing an investment fund when the market sank, harder than convincing his father he had his own path to follow.

A lobster boat, with bony arms extended out over the hull, chugged past, and then a small sailboat skimmed by in the other direction. It was a funny thing about this place by the sea. From this perspective, it seemed as though time stood still and nothing changed. With the exception of the ruined carriage house, everything here was exactly the same as it had been when he left, awash in pain and rage, vowing never to return.

Now a new kind of pain forced him to come back, against his will.

A decade had passed since he'd seen this view, felt this breeze, tasted the tang of salt in the air. Two years after the accident, once Pete recovered, Alex came back to explain everything, but by then it was too late. He hadn't expected Rosa to wait for him and she hadn't. She'd made a life for herself, and that included a boyfriend who happened to be a sheriff's deputy.

From that point onward, Alex welcomed all the myriad distractions of his chosen profession, even cultivated them to pretend his busy life was fulfilling. With dogged determination, he avoided making a fool of himself over a woman he couldn't have.

He cultivated a God-given talent in finance and joined the family firm, becoming a player in the great American investment game. As it turned out, he excelled at it. Clients who signed over their capital were rewarded with returns that exceeded all expectations. Within two years of joining the family firm, Alex earned his reputation of rainmaker.

And it was funny, really, when he thought about it. All he did was put two and two together. He might hear that adding a certain protein to baby formula had been proven to make babies smarter. The rest of the world would be surprised when the stock shot off the charts, but not Alex. He did his research and trusted his gut. He remembered arguing with his father about the IPO of an obscure little internet start-up called Amazon.com. No one had heard of it. Three years later, when that and similar equities soared 3800%, his father gave him his own fund to manage.

Some in the business believed Alex had an uncanny knack for timing. He knew it wasn't so. He read obsessively and knew how to interpret the signs of a company's rise or fall. He didn't do anything special. He just made sure he did it better than anyone else.

Among the funds he managed now was his life's work—The Medical Assistance Private Trust. Its revenues were used to fund health care for the indigent. He'd argued long and hard with his father to found the trust, and only when he threatened to leave the firm did his father agree to it. Alex didn't explain why the fund was so important. It was the one area of his life in which he was unequivocally doing good in addition to doing well, but of course, his father would argue with that.

Even more important was the Access Fund, another he'd created. It was consistently the least productive of the firm's products because he had deliberately created it for people who rarely had money to spare. Unlike all other Montgomery funds, this one had no minimum investment. Some of his clients had given him twenty dollars to start with. His father and colleagues thought he was nuts, that he was wasting his time and the firm's resources. Alex didn't see it that way. He saw it as giving a chance to people who deserved a shot.

His head throbbed.

He dug into the pocket of his cutoffs and fished out the baby aspirin. He shook the tiny pills into the palm of his hand. How much bigger was he than a baby? It didn't matter, he decided. The pills were so old, they had probably lost their kick. He tossed them into his mouth, tasting Sweet TARTS with a slightly bitter edge. He washed them down with a slug of beer. After a few minutes, his headache dulled to an aching thud. The hard blue lines of sea and sky gently melded and blurred.

Nothing like a little beer and aspirin to buzz away annoying reality. Hell, in his family, it was a time-honored tradition.

He heard the crunch of tires on gravel. The slam of a car door made him wince. Maybe the expired aspirin wasn't working so well after all.

He stood up too quickly, and images flipped in front of his eyes like a shuffled deck of cards. Then he set down his beer and went to see who it was.

He came around to the front of the house just as Rosa Capoletti raised her fist to knock at the door.

Before she noticed him, he took a moment to savor the sight of her. He half-hoped that last night's attack of lust and longing had been caused by his drunken state. But no. In the stark light of day, she still had the power to stir his blood. She was earthy and colorful. She wore her dark, curly hair caught back in a ponytail. Even without makeup, her face was a study in vivid color—red lips and large brown eyes, darkly lashed, olive-toned skin that looked soft to the touch.

I suppose she's pretty enough, his roommate at Phillips Exeter used to say as he studied the photograph Alex always kept with him, *in a grape-stomping Old-World sort of way.* Alex couldn't remember whether or not he'd hit him for that remark. He hoped he had.

"Hey, Rosa," he said as she raised her fist to knock again.

She turned quickly. "Alex. You startled me."

He motioned behind him. "I was around back," he said. "Join me?"

She eyed his bare chest, and her stare was so dubious, he thought she might walk away. But then she nodded once and headed for the porch steps. When she grasped the railing, the rotting finial broke off. She lost her balance and pitched forward.

Alex moved swiftly, in spite of his hangover, and grabbed

her arm to steady her. "Hey," he said, getting high on the smell of her hair, "are you all right?"

"I'm fine." Flustered, she disengaged herself from him and stepped back. "You ought to do something about that railing."

"I intend to." He half expected her to flee. Instead she followed him around to the veranda. He couldn't get over how good she looked to him. She wasn't just beautiful, but mature and confident in a way that made him wonder about the lost years between them. Even as a child, a motherless child, she had never been needy. But as an adult, she seemed completely self-possessed. She had transformed herself into an A-list restaurateur whose reputation for fun, food and fashion was unparalleled.

He caught himself checking out her tits. Her smooth skin deepened to shadowy cleavage where a tiny gold cross lay nestled.

"Would you like something to drink?"

Her glance flicked to the beer can parked on the arm of the wicker chair. "No, thanks."

"I couldn't find any coffee in the house." Like that explained it. "I just got here and haven't had time to stock up."

She lowered herself cautiously to the bottom step, clearly hoping it wouldn't collapse. When she turned to look up at him, there was a moment—maybe caused by the slant of light that fell across her face, or perhaps it was the beer and aspirin. But in that moment he saw Rosa as he had always known her. She was a laughing tomboy leading him on wild adventures, a shy teenager looking for her first kiss, a young woman glowing with the power of her big dreams.

Then the moment shifted, and she was a complete stranger again. A stranger who had a hot car, expensive clothes and a look of distrust in her eyes.

You made this happen, he told himself. *You have only yourself to blame.*

The thought prodded his temper. He was mad at himself, mostly, for being here in a place filled with ghosts and no coffee or food. He was supposed to be a respected businessman, established in his field. He didn't like finding himself at a disadvantage.

He sat on the opposite side of the steps from her. Long ago, complete silence used to be comfortable between them. But that wasn't the case now. He watched her fold her hands, open them, fold them again. She didn't feel safe in his world. Maybe she never had.

"I heard about your mother this morning," she said. "Alex, I'm so sorry."

Ah, a sympathy call. He balanced his wrists on his knees and stared out to sea. "So now you know why I'm here."

"Last night, you let me think it was because of me."

"Last night, I had too much to drink."

"Do you do that often?" she asked.

"If I did, I'd be better at it."

"Don't ever get good at something like that."

He looked over at her, searching her face for some hint that she knew more than she was saying. Because, of course, there was so much more to the story than the papers reported. So much more to his magnificent, miserable mother's life. And to her death.

Rosa's expression gave no hint that she knew anything more than she'd read in the papers. "So do you have plans?" she asked.

Last night, before he'd seen her again, he would have sworn he was staying in the big old house for practical reasons. He planned to sell his apartment in New York City and open a branch office of the Montgomery Financial Group just across the Newport/Pell bridge. For now, he needed a place to live. But the moment he laid eyes on Rosa again, he knew his need to be here was much more complicated than that.

However, in his present condition, he was in no shape to explain himself. "The place needs fixing up," he said.

She looked over at the carriage house. "Storm damage?"

"That's right. The house could use some work, too."

"Maybe it's none of my business, but why aren't you with your father?"

She hadn't changed. She'd always been a family-first type of girl, which was one of many reasons they'd been such a mismatch. "I'll be going up to Providence this afternoon to... help with the arrangements." He knew he hadn't answered her question, but that was all he had in him at the moment.

"I take it the two of you never grew any closer," she said, reading between the lines.

Alex's headache kept trying to come back. "I wasn't the kind of son a man like my father knew what to do with." He knew she understood that. She had seen him at his worst with his father.

She held him in that soft, steady regard, the way she used to look at him long ago, never taking his measure, never judging him. And in that moment, she wasn't a stranger at all. She was Rosa, the best part of his boyhood summers.

As a kid, Rosa Capoletti had been more fun than a Ferris wheel ride. As a teenager, she'd set his hormones on fire. Now, as an adult woman, she was lethally attractive.

Alex supposed he'd known women who were more beautiful than Rosa, women who were smarter and more cultured. But none of them—not runway models, Rhodes scholars or concert pianists—affected him the way Rosa did.

"Alex," she said, "you still haven't explained your plans."

His true reasons for coming back to Winslow were rapidly

emerging. It was nuts, completely nuts, but she'd nailed him. Again. Always. He had it worse than ever.

Maybe he was wrong about reconnecting with her. Maybe it was a mistake. Except that it wasn't. It was rare that he knew the truth in his heart; he hadn't felt the rightness of something in a long time but he felt it now. It was time. Events converged as though the universe was telling him to go for it.

"I'm opening an office in Newport." It sounded so sensible, spoken aloud. But the fact was, he would not have come near this place if his mother had lived.

He flashed a grin to hide his pain. "Enough about me. Let's talk about you," he said.

"Alex, you just lost your mother."

"All the more reason to avoid the extremely depressing topic of me." He didn't want to talk about his plans, his problems. He was sick of himself. He leaned back and gave her a long look. "So you're Rhode Island's premier restaurateur. That's what they say in the papers."

She smiled, and her whole being glowed with pride. Most people were too reserved to show the world who they really were, but not Rosa. If she felt it, she wore it on her sleeve without apology. She was living, breathing proof that the hard things of life didn't have to defeat you—or even define you.

"You're really something, Rosa," he said. And before he could censor himself, he added, "You always were."

He recognized the question in her eyes, the same question that had been there twelve years before, when he told her it was over.

What happened to us?

Now, as then, he kept the truth hidden. Years ago, he had lacked the emotional hardware to be the person she needed, the one she deserved. She wanted nothing less than everything from him, and he didn't believe even that was enough for her.

Her penetrating stare was taking him apart. She was so different now; he couldn't figure out what was going on behind those darkly lashed brown eyes. "What?" he asked.

"God, we were so young. I was just thinking about how young we were."

"And now we're old," he said.

"Speak for yourself." She picked a blade of grass, wrapped it around her finger. "Did you know a child laughs an average of three hundred times a day, and an adult just three?"

"No, I didn't."

"I read that somewhere." She uncurled the blade of grass and let it drop.

They sat in silence for a while, watching the waves in the distance, listening to the timeless rhythm of the surf. A seagull landed on the stump of the fallen tree, perched on one leg. Alex started to worry that Rosa would get bored and take off, so he tried to start up the conversation again.

"Celesta's-by-the-Sea," he said. "I like that. You named it for your mother."

"Her cooking inspired the whole concept. Good thing her name wasn't Brunhilde or Prudence."

He lifted his beer can. "To Celesta's." He took a long drink, then noticed her watching him. "What?"

"It's not even noon yet."

"The lady tells time."

"Ah, hostile sarcasm. I don't remember that about you."

"I've been practicing. Anyway, don't worry about me. I'm merely observing tradition. When there's grieving to do, we drink. It's the Montgomery way."

"You call that grieving?" she asked softly. "You haven't even begun to grieve." She watched him with those large, unwavering eyes. It was like looking into a magical mirror, giving him an unsettling glimpse of himself. The truth was there, somehow, in her eyes, the most honest eyes he had ever known. He saw the real Alex, hardened and discontented and immeasurably disappointed in himself. It was an image he ordinarily tried to hide, but this morning he was failing.

"I'm so very sorry about your mother, Alex," Rosa said again. "What I remember about her was that here in the summer house, you were her whole world."

Brand-new grief, as bright and sharp as a fresh knife wound, was taking over, slashing through his control. He felt a squeezing sensation in his chest, and it took him by surprise. People tended to offer their most tender memories of the deceased, and Rosa was no different. The difference was, she understood the dynamics of his boyhood better than anyone he knew. He nodded and looked away, hoping she'd move on to a different subject. In the distance, the horizon line between the sea and sky blurred and pulsed.

"Now that I look back at it," Rosa went on, "making you her whole world was a lot to put on a kid, but I don't think she realized that. I remember how protective she was, how careful of your health. She absolutely adored you."

Rosa didn't understand, he realized. The way his mother adored him was a burden, not a gift. He looked down at his hand and saw that he'd completely crushed the beer can. He had no memory of doing so.

Rosa was looking at him, too. "It's normal to be angry."

He flung the can into the bushes. "I'm not angry."

She smiled at him as though the past twelve years had never happened. "I'm Italian, remember? I'm okay with emotion. The bigger, the better."

The tension in his chest eased like a tight coil unfurling. He didn't have to pretend for her. He didn't have to behave in a certain way. The sweet relief spread through him, more potent than beer and baby aspirin.

He heard another car approach and stood up. "I'd better see who that is."

She stood up, too. "Maybe you should put on a shirt, Alex," she said.

He touched his bare chest. "You're right."

"And I should go," she added.

"No, don't." He blurted out the words. "Please stay." He held open the back door.

She stood there for a moment, then walked to the door and stepped inside. He couldn't read her expression, yet he came to an unexpected realization. The minute Rosa showed up, his headache had disappeared.

He grabbed a sweatshirt from a hook by the door, yanked it over his head and went to the front, stepping out onto the porch just as a car door slammed. He instantly wished he had not insisted that Rosa stay.

"Hello, Dad," he said. "I wasn't expecting you."

"Clearly not." His father looked perfectly tailored and groomed, as though for a board meeting. "That would have meant you were checking your voice mail. I left at least a half dozen messages."

Checking messages had been the last thing on Alex's mind, but of course, his father wouldn't understand that. "I don't get good reception out here."

The passenger side door opened and his sister got out. She shot him a poisonous look. "You should have called," she said. "The medical examiner's report is in. Mother killed herself. We just thought you might want to know."

eleven

Madison's words hammered at Alex, and his headache came pounding back. Oddly, he felt no surprise at the news; in the back of his mind, he'd already known. He looked at them both: his family. They were supposed to be helping each other through this, yet instead they were like three icebergs bumping up against each other, awkward and disconnected.

"Come inside," he said to his father and sister. Even as he spoke, he was aware of Rosa's presence behind him. He held open the door. One look at Rosa's face told him she'd heard. The shock and horror in her expression made that crystal clear.

Alex noticed the same look on his sister's face when she stepped into the musty foyer and spied Rosa. He could see Madison wishing she had kept her mouth shut.

His father masked whatever he was thinking behind his customary icy politeness. "We didn't realize you had company."

He decided not to point out that they might have guessed from seeing the red sports car parked in the front.

"I was just leaving," Rosa said. She headed for the door, paused there and turned back. "I'm very sorry for your loss."

And then she was gone, the door banging shut behind her. Alex's headache roared like a locomotive. Madison glared at him; his father stood as stiff as a suit of armor.

"You didn't waste any time finding someone to comfort you," Madison said. "God, you just dumped Portia van Deusen last week, wasn't it?"

"Last month." Alex massaged his temples. "And she dumped me." He should never have gotten mixed up with her. At first, she'd been a pleasant enough diversion. Their families were close, she was beautiful, convenient and apparently crazy about him. They'd had a few laughs—a few too many—and ended up sleeping together several times. He thought that was the end of it. Portia had other ideas.

"You want everybody to think she dumped you. But the truth is—"

"Enough." Their father's voice brought them up short the way it always had, cleaving like a steel blade through their argument. "We're here about your mother, not Alexander's behavior."

Alex gritted his teeth in frustration. They were a family, for Christ's sake. They should treat each other better, particularly now. Just because they'd never learned how was no excuse. In a neutral tone, he said, "Come and sit down, okay? Please."

He led the way to the parlor, an airy, high-ceilinged room with a bay window framing a view of the sea. There, he peeled back the sheets draping the wing chairs and settee, and motioned for them to sit down.

Alex studied them both for a moment, and a strange notion came over him. He didn't really know these people. Madison was his sister; she'd known him all the days of his life. Yet she had always been a distant figure, tucked away at boarding school, at camp during each summer, then college, followed immediately by a society marriage and a swift conversion to A-list hostess. She was married to Prescott Cheadle, a partner in a Boston law firm. She had two kids Alex liked a lot, Trevor and Penelope. But he didn't know their mother—this strong, attractive woman—and somehow that felt like a loss. He suddenly found himself wishing they all knew each other better. No one had ever told them they might need each other one day, and for some reason, they hadn't figured that out themselves.

And his father... Alex couldn't begin to figure him out. On the surface, he was the epitome of success; the heir to a fortune who had grown the empire beyond all expectations, a respected and influential figure. Now he was a man whose wife had killed herself.

"Dad, I'm sorry," Alex said, stumbling over the hopelessly inadequate words.

"I'm sorry, too."

The three of them lapsed into an uncomfortable silence. Madison got up and plucked at some of the sheeting that covered the furniture, peeking underneath. "So who was that woman?"

She hadn't recognized Rosa. Madison, like his parents, had never realized the significance of Rosa. She was the gardener's girl, and like every other child of the domestic help, she was invisible as wallpaper. Madison had no idea what Rosa meant to him. She'd never known how profoundly the gardener's daughter had changed him, long ago.

But then again, he didn't know much about his sister's heart, either.

"Rosa Capoletti," he said.

Madison had no reaction.

"Pete Capoletti's daughter," their father said, like a game show host offering a clue.

Alex was surprised his father remembered. Madison still didn't recognize the name. Could she really not remember what had happened all those years ago? He glanced at his father and realized he seemed to.

"Mr. Capoletti takes care of the property," their father offered.

"Oh, that guy. Now I remember him. Nice Italian man, wore a flat cap and sang while he worked. Didn't you used to play with his daughter?"

"Yeah, that's right," Alex said, nearly choking on the irony of it. He didn't want to explain Rosa; he couldn't. "She stopped by to pay her condolences. Now, why don't you tell me about Mother?"

Madison looked like a model in a luxury hotel ad, sitting there. Her makeup was perfect, her nails done, every golden hair in place.

Their father cleared his throat and handed him a thick padded envelope.

Alex's heart squeezed as he looked over the papers. The state seal crowned the top sheet, and there were two notarized signatures on the bottom. In between lay an official-looking death investigation report and certifier's forms, the sort you never think you'll see. He scanned the reports, and his gut churned as he read the contents of his own mother's stomach, the levels of toxins in her system, even the placement of objects on the nightstand.

His hands shook as he replaced the papers in the envelope. "Didn't you know she was hurting?" he asked his father. He raked a hand through his hair in frustration. "Couldn't you have done anything?"

"One can always do something," his father stated.

His infuriating calmness caused Alex to snap. "Where the hell were you while she was swallowing all the pills and booze?"

His father gestured at the envelope. "It's all documented. I was in the study."

"You might as well have been on the moon."

"Do you want me to feel guilty?" his father demanded.

"I just want you to *feel*," Alex shot back.

"I feel terrible," his father said. "I am utterly dismayed."

Madison let out a humorless laugh, edged with hysteria. "*Dismayed,* for Christ's sake. Dismayed, as in, 'my stock portfolio dipped.' Or 'I just can't seem to correct that slice in my golf swing.' Or 'my wife just killed herself.' *Dismayed.*"

"Madison," said their father, "that's enough."

"I haven't even gotten started," she said, her eyes bright with tears. "I need to know how to feel about this, and you're not giving me a single clue. You either, Alex."

"Don't you have a therapist for that?"

"Not funny, little brother."

"I'm serious. This is no small thing, and I'm as clueless as you are." Almost, he thought. He actually did have a clue, but he wasn't ready to say anything.

"We're pathetic." She stood and wandered to the kitchen, looking around slowly, as though seeking out ghosts. "Anything to drink?"

"Just beer." He sent a questioning look at his father.

"No, thank you."

"A beer sounds perfect," said Madison.

He heard the fridge open and close, heard the unmistakable crack of a can tab. She returned to the parlor and sat down, then drank what seemed like half the can. She held out her right hand. "I broke a nail opening that."

"It'll grow back." He sat in silence while she took a few more sips.

"So is your girlfriend going to blab?" she asked.

"What?"

"Roseanne Rosannadanna," she said, jerking her head toward the front.

"Jesus, Maddy—"

"I'm serious. Dad and I haven't told a soul."

"I wanted it that way," their father explained. "It's best for all of us. No need to air this tragedy."

What was best, thought Alex with a new flash of rage, would have been for this not to have happened at all. But that was life for you. *You never know what you're gonna get,* he thought in Roseanne Rosannadanna's accent.

"I don't want anyone to know, either," said Madison. "God, I hope that woman won't say anything."

Alex wanted to reassure her, to guarantee her privacy would be guarded, but the fact was, he didn't know. "If she's the same kind of person she was when I used to know her, she won't tell anyone."

"I swear, you are so naive. Everybody changes, Alex. You of all people should know that."

"What do you mean, me of all people?"

Carrying her beer, Madison got up and went over to the mantel, unveiling the objects there with a flourish—vases and framed photographs, a hobnail glass candy dish. "Ah, just as I thought. Pictorial evidence right here. See? If that's not naive, I don't know what is." She selected an old photo in a tarnished silver frame and handed it to him.

Alex felt as though he was looking at a stranger. But he wasn't. On the back of the frame was a label with his mother's tight, neat handwriting: Alexander IV, Summer 1983. The picture itself showed an undersized, pallid boy. He hadn't known at the time how sick he was, of course. His mother never would have allowed him to know. But he could see the ravages of illness now, like a shadow lurking in the background of the photograph.

He was standing in the library of this very house, which had been his favorite place when he wasn't allowed to go anywhere else. He was dressed all in white; his mother had probably been inspired by *The Great Gatsby,* which was the first video movie she had ever bought, and watched constantly. But on ten-year-old Alex, the effect was ghostlike. He had hair so pale it seemed translucent, legs so thin they resembled fragile bird bones. The eyes and cheeks were sunken in a refugee motif. His oxygen-starved skin was pale, his eyes almost unnaturally bright.

Alex put the picture aside, mystified as to why his mother had kept it all these years.

Madison sucked down the rest of her beer and got up to pace the room, stopping in front of a picture of their mother seated in one of the wicker chairs, looking out to sea. Given what had happened, the image seemed to have a haunted quality now.

"I need to know why she did it," Madison said to her father. "Please, tell us why."

The stark desperation in her voice touched Alex, though their father sat motionless. Alex went over to his sister and gave her an awkward hug. His father watched, expressionless; theirs was not a demonstrative family, and neither of them had mastered the proper way to hug.

"I don't know," their father said quietly. "We'll never know. I wish I could give you more than that, Madison, but I can't."

For the first time, Alex felt a flicker of unity with his father as they attempted to console Madison. "She kept things to herself when she was alive," he said.

"What do you mean, things?"

Oops. "She was a private person all her life. You know that."

"Too private," Maddy agreed, "and now this. *Why?*"

"She was unhappy," their father said.

"Who's that unhappy?"

Someone who lived a lie all her life, Alex thought.

"If she was always unhappy, then why would she kill herself on that particular day?" Madison asked. "What was special about it?"

Alex rubbed a weary hand over his unshaven face. "Anything we say would be pure speculation. What's the point of that?"

Madison sank down on a draped ottoman. "What's the point of anything?"

He frowned, worried by the bleak question. He and his father exchanged a glance. "How are you, Maddy?"

She looked startled by the question. "I just lost my mother. I'm a wreck."

"How did the kids take it?"

"They were devastated, of course. They adored Mother. Penelope has slept in bed with me the past two nights."

With me, she said. Not with me and Prescott. But Alex didn't go there.

"I pray I'll never have to tell them about..." She nodded toward the medical examiner's report. "My God, I have no idea how I'd explain that."

As he watched the anguish on his sister's face, Alex felt a fresh surge of fury. Their mother had been fully aware of the impact her suicide would have, especially on Maddy and her two kids. Yet she'd done it anyway.

Somehow, they managed to discuss "arrangements." It seemed surreal to be doing so. Surprisingly, Madison took over. His sister wanted the burden. She was one of the youngest and best hostesses around, and planning events—even her own mother's funeral—was second nature to her. She had very definite ideas on flowers and music. Alex wondered how she could even begin to think about those things. Maybe it kept her from thinking about the harder stuff.

Their father agreed to everything without discussion. Every time Madison asked if he had a preference, he would simply say, "Whatever you decide is fine."

Alex felt queasy. At the end of a thirty-six-year marriage, you'd think there would be more to say.

"What should we do with this file?" Madison asked.

"I don't know. Do we need it?"

"I certainly don't. Did she have life insurance? I'm sure they'll reject the claim after the ruling."

"She never had life insurance," their father said.

Madison looked intrigued. "She didn't?"

"She used to say, 'Dead or alive, I'm worth a fortune, and I can pay my own claim.'"

Madison looked bereft. "I suppose I never really knew her. I wonder if any of us did."

It was a strange and sadly true thing to say. Alex patted her on the shoulder awkwardly. "Not me. Father?"

"This is not productive. It's completely speculative." His cell phone rang, and he looked at the display. "It's the funeral home. I need to take this." He strode outside.

"I'm never going to be a mystery to my kids," Madison declared, dabbing at her face. "I swear that right now. No secrets. No mysteries."

"Good plan. Now. Can I get a lift with you and Dad back

to Providence? I'll help you with the funeral. Then I need to pick up my car and bring some things back here for the summer."

She balled up the Kleenex in her hands. "Don't you have a car here?"

"Friends from Newport drove me." He didn't explain that he'd been in no condition to drive.

"And then just left you? Some friends. Isn't Mother's old car in the garage?"

"Apparently you haven't seen the garage." They walked out back and he showed her the storm damage.

"Oh," she said, examining the caved-in roof, the crushed window frames and split timbers. "So what are you going to do about this mess? God, the whole place is a project." She spread her hands and looked around the vast gardens, the plant-choked pond.

"Alexander, I want you to reconsider this move," their father said in a tone Alex recognized from a hundred childhood lectures. "The house is barely livable. Find a condo in Newport. I can have my secretary find you a place by the end of the day."

"No, thank you. I'll be fine here. There's work to do, and I've got a whole summer to do it."

His father shook his head. "You're going to need more than a summer."

"We'll see." Alex backed away from a full-blown argument. That was one thing his family was good at, so they didn't need any practice.

The three of them left the place together, and oddly, Alex felt eager to head for the city, to get through the ordeal of the funeral. Sometimes he thought his plan was as crazy as his father kept telling him it was. Coming back here was insanity. The entire property was haunted by memories.

Now, finally sober for the first time in a couple of days, Alex discovered something. He wanted to explore the ghosts of memory that drifted through the old, empty house, because a large part of who he was still resided here.

twelve

Down at the Galilee docks, the air was thick with the reek of the day's catch—lobster and bluefish, mussels and quahogs, mounds of striped bass, scrod and tuna. Rosa strolled along with Butch, who marked things on an order sheet attached to a clipboard.

As owner and general manager of the restaurant, she could—and probably should—leave the buying to her employees, but the fact was, she liked coming here. It was a place where nostalgia hung thick in the atmosphere of ice-cooled warehouses. This was her world, and a sense of belonging folded around her felt like a hand-crocheted afghan. She watched the birds congregating on the corrugated rooftops of the icehouses and warehouses, and listened to the chug of ships' engines.

"I love the smell of seafood in the morning," Butch said, inhaling dramatically.

"Me, too." She stepped over a drying net buzzing with flies. "Come on."

"It's true. I used to come here with my mother." She smiled, picturing her mother in a crisp cotton dress, her pocketbook strap looped over one tanned arm, her shopping bag over the other. "Her cioppino was legendary. Guys here fell all over themselves, trying to wait on her."

"Hey, *my* cioppino is legendary," he said.

Chefs, she thought. The good ones all seemed to be made of equal parts talent and ego.

"As a twenty-seven-dollar menu item, it had better be."

"It's the saffron." He wandered off to place his orders.

Rosa waved to Lenny Carmichael, a second-generation lobsterman she'd known since grade school. In his hip-high yellow boots and Red Sox baseball cap, he looked exactly like his father. She owed a large part of the restaurant's success to the fishermen of Galilee, who supplied her with the very best of local seafood. According to one of her myriad psychology textbooks, Rosa was trying to use the restaurant to recreate aspects of her late mother. After she read that conclusion, she shook her head. "Well, *duh*. I know exactly what I'm doing and why. Does that make me a nutcase?"

So she had idealized her mother in her mind. So what? Motherless for twenty years, she felt entitled to declare Celesta Capoletti the most perfect mother a girl had ever had.

She wondered what the self-help books would say about Alex's return. Most experts seemed to believe in confronting unresolved issues of the past. So did her best friend, Linda. Rosa wasn't sure she liked the idea of hauling herself through the old hurt and heartbreak.

The sound of Butch tapping his foot in exaggerated fashion brought her back to the present. "I'll just wait while you collect your thoughts, then."

"What?" She fell in step with him, passing mounds of chipped ice covered with fish.

"You aren't even listening to me."

"I am, too."

"Bullshit, Rosa."

"You just said—" She scowled at him. "I'm not ignoring you. I'm just preoccupied."

"About what?"

"Maybe this summer I'll hire a general manager."

"You say that every summer. That's nothing. You're thinking about Alex Montgomery."

"I am not." They both knew she was lying. She couldn't get him out of her mind—Alex Montgomery with his haunted blue eyes, who had lost his mother in the worst possible way. Even his facade of cool Montgomery reserve couldn't mask a terrible, raw anger. He had some serious grieving to do, yet he was resisting it; she could tell. She couldn't understand that. Why not let it all out?

She pretended to give her full attention to a huge cod laid out on a bed of chipped ice, its mouth open wide, its glassy eyes staring. But that made her think of death, and then she thought of Emily Montgomery and the fact that she had killed herself. Losing a mother was painful enough. Learning it was a suicide added a twist of the knife.

The appearance of his father and sister had been singularly uncomfortable; Rosa couldn't get out of there fast enough. Though she'd known Alex for many years, his family remained a mystery to her. Given what had happened, she wished she'd seen them comfort each other, not bicker. They were supposed to be each other's safe place to fall. That was what a family was for. She'd never seen the Montgomerys do that. Not even now.

"He's back from the city, you know," Butch pointed out.

She tried to act nonchalant, even though her heart skipped a beat. He'd been gone two weeks, three days, an hour and twenty minutes, not that she was counting. "Actually, I didn't. It doesn't matter to me."

"It was in the papers. They buried Mrs. Montgomery in Providence a week and a half, two weeks ago," Butch persisted, watching her like a hawk.

"Yeah?" she said, elaborately uninterested. "So?"

"Must be freaky, knowing your mother killed herself."

A cold weight dropped inside Rosa. *"What?"*

"A suicide. It was in the papers today."

She stared at him. "Can you finish up here by yourself? I need to go."

He looked furious. "Where's your pride, Rosa? Why go crawling back to that guy?"

"I'm not crawling. I'm running."

A flock of seagulls burst skyward as she rushed to the parking lot and got into her car. She needed to find Alex, and fast.

Cioppino

A lot of people think making homemade tomato sauce is too much of a bother. It's not, really. You're ahead in the game if you have some fresh herbs growing in pots on the windowsill. If you get really good seafood, the shells add their flavor to the broth. Just pass around plenty of napkins. Robert and Sal used to get in trouble for practicing ventriloquism with the mussel shells at the dinner table.

Broth:

1/4 cup olive oil
about 6 anchovies, chopped
4 cloves garlic, chopped
2 bay leaves
1 stalk of celery, diced
1 onion, chopped
1 roasted red bell pepper, chopped
1 cup Chianti + 2 Tablespoons red wine vinegar
1 quart fish or shrimp stock
6-8 diced fresh tomatoes (use canned if you don't have fresh)
chopped fresh basil
a good pinch of saffron threads

2 Tablespoons Worcestershire sauce
1/2 cup chopped Italian flat-leaf parsley
2-3 tablespoons fresh lemon juice
salt to taste
1 teaspoon red pepper flakes
2 tablespoons dried oregano, or twice that amount if using fresh
1 teaspoon fennel seeds, crushed with the flat of a knife
1 sprig of rosemary

Seafood: Use whatever is fresh that day, 1/4 pound or more of each variety: prawns (save the shells for making stock), crab, scallops, mussels, firm fish cut in 1-inch pieces (cod, halibut, scrod, bass), fresh clams, fresh oysters (shucked), calamari for the adventurous.

Warm the olive oil and anchovies in a big pot. Add garlic and stir, then add the bay leaves, onion, celery and bell pepper, plus 1/2 of the herbs. Pour in wine, vinegar and Worcestershire and let half the liquid bubble away. Then add tomatoes, basil and the rest of the herbs. Simmer, then add the fish stock and lemon juice, bringing it all to a boil. Finally, toss in the seafood, cover and cook 7-10 minutes. Remove any mussels and clams that haven't opened. Ladle the stew into wide, shallow dishes and sprinkle with parsley. Serve with warm bread.

thirteen

Alex wasn't at the house on Ocean Road, though Rosa knocked long and loud. She left a note wedged in the crack of the front door—*Call me, Rosa*—along with her cell phone number.

Frustrated, she got back in her car and started the engine. She had a hundred things to do today, but couldn't concentrate on anything except the fact that Alex was back, and the press had invaded his family's most private business. She drove past the long string of beaches where candy-colored umbrellas and floppy hats blurred together, creating a colorful lei along the shoreline.

On a hunch, she pulled off the coast road and headed for a part of the beach she rarely visited anymore. Alex knew this place; perhaps he was here.

She clambered past an abandoned stone house whose half-crumbled walls had stood sentinel for years, a silent monument to someone's foolish notion that it was safe to live this close to the sea. Safe indeed. Perhaps it was in the summer when the weather was fine. Whoever had built the place had probably never seen the way a winter storm skirled in from the Atlantic, its winds toppling stout stone walls and dragging trees out by the roots.

Another hundred yards of the beach led to an estuary overgrown with cattails and reeds. And beyond that was a cove as private now as it had been twenty years ago. Back then, when she was an adventurous tomboy and he a lonely invalid, they had discovered this place together. It held more memories than a sentimental girl's diary. But no Alex.

Rosa shaded her eyes and scanned from north to south. A ship's horn sounded in the distance. A group of sea kayakers paddled offshore. Sailboats breezed across the sound.

Suddenly she knew exactly where he'd gone. "Oh, man," she muttered under her breath as she hurried back to her car. "Why there?"

As she drove down an old, tree-lined avenue and passed through the auspicious stone gates of the Rosemoor Country Club, an ancient, bone-deep lump of discomfort took hold of her. She tried to deny it, but the leaden feeling in her gut didn't lie. This place was the scene of one of the most humiliating moments of her adolescence, the sort that haunted her at odd moments even twelve years later. She didn't belong here and never would, no matter how much time passed, no matter how successful she became. This was a bastion of tradition for people whose fortunes had been made many generations ago, preferably by someone who had just stepped off the *Mayflower*.

Wishing she had on something other than a denim miniskirt and a sunflower-yellow top, she crossed the parking lot. A curious, elegant hush surrounded this place; even the seagulls seemed to mute their cries and the *thwok* of tennis balls sounded decidedly genteel. The Tudor-style clubhouse, covered with twining old roses, was nestled between the manicured first teebox and the eighteenth green. The private dock in front of it provided moorage for gloriously restored wooden yachts and sleek racing boats. On the deck overlooking the water, attractive people in breezy tennis whites and visors chatted and laughed together.

Wishing she could be anyplace else, she walked past the Members Only sign and stepped inside. Soft music drifted from hidden speakers. At his podium, the host greeted her. He was polite enough, but she could sense him checking her out, categorizing her as an interloper. A *nonmember.*

"I'm looking for Alexander Montgomery," she said. "Is he here?"

"I believe Mr. Montgomery is on the deck, Miss...?"

"Capoletti." She nodded toward a stairway. "Is that the way to the deck?"

"Yes, but—"

"Thanks for your help." She didn't have to turn around and look at him to know he was staring after her, that he'd probably send someone up to make sure she behaved herself. Fine, she thought. Let him.

She emerged onto the deck and scanned the lunch crowd there, a sea of golf, tennis and sailing togs. All the umbrella tables were occupied. And there was Marcia Brady, regarding her with cool inquisitiveness.

Rosa offered no more than a tight smile. "I'm here to see Alex."

"Is he expecting you?"

"What, do I have to make an appointment?"

One of the guys jerked his head toward the end of the deck. "He went to see if he could get the bar to open early."

Rosa pivoted on her platform sandal and walked away without another word. She hated that she always felt self-conscious around these people. She imagined them regarding her as though she was semiliterate, fresh off the sardine boat.

It wasn't true, of course. People like that simply didn't think of her at all.

She found Alex leaning against the bar, arms crossed over his chest, jaw set as he contemplated the rows of liquor bottles. The late-morning sun glinted off his hair and picked out the perfectly sinewed muscles of his arms and legs. There was no bartender in sight.

Alex didn't look at Rosa, but she saw him stiffen at her approach, as though bracing himself.

"Touché, Capoletti," he said when she was within earshot.

"It wasn't me," she said.

He wheeled on her, seeming to grow larger with fury. Lord, but he was something, she thought. Yet when she really looked at his eyes, she saw loneliness and desperation, perhaps a shadow of the boy who had once been her friend.

"You were the only one outside the family who knew," he stated, his voice low and taut.

"Obviously not."

"My sister's got young kids. This is hurting them, too, or didn't you think of that?"

She felt every ear straining to hear them. "We might not know each other anymore, Alex. But I swear I haven't become the sort of person who would do such a thing."

"I have no idea what sort of person you've become."

"Likewise," she said, holding her temper in check. *And whose fault is that?* She didn't say it aloud. Another time, she might, but not now, not when he was ravaged by fury and indignation on his family's behalf.

"Alex," she said, slowly and solemnly. "On the soul of my own mother, I never said a word."

He pushed back from the bar and stared at her for a long moment. The sea breeze rattled through the reeds along the shore and plucked at his hair. Sunlight glinted in his eyes, and she saw the fury subside.

There were things he would always know about her, no matter how much time had passed, no matter the distance between them. He knew she would never, ever swear by her mother unless she had absolute faith in what she was saying.

"I have no idea who leaked the story, Alex," she said quietly, "but it wasn't me. I would never want the death of your mother to hurt you and your family any worse than it already has."

He flexed and unflexed his hand as though he had a cramped muscle. Then he heaved a sigh. "It would be so much simpler if I could blame you. It's so nice and neat. You knew, and you have a grudge against me—simple."

"It wasn't me."

"Yes, damn it, I know that."

"Why are you so angry?"

"Because if you'd blabbed to the press, I'd have someone to be pissed at."

"Why do you need to be pissed at someone?"

"Because it's easier than being pissed at myself."

The stark honesty that rang in his words reverberated in the air between them. In that moment, she saw him as someone who had lost his mother in a terrible way. Rage was common in relatives of suicide victims. So was guilt. She wondered how he was dealing with it all. He'd led a charmed life that probably did little to prepare him for shock and tragedy.

"How did you know I'd be at the club?"

She stifled a snort of amusement. Summer people had always flocked to places reserved for members only. It was almost instinctual, like salmon swimming upstream to spawn. "Call it a hunch."

She felt for him now. She hadn't forgiven him, not by a long shot, but she felt for him. "Do you think we could go somewhere else?" she asked. "Your friends have had their share of live entertainment today."

"Don't mind them. Let's go for a walk," he said.

She let out the breath she'd been painfully holding in. "All right."

He headed for a flight of exterior stairs that led down to the dock. She could feel his friends glaring holes in her back. They didn't need a reason to dislike her; they simply did. It had always been that way, and her friends had always reciprocated, disliking Alex on principle.

She stole a glance at him, not knowing what she'd see next, but she'd lost the ability to read his mood.

Still, the silence between them was charged. She pretended she hadn't noticed—for a while, at least. They didn't touch but walked side by side along a pebble-strewn path that was probably as old as the more famous walkway along Bailey's Beach.

In the wrack line of washed-up debris that lay along the beach, Rosa didn't see any treasures, just the occasional tangle of translucent fishing line and shimmering heap of brown kelp. Alex used to be good at finding things on the beach—a bit of sea glass or a rare shell.

"What are you thinking?" she asked him. Spoken aloud, it was a strangely intimate question, though she didn't mean it that way.

"I don't know. I wasn't thinking. Just looking at the way the sand blows up against the fence."

"In the winter, it goes in the opposite direction."

"I've never been here in winter."

"I know."

More silence, only the sounds of the sea around them: the muffled boom of the rollers, the hiss of rocks being thrown up on the shore and then rattling down as they were drawn back into the depths. The wind was light, a balmy caress, tousling their hair.

"My father wasn't sure whether or not to send something," she blurted out. "You know, flowers or—"

"There's no need."

"It's not a question of need," she said. "He took care of the property for years, so I guess he—"

"Just drop it, okay?"

The edge in his voice made her frown. It was probably the trauma of the sudden tragic loss, she thought, making him short-tempered. At one time, she would've known. She used to be able to read his face as easily as her own, and he could do the same for her. Those days seemed so long ago.

She felt him checking her out, and she deepened her scowl. "Do I have something on my face?" she asked.

"What?"

"On my face. The way you're staring at me, I thought maybe I had something on my face."

"Sorry. I didn't mean to make you uncomfortable."

"You didn't," she said quickly.

Silence again. She felt something pressing from the inside, straining to get out. She tried to deny that she felt anything, but she did. Here she was with the man who had once broken her heart, and she was consumed with curiosity about him. She couldn't indulge it, not now. He wasn't ready to answer questions. He'd just lost his mother and the world knew it was a suicide.

"Now you're too quiet," he pointed out. "*That* makes me uncomfortable."

"I'm trying to figure out what to say to you. I'm trying to decide if there's anything I can possibly say." She felt an almost overwhelming urge to touch him, and even lifted her hand toward his arm. Then, feeling a shimmer of heat, she dropped her hand, instantly regretting the impulse. "When I lost my mother, I was in a different place than you are. But there are some losses that are always going to be devastating, and this is one of them." She bit her lip and wondered how it might have made her feel to know her mother had wanted to die, had done so by her own hand. It would be all the more horrible to have the world find out, to be the object of gossip and speculation.

She stopped walking. "What are you going to do?"

"I'm not sure."

"Do you have any other theories about who leaked the story?"

"Maybe it was someone from the medical examiner's office. I'm sure we'll have it checked out."

"We?"

"My father and I."

"But if the paper quoted an anonymous source, they won't divulge anyone's name."

"We'll see."

His certainty intrigued her. She didn't want this. Didn't want to be fascinated by him. "Alex, how much does it matter?"

"What, that my mother killed herself, or that the story's in the papers?"

"Both, I suppose."

"Personally, I don't give a shit whether the way she died stays private or it's broadcast on the evening news, but my father's bugged by it. My sister, too. She's going to have to explain it to her kids. That's the part I hate the most."

Rosa noticed he hadn't addressed the first part of her question. And she was a little shocked to feel a deep sense of resentment on his behalf. In general, she regarded the press as her ally, helping her publicize the restaurant. Thanks to syndicated articles by travel writers from all over, her place had been mentioned in papers as far-flung as Miami, London, L.A. Still, she knew how destructive bad press could be.

"I hate it, too," she said. "I'm sorry, Alex." She felt so cautious around him, so awkward. He was just a guy, she kept telling herself. Just a guy she used to know. She tried to remember that he wasn't special.

Even so, she kept sneaking glances at him, wishing he didn't seem so...sexy. She couldn't deny that he captivated her. She could picture him as a boy, and then a teenager. He had excelled at sports—tennis, rowing, cycling, sailing. Having been deprived of anything resembling a life when he was very young, he'd made up for lost time after his health improved. At thirty, he was tall and athletic, with that square-jawed all-American look which he wore as naturally as the sun on his hair.

"Tell me about your life, Rosa," he said out of the blue.

"Why?"

"Because I want to know what you've been up to."

Getting over you, she thought. *Even after all this time, I'm still working on it.* "There's nothing to tell. After Pop's accident, I stayed in Winslow. There was no way I'd leave him, not in the shape he was in."

"Rosa. I'm sorry—"

"Don't say it. I know you felt bad for me." *But not bad enough to stick around.*

She wondered how much he knew about the situation. An anonymous party, through a blind trust administered by the Newport law firm Claggett, Banks, Saunders & Lefkowitz, had paid for her father's long-term care and rehabilitation, which had taken nearly two years. She assumed the angel was one of Pop's loyal clients. And every night, she thanked God for the favor.

"So after your father got better," Alex said, "then what? What about the cop?"

"He's the county—"

"—sheriff now. So you said. That's not what I'm asking, and you know it."

She decided to ignore the question. "And then... I got a raise at Mario's."

"The pizza joint that used to be where your restaurant is."

"Good memory." She tried not to feel defensive. "I moved up to general manager. And Mario was looking to get out of the business. It was tricky, though. The building is the last one standing on the protected waterfront. The property's small, its footprint can never be expanded and the parking lot can never be paved. Still, I wanted it. I wanted to start a restaurant, a really good one. I leased the place from Mario, and five years ago, I launched Celesta's-by-the-Sea." She folded her arms across her chest. "So if I'd gone off to college, I never would have started the restaurant."

Rosa suspected she sounded quite different from the dreamy teenager he had once known. That girl had glowed with shining ideals and high-minded convictions. She was going to be a philosopher, a diplomat, a rocket scientist. She would have scoffed at the idea of running a restaurant. Since then, she'd learned a few things about life and work.

His stare made her wonder what he was thinking. And the accelerated beating of her heart made her question her own motives for coming here.

"Come back to the club with me," he said. "I'll buy you lunch."

"God, you are clueless. Do you know how excruciating that would be for me?"

"Okay, wrong move. Let's get lunch at Aunt Carrie's."

She looked away, trying to hide her vivid memories of the outdoor café. She and Alex had gone there as kids, sunburnt, their hair stiff with salt and their feet bare, to eat clam cakes and blueberry pie.

"What do you say?" He didn't touch her, but she felt his gaze like a caress.

"I say this conversation is over."

"Rosa," he added, "we're not finished."

She burst out laughing, then tossed back her hair and looked him in the eye. "Yes," she said, "we are. You made sure of that a long time ago."

"I made a mistake a long time ago."

It was rare to hear a man admit he was wrong. To hear a Montgomery man admit it was…astounding. "And this just came to you," she said.

"No. I've thought about it a lot over the years." His frankness disarmed her.

"It's too late," she said in a low, rough voice. "We can't just go back to…we can't."

"True," he agreed. "We can do better."

"Alex, for Pete's sake, I don't know what you think I've been doing—waiting, pining away? We had a summer romance. I made the mistake of taking it too seriously. Girls generally do. After you left, I regained my perspective, and I assume you did, too." She felt herself getting overheated and took a deep breath. In spite of everything, she felt vulnerable to him, to his searching blue eyes and his gentle smile, and to her own tender memories of how she'd once felt with him, safe and adored. Along with her yearning and nostalgia came another sensation—fear. She was afraid. She hated that about herself. She wished she could play this for laughs, maybe have some fun with him and then walk away, like Linda said she should do. That was what Rosa usually did with men she dated. But with Alex, it would be impossible.

She said, "Listen. I feel horrible about your mother, and

even worse now that it's in the papers. That's why I came looking for you, not to have lunch and reminisce about the past, which is completely pointless since it's over, and…" She forced herself to stop babbling. "I'm going. I have to be at the restaurant. Okay?"

"No, it's not okay. Damn it, Rosa. It's just lunch."

"And it's not going to happen."

As she walked away, she heard him give an ironic laugh. "Chicken," he said softly.

Don't stop, she told herself. *Don't look back.*

fourteen

Rosa did a great job not thinking of Alex for whole minutes at a time. A few days after their encounter, she managed to convince herself that she'd only imagined the sincerity in his eyes when he'd asked her to come to lunch with him.

Her heart was not so easily fooled, and she felt an odd stumble in her chest at unexpected moments. She had often hoped to feel that half sick, half delicious lurch with regard to other men, but it never worked. Over the years, she'd dated almost too enthusiastically, only to be disappointed, or to disappoint.

Her best defense was to keep busy. Fortunately for her, she had plenty to do. The restaurant consumed half the day and most of the night, and her friends and father filled in the rest. Linda's wedding plans were moving ahead at warp speed, and Rosa found herself delightfully swept away by all the fuss.

After stopping at Linda's to drop off some sample menus for the reception, she went to her father's house, blinking the hall lights to announce her presence.

"In here," yelled Pop.

She followed the sound of his voice to the den off the kitchen, where Pop sat in front of the computer monitor. Behind him, the TV was on, closed-captioning words flickering across the screen of a Red Sox-Cardinals game. The TV was turned up too loud, which didn't bother Pop in the least.

The den, like the rest of the house, was cluttered with old mail, lottery ticket stubs, expired coupons and things her father never bothered to throw away. A stack of newspapers filled the plastic recycling bin nearly to the top. Pop had always been an obsessive news junkie. Online, his browser was bookmarked with a dozen news sites—the *International Herald Tribune,* Rome's *il Mondo,* the *Washington Post.*

Rosa found the TV remote control wedged between the couch cushions and hit the mute button.

"Hey, Pop." She kissed him on the cheek. "You left the front door unlocked. I could have been an intruder."

"An intruder wouldn't flash the lights."

"Pop—"

"Okay, okay," he said, waving his arms to fend her off. "I'll be more careful."

Sure he would. She didn't feel like arguing with him. "Checking your email?"

"I got news from Rob and Gloria." He steepled his fingers together and leaned back in his chair. He had blunt hands, strong and callused from years of hard work, ill-suited to typing at a keyboard. Yet he was remarkably adept at it, and because of his hearing loss, he had embraced the technology of communicating by text message, email and instant messages.

To Rosa, it was a godsend. She could text message his vibrating cell phone or zap him a quick IM to see if he was online, and stay in touch as closely as other people did with their hearing parents.

"So what's up with Rob?" she asked.

"Your brother and his wife are both gonna be deployed to Diego Garcia over the summer. Joey's coming to stay with me."

Rosa was surprised. Normally Rob and Gloria, both career NCOs, alternated deployments and shore duty so one or the other would be at home. They had four kids, though they weren't kids anymore. Their eldest had enlisted in the navy and was stationed in Bremerton, Washington. The twins, Mary-Celesta and Teresa-Celesta, were spending the summer in Costa Rica in a program sponsored by Youth International. The youngest, Joey, would be fourteen now. She hadn't seen him in more than two years, since the whole family had been stationed in Guam.

"I wonder how they both managed to get sea duty at the same time," she said.

"They're patriots, serving their country."

"I bet our country doesn't really need Joey's mother and father at the same time."

"Look at the world we live in." He gestured at the newspapers spread a week thick across the coffee table. "The least we can do is take care of their boy."

It didn't escape her that he said *we*. "Is that all right with you, Pop?" she asked. "Keeping Joey for the summer?"

"Sure, it's okay. He's my own flesh and blood."

"In the past, Gloria's folks have always kept the kids," she pointed out.

"Yeah. Well, they couldn't. They got some kind of conflict," said Pop.

Some kind of conflict, thought Rosa, like not wanting to look after a teenage boy all summer.

"Gloria's mother had to have female surgery," said Pop. "I didn't ask for details."

She instantly felt guilty for the thought. The Espositos were perfectly fine people as far as she could tell. They lived in Chicago and she didn't know them very well.

"When's he coming?" she asked her father.

"Day after tomorrow."

Way to give us advance notice, Rob, she thought. "I'll go with you to pick him up at the airport."

"You don't have to."

"Pop. I'm going." She had learned not to argue with him. It saved time to simply dictate.

He had learned to save time, too. He turned his hands palms up and looked at the ceiling. "You're a bossy girl. Just like your mother, you are."

Rosa loved being likened to her mother, which Pop knew very well. "I'll have the restaurant's cleaning service help you get the house ready."

"What, ready? He's fourteen. He's a guy. He doesn't care what the place looks like."

"I care." Rosa shook her head. "Fourteen…and he was just eleven the last time we saw him." She remembered an apple-cheeked boy with chocolate-brown eyes and a shy smile, nervous and excited about moving overseas. It would be fun to have him here for the summer, she decided. Still, she didn't know if her father was up to having a half-grown boy living with him. On the other hand, it might be good for them both.

"So anyway," she said, "we should get started. I'll help you."

Pop scowled. "What help? I don't need any help."

She eyed the cluttered room, the cardboard boxes stacked on the stairway as they had been for weeks, waiting to be taken up. She stood and pushed in her chair. When she was certain he was looking at her, she said, "I'm going to get the boys' room ready for Joey."

He didn't object as she seized one of the boxes and headed

upstairs. She hadn't been up here in ages, and neither had Pop, judging by the cobwebs in the stairwell.

A curious sensation came over her. She was not just walking up a flight of stairs in the house where she'd grown up. She was ascending to a place where old memories shimmered like dust motes in the air around her. The boys' room, as it was still called even though the "boys" hadn't lived here in twenty years, was frozen in time, a snapshot of their world the day they had both left for basic training.

Robert had been eighteen, the ink barely dry on his high school diploma. Sal was a year older, though he'd stayed home the year after high school. Rosa had been too little to understand why he had stuck around while all his friends were heading out into the world to find their lives. Now, as an adult, she knew exactly why.

He had stayed home because that was Mamma's last year on earth. He, Rob and Pop had known. Mamma had known. But no one had told Rosa.

Sal had spent more time than anyone else with their mother. Along with the nuns and a visiting nurse sent by their church and funded by St. Vincent de Paul, Sal became Mamma's primary caretaker. Rosa could still picture him smiling gently as he spooned lime Jell-O into her mouth when she was too weak to feed herself. He had unflinchingly emptied and cleaned the tubes and bags that had become her prison in the end. Sometimes he would go to another room and sit down and cry in rough, jagged sobs that made his whole body shudder. But he never cried in front of Mamma.

Mostly, he sat by her side, held her hand and read to her, everything from the Bible to James Herriot books to a new novel called *The Color Purple*. Those times, Rosa believed, had brought him to a state of grace. At the side of his dying mother, he discovered the path his life was to follow. He found the strength of his convictions, and he made her a promise. He would be a priest. And he'd done it, attending seminary courtesy of the United States Navy, because they needed men of faith. Now he was a chaplain, and as good a priest as he was a warrior.

Rosa's brothers had left on a clear morning in June. She and Pop had driven them to the train station in Kingston, had stood numbly on the platform, waving goodbye. They'd returned to a house that was eerily quiet and diminished by loss, the same way it had been when Mamma died.

That afternoon, Rosa had gone to work with Pop because she was too young to stay home alone. It had been that same afternoon, she recalled, that she met Alex Montgomery for the first time.

The boys' room stood virtually untouched, as though Rob and Sal had just walked out of it five minutes before. There was a Winslow Spartans pennant on the wall, a shelf of baseball and Greco-Roman wrestling trophies, a dresser covered with photos yellowing in their frames. There were shots of Rosa at six, dressed like a miniature bride for her first communion, and at eight, proudly holding aloft a bluefish she'd caught while out on the Carmichaels' boat. The photos of her mother formed something of a shrine, and the faded quality of the prints seemed to enhance the deep, ethereal beauty of Celesta, haloing her with a look of untouchable grace.

Rosa cleared out the closet—Levi's and Chuck Taylor sneakers and shirts with pointy collars—and threw everything into plastic sacks for the dump. She was not about to burden the Salvation Army or Catholic Charities with old gym socks and *Dukes of Hazzard* T-shirts.

Eventually some combination of curiosity and guilt brought her father to the room with a dust mop, a can of Pledge and a roll of paper towels. He said nothing, but started on the floor in desultory fashion. They worked together in companionable silence until Rosa stripped the bunk beds and bundled up the sheets to take to the basement for washing.

"What are you doing that for?" asked Pop. "Those are clean sheets."

"They need freshening up." He didn't seem to catch "freshening" so she signed it.

"Suit yourself," he muttered, moving the things off the dresser to squirt it with Pledge. He wiped down the surface and then dusted each photo with care, smiling a little at the images.

She waved to get his attention. "What are you thinking about?"

He set aside a photo of Rob and Sal in their Little League pinstripes. His face was creased by lines of sentiment. "Thanking God for all of this, thanking God that it happened to me."

She ached for him, knowing he could recall a time when his hearing was keen and the house rang with laughter, when disease and disaster were things you read about in the newspaper. The accident twelve years ago had changed him, darkened his spirit.

She helped him arrange the pictures. "There are plenty of good times ahead, Pop."

He patted her hand. "You bet." Then he studied her face, and she could feel him reading her; he'd always been able to guess at her thoughts. "You are going to start seeing him again, eh? The Montgomery boy."

"I'm not sure. Maybe." She had no idea why she said that. She kept telling herself it was long over; she didn't want to see Alex again. But Pop had a way of getting her mouth to speak up before her brain could censor her.

"Rosa. This is a boy who hurt you. He did a terrible thing and the heartbreak nearly—" He stopped himself, she could see, with sheer force of will.

She knew he was thinking about her extreme reaction to the accident and Alex's departure. "I was a kid," she said. "I didn't have good coping skills."

"Well, now you got a perfectly fine life. Don't go messing with a boy like that. He'll do you no good at all."

Alex would always be a boy to Pop, a spoiled rich boy.

"Everybody changes," she pointed out, wondering even as she spoke why she was taking Alex's part. Probably because Pop took the opposite side, and the two of them loved to argue.

"His wedding got called off and he's just lost his mother. He's looking for a shoulder to cry on."

She paused, Windex bottle in hand. "Sounds like you've been keeping up with all the gossip."

"I read the papers."

"Then maybe you've read that he manages a trust to provide health care for the needy."

"Montgomerys are good at making money. They can't help it."

"You say that like it's a bad thing."

"Never mind that boy, Rosina. You got better things to do with your time."

She went downstairs and got some new lightbulbs; most seemed to be burned out in here. As she unscrewed a corroded bulb from the ceiling fixture, sparks shot from the socket. She nearly fell off the chair she was standing on.

"The wiring's terrible in here, Pop," she said. "This place is a firetrap."

"I'll get Rudy to come take a look at it." Rudy was a retired electrician who lived down the block.

"You do that, Pop. Tomorrow."

fifteen

The main street of Winslow was lined with shops that catered to summer visitors and well-heeled browsers. The hardware store hummed this time of year, peak season for gardening and home improvement. Business was always brisk for Eagle Harbor Books, the Twisted Scissors Salon, the Stop & Shop and Seaside Silversmith. At the end of Winslow Way was a beach-access parking lot bordered by summer-only stands called "She Sells Sea Shells" and "I Scream For Ice Cream."

There were three dress shops, one that attracted the matronly golf set, one for tourists and trends, and a bridal boutique owned by a local woman named Ariel Cole. Her mother, a Portuguese immigrant, had started a tailor shop decades before, and Ariel still did a decent trade in alterations, but the larger part of her business was Wedding Belles, the bridal shop.

Linda's bridesmaids gathered at the boutique to try the three options Ariel had selected for them. Wearing strapless A-line gowns in aqua silk shantung, Rosa and Linda's sister, Rachel, stared at their reflections in the boutique mirror while Linda and Ariel stood back, examining them with a critical eye.

"This can't be right, Ariel," said Rosa. "This is a great dress. It actually looks good on us."

"And your point is...?"

"Bridesmaid gowns are supposed to be ugly so they don't outshine the bride. Isn't that a rule or something?"

"Not in my shop, it isn't," Ariel said with a sniff. She had always taken pride in her exquisite taste. She turned to the other bridesmaids, Linda's sister Rachel, and Sandra Malloy, a local writer who had become fast friends with Linda. "Well?"

"We love it." Sandra, who hadn't tried on the dress, patted her hugely rounded stomach. "This is our favorite. Now all I have to do is make sure the baby comes before the wedding. No idea what size I'll be, though."

"I'm doing the alterations myself," Ariel said.

"You look like a fertility goddess," said Linda, holding the gorgeous fabric against Sandra's pregnant belly.

Rosa was blindsided by a swift, sharp pang of yearning. Oh, she wanted to feel the way Sandra must be feeling now, as a contented wife with her first baby on the way. She wanted that with all her heart. She had for a long time, but the distance from the wish to the deed was vast.

"Earth to Rosa," Linda said, nudging her. "Last chance to cast your vote."

"I don't know," said Rosa, shoving away the painful thoughts. "It seems too easy. We're not objective enough. I want to go show Twyla." She went outside and headed for the Twisted Scissors Salon a few doors down. Rosa had always given Twyla full credit for rescuing her from the world's worst haircut when she was thirteen, and she'd been Rosa's stylist ever since.

As she hurried down the sidewalk, she noticed a tall man in

painter's pants and a paint-spattered T-shirt and cap, carrying a five-gallon bucket out of the hardware store. Rosa slowed her pace. She was not in so much of a hurry that she couldn't stop for a moment to enjoy the view. She'd always been a sucker for a guy in work clothes.

She was thinking seriously about having her condo repainted when she realized who she was staring at with such lust. As he lowered the tailgate of a white SUV and loaded the paint in the back, she knew that perfect male butt could only belong to one man.

Rosa ducked her head and started walking again. But being inconspicuous on the street while wearing a strapless turquoise gown was impossible. A wolf whistle from the direction of the truck alerted her that she'd been spotted. She stopped before he could do it again, drawing even more attention to her. He closed the tailgate of the truck and walked over to her.

"Rosa." Alex's gaze slipped down and up, twice. "Nice dress."

His look alone gave her goose bumps, which she tried desperately to will away before he noticed. "Thank you. So anyway... if you'll excuse me..." She edged toward the salon.

He stepped in her path. "I've been thinking about our conversation...at the club last week."

The club. He had no idea how that sounded. "I'm sort of in a hurry here."

"I meant what I said about seeing you."

"Look your fill." She spread her arms and faced him with reckless confidence, goose bumps and all, even though she knew he'd dated women far more beautiful than she. Pictures of his glossy public life sometimes ran in the "Evening Hours" column of the *Times*. He always favored a "type." Patrician, fair and WASPy, his dates were as tall and thin as uncooked spaghetti.

Judging by the expression on his face now, Rosa suspected

he might be willing to keep an open mind about his type. His eyes didn't just look, they touched. She felt a swift phantom caress on her lips, her throat, her breasts, as his gaze slipped over her.

"That's not enough," he said.

"That's all I'm offering." She brushed past him. "I have to go."

He took her by the arm and pulled her back to face him. "Not so fast."

Rosa hated herself for feeling that touch all the way through her, like a jolt of electrical current.

"It's not a lot to ask," he urged her. "I need to see you again."

As always, this was about his needs, not hers. He hadn't changed one bit. In spite of herself, Rosa remembered how she had ached with missing him, how she'd grieved for the future they'd never have together. To her horror, all those feelings came rushing back at her now, swirling around and engulfing her like a powerful undertow, pulling her feet out from under her.

How could this not have changed? she wondered in a panic. *We're different people now. Why do I still feel this way?*

Neurolinguistic implantation, she thought, dredging up something she'd learned in a cognitive science course. An event in the present evokes past sensations. But science couldn't explain how a foolish heart had the power to overrule common sense. *Run, Rosa, run,* she urged herself, yet somehow she stayed planted right in front of him. Maybe if he wasn't touching her, she'd be able to think straight.

"Let go of me, Alex."

He didn't, but rubbed his thumb along the inside of her elbow until she felt the heated sting of temptation.

"I don't want to."

She caught her breath and asked, "What about what I want? You don't even know whether or not I'm spoken for."

"You're not. I checked."

She pulled her arm away. "You've been checking on me?"

"Not really. I was bluffing, and you just told me what I want to know."

Oops. "I don't need you—or anyone—in my life. I'm perfectly happy with the way things are," she snapped.

He met her furious glare with a calm smile. "Remind me not to piss you off."

"Too late," she said with a small laugh. "I believe your exact words to me were 'We're not going to happen.' I think that still holds true, don't you?"

The expression on his face told her that he recalled the conversation, probably as clearly as she did. They both still remembered exactly what he'd said the night he had told her goodbye forever.

"Don't you believe in second chances, Rosa?"

Refusing to answer that, she studied him for a moment, subjecting him to the same scrutiny he gave her. There was a time when she had known every thought in his head, every wish in his heart. Where was that brilliant, lonely boy who had opened himself to her, who'd been the keeper of her deepest dreams and secrets? For a second, she thought she saw the boy's yearning and desperation in the man's blue eyes, but that was probably just a trick of the light.

"What?" he asked her.

"You're getting too skinny," she said, and that was true, judging by the gaunt shadows under his eyes. He clearly wasn't treating himself well, all alone at the beach house. She tried to imagine what it was like for him, grieving alone, wondering what had driven his mother to take her own life. The bleakness of that image touched her in spite of herself. "You should eat."

"So feed me."

"Book a table at the restaurant, and I'll feed you."

"Your friends there are overprotective."

"There are other restaurants in town," she said. "Or—here's a concept—you could learn to cook."

He shook his head and gestured at the buckets in the back of the truck. "I have other projects going on."

"Why are you painting your own house? Couldn't you hire someone to do it?"

"Stop by and I'll explain it."

Rosa realized they were garnering stares from passersby. "I have to go." She turned and fled to the salon. He wouldn't dare follow her there.

She was wrong. She stepped inside, and just as she began to think she'd made a clean getaway, the bell over the door jingled lightly. Even before turning around, she knew it was him.

"Look, Alex—"

"I'm looking." He took off his painter's cap and offered everyone a friendly grin, stirring up a flurry of female sighs among Twyla and her customers. "Pardon me, ladies. I was just trying to make a date here—"

"I already told you no," Rosa snapped in frustration.

"What are you, nuts?" asked a woman whose head was covered in strips of foil. "The guy's asking you out."

"So you go out with him," Rosa said.

"I'm asking you, Rosa," Alex said. "And not for the first time."

"Then you should know you're wasting your breath. I won't change my mind."

He stood very still with his cap held over his heart, and she thought that at last she'd gotten through to him. For a second, she felt the tiniest twinge of regret.

Then he grinned again, put his hat back on and headed for the door. "Sure you will, honey," he said, loud enough for everyone to hear. "Sure you will."

sixteen

"My God, Alex," said Gina Colombo, getting out of her rental car and goggling up at the place. "You live in a frigging ark."

Alex came down the porch steps to greet his most trusted colleague at the firm. "But you don't have to come aboard two-by-two."

She gave a happy little yell and hugged him with unabashed affection. "It's good to see you. How are you doing?"

"I live in an ark. I'm drifting."

"That's what you're supposed to do when you take time off. Oh, that's right. You wouldn't know what that's like."

"I'm not so sure I'm cut out for a life of leisure," he said, wondering if he should admit that he'd spent the past eight hours painting the fascia boards with nothing but a transistor radio for company. Since joining the family firm six years before, he had never taken time off. He wasn't sure why this was the case. There were plenty of places for him to go. In addition to the beach house, the Montgomerys had a ski lodge in Killington and a cabin in the Catskills. He could travel to Monte Carlo or Rome or anywhere in the world if he felt like it.

He didn't ever feel like it. Usually he just worked. When he worked, he was in his right place, doing something that mattered. "How is Don?" he asked.

"Fine. We're both fine. I can't wait to get him to Newport. I'm so glad we're making this move, Alex."

His associate was as capable and trusted as Alex's own left brain. It was coincidence, pure coincidence, that she happened to have a name like Gina Colombo, dark curly hair and olive-toned skin, and that she was short and compact, with perfect breasts and a sexy mouth. The attitude was all her own, however. As was her degree from the Wharton School of Business.

Alex's mother had called her the Bride of Frankenstein when she first met her, "Because you're trying to build a substitute Rosa."

The memory made him wince. His mother had always seen him too clearly; he only wished he'd understood her heart half as well.

Despite his mother's skepticism, he forged a deeply intimate partnership with Gina. She knew what he thought, could anticipate his desires in any situation. In practically every way, she was the perfect woman for him. Except she happened to be in love with her husband, a freelance photographer.

Gina embraced the challenge of opening the Newport office. She was on track to earning a promotion to partner in the fall.

"Tidying up an abandoned ark after your mother passes away hardly qualifies as a leisure activity," Gina pointed out with her typical bluntness. "You've lost weight. You look like shit, by the way."

"I feel like shit. How would you expect me to feel after my

mother's death? Which I'm not ready to talk about, so don't even start."

"All right," she said easily, heading for the front door. "Let's talk business instead. I'll take equity risk premiums and p/e ratios over depression and suicide any day."

Alex thought it was curious that she had thrown in depression. No one else had mentioned it, but that was Gina. There were no roadblocks between her heart and her mouth. She was only voicing something Alex had been thinking about ever since the phone had rung that morning. If his mother was in treatment for depression, why wasn't it working? And why that particular day of all days?

"So," Gina said, stepping through the door and heading straight for the parlor, "this is the Montgomery family compound."

"Once upon a time. Would you like something to drink?"

"No, thanks." She sighed, gazing out the bay window. She made a leisurely stroll through the downstairs, oohing and ahhing at the tall Carpenter Gothic windows, the antique woodwork. "I could live forever on this view. Boy, Alex. This is some place."

In the kitchen, she laid a thick legal-sized envelope on the window seat. "Earnings reports, forecasts, meeting minutes. Nothing urgent. I was feeling nosy, so I used this as an excuse to spy on you." She folded her arms across her middle and stared at him.

"What?"

"You look different as well as skinny."

He grazed his fingers through his hair. "I need a haircut."

She frowned and tilted her head to one side. "It's not that. It's—"

"Alex? It's me, Rosa," called a voice from the porch.

Gina raised one eyebrow.

Great, thought Alex, excusing himself and heading for the door. The two of them together should be interesting. Ever since making that scene in the beauty parlor, he'd been hoping Rosa would break down and stop by, and finally something had prodded her to come. But her timing was unfortunate. Still, Rosa at the wrong time was better than no Rosa at all.

He opened the door and she stepped inside, holding a foil-wrapped parcel like a holy offering.

"I brought you something to eat," she announced.

Aha, he thought. This was the key to Rosa—she couldn't resist a starving man. He couldn't help it; he laughed. "You really want to feed me?"

She sniffed at the question and headed for the kitchen. Alex felt like a deer in the headlights, but she didn't seem to notice as she breezed through the house. "You're clearly not doing it for yourself. You have to promise to eat this while the sun is still up. My mother used to say a well-made lasagne keeps away regrets and bad dreams if—oh." She stopped in the doorway and stared at Gina. "Hello."

Standing across from each other, they looked eerily similar—dark, rounded, so very female. The two of them together were a men's magazine fantasy.

"Rosa, this is Gina Colombo, my associate at the firm. Gina, Rosa Capoletti. She runs—"

"Celesta's-by-the-Sea," Gina finished for him. "I read that profile of you in *Entrepreneur*."

"Really?" Rosa's smile shone with pride. "Thanks. You have a good memory." She indicated her parcel. "So I'll just drop this off and—"

"I was on my way out," said Gina, swishing past Rosa. "I need to get over to Newport to look at the rentals. It was nice to meet you, Rosa. I hope to see you again sometime."

Alex escorted Gina outside, saying to Rosa over his shoulder, "Be right back."

As he held open Gina's car door, he tried to avoid her gaze, but couldn't. "All right," she said. "Spill."

"Go away, Gina. Go to Newport. Call me next week."

"I want to know—"

"There's nothing to know, okay?"

"Oh, right. She's wearing red, she's bringing lasagne, she can't take her eyes off you… I wouldn't call that nothing."

"What would you call it?"

"Hello?" She playfully knocked on his head. "I might even approve of this one, Al." She twitched her skirt out of the way of the door. Lowering her voice an octave, she said, "I'll be back."

"You're not invited."

"Like that's going to stop me." She gave him a quick hug and got into the car. With the stereo blaring an Eva Cassidy tune, she pulled out of the driveway.

When he went back inside, Rosa was in the kitchen. She stood in the pale light of the sun, looking out the window at the lawn her father had cultivated and groomed over the course of decades. *Her father.* Alex considered asking her how Pete was doing. He didn't, of course.

Rosa turned to face him, hands on hips, and he could picture her in this house years ago, a dark, wiry little girl with bright eyes and a brighter smile. There had been magic in their friendship, but he couldn't sense it now. She was no more than a lovely stranger, standing in his mother's empty house.

"Gina really was just leaving," he said.

"Look, I came because I thought you might need something decent to eat," she explained. "And I suppose because, under the circumstances, I thought you shouldn't be alone. Both times, you weren't."

"Yeah, sorry."

"Don't be. Never apologize for having friends and family around when you need them."

He searched for hidden meaning in her words. Did she intend to remind him of how alone she'd been at the end of their last summer together? He could still taste his guilt over that even now, all these years later. "Look, about Gina—"

"I don't need an explanation."

"Just so you know. She works with me. That's all."

"Fine. I really don't... It's none of my business, Alex." She indicated the covered dish on the counter. "All I'm doing is bringing you a lasagne."

She turned on her heel and headed out through the nearest exit—the back door. He followed her out into the yard and noticed the way she studied the pond, the lawn, the big gnarled tree where she'd once hung a rope swing. He wondered if she, too, felt that bittersweet pang of memory. Their lives—their love—had been so simple then.

"Thank you for bringing the lasagne." He didn't know what else to say. "I promise I'll eat every bite."

"It's a lot of food."

"Then stay and help me eat it." He stood in her way, blocking the path to the front drive. They stood very close, staring at each other. The rose-tinted sheen on her lips would give him something to think about for the rest of the day, he thought.

He caught her scent and was shocked to discover that he recognized it even after all these years. It was some kind of fruity shampoo or skin cream, and on Rosa it was as heady as a shot of whiskey. He could feel the warmth of her even though they weren't touching, and he imagined the smoothness of her skin under his hands. For a moment, the urge to touch her crackled like lightning between them. Recognition flashed in her eyes, and he knew she felt that unseen current of heat, too.

"Rosa," he said.

"I have to go."

"It's kind of inconsistent for you to show up and then say you don't want to see me." He risked pointing out the obvious. "You came to my house, not the other way around. The casserole's nice, but it's just an excuse. You do want to see me."

"I wanted to make sure you're okay," she insisted. "You've had a terrible loss and you're all alone out here. In that sense, I suppose I came to see you, but not in the way you mean."

Out here at night, lit only by the stars and the moon, with the wind soughing through the reeds and the waves swishing up from the sea, he discovered the true meaning of being alone. And each night, he searched for some way to make sense of what his mother had done, but the answers eluded him. The only thing that made sense was what he was feeling for Rosa.

"You want to stay." He took another chance and said it.

"That's bull—"

"Then why are you still here?"

That ticked her off. She shook back her curls and glared up at him. "Because you won't stop talking. Ah, but now you have. So if you'll excuse me…"

"I'll call you," he said. "You can handle that, can't you?"

She yanked a cluster of keys from her purse. "I'm busy."

"I know. At the restaurant, surrounded by guys who want to break my kneecaps."

"That's the one."

"Look, all I want to do is talk."

"About what?"

"About everything." Then he told the truth. "About our last summer together." He'd tried that once before. It hadn't worked then; why would it work now?

Her cheeks turned bright red, and he should have felt gratified that she remembered. Instead he felt like a heel. "I shouldn't have left you like that, Rosa," he said. "I was young and stupid, and I handled it badly. I didn't know what else to do. I've always wanted to explain it to you."

"We were both young," she said, pointedly not calling herself stupid right along with him. "Everybody knows that relationships like that never work out."

"Everybody but the young." A silence, heightened by the sound of the wind and the waves, rolled out between them. "Anyway," he said, "we're different people now."

"So?"

"So, we should get to know each other again—as adults."

"Why?"

"Because...we might be good together, Rosa."

"We might be a disaster."

"Are you afraid of that?"

She studied his face for a long moment. "Yes," she admitted. "Maybe I am."

Lasagne Magro

In the old country, if you can afford meat, you don't hide it in a lasagne. The original recipe is meatless. This delicious lasagne is commonly found in southern Italy.

Ingredients:

At least a quart of good tomato sauce, preferably homemade
1 large carton full-fat ricotta cheese
1 cup grated parmesano reggiano cheese
1 cup shredded mozzarella cheese
1 large fresh egg
1/2 onion, chopped
1/4 cup chopped parsley
1/4 cup chopped fresh basil
1/2 pound chopped fresh spinach
8 ounces additional mozzarella cheese, sliced thin

4 ounces additional grated parmesan cheese
1 package dry lasagne noodles

Mix the ricotta and grated cheeses together with egg,
onion, spinach and herbs. Cover the bottom of a large
lasagne pan with olive oil and then sauce. Add a little
water and mix. Make an overlapping layer of the dry
noodles across the bottom of the pan. Spread sauce on top,
making sure the pasta is covered. Add a layer of the ricotta
mixture and mozzarella slices. Continue in this manner
until you run out of pasta. Top with sauce, add another
layer of mozzarella, then sprinkle on the parmesan.
Cover with foil and bake at 375° F for about forty
minutes. Check occasionally, and add boiling water
around the edges if the pasta seems too dry. Remove the
foil and cook another 10 minutes. Let rest an additional
10 minutes. Serve in squares, topped with a basil sprig.

seventeen

Rosa fumed as she drove over to her father's house. What kind of idiot was she, anyway? *Are you afraid? Maybe I am.* What in God's name was she thinking, talking to him like that?

"I was being honest," she said, taking the turn onto Prospect Street a little too fast. "As if that ever did me any good. I don't know any other way to be. I never should have taken him that stupid lasagne."

She let herself in, flicking the lights to alert her father. "Let's go, Pop," she yelled, mainly for her own benefit. After seeing Alex, she definitely needed to yell. "Come on." She paced back and forth, eyeing the ancient school photographs that hadn't been changed in years, the boot tray with her father's mud-encrusted boots and a tiny holy water font with a frieze of St. Francis installed by the door.

The moment her father appeared in the front hall, she felt guilty about her impatience. Eager to see his grandson, Pop had dressed up in his good Cordovan leather shoes and his one perfectly tailored suit. The white shirt was as clean and crisp as newfallen snow. His salt-and-pepper hair bore the furrows of aggressive combing, and he'd done a precision job trimming his mustache.

"You look wonderful, Pop," she said, signing as she spoke, for emphasis.

"I'm gonna get all messed up in your convertible," he grumbled.

"We're not taking the convertible. It's only got two seats."

"I knew that." He took his hat from a peg by the door.

"I borrowed Vince's Camry."

At Green Airport in the baggage claim area, they sat on a padded bench, nervously flipping through Rosa's purse-sized photo album, something she always carried. The pictures of Rob's kids had come enclosed in Christmas cards over the years. Her nephew, Joseph Peter Capoletti, had started out with that special angelic quality small children seemed to possess in abundance. As the youngest of four, he had been an adored little boy with a charming smile.

Around Joey's twelfth year, it seemed the novelty of him had worn off, because the pictures dwindled. Rob and Gloria had both been promoted and were busier than ever, living overseas. Rosa remembered Joey's shy smile, dreamy brown eyes with lashes so long they were wasted on a boy, and an acute fear of spiders.

The flight from Detroit, where he'd connected from L.A., landed. A wave of passengers emerged from the concourse. Rosa sensed her father tensing up as he scanned the crowd. There were business people with sleek luggage, young families juggling strollers and diaper bags, students and foreigners. She saw a couple reunited, radiating happiness and oblivious to the world as they embraced. From where she sat, Rosa could see the woman's eyes close as though to keep in the joy. Rosa looked away, burying a pang of sentiment.

The flood of passengers became a trickle, and she consulted Joey's hellacious-looking trans-Pacific itinerary. With a feeling of foreboding, she turned to her father. "He didn't make the flight."

Pop merely sat there, unmoving, watching the exit at the end of the concourse. His face betrayed nothing, and she looked again. The only passenger walking toward them was a lanky stranger with a pink Mohawk, dark glasses and a variety of uncomfortable-looking facial piercings. Under his breath, Pop emitted a string of curses in Italian, and Rosa nudged him to get him to behave. Really, she didn't blame her father. His adorable young grandson had morphed into a stranger.

Rosa prayed he hadn't seen her quickly rearrange her face from shock to delight. "Joey! You're a foot taller!" She opened her arms. He permitted her a hug that was brief and awkward, nothing like the exuberant embraces of his youth when he'd clung, monkeylike, as if he would never let her go.

"Hey, Aunt Rosa," he muttered, keeping his head down as though he'd dropped something. "Hey, Grandpop."

"Pop doesn't know what you're saying unless he can read your lips," she reminded him.

Joey tossed back his head and slowly, deliberately peeled off his shades. "Hiya, Grandpop," he said.

Rosa was grateful her father couldn't hear the sarcastic inflection in Joey's voice. Pop grabbed the boy by the shoulders and stood on tiptoe to give him two resounding kisses, one on each cheek, Italian style. Then he said, "You look like a freak."

Joey glared at him, his face burning with a blush from the kisses. "You got a problem with that?"

"Not as long as you don't act like a freak. Let's go get your bags."

His luggage consisted of a camouflage duffel bag patched

here and there with duct tape. *Aw, Rob,* thought Rosa. *You couldn't get the poor kid a decent bag?*

As they walked to the car, Pop touched the stiff spikes of the Mohawk. "I bet your parents didn't see this."

Joey's ears and cheeks turned red. "That's right."

"They're gonna tan your hide when they see you."

"I'll risk it."

In spite of herself, Rosa felt a grudging admiration for the kid. "I'm glad you're here, Joey," she said. "It's going to be a great summer."

eighteen

Alex wasn't much for shopping, but Rosa's lasagne, which he still dreamed about, was long gone. If he was going to spend the summer in a house by the sea, without a deli around the corner or a pizza delivery service, he would have to pay an occasional visit to the Winslow Stop & Shop.

In search of shaving cream, he stumbled into the wrong aisle and was confronted by a frightening display of feminine products. Eager to escape the panty liner zone, he tried walking briskly away—too briskly. At the end of the aisle, he took a corner fast and sharp, T-boning an unsuspecting cart with his own, causing bottles and cans to rattle and roll.

"Sorry," he said, but when he recognized his victim, he grinned in delight. "Hey, Rosa."

"Hey, yourself." Her smile, in contrast, was merely polite.

"Imagine running into you here," he said lamely. He had a reputation as a smooth talker, but he couldn't think straight when she was around. She wore a black top with skinny straps, low-slung jeans that showed a perfect olive-toned inch of skin above the waistband. And, God love her, she had a navel ring. Alex was a goner for them, and had actually seen very few up close and personal. The women in his world didn't self-mutilate, as they liked to call it. A tiny golden ring in a gorgeous female belly button was high art as far as he was concerned.

He felt like an idiot, standing there while an invisible hormone rush bathed him in painful lust. He distracted himself by checking out the contents of her cart. Tomatoes and grapes, a lot of leafy green bunches, cartons of ricotta and yogurt, three paperback romance novels. A bag of Cheetos—"Dangerously Cheesy"—seemed out of place, as did the two gallons of milk and the package of Oreos.

She noticed his inquisitive stare. "I bet you're thinking I'm a closet junk-food junkie and romance novel addict."

"Are you?"

"Yes and no. I'll pass on the junk food, but don't get between a girl and her romance novels."

"Yeah?" He picked one. "*Cattleman's Courtship* by Lois Faye Dyer. 'Will a sophisticated city slicker find love with a rugged rancher?'" he read from the back cover. Tossing the book back into her cart, he said, "Bet not."

She sniffed. "Shows how much you know. They'll work it out."

"Why read it if you know the ending?"

She fixed him with a you're-too-dumb-to-live stare. "Because it's wonderful, every time."

Okay, so maybe she was in love with falling in love. Alex supposed he could understand that. It was all heady stuff— the blast of emotion so intense it made you light-headed, the physical burn of passion, the yearning so strong and sweet it made your heart ache. Alex was familiar with the symptoms. He'd experienced them all.

But only once.

"So the junk food's for...?" he asked. "You have a pet on a strange diet or something?"

"Nosy, aren't you? Actually I'm—" She broke off as a lanky, half-grown boy emerged from the magazine aisle. "There you are, Joey," she said, then turned to Alex. "Alex, this is Joey Capoletti."

Holy crap, he thought. Her son? He panicked as his mind raced through a swift calculation. Could this giant, spike-haired, nose-ringed kid be...no way. Alex rejected the notion. The kid was thirteen if he was a day.

Relieved, he reached out to shake hands. "Alexander Mont-gomery. Nice to meet you."

"Hello, sir."

"Joey's my nephew," Rosa said, and her wickedly amused smile indicated that she'd seen Alex's momentary panic. "He's spending the summer with my dad."

Joey was a punk, Alex saw, his sagging black jeans hung with chains from pocket to pocket, his T-shirt emblazoned with some sort of tribal symbol. He'd apparently inherited his aunt's penchant for piercing, only on Joey it had run amok. There was enough metal attached to him to set off alarms at airports.

But Alex knew appearances could be deceiving. For Rosa's sake, he hoped that was the case with this character. He sus-pected he was right when he saw the magazine Joey held— *Scientific American.*

"So, what do you think of Winslow?" Alex asked him.

"It's okay." The boy's gaze wandered to a blond girl shopping the aisle with her mother. She looked to be about his age and had the sort of long-legged, flowerlike beauty of a girl in the mysterious process of becoming a woman. They made eye con-tact, a message passing between them. "It's pretty nice here."

Rosa nudged him. "You're liking it better and better, huh?"

His ears turned red and Alex felt sorry for him. He thought

he recognized the girl's mother from the club—somebody Brooks. But the moment to introduce them was past, so he changed the subject. "When I was a kid, I spent every summer here. I've known your aunt since she was nine years old."

"Uh-huh."

"I'm working on our family's old house," Alex went on, trying to figure out how to engage the boy's interest. This was his first real break with Rosa. If he could make friends with the kid, maybe she'd give him the time of day. He glanced again at the magazine. The cover story was something about planetary transits. "You know, I used to have an old telescope." It had been stashed in a window seat of the parlor, and as far as he knew, it was still there. "I was going to see if someone at the high school wanted it, but if you're interested—"

"That'd be great," said Joey.

"I don't think so," said Rosa.

Alex ignored her. He had an ally now. "Why don't you come by this afternoon and I'll show you what I've got?" He sensed Rosa winding up for a protest, and quickly added, "You're not busy this afternoon, are you?"

"Nope," said Joey, also ignoring Rosa. "I've got a job at the ice-cream place, but I'm off today. What time?"

"Will two o'clock work?"

"Sure."

"Your aunt knows where I live. She won't mind giving you a lift." Alex didn't want to give her a chance to back out, so he said, "I'd better get going. See you this afternoon, Joey. You, too, Rosa."

"Bye, Alex." She aimed her cart and sped toward the baking aisle.

Pretending great interest in a display of bagels in cellophane, he furtively watched her go. Then he threw a few frozen dinners and bags of pretzels into the cart, followed by milk and cereal, juice and beer. His major food groups covered, he checked out and started loading his purchases into the back of his Ford Explorer. On the far side of the parking lot, he saw Rosa and Joey getting into her red convertible. She wore sunglasses and a long polka dot scarf to protect her hair from the wind, and she was using the rearview mirror to put on a stroke of red lipstick.

That was too much. Alex grabbed his cell phone and dialed her number—the one she'd left stuck to his door the day the papers reported his mother's suicide. He'd immediately programmed it into his phone.

"Rosa Capoletti," she said in a businesslike tone. Alex could see her holding the tiny phone to her ear with one hand and clipping on her seat belt with the other.

"Have dinner with me," he said.

There was a beat of shocked silence. Then she cleared her throat. "I'm afraid that won't be possible."

"What's your schedule like?"

"It's full. Forever."

She was pissed that he'd invited Joey over, Alex thought. Too bad. "I won't accept that."

"Then I suppose," she said as she put the car in gear, "you'll have to find a way to deal with it."

"Stalking," he said with a laugh. "Would stalking work for you?"

"I have to go," she said, steering toward the parking lot exit.

"All right. But you might want to fix your scarf," he said. "It's caught in the door."

Her brake lights flared as she hung up and craned her neck around. She didn't spot him, though he stood in plain sight, leaning easily against the back door of the Explorer. She opened her car door, liberated the scarf and sped off.

Okay, thought Alex. Time for Plan B.

nineteen

The minute they pulled into the driveway of Alex Montgomery's house, Joey felt like he'd entered a different cosmos. The place looked like it could be haunted, a classic old New England house with tall, narrow windows and peaked gables, a porch wrapping around three sides and a huge garden with a pond. About fifty yards beyond that was a beach.

The guy called Alex, who had been hitting on his aunt, came hurrying out of the house like he couldn't wait to see Joey. But of course, his face fell when he saw it was Grandpop, not Aunt Rosa, who had driven Joey over. Clearly Alex had been counting on seeing her. He totally dug her. You could tell that a mile off.

"Hey, Joey." He was acting cool now, like he didn't even mind that Rosa hadn't shown up.

Then when Grandpop got out of the car, it was like the hot summer day turned winter-cold. "Hello, Alexander," said Grandpop.

"Mr. Capoletti."

"I'm sorry for the loss of your mother."

Aw, jeez, thought Joey. He'd hoped the subject wouldn't come up. Now everything was going to be all awkward.

"I appreciate that," said Alex.

Grandpop nodded and then said, "I will wait out here, Joey."

Joey figured Alex would insist that Grandpop come in, sit down, have a drink, whatever, but Alex just headed for the house. Must be some bad blood between the two, Joey figured.

"I've got the telescope right here," said Alex, walking over to a giant bay window. The lid of the window seat was propped up with an old fishing pole. Alex shone the beam of a flashlight into the cobwebby depths of the storage space. When he straightened up, he was holding an old telescope by the optical tube.

Joey felt a little beat of excitement, but he was careful not to let it show. Once you show how much you want something, it could get taken away. Joey was the youngest of four kids, and he'd learned that the hard way.

"Could I...see that?"

"Sure." Alex handed it over. "There are some other pieces and accessories in here. I'll just see if I can find them..." He turned and started rummaging in the window seat.

Joey checked out the telescope, rubbing his thumb over the tarnished brass latitude scale on the equatorial mount. It was a Warner & Swinburne, and he didn't know that much about it except that it was a valuable antique.

"So there's this," Alex said, handing him a tripod and brass finderscope. "And I found these lens boxes..."

"Are you sure you want to let me use this?" Joey asked.

"No." Alex spoke over his shoulder as he kept rummaging. Joey's heart sank. "Then—"

"I want to let you *have* this." He pulled out a long black case. "For keeps."

"Uh-uh." Joey shook his head. "You don't want to do that. You don't know what you have here."

"A Warner & Swinburne refracting telescope, made in Boston in the 1890s," Alex said. "It's worth a few hundred bucks to collectors. I'd rather give it to someone who might use it and maybe even learn something. It's nowhere near as good as a modern scope, but Maria Mitchell used one like this at her observatory in Nantucket. It's all yours. The best place for viewing is Watch Hill. It's about a mile north of town."

"Why me? You don't even know me." Just then, Joey got it. "Oh, I see. You're being nice to me because you have the hots for my aunt."

"Did Rosa tell you that?"

"Nope."

"Then how—"

"Duh." Joey shook his head.

"What did she say about me?" Alex asked.

Joey snorted. "I thought I was finished with junior high."

Instead of being offended, Alex laughed. "When it comes to women, you're never finished with junior high. Hang on a second while I make sure I gave you everything." He pulled a bunch of old stuff out of the window seat—flat vinyl records by groups like The Byrds and the Herb Alpert Band, clothes someone probably should have thrown away decades ago, a stack of old piano music, copies of *Life* and *Time* filled with past history.

"Check this out." Alex handed him a clear plastic bag filled with political buttons with slogans like Nixon. Now More Than Ever. and Goldwater in '64. Joey wondered who the heck they were. Old failed candidates, probably.

Joey picked up a framed picture of some woman and dusted it off. She had long red hair, and she was leaning against a blue car and laughing into the camera. "Who's this?"

Alex's face changed. Not a lot, but it hardened as if he'd just gone into the deep freeze. He took the photo and stared at it for a few seconds. "My mother, about twenty years ago."

"I'm sorry she died." Grandpop had explained the situation to him on the way over and it was a total bummer. The woman had killed herself. "It sucks," he added, and then he made himself shut up. Every word in the English language was lame in a situation like this.

"It does suck," Alex agreed. "I suck at dealing with it, too. I try not to think about it, and then all I do is think about it."

"So you should think about it," Joey said. "Maybe you're supposed to."

Alex grinned a little. "Maybe." He quickly dumped the old papers back into the box. "Anyway, I think you've got everything, Joey. Go see if you can get the thing to work."

Rosa was keyed up and distracted at the restaurant that evening, but she tried not to let it show. She greeted customers, monitored the kitchen and generally conducted herself as though this were any other night. No one could tell how rattled she was about Alex Montgomery.

Or so she thought.

Vince cornered her in the prep area of the kitchen. "All night you've been acting like you got a bug up your ass."

"How would you know how I'd act if I had a bug up my ass?" she asked. "For your information, I've never had one, so even I don't know how I'd behave."

"Just like you are now," he said without missing a beat. "Testy and maybe a tad distracted. I know I would be."

"Sicko." She brushed past him and headed toward the insulated double doors to the dining room. But before going out, she glanced at the monitor, which panned over the dining room, foyer, deck and parking lot. She squinted at the parking lot view and jumped back. "Oh, shit."

"I thought you were done with this conversation," Vince said. He glanced at the video monitor. "My, my," he said. "Miss Rosa has a suitor." He planted his hands on his hips. "Leave this to me. I'll make him go away."

Rosa cursed herself for not keeping a poker face when she'd spotted Alex. She was terrible at playing it cool. She always wore her emotions with the flash of the latest fashion accessory. "That's okay, Vince. I'll deal with him."

Vince kept watching the monitor. "No need. Teddy beat you to it."

She looked up to see Teddy and Alex in the parking lot, nose to nose, chest to chest, like an umpire and an irate player. Teddy was a large, formidable man. Most people knew better than to mess with him. His thick finger jabbed at Alex's face, but Alex didn't back down.

"Shit," Rosa said again, and rushed for the back door. She burst out into the breezy summer night. Her work clothes— a formfitting black dress and spike heels—were not designed for sprinting. Scurrying, maybe, if she was careful.

She scurried as fast as she could to the front parking lot, arriving in time to see Alex trying to push past Teddy toward the restaurant. He didn't get far. Even as Rosa called out "No…" and lunged toward them, Teddy coldcocked Alex. She watched helplessly as Alex toppled like a heap of unmortared brick, and a puff of dust rose around him.

"For Pete's sake," Rosa yelled, "what are you doing, Teddy?"

"Guy wouldn't take no for an answer," he said, glaring at the groaning, groggy man on the ground. "He upsets you."

She started to say, "He does not…" but that would be a lie. Alex Montgomery upset her in the most fundamental way, making her body tremble and her palms sweat. But that was her fault, not his.

"Help him up," she said.

Teddy held out a hand to Alex, who looked dazed as he tentatively shifted his jaw from side to side. When he saw Teddy's beefy paw outstretched, he leaned away.

"He won't hit you again," Rosa promised.

"He doesn't need to." Alex eyed Teddy ruefully. "He got me the first time." He stood up and dusted sand and gravel from his tailored beige slacks.

Rosa turned to Teddy. "Why don't you go back inside?"

"But—"

"I'm fine, Teddy. Promise."

He ambled away, casting glances over his shoulder, and she knew he and all the others would be glued to the security monitors. It was stupid, she told herself, yet she felt like some sort of damsel in a joust.

"Are you all right?" she asked Alex.

"Just peachy." He rubbed his jaw, wincing at his own touch.

"I can't believe you came here and picked a fight with Teddy."

"He picked one with me."

"He wouldn't have if you hadn't shown up."

Alex leaned against a lamppost. "I didn't come here to make trouble," he said. "I'm sorry this happened." He touched his jaw again. "Real sorry. I should have walked away."

"Yes. You should have."

"Now it's too late." His eyes were hooded by the night shadows. "I'm not going to hurt you, Rosa."

She prayed he couldn't see that he already was. His very presence opened old painful places inside her, places she used to believe had healed. "I'll pass that message along," she said.

"Thank you." His gaze flickered around the parking lot

until he found a security camera mounted on the center light pole. "Think he'll believe you?"

"I'll make sure he does." She glanced over her shoulder. "So...are you here for dinner?"

"I'm here for you, Rosa."

A chill that had nothing to do with the evening breeze slipped over her skin. She had a hundred reasons not to be with him; she'd lain awake at night dreaming them up. At the moment, she couldn't think of a single one. Best not to let him know that, though.

She laughed as if he'd made a joke. "Oh, I'd nearly forgotten. You're stalking me."

He offered a lopsided grin, favoring his injured jaw. "If that's what it takes."

She ignored the extra beat of her heart. "You're wasting your time. We don't belong together, and you were smart enough to figure that out years ago. Let's leave well enough alone. That's what *I* want—to live my life and run my restaurant."

"You don't want to live happily ever after?"

"It is *after*. And I'm happy," she retorted.

"So you've said before. I'd hate to see you when you're mad."

"Look, Alex. We're not kids anymore. Whatever happened in the past...it doesn't matter now."

Without warning, he cradled her cheeks in his hands. "My thoughts exactly."

She nearly melted right then and there, her whole body warming to his touch. "This is a bad idea."

Keeping his hands in place, he glared up at the security camera. "I'm going to have a seat at the bar—"

"I'm working. I don't have time to have a drink with you."

"That's not what I'm asking. I need to have a chat with your friends Vince and Teddy."

She stepped back. "No way."

"I'm not going to spend the summer sneaking around like teenagers."

"There's no need to sneak, Alex. Just walk away in plain sight."

"That's not going to happen." He started toward the entrance.

Her heart tripped over the possibility he held out. To be with him again, after all this time. She loved the idea; she hated it. She had made herself into a pillar of female strength, and now he was back, chipping away at her. "Are you crazy?"

"Maybe. I'll be in the bar if you need me." He paused and looked back at her. "It'll be all right, Rosa, I swear it."

She glared up at the camera and then went inside. When she stepped into the steaming, clattering kitchen, everyone was hard at work, as though they had not just been glued to the monitors, spying on her for the past ten minutes.

"If he decides to come inside," she said tersely to anyone who would listen, "let him."

Unable to resist, she kept an eye on the video system and noticed that Alex had indeed gone into the bar. He was not alone. Somehow he had persuaded Vince and Teddy to join him. Alex held a plastic bag of chipped ice against his jaw. The other two were both talking at once, leaning across the table, occasionally making a point with the pounding of a fist.

Rosa could still feel Alex's hands cupping her cheeks. She felt dizzy with the sensation of it. He was back, and willing—perhaps foolishly willing—to fight for her.

This was not the Alex Montgomery who had stolen her heart long ago, then walked away with it like a thief, leaving her empty. This was a different person.

twenty

"Thanks for meeting with me," Alex said to the two formidable, skeptical men. He knew he looked ridiculous holding the bag of ice on his face, chilly drops streaming down his arm. Plan B had seemed like a good idea at the time, but maybe he should have worked it out in a little more detail.

"We don't like what you have to say, we'll kick your ass," Teddy warned.

Christ, where did Rosa find these characters? Alex wondered. *The Sopranos?*

"You already did that," he said genially, "but I'm not changing my mind about seeing Rosa again. It's that simple. That's why I'm here."

"No, you're here because Rosa said to let you in," said Vince.

Alex remembered him as a skinny, pimply-faced punk. He'd turned into a fashion plate in an Italian suit. There was a fierce affection in his eyes when he spoke of Rosa.

"Okay," he said, "so she's lucky to have friends like you. But

I have to ask, do all the guys she goes out with get the same kind of royal treatment?"

"No, of course not," Vince said with a wave of his hand.

"What's so special about me?"

Vince's glare was an arctic blast.

"We were young," Alex said. "Kids break each other's hearts every day. It happens, okay?"

"Not like that."

"Like what?"

Teddy and Vince shared a look. "This was not your ordinary broken heart," said Teddy.

"It's not like she took to her bed and ate a pound of chocolate," Vince added.

"Didn't eat anything, more like," Teddy added.

"Slow down," said Alex. "You've lost me." He tried to piece together the shattered memories of that time. Clearly these two thought they knew something he didn't. "You're saying she went on some sort of hunger strike and it's my fault?"

"She could have died," Teddy said, ignoring his question, "but you wouldn't know that. You were long gone."

A sick lump formed in Alex's gut. Running away from responsibilities—wasn't that what his father used to accuse him of? Was that what he'd done?

Vince folded his hands on the tabletop. "She was all alone after her father's accident. Her brothers tried to help, but they were in the service and couldn't stay. She stuck around while Pete learned to walk and talk again. It took two years, and he got better eventually. Except for his hearing."

"His hearing?"

"He's totally deaf. Does fine, but Rosa worries like crazy about him."

Alex reeled from the news. When Pete had brought Joey over the other day, Alex hadn't noticed a thing. Deaf. Pete

Capoletti, who adored opera and jazz, had lost his hearing. One night. So many lives were changed by that one night.

"But the thing is," Vince went on, "she worked herself into exhaustion, all alone, trying to do everything on her own. She never admitted there was anything wrong until she collapsed at work one day. Someone called 911 and she had to go to the hospital."

He set down the bag of ice. His jaw was completely numb. "So where the hell were you guys while this was going on?" He could tell they felt guilty, too. Maybe that was why they were so protective now.

"At first, nobody noticed," Vince said. "Nobody realized she was staying at work until after midnight, getting up at dawn to go to the hospital, working weekends and trying to manage on her own."

He felt sick. Everything had gone so wrong for her. That wasn't supposed to happen. With only good intentions, he'd walked away from the love of his life. He thought it was the right thing to do under the circumstances. But when he considered what had happened in the aftermath, he wondered if he should've done something differently. But what? he wondered. What?

"She got better," he said, desperate to know her suffering had been brief.

"Hell, yes, she got better," Vince said. "She scared herself into getting well. She realized her father would be completely alone if something happened to her. But she's different now."

He tried not to crane his neck around, looking for her. He longed to see her through new eyes, with this new knowledge. "What do you mean, different?"

"You can't go through all that and not be changed by it. Her father was nearly killed by a hit-and-run driver. She lost out on her chance to go to college. You walked out when she needed you most, and she almost didn't survive. A few life-altering events, I'd say."

Alex crushed a cocktail napkin in his fist. She never knew he had thought about her constantly. From a distance, he'd followed Pete's recovery progress as much as he was able. Clearly, he'd missed a few things. No wonder she was so bitter when he came back the last time. No wonder she'd sent him away.

"So," Vince said, "we don't like people coming to town and upsetting her."

Alex's jaw felt hot now, as the numbness tingled to life. "She's a grown woman who can take care of herself. So how about you let her make up her own mind about whether or not she wants to see me again?"

"She doesn't," Vince said quickly.

"Have you asked her?" Alex shot back.

Vince's hesitation and the glance he exchanged with Teddy indicated that he hadn't. "Just what are your intentions?" he asked.

Alex burst out laughing, then winced in pain. "I'll answer that question when it comes from Rosa."

"We don't trust you," said Teddy. "What the hell are you doing back here? You're rebounding. Your fiancée just dumped you."

Yet another charming aspect of being a Montgomery. Your personal life made the gossip columns. "That has nothing to do with Rosa and me," he said. "And frankly, neither do you guys. So back off."

Teddy glowered at him. "We'll do whatever Rosa wants us to do."

They sat in silence for a few minutes. Alex picked up the ice pack again and held it to his jaw. He was starting to question his own sanity now. *Sanity*. He hadn't even begun to deal with his mother's suicide. He and his father were like cordial strangers, willingly engaging in a conspiracy of denial. The Montgomery way, he thought. Sometimes it was probably better to haul off and punch someone.

"You want a beer or something?" Teddy offered in a conciliatory tone.

"No, thanks." Alex intended to stay sober. He didn't want to be poured home, as he had his first night here.

Rosa appeared at the bar. Her black dress was probably meant to be conservative. On Rosa, it looked like a Victoria's Secret ad. Alex had a swift, almost brutally carnal reaction. He hoped it didn't show as he stood to greet her.

"You're just in time to rescue me."

She looked bemused. "Do you need rescuing?"

Alex eyed Vince and Teddy. "They say they'll do whatever you want."

Her eyebrows went up. "Excellent. I want you guys to get back to work. How's that?"

They exchanged a glance, then subjected Alex to a final threatening glare and went to their stations. He held a chair for her. "What can I get you to drink?"

"A nice little espresso," she said, although she didn't sit down. She paused and looked him straight in the eye, her expression both frank and mysterious.

"At my place," she added.

twenty-one

Every bit of Rosa's common sense shrieked Danger as she drove toward her condo with Alex's headlights beaming in the rearview mirror. Everyone kept telling her she should deal with him so she could move on, once and for all. She was going to do her best to accomplish that tonight.

She had never been nervous about bringing a man home before. But Alex was different in every possible way—and *she* was different when she was with him.

They had started this meeting—date, rendezvous, whatever it was—with a debate about the cars. He wanted to drive her, but she wasn't about to leave her Alfa behind at the restaurant parking lot, thus informing the entire staff as to exactly how much time she was spending with Alexander Harrison Montgomery.

"At my place," she muttered under her breath, mimicking herself. "I've had better ideas."

Still, anything was preferable to being with him at the restaurant with everyone hovering.

She tried to remember how much of a mess she'd left her place in. If he didn't go near the bedroom or closet, she was safe. And she wasn't about to let him get anywhere near the bedroom, she told herself firmly, no matter how incredible he looked or how much she hyperventilated at the sight of him.

"Big deal, so he's coming up for coffee," she said, slowing down as she turned on to her street and into the parking alley. He pulled into a Visitor spot and they both got out at the same time.

The condos in her building had a commanding view of the bay. On a clear day, she could see the ferry steaming back and forth between the mainland and Block Island and the fishing fleet from the port of Galilee heading out to the banks. At night, the lighthouse beam swung out over dark water dotted with tiny lights from the fishing vessels.

"I bought this place three years ago," she said, trying to be smooth as she unlocked the front door. The historic building, once a Victorian resort, was now a beautifully refurbished condo complex. "It's small, but..." She forced herself to quit babbling. No need to explain or excuse anything.

She stepped inside and flipped on a light switch. Her place had a view of the sea and was filled with the things she loved. Unfortunately the things she loved were a haphazard collection, and a perpetually work-in-progress air hung over the apartment. The restaurant consumed her, and she'd never gotten around to serious decorating.

She did have a motif, at least. She'd created it around her favorite item—a tablecloth Mamma used in the kitchen for everyday. Its colorful design of flowers and roosters had influenced the other choices—painted vases, chintz curtains and white bead board trim everywhere. One of these days, she told herself, she'd get around to pulling it all together.

Still, even in this state, it was all terribly personal. Her house was...her home. It revealed so much about her. It would be like standing before him naked.

Although she suspected it would be less of a turn-on.

"Make yourself at home," she said. "I'll fix us an espresso."

"Thanks." He stepped inside and looked around. From the kitchen, she watched him as she took out the coffee and got to work. She used the same coffee served at Celesta's— estate-grown organic beans from the Galapagos Islands. The La Pavoni Romantica espresso maker had been one of her few extravagances for the apartment—a classic lever-style machine with polished brass and hardwood handles.

Alex wandered into the tall-ceilinged main room. She saw him looking around, but couldn't read his expression. She wanted him to see that she'd done fine for herself, that she had a great job, friends and family around her.

The furniture consisted of an overstuffed chintz sofa, a matching chair and ottoman. At present, the ottoman was occupied by a pair of cats who eyed Alex with blasé effeteness. He stuck his hands in his pockets and eyed them back.

"Romeo and Juliet," she told him. "They used to be lovers, but since that visit to the vet they're just friends."

"Are they friendly?" he asked, stretching out a hand to Romeo's funny pushed-in face.

"They're cats," she said, grinning as Romeo turned up his nose at the outstretched hand. Juliet wasn't interested, either. They poured themselves off the furniture, then minced away.

"I think they've been talking to your friends at the restaurant," Alex said.

"They don't talk to anyone." She saw him glance at the terrarium on the windowsill. "The turtles are Tristan and Isolde, and their offspring are Heloise and Abelard."

"So where are Cleopatra and Mark Antony?" he asked.

"In a tomb in Egypt, I imagine. But you can look in the

fish tank and see Bonnie and Clyde, Napoleon and Josephine, and Jane and Guildford."

He bent and peered into the lighted tank. "Fun couples. Is it a coincidence that they all ended tragically?"

"Not a coincidence, just poor judgment."

"Isn't it bad karma, naming your pets after doomed lovers?"

"I don't think they care."

"Do you mind if I put on some music?" he asked, picking up the remote control to the stereo.

"That's fine." She racked her brain, trying to remember which CD she had left in the slot. He hit Play, and it was worse than she'd feared—Andrea Bocelli at his most achingly sentimental.

So big deal, she thought. *I like mawkish Italian music. So sue me.*

Rosa refused to allow herself to cringe as she watched Alex peruse her bookshelf, crammed with paperback romance novels. She couldn't bear to part with her favorites, and her collection filled the space from floor to ceiling.

He moved on to another shelf, this one filled with books that were decidedly not romance novels. He turned to her. "Textbooks?"

"That's right." The grinder whirred as she ground the beans.

"You're going to school?" he asked when it was quiet again.

"Constantly." She put the ground coffee in the portafilter and assembled everything.

"Where?" he asked.

"Where what?"

"Where are you constantly going to school?"

"Any place that'll have me." She laughed at his expression. "I'm not enrolled anywhere. I monitor courses that interest me. In the fall I'll be checking out Georgetown and the University of Milano. It's just something I do."

"You're kidding."

"Would I make this up?"

"No one would make this up. You're really something, Rosa."

She pulled the lever to force the water through the heat exchanger, and a loud hiss of steam interrupted the conversation. The espresso trickled into two white demitasses; then she added a bit of Frangelico to give the coffee a hint of hazelnut. Lord knows, after getting socked in the jaw, he'd earned it. She put the cups on a tray, laid a crescent-shaped pignoli cookie on each saucer and joined him in the living room. The couch or the chair? she wondered with a sudden flutter of nerves. The simple matter seemed a critical decision.

Alex took the tray from her and set it on the white-painted coffee table. Then he took her hand and brought her to the sofa, smoothing over the awkward moment with ease.

"Thank you." He smiled, though not without pain. His jaw was visibly swollen.

"You're welcome. How's your face?"

"I'll live." He sampled the coffee and a look of delight came over him. "This is fantastic."

Relax, she told herself. It's just coffee. "Thanks," she said. "I wanted to thank you for loaning Joey that telescope."

"It's not a loan. I want him to have it."

"It's a valuable antique."

"How can something have value if it's not being used for its purpose? He found his passion and it's a good one. Nurture it."

"He's also a kid. What if he breaks it, pawns it, sells it on eBay?"

"It's up to him. No strings attached."

"Thank you. Pop says he's got it all taken apart with the parts labeled. It'll be a good summer project."

A comfortable silence settled over them. Surprisingly comfortable. So his next question caught her unawares. "What's on your mind, Rosa?"

She could lie, but she'd never been good at deception. "That I feel comfortable with you. For the moment, that is."

"There's a reason for that. We've known each other twenty years."

She took a deep breath and reminded herself that she'd invited him here. It was all her brilliant idea. She shut her eyes and felt an old hurt start to throb. He had once held her heart in his hands. Perhaps that was why she'd felt so betrayed by him in the end.

Bocelli's voice swelled dramatically into the silence. She opened her eyes and watched Alex over the rim of her cup. He seemed to be listening to "Con te partiro" with deep appreciation. You never knew.

"Did you study Italian, too?" he asked her. "In your course work, I mean."

"Sure."

"'Time to say goodbye,'" he translated the song on the stereo.

She raised an eyebrow. "You speak Italian?"

"No," he said. "I have this album, too."

Maybe that was when she started to be afraid. Because she felt herself starting to love him again.

Panic set in. Love him? Loving this man was the emotional equivalent of stepping off a cliff in the dark. No rational woman would do it.

But she couldn't help herself.

Like a lab rat in one of those horrid experiments, she kept going back to the source of her hurt.

"Are you all right?" Alex asked her.

"No." With unsteady hands, she set her cup and saucer on the table.

"What's the matter?"

"I shouldn't have invited you over. I'm sorry, but I think you should go. You know, *con te partiro* and all that."

"Hey, this was your idea."

"It was a bad one. I made a mistake."

He took her hand, and his eyes turned soft. "I'm here, and the world hasn't come to an end."

She knew it would look foolish and petty to snatch her hand away. Besides, she didn't want to. In that moment, she felt utterly mesmerized, still falling off that cliff into the unknown. He was not the one who could save her. Quite the contrary, he was the one who had pushed her.

With one hand, he gently tipped up her chin so that their lips were nearly touching. Her heart sped up and chills rushed over her.

Kiss me, she thought wildly. *Kiss me. Kiss me. Kiss me.*

He didn't. He couldn't hear her yearning thoughts and she was too afraid and vulnerable to speak them aloud.

Sometimes, she thought, a freefall was fun—until she hit the ground.

She reminded herself of all the reasons that this was impossible. He probably saw nothing wrong with killing a summer pursuing an old girlfriend. He was on the rebound from a broken engagement, grieving for his mother, sorting through a house that had stood unchanged for a decade. Flirting with her was probably a diversion for him.

"You can stay until we finish our coffee," she heard herself say.

"I'm a slow drinker."

She looked down at their joined hands. "I simply don't understand why you think this is a good idea."

"Maybe it's not. But then again, maybe it is." He let go of her hand and then did something worse. He slid both arms around her. "I have something to tell you, Rosa. I never had a chance the last time we were together."

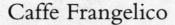

Caffe Frangelico

Frangelico is a liqueur made from hazelnuts grown in the orchards of Lombardy. It's clear and sweet and so delicious, it's said to cause the teeth to sing.

2 parts Frangelico
5 parts hot coffee

Top with whipped cream and crushed hazelnuts.

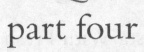

part four

PASTA

There once was a time in Italy when a traitorous poet named Marinetti claimed that pasta "…induces scepticism, sloth, and pessimism and…its nutritive qualities are deceptive." In the ensuing pandemonium, one fact rang clear: Italians love their pasta for all its best qualities as a food. It's abundant, simple to store, delicious to eat and, with no regard for Marinetti's opinion, nutritious and adaptable. In the summer, use the freshest ingredients in nature and see for yourself.

Penne Pasta With Fresh Arugula, Tomato and Mozzarella

Success depends on fresh tomatoes and arugula and basil. And don't even think about using anything but the freshest mozzarella. You don't need much, so go ahead and splurge on the good stuff.

1/2 pound penne pasta
4 ripe tomatoes, diced
about 10 ounces fresh mozzarella, drained and diced
5 ounces arugula, torn into bite-sized pieces
a few fresh basil leaves
1/2 cup extra virgin olive oil
salt and red pepper flakes to taste

Cook the pasta. Put the tomatoes, arugula, basil, mozzarella, olive oil, salt and pepper in a large bowl. When the pasta is ready, toss it with the tomato mixture and serve.

twenty-two

Summer 1992

"So how'd the interview go, kiddo?" asked Mario Costa. "Did you get the scholarship?"

Rosa tied on her apron, emblazoned with a whimsical winged pizza, the Mario's logo. "All right, I guess," she said. "It's up to the committee now." The mere thought of the whole intimidating process made her queasy with nerves. She was on the brink of going to college. And not just any college. Brown University in Providence, that three-hundred-year-old, ivy-covered bastion of higher learning. She'd been accepted and offered a financial aid package that was adequate, though not generous. If she won the coveted Charlotte Boyle Prize, a large grant for which she'd just interviewed, the burden would be lightened considerably. All through spring she'd dreamed of going away to college, wondering which classes she would take, which professors would teach and guide her.

Her brothers had urged her to join the navy as they had.

Rob was married with two boys and twin daughters, Sal was a chaplain, and their lives were filled with adventure. But Rosa couldn't see herself in the service. She intended to fight for her education, too, but she was no warrior. Still, it would be wonderful, she thought, not to saddle Pop with more bills than he already had.

He'd hidden his financial situation from her for years. As she grew older and took on more responsibility, she traced the problem to its source, and the source did not surprise her. Her mother's three-year ordeal, with all the attendant surgeries and treatments, had wiped him out when Rosa was nine. Lacking medical insurance, he was obliged to pay for every penny of her treatment.

Rosa had discovered all that and more when she took over the bookkeeping for her father. She'd come across records of three clients who never paid a cent for the work Pop did. At first, he had resisted her questioning. But finally, he admitted the clients were Mamma's doctors—an oncologist, an anesthesiologist and a surgeon. He repaid them by maintaining their property and would probably do so for many years to come.

She wondered if it made Pop bitter to keep working for them long after Mamma was gone.

In the spring when the college letters had arrived, she'd offered to attend the state college in Kingston to save money, but Pop wouldn't hear of it. He proudly insisted that she attend Brown, that it would be worth the sacrifices they'd both make.

She scrubbed her hands at the big stainless steel sink and pushed her nerve-racked doubts away. Then she stood before a small mirror and checked her hair, which was pulled ruthlessly into a bun and covered with a regulation net. Since that summer five years ago, when Alex Montgomery had cut it all off, she'd let her untamable curls grow down to the middle of her back.

"You ready for the lunch rush?" Mario asked her.

"You bet."

They still had a half-hour before the place opened. The ovens were roaring, the giant steel mixers churning out smooth, pale mounds of pizza dough.

"I wanted to show you this," she said, reaching into her pocket. "Two things, actually."

Mario put on his reading glasses. "What's that?"

"A new seating grid for summer. If you arrange the tables in this layout, you'll increase your capacity by eighteen. Twenty-four, if you add two tables to the deck. It will help move the summer crowds faster, not to mention increase the till."

He studied the sheet of graph paper with deep absorption. Rosa had stayed up late last night, figuring out the arrangement. Mario always encouraged her to make suggestions for improvements around the place. Over the years, she offered her opinion here and there, ways to improve efficiency or cut costs, maybe save on expenses or overage. A glass front for the self-serve soft drink case had increased sales by fifty percent. The addition of a salad bar raised the average tab by three dollars. Plastic number tents for each table increased accurate orders.

The minor adjustments were all obvious to Rosa, but Mario always acted as though they were revelations. He was, she had come to realize, a wonderful person but a mediocre business-man.

Fortunately, because of the summer crowds and the prime location of the restaurant, mediocre was good enough for Mario.

"Perfect," he said. "I'll tell Vince and Leo to come in after closing time tonight and do a reset."

"Vince hates doing resets," she said. "Don't tell him it was my idea."

Mario tacked the grid to the bulletin board over the clock.

"Rosina, *cara ragazza*," he said. "Don't be so modest about being good at this. It's a gift."

Big deal. Who wanted to be good at running a hot, greasy kitchen and feeding people who were often rude to you? What the heck kind of a gift was that? She longed to be good at calculus or philosophy or nuclear physics, not feeding people.

She handed him a computer printout. "Take a look at this. I was talking to one of the vendors about our paper goods order. If we increase our quantity of pizza boxes by just two hundred, they'll give you a price break."

He gestured at the already busy, overheated kitchen. Stainless steel shelves were stuffed to the ceiling with supplies, some of them years old. "I got no more space."

"I'll make space. I promise." Rosa knew she was creating extra work for herself, but inefficiency drove her nuts. "And also, if you order the supplies on the internet, they'll ship from out of state and you won't owe sales tax."

"The inter-what?" Mario frowned.

"The internet. It's…an electronic network." Rosa had no clue how to explain it. "Sort of like ordering from a catalog, but it's through the computer."

"And this is legal?"

"As far as I know."

Mario beamed at her. "Such a smart girl. That scholarship committee will give you anything you want. You'll see. Did you show them my letter of reference, eh?"

"If I was five years dead, they'd think you were trying to canonize me."

"Nah. I just told the truth."

Rosa smiled, but her stomach was churning. She had prepared carefully for the interview. She'd borrowed a perfect outfit from her friend Ariel, whose mother had an alterations shop. She had reviewed her qualifications and practiced in front of a mirror, trying to figure out the proper way to sit. She wrote a list of talking points on index cards and memorized each one.

Despite all the preparations, the interview had been singularly intimidating, particularly since Mrs. Emily Montgomery sat on the committee. Both Mr. and Mrs. Montgomery were alumni of Brown. It was strange to see her sitting there, judging Rosa, knowing all she knew. Not that she knew anything bad about Rosa, or good for that matter. It would have been nice if Mrs. Montgomery would vouch for her, but that would be the day.

Maybe she honestly didn't know the first thing about the gardener's daughter. The two of them were linked by a single tenuous common thread. Alex. And Rosa hadn't seen him in ages.

Alex didn't come to Winslow in the summer anymore. Not since junior high, although she thought of him more often than she probably should. After the first time he'd kissed her, they had done a lot more kissing that summer. Then he had gone away to boarding school, because the doctor said his asthma was so much better that he could live in a school dorm.

Rosa thought it surprising that Mrs. Montgomery would let him out of her sight. She was normally so overprotective. Maybe he'd rebelled, told her to quit hovering. Rosa could picture that. Alex was a scrawny kid, but when he made up his mind, he could be really stubborn.

He'd written to her a couple of times in the beginning. He liked school, but more than that, he loved the freedom of being away from home. She wrote back that she'd started a part-time job at Mario's and was saving her money for college. Despite their best intentions, the correspondence quickly dwindled along with the autumn leaves that year. And Alex never again came back to the beach house.

After her fourteenth summer had come and gone, Rosa

made herself stop hoping he'd return. Still, whenever she saw Mrs. Montgomery, who came to Winslow by herself and had garden parties and cocktail hour for her friends, Rosa couldn't resist asking from time to time: *Is Alex coming this summer?*

He had other things to do, his mother reported. There was summer camp, one that seemed to last for three whole months. He stayed with friends from boarding school. One year he went on a trip to Europe—a study trip, Mrs. Montgomery called it, but Rosa pictured Alex goofing off on a train or drinking pastis and smoking Gauloises somewhere on the Riviera. Then there was a Wall Street internship, which sounded really important, though Rosa imagined him standing around a Xerox machine, bored out of his gourd. Finally she forced herself to stop asking. She didn't want to seem too transparent or, God forbid, pathetic.

She wondered if he was enjoying all the travel, the summer camp, the visits with friends. She wished he'd send just one or two postcards from places like the Isle of Man or Mykonos, but that was dumb. What would he say to her on a postcard? What would she say to him?

As kids, when they were together, they never ran out of things to talk about. Even their silences were filled with wordless exchanges and shared feelings they both understood.

But that, she reasoned, was the nature of summer friendships. Now that she was older, she understood. A summer friendship flourished lavishly but temporarily under the extravagant brightness of the summer sun. At the season's end, the relationship simply stopped. Like a beach umbrella, it was folded up and stored away until the next summer returned.

She smiled a little at her own thoughts as she inventoried the supply of takeout boxes. Maybe she'd study things like this in college—the psychology of friendship. There was probably a course on that alone. If she was honest with herself, she'd admit she was pretty daunted by the phone-book-sized course catalog. College was going to be hard, that was for sure. Still, it was necessary to her success. She didn't want to spend the rest of her days hanging around Winslow.

Humming along with the radio while she worked, she re-organized the supply shelves. The phone started ringing as requests for deliveries came in. Mario's wood-burning oven, which he'd built himself brick by brick, was modeled after the one in his father's trattoria in Naples. It exuded a fragrant heat that would, by midafternoon, make the kitchen an unbearable hell. The two cooks, Vince and Leo, would take turns stepping out back to cool off with a wet towel and a Newport cigarette, littering the ground around the Dumpster with butts.

Note to self, she thought. Put out a bucket of sand for an ashtray. She kept meaning to do that.

As the first pizzas of the day went into the ovens, she shut her eyes and inhaled. This, she thought, was why she worked at Mario's year after year. Lots of local girls worked in bou-tiques or as lifeguards at Town Beach. Some went all the way to Newport to be waitresses or hotel clerks. Rosa, with her reliable reputation, could have landed a more challenging job, maybe even an internship at a radio station.

She was comfortable right here in the clattering, over-crowded, overheated kitchen with Tony Bennett crooning on the radio, the smells of baking dough and marinara sauce spicing the air.

There was a spring in her step as she went to the counter to power up the register and credit card machine. Through the front window, its glass painted with—what else?—a winged pizza, she could see the first customers of the day gathered on the sidewalk outside.

She went to flip the sign on the door from Sorry, We're Closed to Come In, We're Open, turned on the neon lights and opened the door. A crowd of half-grown boys, all in green YMCA Day Camp T-shirts, pushed inside, each straining to be first. The kids were all shapes, sizes and colors, probably on a field trip to the shore for the day.

They were shepherded inside by a tall, broad shouldered camp counselor who wore a baseball cap over his sandy hair. The surging pack of hungry boys streamed toward the counter, and Rosa hurried after them.

Taking an order pad and pencil from her apron pocket, she said, "Welcome to Mario's Flying Pizza. What can I get for you?"

"Man, it smells good in here," said a boy wearing a stick-on name tag that read Cedric.

"I could eat a bear," said another.

"You look like a bear," his friend teased.

"Do not."

"Do so."

"Got any bear pizza?"

The conversation disintegrated into boyish banter, and Rosa looked to their camp counselor for help. He took off his baseball cap, and their eyes locked. His were ocean-blue, and they crinkled when he grinned at her.

She blinked to break the spell, but he was still there.

Alex.

A smile started deep inside her somewhere. She felt it rise up through her slowly like a rainbow-colored soap bubble on a breeze and then unfurl on her lips.

Alex Montgomery. Alex was back, at last. He looked so... different.

"Hi," she said.

"Hi," he said, and his voice nearly laid her out flat. It was a deep, almost musical baritone, the voice of a stranger. "I heard you worked here."

"You heard right." She sounded like a dork.

The natives were getting restless. And noisy. Clearly this was not the moment to ply each other with questions.

She burned with curiosity as he ordered four extra-large pizzas, two cheese, one pepperoni, one sausage. Soft drinks all around.

"For here or to go?" she asked Alex, then waited as though he was about to reveal the meaning of life.

"Here." He gestured. "I'll take them out on the deck."

Mario's deck was set with a few picnic tables shaded by Campari umbrellas. The place didn't have a beverage license, but Mario's cousin Rocky had a distributorship which kept him well-supplied with umbrellas and lighted clocks.

"What do I owe you?" asked Alex.

An explanation, she thought as she punched buttons. Where have you been for the past four summers?

She gave him the total and he reached for his wallet.

"Oh, man," said one of the kids, "Alex is making googly eyes at the waitress."

"Get on outside," Alex said. "And don't feed the seagulls."

They pushed and shoved toward the side door leading to the deck, and Tony Bennett sang into the ensuing silence.

"I am, you know," Alex said as she counted out his change.

"What?"

"Making googly eyes at you."

God, he was flirting. In a baritone voice. She tried to be cool, hoped he couldn't tell she was blushing.

"Where are your glasses?" she asked. "You might be mistaking me for someone else."

He winked. "Contact lenses. Now, what time do you get off work?"

"Seven o'clock."

"That's forever. I'll be done with the hooligans by five. I'll come by then."

Don't give in too easy. That was her friend Linda's motto. "I'll still be working."

"Take off early."

Oh, she was tempted. Mario would let her take off if she asked him. But she wouldn't. Not even for Alex.

"Seven o'clock," she reiterated.

twenty-three

The day dragged, each minute longer than the last. When the hour lurched to 5:00 p.m., she called herself an idiot for not getting off sooner. It was a weeknight, still early in the season, and business was slow.

During the long periods when no one was around, she took a paperback novel from her purse, perched behind the counter and indulged herself. If anyone came, she slipped the book under the counter and hoped no one noticed the hot-pink cover emblazoned with an embracing couple. Someone who was going to Brown couldn't possibly be reading romance novels.

Several times she reached for the phone, intending to tell her best friend Linda who was back in town. But she wasn't ready to share Alex's reappearance with anyone just yet. Instead, she phoned home and left a message on the answering machine, letting her father know she would be late.

If only she had a mother or a sister, she thought wistfully. There were certain things for which a girl needed her mother.

Getting your period or shopping for your first bra, for example. Those just weren't the sort of issues you wanted to discuss with the nuns at school or your dad. And sometimes you
were bursting to tell her everything inside you, like when Alex
Montgomery came back to town, having transformed himself
from a geek to a Greek god.

She served a noisy family who had just taken a beach rental
on Pocono Road. Then a skinny woman with complicated special instructions about anchovies arrived. Rosa chatted with the
retired guy who delivered the Chamber of Commerce papers
for the rack by the door, but her mind kept wandering to Alex.
She couldn't believe how much he'd changed. She wondered if
he knew he looked like a guy on the cover of a romance novel.
Probably not. He was reading *Bulfinch's Mythology* at age ten.
He was probably reading Proust now. In French.

The clock somehow dragged toward evening. From her station at the counter, she watched the beachgoers pick up their
straw bags and ice chests and head for their cars. In the slanting
rays of the setting sun, the water turned to flickering gold. Far
down the coast, the lighthouse blinked its signal—two long
and two short, nine seconds in between.

And finally seven o'clock rolled around. A girl named Keisha came on duty to take Rosa's place because, in the summer,
Mario's was open until midnight, seven days a week.

"Slow tonight, huh?" asked Keisha.

"Yes." Rosa tried not to look hurried as she peeled off her
apron and hair net.

Technically, Keisha was a summer person; her family lived
in Hartford during the school year. Her grandfather had been
a Black Panther, a fact that seemed to embarrass Keisha. Then
he wrote a memoir and got himself elected to Congress, and
suddenly they were a middle-class family. Her parents were
both lawyers, and, fiercely intellectual, she was headed for

Amherst College. Still, she never acted like the summer people who strolled around in their tennis whites. She fit in with the townies just fine.

"See you tomorrow," Rosa said.

"Bye." Keisha settled herself on a stool behind the counter. It was then that Rosa remembered that she'd left her book under the counter. To her dismay, the girl found it and studied the cover, flipped a few pages and said, "Cool." Then she settled down to reading it.

You never knew, thought Rosa. She stepped outside and was hit by sea breeze and salt air. A bonfire burned on the beach, illuminating tall girls with tanned legs and sleek ponytails. They were roasting marshmallows and talking nonstop. A few shirtless boys tossed a football back and forth. Summer people, oblivious to the locals heading home from work.

Alex was nowhere in sight. She scanned the parking lot and saw only a few cars. A couple strolled past, holding hands and leaning on each other in a way that made her feel wistful.

Still no Alex. Maybe he'd been a figment of her imagination. The guy who'd come into Mario's did not look or sound anything like the Alex she remembered.

The Alex she remembered was skinny, awkward and funny. He had a high-pitched voice and an infectious laugh. This Alex was—

"Sorry I'm late," he said, breathless as he jogged across the parking lot toward her. "One of the kids' mothers never showed up, and I ended up driving him to Pawtucket."

"That's okay." It was all she could do not to stare. Burnished a deep red-gold by the sunset, he seemed like a figure out of a dream.

Then she realized something. He was studying her as intently as she was studying him. She felt self-conscious as his gaze touched her hair and eyes and lips, then slipped down-ward even though he clearly seemed to be trying to play it cool.

"You're staring," she said softly.

"So are you."

She blushed. "You've changed a lot."

"So have you."

The last time they'd been together, he was undersized, pale, often bright-eyed with medication and oxygen deprivation. She had been small and dark, her hair wild, her tomboy phy-sique stick-straight. Now he looked like an Olympic athlete, and she had the kind of figure that drew rude sounds from boys on the beach. She liked it, and she didn't like it. Some-times she lay awake at night wondering how to deal with her ultra feminine body. Should she hide it or accentuate it? Feel pride or shame?

"Well," he said, "what would you like to do? Do you need to go home first, or…?"

"No. I called my father and said I was going out after work." She smiled uncertainly. "So I'm out."

"My car's over here." He gestured at a shiny two-seater MG convertible. "Unless, um, you have a car you need to—"

"No." She gestured at a much-used Schwinn La Tour lean-ing against the side of the building. "I ride my bike to work. I drive my father's truck sometimes, but we share it." Rosa made herself stop babbling. She hated the feeling of embar-rassment that crept through her. She didn't have her own car. With her going away to college, she and Pop had to be careful with money. "Anyway, you can just bring me back here after we…after our…" What? She didn't dare call it a date.

"No problem." He grinned at her.

She smiled back, feeling a curious sort of relief. She had seen a glimpse of the old Alex, the boy who had been her best friend each summer. He might look like a hunk, but he was still Alex.

Then, with an unexpected air of gallantry, he held open
the passenger side door for her. As she climbed in, she faintly
regretted not treating this like a real date. Maybe she should
have gone home to primp and try on different outfits and do
her hair. Here she was, in her jeans and white shirt with *Mario's* stitched on the pocket, the smell of pizza sauce infusing
her hair and even the pores of her skin.

He pulled out of the parking lot and drove along the coast
road. It was a clear night, and the breeze felt heavenly as it rip-
pled over her, sweeping away the last vestiges of the pizza joint.

They both reached for the knob of the radio at the same
time and their hands bumped awkwardly.

"Sorry," she said, drawing her hand back.

"It's okay. Do you have a station you like?" He turned on
the radio and The Heights, singing "How Do You Talk to an
Angel?" drifted out.

"I think that's probably it—92 Pro out of Newport."

They drove along, listening to music and feeling the warm
summer breeze. She wondered if he was as lost in memories
and as full of questions as she was.

As they headed away from town, he asked, "What's North
Beach like these days?"

"Exactly the same."

"Deserted, you mean."

"Usually."

"You want to go check it out?"

She knew then exactly what he was asking. It wasn't about
the beach but about them. He wanted to know if it was time to
go back to the past, back to the friendship they'd once shared,
and then maybe go forward from there.

"Yes," she said. "We should definitely check it out."

He drove by his family's house, and Rosa saw the porch
light glowing and lamps brightening the upstairs windows.

"Your family's here?" she asked.

"Just my mother. My father's in the city and my sister got married in May. She lives in Massachusetts now."

"One of my brothers is married, too. Rob married a fellow officer in the navy. I have two nephews and two nieces. A set of twins and two boys."

"All in the last four years?"

"His wife's Italian, too."

He took his eyes off the road for a second to glance at her. "You're an aunt."

"Aunt Rosa. Pretty wild, isn't it? My other brother Sal is a priest. A navy chaplain."

"Tell me where to turn," he said. "I haven't been here in a while."

"I know." She cringed, hoping he hadn't caught the note of wistfulness in her voice. She directed him to the gravel pull-out by the side of the road. On rare occasions she came here to walk and think, sometimes to rake quahogs to surprise Pop with his favorite meal of spaghetti alle vongole.

The sun was nearly gone as they got out of the car. The tall marsh grasses were painted in deepest black against the fire-colored sky. Out over the water, darkness gathered and melded with the horizon line.

He led the way along the sandy footpath. Beach grasses nodded as they passed, and wild rose branches snatched at their shirts. Then the path widened, opening to the beach, which spread out before them in splendid isolation.

A sense of wonder welled up in her the way it always did when she came here. All her life she'd found solace down by the sea where its power and vastness diminished everything. It was a place where the will surrendered. Here was a force that would not—could not—be controlled. She found a strange comfort in that.

"First time I ever flew a kite was right here," Alex said.

"I know," Rosa said, startled that he would mention it. "I was there."

"First time I went wakeboarding, too, and you were there."

"And scared to death."

"That didn't stop you from doing it," he pointed out.

"Being scared never does," she said. Then she felt him staring at her, and his look made her blush. "Let's walk," she suggested. Her legs were tired from the day's work, but being with Alex filled her with nervous energy. They headed down to the water's edge and took off their shoes.

She sneaked a glance at him and caught him still staring. She gave an embarrassed laugh and tried to smooth down her hair, hopelessly tangled by the ride in the convertible.

"What?" he asked.

"This is just so weird, seeing you again."

"Good weird or bad weird?"

"Good. Definitely good." She moved a little closer to him so their shoulders were nearly touching. "So why haven't you been back here?"

"Once I started high school, I finally got to have a life."

"What, you didn't before?"

"My mother never used to let me out of her sight."

"I remember that."

"She backed off when my asthma got better."

"Better. You mean it went away?"

"Not exactly. The symptoms went away. The doc said that's pretty common during a growth spurt. He was hoping for it all through my childhood. I'm still an asthmatic, but I outgrew my asthma. In three years I've had just two attacks. I'm on an experimental drug that's working, so I'm not planning on having any more."

"Alex, that's fantastic." She was amazed and thrilled for

him. A miracle had transformed a sickly little boy into...into Brad Pitt.

"I can't explain how it felt to suddenly be able to do things like a normal kid," he said. "I played sports, didn't have to lug around a breathing apparatus. It was like getting out of jail, finally. I wasn't keen on spending summers under my mother's thumb."

"It's great that you're better, Alex." She was on the verge of admitting that she'd missed him, that summer wasn't the same without him, but she kept quiet. Too much information.

He slowed his pace as though he wanted to prolong their walk. "How about you?" he said. "You've changed, too. I mean, I can't help noticing it."

"I haven't been to Europe or Costa Rica or Egypt," she said, then blushed because she'd all but admitted she'd been asking about him. "I haven't been anywhere. Just here."

"Here's fine."

She nearly told him about Brown, but changed her mind. Not yet.

They stopped to look at the water, reflecting the last colors of the sunset. A long way down the beach, the lighthouse beacon swung its beam out into the night. There was no sound except the waves hissing up to their feet, rattling over rocks.

"I sure missed coming here," Alex said. "I just didn't miss my mom watching me like I was a lab rat."

"So what did you do with all that freedom?"

"I went to a very boring high school. Phillips Exeter Academy in New Hampshire. My father went there, and his father, and so on, right down to old John Phillips himself, as far as I know."

"It's supposed to be a terrific school," she said. "I can't believe you were bored." He was extremely smart, she remembered. Maybe classes moved too slowly for him.

"All right, I wasn't that bored. I was so ready to get out of the house, I would have gone practically anywhere."

Rosa could certainly understand that. "Because of being sick?"

"Yeah. I needed a different life." He met her gaze and held it steady. "But there was something I missed about spending the summer here."

Goose bumps rose and spread over her skin. "Yeah?"

He grinned. "Definitely."

"Are you staying until fall?" Great, Rosa, she thought. Way to sound eager.

"That's the plan. I'm working full-time at the Y."

She shut her eyes and suppressed a shudder of delight. Then she had to ask: "You're going to college?"

"That's right. You?"

"Yes." She folded her arms across her middle. "I'm going up to Providence. To Brown."

Even in the dark, she could see his grin, and she knew then that he was going there, too. "No kidding."

"No kidding." Once or twice, Rosa had asked herself why she'd chosen Brown. Was it because it was the best school in the state? Because she'd been given a good financial aid package? Or because somewhere in the back of her mind, she knew Alex would end up there? It was where his mother had gone, his father and grandfather. It was where all Montgomerys went. There was a photo in the library of Alex's house of his parents, sitting on the chiseled stone steps of Emery Hall.

Suddenly her future, which had seemed unbearably exciting ever since the coveted acceptance packet had arrived in the mail, felt real. For the first time, she could actually picture herself there, walking across a quad, sitting in a lecture or lab. And now Alex was part of the picture.

"Remember this place?" he asked, clearly not as excited as she was. He probably wasn't, because it was so…expected.

"No," she said. "What about it?" Inside, she was dying. She remembered this with every cell of her body. She dreamed about it, thought of it with the frequency of obsession. Here. It had been here. With the sunlight warm on their faces and the breath of the wind in their ears, her relationship with Alex had turned from friendship to something else. Something more.

Then he was right in front of her, very close, and she caught her breath at the full impact of his height.

"Liar," he said. "You do so remember."

She felt her cheeks grow warm. "We were a couple of dumb junior high kids," she said. "That's what I remember."

"Don't tell me you don't remember your first kiss."

"What makes you think you were the first? You weren't, you know."

"Was so."

"Were not." But she was lying, and he knew it. In seventh grade, Paulie diCarlo had tried to steal a kiss at a school dance, but she hadn't let him succeed, and after that she didn't speak to him the rest of the school year.

"It's kind of cool that I was first," Alex whispered.

"I could say the same." Rosa never used to ask him much about his school in the city, but she was pretty sure he was a loner. The one time she'd asked him, he had dismissed the question with a wave of his hand. "I don't have any friends there," he said. "Everybody calls me a freak." Now, she knew without asking that the situation had changed for him.

"Rosa, do you have a boyfriend?"

"If I did, I wouldn't be here."

"That's good." He took her in his arms and pulled her close. She felt the surprising strength of his body, the hardness of his muscled limbs. Her senses filled up with him, and she felt strangely helpless, strange because she was usually in control of herself.

She looked up at him as he bent to close the distance between them, and felt a sudden ripple of apprehension. "I'm not looking for a boyfriend, Alex."

"Not anymore, you aren't," he said, just before he kissed her.

Spaghetti alle Vongole

4 dozen littleneck clams in their shells, the smaller the better.
(If you use quahogs, you only need a dozen; just chop the clam
meat fine.)
2 Tablespoons of sea salt
1 pound dry spaghetti
1/2 cup olive oil
4-8 garlic cloves, minced
1/2 cup white wine (Principessa Gavia is preferred)
2 Tablespoons chopped flat-leaf parsley

Scrub the clam shells under cold running water. Cook the
spaghetti until al dente. In a heavy pan with a lid, heat the
olive oil and sauté the garlic. Add the clams in their shells
and the white wine, bring to a boil, cover the pan and cook
until the clams open. This should take a few minutes, and
feel free to add more wine. Discard clams that do not open;
you'll find a few rejects in every bunch. Remove the clams
with a slotted spoon. Add the cooked spaghetti to the sauté
pan, stirring it into the sauce. Add the parsley. Serve in
individual bowls, topped with the clams.

twenty-four

Rosa floated. She was lighter than the clouds of the marine layer that drifted in with the morning sunshine. She was lighter than the pink cotton candy spun in big silver pans at a booth at Town Beach, lighter even than the tunes played by The Cranberries floating out of the kitchen radio.

Pop was already gone for the day. He'd had to leave his truck at the mechanic's, and today he was commuting on his familiar old yellow bicycle. That bike was such a powerful reminder of the past. He used to ring the bell when he got home from work, and Mamma would go flying out the back door to greet him.

Maybe he'd be working at the Montgomerys' house today.

"Alex is back," she said to the photo of her mother propped on the windowsill. "Alex Montgomery is back for the summer."

They had arranged to meet at the beach, which would be busy and crowded today. Their work schedules conflicted, but they discovered they could see each other in the morning if they got up early enough. She had promised to be there by eight, and said she would bring something to eat.

As she fixed breakfast, she relived last night's kiss over and over again, and it was wonderful, the pleasure and the dizzy burn of his lips against hers. She probed each moment, each heartbeat, on a molecular level, trying to figure out why it was so magical. Their kiss had been familiar enough to feel safe—this was Alex, after all—yet new enough to tantalize her with a fine sharp edge of risk. She felt something brand new for an old friend. Until now, she hadn't realized such a thing was possible.

She hummed along with the radio while cutting thick slices from the ring of ciambellone bread she'd made earlier. It didn't taste exactly like the ciambellone she remembered from her childhood, but it was close. She fixed the sweet, lemony bread the way she always did, the slices spread with mascarpone and sprinkled with cinnamon and sugar.

"You're a natural in the kitchen," Pop always said.

Being good at cooking was nothing special. She wanted to be good at Latin, at vector analysis, at Jungian psychology. Not cooking.

Yet she always seemed to be feeding people in spite of herself. In high school, she was the one who brought snacks to study tables or booster meetings. By senior year, she had football players eating cicchetti and the student council debating the merits of different types of olive oil.

She took along some fresh berries to eat with the bread, added two round, squat bottles of Orangina, loaded everything into the basket of her bike and took off. She floated all the way there. It was amazing how Alex filled her mind. Simply amazing. Only yesterday, thoughts of moving away and getting an education had consumed her. Now she could think of nothing and no one but Alex.

He wasn't exactly waiting for her, she observed as she glided under the stone archway leading to the beach. But he was there, already engaged in a game of volleyball on a team of visitors against a team of locals. Unnoticed, Rosa watched them. Or rather, she watched Alex. He looked incredible with his shirt off, hanging from the waistband of his shorts. It was hard to believe skinny, pale, wheezing Alex had turned out this way. She felt a strange shiver of heat as she studied his muscular chest and flat middle and the way his golden hair fell over his brow. On long, strong legs and bare feet, he moved with an assurance that was nearly a swagger.

No matter where they were from, all guys tended to turn a simple volleyball game into a life-or-death struggle. The locals were boys she knew from school or work—Vince, Paulie, Leo and Teddy. They wore cutoffs and muscle shirts, and some of them sported tattoos and mustaches or goatees. They talked and jeered in loud voices, and Rosa found herself wishing their differences from the visitors were not so noticeable.

The other team was made up of summer people, instantly recognizable by their patrician looks, their casual clothes that cost a fortune, their shiny hair. Three other girls also watched from the sidelines. Rosa didn't know them, but she knew their type. They would have names like Brooke or Tiffany, and they probably attended schools with zero church affiliation. Their silky pale hair, caught back by hairbands, swung as they moved. They wore khaki shorts and oxford blue shirts rolled back to the elbows. Their negligent sense of style set them apart from Rosa and her friends, who studied every issue of *Glamour* and *Cosmopolitan* and hopped on each passing trend like short-haul truckers.

"Hey, Rosa," yelled Vince, all but beating his chest.

Finally, she thought. It was about time someone noticed. She waved at him.

"I'll be through in a minute," Alex said.

The volleyball match turned into an all-out battle. You'd think the state championship was at stake, the way they went at it.

Linda Lipschitz, Rosa's best friend, arrived and sat down beside her, and they dangled their bare legs against the concrete wall. Linda was eating a banana and drinking a Diet Dr Pepper. This was her latest fad weight-loss scheme. Yet as hard as she tried, Linda never changed. She was born round and seemed destined to stay round. And she was cute that way, with a bright smile that made her endearing no matter what.

"How was that interview?" she asked.

"Fine."

"I can't believe you're leaving us to go away to college."

"I'm not leaving you." But it occurred to Rosa that she might be lying.

"That's what they all say. You'll probably wind up in Europe or California and I'll never see you again."

"Why would I go to Europe or California?"

"That's where people go with a fancy schmancy education." Linda watched the game for a while. "Someday, years from now, you'll be on their team." She jerked her head toward the summer people.

Rosa laughed. "They'd never have me."

"True. You would need to bleach your hair. Oh, and grow taller and flatten your boobs," she added.

"That's Alex Montgomery." Rosa pointed him out and savored Linda's look of astonishment.

"No way. You mean that geek you used to hang around with in the summer?"

"The very same."

Linda put her hand to her heart. "Oh, my God."

Rosa leaned back on the heels of her hands. She thought

she was being nonchalant, but the expression on her face must have given her away.

"Holy cow," Linda said in a stage whisper. "You hooked up with him."

Rosa stared straight ahead. "Whatever gave you that idea?"

"Come on, Rosa. Spill."

"There's nothing to spill." She couldn't keep the grin from her face. "Yet."

"Holy cow," Linda said again, elbowing her playfully.

Alex spiked the ball to score, punching it down right next to Paulie diCarlo's head. "Game point," a boy shouted as he prepared to serve.

Paulie ripped off his muscle shirt and hurled it at the ground. "Screw it."

"No, thanks," Alex muttered.

With a roar of fury, Paulie charged the net, ducking under and bearing down on Alex.

Laughing, Alex sidestepped him and started to run, but Paulie dove, grabbing hold of his ankle and yanking his foot upward. Alex came down hard on his back, and even from where she sat some distance away, Rosa could hear the air rush out of him.

"Oh, no," she said, instantly fearing an asthma attack. She could see the panic and confusion bright in his eyes, and she was terrified for him. But even before she jumped down to the sandy volleyball court, he'd regained his breath without the aid of an inhaler. He moved so fast it was a blur, but through the cloud of dust, she could see that he had flipped Paulie to his back and held him pinned.

"You lose," he said. "Again."

"Big mistake," Linda murmured. "He should apologize."

"Oh, like that's going to happen."

"Come on, Paulie," said Teddy. "It's time for work, anyway." They were on the beach patrol for the parks department. They drove a county truck and wore uniforms, cleaning up the beaches and roadsides and parks. But they strutted around as though they were extras on *Baywatch*.

The girls watched them, whispering among themselves. Rosa didn't miss the looks they shot at Alex—adoring, possessive looks. She felt an awkward moment coming on.

"Hey, Alexander," said the prettiest, blondest one of all, "let's go over to my place. My parents are gone for the day."

He looked at them, then over at Rosa. She wanted to die, completely die. She never should have come here, never should have agreed to meet him in town. They were from two different worlds, and unless they were alone, they made no sense together.

"Thanks, Portia, but I can't," he said with a grin. "I'm busy." With that, he brushed the sand off his arms and chest and walked over to Rosa. "Ready?" he said.

Behind her, Linda sighed audibly.

"Completely," Rosa said.

twenty-five

One Saturday morning, Rosa heard the mail drop through the slot and went to get it. She'd been on pins and needles, waiting to hear about her scholarship. She shuffled through the usual junk mail and bills, then caught her breath when she came across an elegant envelope of cream stock, hand addressed. It was from the Charlotte Boyle Center.

The rest of the mail drifted to the floor. She tore open the envelope, trembling as she read the committee's decision.

Oh, no, she thought.

She found her father in the driveway, putting a new chain on his bicycle. "I need to talk to you, Pop," she said.

He wiped his hands on a red handkerchief. "What's the matter?"

"Everything's fine, but… I heard from the scholarship committee. I didn't get it, Pop. I didn't get the scholarship." She stared at the cracked concrete driveway. She felt terrible. The generous prize would have taken a burden off her father.

She told herself that there were many other girls more qualified and probably just as needy. Still, a tiny voice inside her whispered that perhaps Emily Montgomery's influence had affected the decision. Mrs. Montgomery had never liked her.

"Anyway," she continued, "I was thinking I...could wait a year." She tried to sound upbeat as she said it. It was the most practical course of action. "I could stay here and work full-time."

"What, wait?" He shook his head, and when he looked at her, there was a gleam in his eye. "You're not gonna change your plans now. You go to college, Rosina."

"Really? Really and truly?"

"It is what my Rosa wants, it is what you worked so hard for, of course you are going."

She flung her arms around him, inhaling his familiar, comforting scent. "Thank you, Pop. Thank you so much."

"You're gonna get all dirty," he said.

The summer days sped by far too quickly, and Alex and Rosa found too little time to be together. Most days, he was busy with his boys at the Y. Most nights she was at Mario's, earning every penny she could for college.

One hot July day, Alex and Rosa both managed to get the whole day and evening off, a rare occurrence given their busy work schedules. They met for coffee, and she was thrilled that he remembered how she took hers, with lots of cream and sugar. Alex borrowed a sleek Club 420 sailboat from the Rosemoor and they sailed clear out to Block Island. Rosa was happy to lean back, clasp her hands behind her head and let Alex do the work.

The sky was an endless arch of brilliant light over the small, fast-moving boat. Rosa could think of nowhere else she would rather be than out here in the blue Atlantic, where the water was veined with the white whorls of undercurrents. The craggy island was cloaked in a mantle of wildflowers and blueberry shrubs, and the sweep of scenery dazzled Rosa. They moored in a sunny cove and went ashore for a picnic by Settlers Rock, which was engraved with names from the seventeenth century. They collected jingle shells and bits of sea glass, and Rosa found a rare mermaid's purse.

Alex scrutinized it. "That's the egg case of a skate."

"Huh. It's a mermaid's purse. It has magical powers." She handed it over. "Here, you keep it."

He put it in his pocket. "I need all the magic I can get."

She considered telling him she still had the nautilus shell he'd given her the first day they met, but decided against it. He would think her hopelessly sentimental. Especially if she admitted that not only had she kept it, but she'd put it in a special place on a glass shelf in her bedroom window, where the sunlight shone through it from behind.

"It's nice, getting away for a day," she said. Here, walking the Mohegan Bluffs among tourists and strangers, she didn't feel like a misfit at all as she held hands with Alex. She just felt like... Alex's girl.

He had no idea about the scholarship prize. Maybe he didn't even realize his mother was on the committee. She pushed the thought from her mind and hid her thoughts behind a bright smile. Just for today, she wasn't going to let herself worry about it.

In the afternoon, they headed back to the mainland. "You're good at this," she told him as he turned into the wind.

"You're just saying that because you want me to do all the work."

She leaned back and trailed her hand in the cool water. "I'm saying that because it's true." He'd never been much of an athlete as a sickly boy, but clearly he'd made up for lost time. He maneuvered them expertly out onto open water, the sun glittering over the surface. Yet for all of nature's beauty around them, Alex seemed distracted. His attention kept returning to one spot in particular.

He was staring at her boobs, she was sure of it. So maybe her white shirt, blowing open to reveal her tomato-red bikini top, needed buttoning. But she didn't button up or even buckle her life vest. Because if she was completely honest with herself, she liked the way he looked at her. That was the whole idea behind wearing a red bikini in the first place.

She liked staring at him, too. With the passage of summer, his coloring deepened, and the contrast of his light hair against his skin was striking. His mouth was perfectly chiseled, like a Donatello masterpiece. She loved the way his lips felt and tasted when he kissed her, which he didn't do nearly enough as far as Rosa was concerned.

"What are you thinking?" he asked.

The unexpected question drew a blush to her cheeks. She was trapped, and she was an incredibly bad liar. "Actually, I was thinking about you." Maybe he wouldn't make her elaborate.

"What about me?"

"I'm just glad you're spending the summer here."

She wished they had more time to laze around in the boat, but the light had deepened to a fiery golden glow and evening was coming on. It was a bad idea to sail at night without proper equipment. Working together, they sailed into the channel at Galilee and tied up at the dock of the Rosemoor.

They stopped in Winslow at the ice-cream parlor. Rosa was so busy perusing the huge buckets of mocha almond and caramel fudge that she scarcely heard the bell of the door jingle.

In walked two of the summer girls who clearly recognized Alex. One of them had three small dogs attached to a single leash. It probably violated some health code, but the guy behind the counter didn't object.

"Hi, Alexander," said the girl with the dogs, beaming at him and showing off a set of freshly lasered teeth. She looked perfect in a denim skirt and Weejuns, a cotton sweater slung around her shoulders. They were both so incredibly stylish. How did they do that, making it look so simple? Rosa wondered. She herself was at a hideous disadvantage here. In addition to cut-offs, bikini top and flip-flops, she wore the sweat and brine of a long day out on the water. Her hair looked like a troll doll's.

"Hey." Alex stepped back to include everyone. "Rosa, this is Hollis Underwood and Portia…"

"Van Deusen," said the taller girl, sending Alex a moue of chagrin. "Don't tell me you forgot, Alexander. Our fathers are best friends."

"Right," said Alex, clearly not on the same page as Portia.

"You work at that pizza place, right?" the girl named Hollis asked Rosa.

She nodded, wondering what that had to do with anything. "Are those your dogs?" she asked, hoping to change the subject.

"Temporarily. These are rescue dogs. I'm socializing them so they can be adopted." She bent down and petted each one. "Aren't I, Wizzy Kizzy," she said in a baby voice that made Rosa want to cringe. Then she straightened up. "Would you like to adopt one?"

"I would, but I'm going to college at the end of the summer." Yet as she looked at the furry little herd, Rosa felt an unexpected softness. They had never had a dog in their family. Pop said they were expensive and too much trouble.

"You are?" asked Portia. "Which college?"

"Brown," Rosa informed them, trying not to sound smug. But she didn't even bother concealing her satisfaction at the expressions on their faces.

Alex turned back to placing his order. Despite his dismissal, Portia leaned on the glass case, blocking his view of the ice cream. "So are you planning on going to that charity formal at the club?"

Portia, thought Rosa. Portia Schmortia. She called it "the club."

"I'll be there," Alex said, taking out his wallet to pay for the ice cream.

Rosa hid her surprise. He hadn't said anything about a formal at his country club. Not to her, anyway.

Portia glanced at Hollis, then back at Alex. "Do you have a date?"

"Yeah. I do."

Rosa tried not to choke as he handed her an embarrassingly large cone of maple nut crunch. *All right,* she told herself. *Don't panic. It's not like we're a couple or anything. If he's got a date, I'm fine with that.*

As she left the ice-cream shop, she felt about an inch tall. She was as insignificant as a house fly, an ant. An ant with boobs.

But the feeling of insignificance vanished as Alex opened the car door for her. When she was with him, she felt like the most important person on earth.

"Friends of yours?" she asked, licking her ice cream and acting nonchalant.

"I know them from school."

She was burning up with curiosity about the charity event. Even worse, she was dying to hear about this date Alex supposedly had.

She savored her ice cream and acted like it didn't matter, but she was about to explode. Finally she couldn't stand it anymore. "So do you really have a date to that thing?" she blurted out.

"Depends," he said, then took an infuriatingly long time

to finish his ice cream, crunching the last of the waffle cone with a satisfied look on his face.

"Depends on what?" she asked, a slow burn of frustration rising through her.

"On whether or not you say yes." He looked at her for a moment and then burst out laughing.

"You rat," she said, punching his shoulder, but she couldn't contain her grin. She smiled all the way through town. A formal dance. Not a prom, either, but an actual event with a purpose. And she was going. He explained that his mother was chairman this year and the goal was ambitious. They wanted to raise a hundred thousand dollars for the Sandoval Art Museum.

Glancing at the clock on the dashboard, she said, "I promised my father I'd be home early tonight."

"I'll drive you," he said.

Rosa hesitated. She hated that hesitation, that moment of thinking *I don't want you to see where I live.* That impulse to say lightly, *That's okay, I can walk.* There wasn't one thing wrong with her house. It was just different from what Alex was used to.

"Thanks," she said. "That'd be great."

"You're going to have to give me directions," Alex said as they left the main drag.

"Right at the stoplight." Nerves jumped inside her. In all the summers they'd spent together, Alex had never seen where she lived. As the road wound away from the shoreline, the neighborhoods grew weedier, the houses smaller. "Take a left here, on Prospect Street."

The street where she'd grown up was lined with clapboard houses with fading paint, overgrown yards with toys left out, driveways with too many nonworking cars.

"Up there?" he asked. "Isn't that your dad's truck?"

"That's the one."

He pulled alongside the curb and opened the door for her. Across the way, a curtain stirred in the window. Mrs. Fortenski was at her post.

"Thanks for the lift," she said.

"You're welcome."

Okay, she thought. In for a penny, in for a pound. "Would you like to come in?"

"Sure."

She adored him for not even hesitating.

Her father, bless him, was a world class gardener. The front yard and walkways were as beautiful and neat as the neighbors' were untidy. She wished she could say the same about the inside of the house, but the fact was, Pop was kind of a slob. Rosa kept the kitchen and her own room clean, and she did her best with the rest of the place, but Pop had a habit of leaving a trail of litter behind him—old newspapers, empty glasses, effluvia from his pockets.

Rosa knew a moment of wistfulness. If her mother were alive, she'd go bursting in, full of her news about the formal, and Mamma would be just as excited as she was. Pop was a guy. He wouldn't get it.

She took a deep breath, made sure her blouse was buttoned over the bikini and opened the front door. "Pop, I'm home," she yelled.

"There you are," said Pop, coming from the den. "How did—oh." He stopped when he saw Alex.

"Hello, Mr. Capoletti."

"Is everything all right?" asked Pop. Clearly he misunderstood Alex's presence.

"Everything is fine, sir."

"Alex gave me a ride home. We went sailing today."

Pop took his measure in that fearsome way of his. There was something about Pop's thick eyebrows, his sharp eyes, his compact, muscular build, that was designed to intimidate. But Alex didn't flinch.

"Come in and have a seat," Pop ordered, and led the way to the den.

"I'll get us something to drink," said Rosa.

In the kitchen, she went into what Linda called her Martha Stewart mode, putting crescent-shaped pignoli cookies on a plate and little sprigs of rosemary in the lemonade glasses. Actually, Rosa secretly admired Martha Stewart, who had her own magazine. According to *People* magazine, some publisher had turned her into a media figure, whatever that was.

When Rosa arrived at the doorway to the den and saw Alex sitting with her father, a strange and powerful feeling came over her. It was an extraordinary emotion, so strong that she scarcely remembered to breathe. For a few seconds, she didn't bother trying to put a name or a value on the feelings rising inside her. She just watched Alex for a moment, knowing the world was changing in some silent, secret way.

There he sat with her father, in a dingy living room littered with old newspapers, and he was completely, utterly at home. He was as comfortable and nonjudgmental as a parish priest or a really good doctor. This boy, whose family had homes and villas all over the world, who dined on fine china every night, whose family had more money than some third-world nations, looked utterly content in the company of Rosa's father. Alex was, she reflected, the most sincere and unpretentious boy she'd ever brought home.

Finally she understood the feeling that struck her with such force. In that moment, with all the power of her young, yearning heart, Rosa fell in love with Alex Montgomery.

Rosemary Lemonade

In the Old Country version of "Sleeping Beauty," the princess was awakened from her enchanted slumber with a whiff of rosemary-scented water. The prince was probably miles away, lost.

2 cups water
2 cups sugar
2 cups lemon juice
Grated rind of one lemon
Two sprigs of rosemary
Ice cubes
Cold water or club soda

Combine the water and sugar in a pan and bring the mixture to a strong boil. After three minutes, remove the pan from the heat and stir in lemon juice, lemon rind and rosemary. Cover and steep for an hour. Strain the mixture into a jar. To fix a glass of lemonade, fill a drinking glass about a third full with the lemon syrup, add ice and water or club soda to the top of the glass, and stir. Makes about 4 cups.

twenty-six

"This boy," Pop said the night of the dance at the country club, "he's got to have you home by midnight."

"You bet, Pop. Otherwise I'll turn into a pumpkin." Rosa paced up and down in front of the hall mirror as she waited. She wasn't nervous, but excited. She'd never even seen the inside of the Rosemoor Country Club, much less danced on its hundred-year-old parquet floor.

She patted her hair, which she wore swept up and held in place with spangled pins. The dress was a dramatic strapless red sheath she and her friend Ariel had found in a church thrift shop. Ariel swore that, after alterations, the dress would look as though it had been tailor-made for Rosa. The bright cherry-red was delicious, the open-toed ruby and rhinestone sandals made her look taller and she felt wonderful.

She turned to her father. "I guess I'm as ready as I'll ever be."

"You look very beautiful. That boy, he better treat you like a lady."

"Of course, Pop. It's Alex, for heaven's sake. We've known him for years."

"Makes no difference. Something happens to a boy when he is with a beautiful girl. His brains, they quit working. They run right out of his ears or something."

"Alex is a perfect gentleman," she said. "Oh, Pop. He's just as smart and kind and funny as he was as a kid. And, I don't know, he seems to have no idea how incredible he is. I've seen girls fall all over themselves to get his attention, and he doesn't even notice."

"You don't need to be falling all over anything," he said. "This boy, he—"

"We're just friends," she said quickly. She didn't know why she said it. Alex was so much more than a friend. But she didn't want her father to know. Not yet, anyway. What she felt for Alex was as fragile and elusive as spindrift. She felt the need to protect it, to keep it to herself and nurture it in the privacy of her own heart, at least for a while.

The sound of a car door slamming ended the discussion. Alex came up the walk, resplendent in a black suit with a crisp white shirt, gleaming shoes and a glorious smile that shone even brighter when he saw Rosa.

"Wow," he said. "You look great."

"So do you."

He shook hands with her father. "Hello, sir."

"Alexander." Pop smiled, but there was something in his eyes, a concern Rosa didn't quite fathom. "You wait a minute. I'll get the camera."

He took a picture of them at the foot of the carpeted stairway, and then one in front of the roses in the yard, and finally a shot of them standing beside Alex's car. Rosa was happy and excited about her evening. Yet between her father and Alex she sensed a curious disconnect as though they lived on different planets.

Alex kept glancing over at her as he drove. "You are really something," he said.

"Yeah? Maybe you are, too."

"You used to be all skinny and messy."

"I was not messy," she said with a laugh.

"You had scraped knees and dirt on your face. Your hair was always wild."

She studied the French manicure Linda had given her. "I guess I clean up pretty good."

He drove in silence, the smile lingering on his lips. He pulled the car under the porte cochere of the venerable old country club.

A valet opened the door for her, and she smiled up at him. He looked sweaty and uncomfortable in his black suit and white gloves, but his eyes lit when he saw her. "Good evening, miss." Then he did a double-take. "Rosa?"

She felt hideously awkward as she offered a lame smile. "Hey, Teddy," she said. It felt weird to have a guy she knew from school waiting on her.

Alex came around the car, offering her his arm, and they entered through the tall glass and brass doors. She felt like she was stepping onto a luxury liner, into a world so beautiful and rich that it seemed made out of spun gold and fairy-tale dreams. The sound of a swing band blared from the main ballroom. Rosa's heart fluttered with excitement as she entered on Alex's arm. Tonight, she promised herself. Tonight she would tell him that she loved him. He didn't need to say it back. She'd make sure he understood that. She wanted him to know what was in her heart.

She half expected to encounter the Great Gatsby and Daisy, but at the arched doorway of the ballroom the Montgomerys were waiting. They greeted guests, chatted, sipped martinis, shook hands and air-kissed. As chairman of the event, Mrs. Montgomery probably had plenty to do. Rosa and Alex waited their turn. She had not seen much of Alex's father over the years. He was a financier who always seemed to be busy with meetings. He almost never went to the house by the sea, and when he did, he tended to work in the study with his briefcase open on the desk and a phone held to his ear.

She took the opportunity to study him now, and she could see that he was younger than her own father and quite handsome. Like Alex, he had light hair and eyes, broad shoulders and strong, squarish hands. Unlike Alex, he held himself with stiff dignity and his smile seemed forced, as though his shoes were too tight.

She wondered what he was like, this man whose son was so important to her. Later, perhaps, she would ask Alex. He never said much about his parents, although he'd once told her there was no pleasing them. She was mystified by that; he seemed like the perfect son.

They moved to the head of the line. Alex presented her to his parents, sounding formal and old-fashioned. His parents were equally formal, his father clearly unaware of who she was. His mother recognized her, of course.

"Well," she said. "Rosa Capoletti. What a surprise."

And not a pleasant one, Rosa suspected. Mrs. Montgomery held her smile in place as she turned to a linen-draped tray, picked up a martini and took a drink.

Rosa felt a wicked urge to mention the scholarship, but she held her tongue. It was already decided, and speaking up was not going to change anything. Besides, it was a big night for them all.

"Straighten your tie, son," murmured Alex's father.

Alex glared at him and jerked the knot in place. "How's that, sir? Good enough?"

The tension crackled between them, and Rosa couldn't stand it. She wished he had the easy trust and intimacy she'd always shared with Pop. Life was simple when you knew you could count on someone.

She slipped her arm into Alex's and said, "Why don't you show me around?"

As they entered the glittering ballroom, she was burning up with self-consciousness. She felt as though everyone in the whole room was staring at her. "You might have warned your parents that I was your date."

"What, and spoil the surprise?"

Blazing anger stung her. "Is that all I am? A prank you're pulling on your parents?"

"Aw, come on, Rosa. These days, everything I do gets at them. I can't please them."

She noticed he didn't deny it. "You set me up, Alex," she said between gritted teeth. "I don't belong here, and you knew it all along."

"That's bull," he said, his eyes narrowing. "You have every right to be here. I don't know why you're so paranoid about being at a stupid party."

Before she could reply, two girls approached them. Hollis Underwood, Rosa remembered, and Portia Van Deusen. The dog trainer and the one with the hots for Alex. Hollis looked chic in a gown patterned with stylized black poodles around the hem. Portia was in pure white, debutante style.

"Hello, Alexander," Hollis said, then turned to Rosa. "I don't remember your name."

"That's Rosa," Portia informed her. "You know, the pizza girl."

"Excuse us." In the blink of an eye, Alex managed to slip

his arm behind her waist, send a dismissive smile to the girls and steer Rosa out on the dance floor.

She should have been grateful, but instead she felt a dull thud of panic knocking in her gut as she looked around the ballroom. Dancing with him was only a reprieve. The whole evening was going to be a series of awkward encounters and veiled insults. Even her red strapless gown, which had seemed so perfect just a short time ago, branded her with bad taste. She wanted to sink out of existence. She wanted to melt down between the cracks in the parquet floor.

"What's the matter?" asked Alex, gazing down at her.

"I look like a painted fire hydrant."

"You look hot."

"You're such an idiot. If you need to thumb your nose at your parents, that's your business. You shouldn't have used me to do it."

"I didn't use you. I have no idea why you'd think that."

"Now you're treating *me* like an idiot. You knew, Alex. You wanted to see your mom have a cow at her event, so you brought a townie as your date. Is that why you're dating me?" Rosa felt the icy burn of tears in her eyes, but she blinked fast and conquered them. "Is that what you've been doing all summer?"

He stopped dancing, right there in the middle of the floor. He tightened his grip on her, perhaps sensing she was inches from running away. He pinned her with his stare. "Where the hell is all this coming from?"

"From the fact that you didn't tell your parents I was coming and you didn't tell me not to go strapless and you—"

He touched his fingers to her lips. "My God, Rosa. I had no idea you were so insecure."

Neither did I.

"And you have no reason to be," he said. "You belong here. Right here with me."

She shut her eyes briefly, then looked up at him.

"Do you want to leave?" he asked.

"Are you kidding?" Somehow she managed to summon up a smile. "Let's keep dancing."

And they did. And for a few seconds Rosa forgot herself and had a wonderful time. But mostly, she felt so awkward she wanted to scream. A boy named Brandon Davis danced with her, grinning as he said, "I heard there was some local talent around here."

"Talent?"

"You got any girlfriends?" His hand slipped downward. Rosa pushed him away so hard that he stumbled.

"You creep," she said.

He laughed, but there was an edge in his voice. "Ooh. Boobs *and* a mouth."

At that, it was Rosa's turn to laugh, and that was how Alex found her.

"Having a good time?" he asked.

She laughed harder and hoped the tears of mirth wouldn't ruin her makeup. "Oh, yeah," she said. "Just dandy."

After that, things improved. Brandon Davis had done her a huge favor. He had made her realize that there was nothing special about this crowd. Like any other roomful of people, they were everything: Petty, generous, insecure, gregarious, mean, kind...and in spite of her misfit status, she liked it. She liked the elegant setting and the discreet waitstaff, the heaviness of a crystal glass in her hand and even the congregation of valets outside, smoking cigarettes and telling jokes to pass the time. She took in everything around her, right down to the smallest detail. She noticed the quality of linens on the tables, the sound system, the enormous vases of flowers, even

the arrangement of canapés on the platters of servers circulat-
ing through the crowd.

She sampled several bites and kept her expression bland. But
Alex knew her too well.

"You hate the food," he said.

"No, it's really—"

"That's okay. I hate the food, too."

"I thought it was just me."

He slipped his arm around her waist. She noticed his mother
watching them with laser-beam eyes, the ever-present martini
in hand. Next to her stood a stout, balding man. "Who's that
man with your mother?" she asked.

"Some lawyer. I think his name's Milton Banks."

"Is she in trouble?"

Alex frowned. "What?"

"People don't have lawyers unless they're in trouble."

"Sure, they do. My folks have lots of lawyers. So does the
company. I think their job is to keep us *out* of trouble." His
mother polished off her drink and took another from the tray
of a passing waiter.

"Let's get some air," said Alex. He led the way through the
French doors to a flagstone patio surrounded by a low stone
wall.

Groups of people congregated here, and their conversation floated gently on the breeze. Lights glittered from boats
moored at the yacht club marina, casting a glow upon the water
lapping up against the shore.

Rosa discreetly wrapped a paper napkin around her can-
apé—a dry affair of puff pastry and greasy smoked salmon—
and deposited it in a wastebasket. She wasn't discreet enough;
Alex noticed.

"Too bad about the food."

"I bet it cost an arm and a leg, too. Boy, these people would probably kill for a piece of pizza right now." Before any important gathering or holiday, her mother used to work on the food for days. Rosa would stand on a stepstool at the counter beside her, shaping meatballs or cutting dough. In the summer, she and Mamma would wrap paper-thin slices of prosciutto around melon balls and serve them on toothpicks. There was nothing wrong with keeping food simple.

"What do you say we get out of here?" asked Alex.

"Won't your parents expect you to stick around?"

"This is for their crowd, not mine." He looked around the patio area at the elegant people, sipping drinks and making small talk. "Once we're at Brown, I'm thinking the parties will get better."

At Brown. An invisible thrill went through her. In the fall they would be in a whole new world. On that venerable, leaf-strewn campus, the sense that they came from two different places would simply melt away. How amazing that was to her. To be in a place where it made no difference if you were rich or poor, an immigrant's daughter or a descendant of the founding fathers.

"If the parties don't get better," she said, "I'm going to have to rethink college."

Before leaving, she sought out the Montgomerys and thanked them. Mrs. M's disdain was nothing new to Rosa. She had always been disapproving, only tolerating Rosa at Alex's firm insistence. When Rosa and Alex were little, his mother used to worry that he would be lured into doing something dangerous to his health. Now that they were college-bound, she looked just as worried.

Get over it, lady, Rosa wanted to say. Instead she said, "Congratulations on this event. I know the art museum is going to be so grateful."

Mrs. Montgomery looked startled by the comment. "A thriving art collection is gratitude enough."

Rosa smiled, but deep down she couldn't help but think about how much all this money could benefit cancer research. The world needed art, too, she supposed.

"Thank you for having me," Rosa said.

"You're welcome, my dear."

I'm so sure, thought Rosa.

She wanted to thank Mr. Montgomery, too, but he was surrounded by well-dressed people who all seemed to be vying for his attention.

"Your dad sure has a lot of friends," said Rosa.

"He makes them ungodly amounts of money."

"He must be really smart."

Alex's eyes narrowed as he watched his father, so smooth and impeccable in his tuxedo, with his martini. "His clients were rich to start with. What would really be smart is if he could make a poor man rich."

"If there was an easy way to do that, everyone would be wealthy." She regarded him thoughtfully. The tension between Alex and his father was a tangible force. "Which is definitely not a bad thing."

"Just because something's hard doesn't mean it shouldn't be tried."

She looped her arm through his. "I think that was a triple negative. Let's go."

Alex escorted her outside and sent for the car. "Well," he said under his breath. "That sucked."

She bit the inside of her cheek to keep in a giggle. With a curiously adult smoothness, he tipped the valet and slid into the driver's seat. Once the doors were closed, he said, "I can't stand valet parking."

"Why not?"

"It's stupid unless you're disabled or something, which I'm not."

Guys didn't like other guys being in charge of their cars, she reflected.

"Where are we going, Alex?"

"I haven't decided yet."

"You don't have to entertain me," she said.

"I know. But you're too pretty to take home."

She nearly melted into a puddle on the floor. In high school, she'd never had a steady boyfriend and her friends often asked her why. She didn't really know the answer until now. She was waiting for Alex.

He headed into Newport, where Thames Street teemed with tourists and glittering restaurants and shop windows. The whole area was filled with strolling couples, and jazz music drifted from clubs or open air decks. He found a parking spot and hurried to open the door for her. "You're even too pretty for this," he said, "but it's the best I can do."

"I love you," she said, before she lost her nerve. She stood up and faced him, her back pressed against the car. "I really do, Alex. I love you."

For a moment he just stared at her. She couldn't quite decipher the expression on his face. He looked either like someone who had been kneed in the groin, or who had just won the lottery.

"Is it that shocking?" she asked, beginning to regret her admission.

"Yes," he said. "Yes, it is."

"Well, I can't help it. I wanted to tell you. You don't have to…" Her voice trailed off. She was at a complete loss.

"Don't have to what?"

Now she was in trouble. *Me and my big mouth,* she thought. Suddenly she was fighting tears. *Oh, that's swell,* she scolded herself. *First throw your love at him and then burst into tears. That's got to be every guy's dream.*

He was looking at her with that endearing crooked grin that reminded her so much of the young Alex. But she still didn't know what he was thinking.

"You don't have to do anything," she managed to say in a husky voice. "I mean, just because I said that doesn't mean you have to say it back to me."

"No, I don't have to say it back." He cradled her cheek in the palm of his hand, caught a renegade tear with his thumb. "I wish to God I'd been the one to say it first."

And just like that, all of Rosa's fears and insecurities slid away on a warm tide. "Really?"

"I've always loved you, Rosa, from the very first moment I met you. I think I knew it back then, even though I had no idea what to do about it. But now..." He bent down and kissed her long and deeply. Then he came up for air and added, "Now, I do."

twenty-seven

On Labor Day weekend, Rosa invited Alex to the annual picnic of Mario's Flying Pizza, which Mario hosted for his workers, friends, family and guests. Employees took turns keeping the restaurant open that Monday, but Rosa had the entire day off. Mario seemed to understand that this was a special period for her. In a week, she would set off for Providence and college.

The event took place at Roger Wheeler State Beach, and it had grown to accommodate well over a hundred people. Rosa promised Alex he would not have the same problems with the food that they'd experienced at his country club.

She found her father in the garage, working on his truck. "Hey, Pop," she said to the propped-up hood.

He emerged from beneath the hood. "I hope you're not gonna need the truck today," he said, wiping his hands on a rag. "The clutch keeps going out."

"Alex is driving me to the picnic."

Pop scowled as he sprayed the rag with solvent. "What's he want to go to Mario's picnic for? It's not his crowd."

"Alex doesn't have a crowd." Rosa was instinctively cautious when discussing Alex with her father. She wasn't quite sure why. "He gets along with everyone."

Despite that assurance, her first glimpse of him when he showed up made her uneasy. He was dressed as though he'd stepped from a J. Crew catalog, in khaki shorts and a crisp blue shirt with the cuffs rolled back. He looked so… WASPy.

"What?" he asked.

"People wear really casual clothes to this picnic, Alex." She gestured at her shorts and Flying Pizza T-shirt.

"Who cares? You make such a big deal about stuff like this, Rosa. Why is that?"

She flushed. "I have no idea. Come and help me finish up the ciabatta bruschetta."

As they put sprigs of basil on the appetizers, he stole one from the tray. "That's about the best thing I ever ate."

"Really?"

"Pretty much."

"Then you're in for a treat today." She hugged him hard. Her father chose that moment to walk through the back door. She practically jumped away from Alex as she spun around. "Hi, Pop."

"Hello, Mr. Capoletti." Alex's ears turned bright red.

Pop nodded. "Alexander."

The phone rang and Pop picked up the handset. "I'll see you there," he said and then answered the phone. "Yes, ma'am," he said and turned away.

One of his clients, Rosa thought. "We should go," she said hastily, wrapping the tray with plastic. "Are you ready?"

As they drove to the state park, she wished she could find a way to make Pop and Alex like each other. It was important to her. *They* were important to her. And so were the people who jammed the picnic area, she realized as Alex parked in one of the few remaining spots.

On the smooth, tree-shaded lawn donated by the Winslow Knights of Columbus, a group of older men played a serious match of bocce balls. Working together under the oblong picnic shelter, women laid out the feast while their husbands grilled Italian sausages so spicy the aroma made Rosa's mouth water at a hundred paces. Children raced through the surf while their parents watched.

Rosa felt a rush of love for this world, this rich place of grandmothers who spoke only Italian, women who lived to feed people and men who grew loud and boisterous and competitive for no apparent reason except that they were men. For the first time, she actually felt a pang of apprehension about leaving.

"You ready?" she said brightly to Alex.

"Sure."

Pop arrived on his bicycle and leaned it against a tree. He probably hadn't finished fixing the truck, then. He waved to Rosa, then headed over to the bocce ball court and was greeted loudly and heartily.

Alex stuck out like a white-bandaged sore thumb amid the guys in their black jeans and muscle shirts. It was the Sharks versus the Jets, but Alex had only one on his side. As Rosa led the way to the pavilion, she pretended not to see a group of her school friends eyeing them.

"Hey, Rosa," said Paulie diCarlo, refusing to be ignored. "We're having a game of flag football."

Rosa put her hand on Alex's arm. "You don't need to—"

"I don't mind," said Alex, then turned to Rosa. "How about you?"

"Okay," she said, sending Paulie a look of defiance. "Let's go."

"One team takes their shirts off, the other leaves them on," said Paulie. "I vote Rosa is on the shirts-off team."

"In your dreams," she said.

His gaze gave her the once-over. "You guessed it."

"Go shampoo your brain, Paulie," she said, then lowered her voice to warn Alex. "You know they'll play target practice with you."

He grinned. "They're going to need some luck."

Alex played as hard as he'd promised. And true to Rosa's warning, the ball drilled right at him time and time again. He managed to catch most of the passes, giving the opposing team multiple opportunities to attack. Even from a distance, Rosa could hear their grunts on impact as Alex was tackled, the whoosh of wind being knocked out of his lungs. The third time it happened, she decided to say something.

"Paulie, this is supposed to be flag football."

"It's fine." Alex peeled himself up off the ground and shoved his flag back into the waistband of his shorts. He gave as good as he got, elbowing and shouldering a tortuous path toward the goal line, earning a small measure of grudging respect from some of Rosa's friends.

The game didn't end; it was declared over by Nona Fiore, calling everyone to eat. There was a stampede to the food— panzanella with tomatoes and bread, every conceivable variety of pasta, grilled sausages, fresh fish roasted in foil, Napoleon pastries and reginatta made with creamy half-melted ice cream. The older people drank Chianti from juice glasses and spoke Italian among themselves. Every once in a while, Rosa heard them mention *quel ragazzo;* Alex was being discussed. She wondered what was so wrong, that he couldn't simply be welcomed and accepted by the people she loved.

"Here, you eat that, you're too skinny," said Nona Fiore, Mario's elderly mother-in-law. Rosa turned to see her give Alex a big piece of *trippa marinata* on a toothpick. Before Rosa could warn him, he thanked the old lady and ate it.

"It's delicious," he said, holding a napkin to his mouth because he was still chewing. He would be chewing for a very long time, Rosa knew. When Nona smiled, then nodded and moved away, he asked Rosa, "What am I eating?"

"Pickled tripe. Made from cow's stomach."

He swayed a little and chewed faster, his eyes bugging out.

"Chewing doesn't help," she explained. "You chew and chew and chew, but it doesn't get you anywhere. Just swallow."

He made a loud gulping sound. "Let's go get something to drink."

He went to an ice-filled chest and pulled out two Cokes. Mario and his brother-in-law Theo tried to include them in a conversation. Alex seemed stiff and unnatural as he spoke with them, and he ducked away as soon as he could. There were lots of moments like that throughout the day. Rosa didn't want it to be so, but as the day progressed, the truth emerged like a storm cloud. He didn't fit in with the people she loved any more than she fit into his world. He sampled the hot, rich food, laughed politely at incomprehensible jokes, gave his undivided attention to grandmothers who barely spoke English. The harder he tried, the more foreign he seemed. And the more she loved him for trying.

She loved him for accepting a plate of pasta so big it took two hands to hold it, for pushing child after child on the swings, for trying to win her father's approval even though Pop made it clear he didn't approve of anything about Alex. Rosa could think of only one reason for Alex's efforts—her.

Afternoon stretched into evening, and fireflies spangled the darkness while someone gathered the kids to roast marshmallows over the grill. Rosa looked at the glow upon the faces of her friends and neighbors and then at Alex beside her, and she felt another wave of contentment, shutting her eyes to keep it in.

To be surrounded by such things, she thought, boldly leaning her shoulder against Alex's, was the very essence of happiness.

Mamma would love this, she thought, listening to the women chatting in Italian. Then it occurred to her that perhaps her mother wouldn't be thrilled with Rosa falling in love with a rich Protestant boy from the city.

"Let's get out of here," Alex whispered to her.

"All right."

Parents trundled their sleepy little ones into station wagons. Men dumped the ice from coolers while women packed away empty Pyrex dishes and pasta bowls. Rosa and Alex found Pop smoking his pipe and gossiping with the older men.

"Good night, sir," Alex said. "Thank you for including me."

"That was Rosa's idea," Pop said.

Rosa bridled. "What my father means is you're welcome," she said. "You're very, very welcome. Right, Pop?"

The darkness masked his features, but his posture was stiff, formal. Anything but welcoming. "Yeah, okay," he said. "You be careful driving."

Rosa and Alex exchanged a glance. "We're going to the movies in Wakefield."

"Now?" asked her father. "It's late."

"No, it isn't. It's not even nine o'clock." She didn't want to fight with him about it, not now. Not in front of Alex. But the expression on Pop's face tore at her heart. She was leaving home and her father would soon be completely by himself. The prospect sat uneasily inside her.

Don't do this, an inner voice whispered. And yet she must. She had to go out into the world and find her life, and leaving Pop was part of the process. People did it every day. They left home and they were fine, and their families were fine, and that was exactly how it would be—fine.

twenty-eight

Rosa and Alex escaped the picnic, exiting through a gauntlet of people before making it to his car.

"That was awful for you," she said. "I'm sorry."

"It was fine."

"Liar. You're a terrible liar, you know," she pointed out.

"I know. That's why I always tell you the truth, Rosa. I was going to say today was no picnic, but it was. Just not my kind of picnic."

It was my kind, she thought.

"I'm sorry about Paulie diCarlo," she said.

"Don't be. Open hostility I can handle. Just..." He turned up the radio, which was playing "Walking on Broken Glass."

"Just what?"

He pulled slowly out of the parking lot. "I can't wait until we're away from both our families."

Again that wave of unease rolled over her. He probably wasn't used to the intimacy and openness of the familial atmosphere at the picnic; maybe it made him uncomfortable. She wasn't sure she felt the same way, but she said, "Yeah. Me, too."

She leaned back against the headrest and watched the night flow past. She saw the long, thoughtful wink of the light-house beacon and wondered what it would be like to live surrounded by city lights. She'd never spent a single night away from this place, and though she knew she wanted to, the idea still unsettled her.

"What?" asked Alex.

She looked over at him and smiled. He was so good at reading her moods. "I'm not like you," she confessed. "I've never been anywhere."

"Are you saying you don't want to leave here?" He sounded incredulous as he turned the volume down on the radio.

She winced. "What's so bad about this place?"

"Nothing, except that there's a whole world out there."

There's a whole world right here, she thought, watching shadows flicker in and out of the big salt marsh as they passed. "It's different for you," she said. "After you're gone, your parents will still have each other, but my father will be all alone."

He stared straight ahead, his wrist balanced on the top of the steering wheel. "That's not exactly right, about my parents."

"What do you mean?"

"They won't have each other. They never have."

A chill licked down her spine. Were they getting a divorce? Plenty of her friends' parents got divorced. Everyone always said it was for the best, and maybe they were right. But things were never the same, no matter what. Vince, whose parents had divorced a few years earlier, said it was like trying to re-build a house after a fire. In a way, the family was as disrupted as Rosa's own had been after her mother died.

"Are they splitting up?" she asked.

"No way. She'd never leave him, not in a million years." He pulled off the road at a gravel turnout and cut the engine.

"Then that's good, right?"

He shifted sideways to face her. "It's not good or bad. It's just…it's the way things are."

"So they're not happy together," she said.

"They're happy apart. My father spent one weekend here this summer. He came down for the Rosemoor ball."

"I assumed he stayed in the city because he had to work."

Alex gave a short, unamused laugh. "Ha ha." He rubbed his chest in an unconscious gesture, the way he'd done when he was little and felt an asthma attack coming on. "I used to think their marriage was normal. Every kid thinks his situation at home is normal. They're incredibly civil, but they don't really have conversations. Just planning sessions about business or travel or my mother's charity work."

"Why did they marry in the first place?"

"No one ever said anything, but Madison was born seven months after they got married."

It sounded so bleak that she ached for him. Rosa wished he'd had parents like hers, who were utterly at ease with one another, laughing or simply sitting together in the garden in the evening. "I'm sorry, Alex." She leaned across the seat and kissed him. "They did something right," she added. "Somebody must have taught you about love."

He held her by the shoulders and looked deep into her eyes. "You did that."

She felt a shiver of emotion. "My mother used to always say we only get one shot at life, and it's a shame to spend it being unhappy."

"I guess my father gets his kicks from the family firm, and my mother from doing her good works. And from drinking. Mustn't forget that."

It was the closest he'd ever come to talking about the fact that his mother was probably an alcoholic. She sensed his mood darkening like a cloud moving in front of the moon. "What is it, Alex? You're really down on your mother."

"It's not...ah, shit. Right before I picked you up, she and I kind of had words."

"Words about me," Rosa said, knowing it in the pit of her stomach. She pulled away and stared straight out the windshield. "About us."

He made a fist around the steering wheel. "She'd had a few too many mint juleps or whatever was being served on the lawn today. Sometimes when she drinks, she says stuff..."

"Stuff she doesn't mean?"

He shook his head. "No, but things she wouldn't ordinarily say."

Finally she said it aloud. "Like the fact that your mother doesn't think we should be together." Rosa thought about the phone call to Pop earlier. Maybe it didn't have anything to do with gardening.

"It's all such bullshit," he said. "And I told her so. I'm tired of her nagging me."

Rosa suspected it was a bigger fight than Alex was admitting, and that it had been going on all summer long. She also suspected he would never tell her everything, like the precise details of his mother's opinion of her.

She hated the idea of them fighting because of her. "You should apologize."

"No way. She's completely wrong about us. She doesn't understand. Rosa, I told her I'm in love with you, and I told her I wasn't ever going to stop. And she freaked, completely freaked."

His fierce declaration was both thrilling and vaguely frightening. "I still think you should apologize for upsetting her. It's horrible having your mother mad at you."

He got out of the car and went around to open her door for her. "I am officially changing the subject."

She stepped out of the car. "To what?"

He slipped his arms around her and leaned down to whisper in her ear. "Let's not go to the movies tonight."

She pressed her cheek against his chest. "Let's not. Let's just be together." When she was alone with him like this the whole world fell away. Their rival groups of friends, their totally different families, ceased to matter.

She pulled back momentarily to study the deserted road, a black ribbon that disappeared into the night. Then she looked up at Alex and saw the moon reflected in his eyes. And finally, she opened the trunk of the car and took out the thick Tattersall blanket she knew he always kept there. "Let's go," she said, and led the way to the beach.

They didn't speak as they walked along the moonlit path, but Rosa suspected they were each thinking about the same thing. Their hands were clasped tight—in desperation, anticipation— and their footfalls barely made a sound on the sandy track.

The deserted beach welcomed them. The Montgomery house was within shouting distance but lay around the curve and out of sight. Stars created a thin, misty sweep of light across the sky, and the waves held the glow of the moon in their restless, foamy crests.

Rosa stopped walking. "Right here is fine."

"Are you sure?" he asked her.

"Yes, absolutely. One hundred percent." She pushed every misgiving from her mind as she turned to look at him. How tall he was. Limned by moonlight, he was as handsome and sincere as a prince in a fairy tale.

He cupped her cheek in his hand and leaned down to kiss her lips. She felt...peculiar, feverish, as though he had somehow magically slipped inside her and turned up the heat.

She couldn't bear it. She needed him, all of him. She needed the mysteries and dreams and fantasies she had woven about him, about them both. Making a wordless sound of yearning, she stepped back and disengaged herself from his arms.

"Rosa?" He stood still, though she could see the rapid pulse in his neck and the quick rise and fall of his chest.

"It's okay." She studied his face and detected a flicker of uncertainty in his eyes. Then, before she could change her mind, she unbuttoned her sleeveless blouse and let it slip to the ground.

His eyes widened briefly as he recognized the blatant invitation. In one swift movement, he took off his shirt. But when she reached behind to unhook her bra, he said, "Don't."

Rosa froze, mortified. Had she made a mistake then? Read him wrong?

He smiled gently at her confusion. "I've always wanted to do this." His arms slipped around her. She felt his fingers unhooking the bra, and even that light touch caused a wild leap of fire inside her. She shut her eyes and pressed her lips to his bare skin, and slowly, deliciously, her hesitation slipped away. She was a woman now; this was what she was made for. She trusted Alex, and this felt right. She was exactly where she was supposed to be, safe in his arms.

He stepped back a little and looked at her, and the expression on his face gave her a keen sense of…she wasn't sure what. Power and gratification, perhaps.

He drew her down on the blanket and lay beside her. She trailed her fingers over his chest. A shiver passed through her because he was so different from the Alex she had once known, and those differences were never more apparent. In childhood, he had been open and funny and fragile. He cherished their friendship and made no secret of it. The new Alex was still funny, but sometimes he was completely unfathomable and not fragile at all.

Yet when she looked up at him and saw him gazing in awe at her, she recognized the Alex she knew, even though his frank stare made her blush.

When he realized he'd been caught staring, he seemed to blush, too, though in the dark she couldn't be sure. With slow deliberation, he took a condom from his pocket and set the packet on the blanket, a wordless declaration of intent. There in the moonlight they shed the rest of their clothes and came together in a fierce clash of wanting. They kissed again, long and hungrily, and she felt his hands on her everywhere. A storm swept through her body.

All the times she had daydreamed about this could not have prepared her for what it was really like. It was awkward and wonderful and mysterious. She surrendered her free will, and gladly. She disappeared into the moment and lost herself. She made a sound in her throat as though she was about to explode. A pounding surge, a force she didn't want to resist, pushed her toward him. She touched him in ways no one had ever taught her, but she seemed to know with mysterious instinct, and so did he. She felt pressure build and then a flash of pain and then nothing but the exhilarating upsweep of intensity. She heard herself cry out, and then at last Alex went rigid, let out his breath in a long, groaning rush and held her so close she could scarcely breathe.

Everything slowed down—their breathing and heartbeats, the sigh of the night wind and maybe even the shush of the waves licking up on the sand. She wished she could freeze this moment forever. She wanted to hold it in her heart, to cherish this feeling of wonder and joy, to savor this burn of love so pure and true that it changed the very color of the world.

She had no idea what was going through Alex's head. He

sat up and handed Rosa her shirt, then tugged on his shorts. "Are you all right?" he whispered.

"Yes," she said. "Shouldn't I be?"

"Well, sure, but… I thought I should ask."

"I'm fine," she said. "What about you?"

He laughed.

"What's funny?"

"I've been asked that before but never in this situation."

She bit her lip. "Meaning…you've been in this situation before."

"I went to boarding school. Well, but not like—wait a minute." He pulled back and the night breeze chilled her skin. "You mean you haven't—you've never—"

"No." She rescued him from having to complete the question.

He pulled the edge of the blanket over them. "God, Rosa. I swear I didn't know."

She turned and lay sideways to face him. "Does that mean you assumed I wasn't a virgin?"

"Nobody is." He brushed his hand in the sand. "You should have told me. Are you sure you're all right?"

"Shouldn't I be?"

"I don't know. God, I'm sorry." A worried frown creased his brow.

"Sorry for what?"

"Well, that I…you know." He held her closer, stroked her hair.

She smiled at his awkward tenderness toward her. "Don't apologize. I'm glad you were the first."

"Honest?"

"I'm always honest with you. And I thought you were with me, but apparently that's not the case."

He looked away, resting on his elbows and staring at the open water.

"Come on, Alex," she said. "I can't believe you didn't tell me."

"It's private."

"I thought we told each other everything."

"Maybe you did."

She pushed away from him and hurried into her clothes, suddenly eager to cover up. "No maybe about it. I just never considered the idea that you've kept secrets from me."

He sat up and pulled his shirt on. "We've only ever been together in the summer. I have a whole life separate from you."

That was true. He knew everything about her because he came to her world. She had never been to his. Still, that didn't mean he was right to conceal something as important as this. "All right," she said, "spill."

"I just did."

"Very funny."

"Was it?"

"No." She shivered. "It was…" *Wonderful.* But she felt cautious now. How could she tell him anything if she didn't know how he felt? He claimed he loved her, that he had always loved her, yet he was a stranger still, in so many ways. Their differences hung between them like poison ivy on a wall.

"It was what?" he prompted her.

"My first time," she said. "I don't know why I assumed it was yours. I have two brothers. I should know it's different for a guy. So do you have a girlfriend somewhere?" She braced herself, waiting for his answer.

"Of course not. Come on, Rosa. There was just a couple of times, back in school and one time at summer camp… I wish you wouldn't think that it matters. It was special with you."

He stroked her hair and scooted toward her on the blanket. "I knew it would be."

"I knew it, too," she admitted, trusting the tenderness she saw in his eyes. "I'm glad I waited for you."

He opened his arms and she leaned back against his chest, lifted her gaze up to the stars. "It's going to be perfect once we're at school."

She swallowed hard. It all seemed so surreal, heading off to the strange new world of college. "I guess," she said.

Somewhere in the distance, a siren wailed. Labor Day partying had probably gotten out of hand.

"What do you mean, you guess?" he asked. "You can't change your mind now."

"I'm not. I'll probably go up to Providence a few days early to get a job."

"Get a job where?"

"I don't know yet. Waitressing. Or something at night." She smiled at his groan of disappointment. "What?" she teased. "I can hardly hear what you're saying around that silver spoon in your mouth."

He didn't take offense. How could he, when he knew it was true?

"It's going to be hard, working and going to school."

"Beats joining the navy. I've been working since I was fourteen," she said, to herself as much as to him. "It's no big deal."

"It sucks."

"It's reality." She couldn't keep in a sigh of frustration.

"What?"

He seemed to read her mood even in the dark, perhaps from the way she felt in his arms. "Nothing. I'll be all right. I feel lucky just to be going."

That was certainly true. The town of Winslow didn't offer a lot of escape hatches. Her best friend Linda would be working for a bookkeeping firm. Ariel was helping out at her mother's alterations shop. Vince would be heading to Newport to bus tables at a high-end restaurant. Paulie diCarlo was joining his uncle's waste management business. Some of her friends were getting married—a mistake, in Rosa's estimation, but when people were in love, you couldn't tell them anything. Only a few graduates of her high school were headed for college. Rosa was grateful for the shot, and moonlighting was a small price to pay.

She turned in his arms. "Tell you what. Let's change the subject again."

"Good plan." He gave her a long, slow kiss and she ran her hands up under his shirt. He started searching his pockets for another condom, but she had the presence of mind to check her watch. "I have to get home."

"Stay with me," he whispered, and tightened his arms around her.

"I promised my father I'd be back by eleven," she said. "It's eleven o'clock now."

He grumbled in frustration but didn't argue further. At the front door of her father's house they kissed goodbye, its sweetness unexpectedly piercing. She felt a sting of tears in her eyes as she lifted up on tiptoe and said, "I love you, Alex."

He kissed her again, longer, harder. "Bye, Rosa."

She floated into the house. "Pop! I'm home!"

He didn't answer, but that wasn't unusual. He went to bed early and was a heavy sleeper. All the same, she headed to his room to nudge him so he'd know she was home.

His bed was empty. She frowned, not overly concerned. He'd probably gone to the Fiores' after the picnic and was still talking and smoking his pipe on their back porch, late into the night.

So she'd cut her date with Alex short for no reason, she reflected, scowling. The minutes with him were precious, but at least they had college to look forward to. Finally their lives were about to converge. They could be together without having to deal with their families and friends. Maybe it would last forever. Judging by the way she felt tonight, that was exactly where it was headed.

She stood in front of the hall mirror and contemplated her reflection for a long time. It was so strange that she looked the same even though her whole world had changed. She'd made love for the very first time and it was unexpected and bumbling but completely wonderful. So what if he wasn't a virgin, too? There was no sense in trying to change the past.

She was filled up with love for him. She had given him everything she had, all of her heart. She hoped that was enough.

I love you, Rosa. I always have.

She clasped the invisible gift of his words to her heart. Then, too dizzy with elation to sleep, she went to the kitchen and poured a small glass of Mosto d'Uva. She took a sip of the intensely flavored grape juice, then went to the den to watch TV and wait for Pop. There were things she would never share with him, but happiness burst from her, and she could certainly share that. She was brimming with excitement about school, about her future. She knew Pop worried about her leaving home, probably even more than she worried about leaving him.

Tonight she finally knew for certain that everything would be all right, and she couldn't wait to tell him.

She flipped through a few channels. There were probably things in this world more boring than a telethon, but for the life of her she couldn't think what those things were. The first time she nodded off, she caught herself and tried to follow the telethon totals, but the second time she gave in and stretched out full-length on the sofa.

Alex was everywhere, surrounding her, whispering *I love*

you into her ear, and she was annoyed when an insistent ringing sound awakened her.

The phone. She lurched up off the sofa and stumbled to the
nearest extension in the front hall. "All right, all right," she
muttered. "I'm coming." It was probably one of her brothers
calling from overseas. Or better yet, it might be Alex, who
was still thinking about her.

She grabbed the black receiver in the middle of a ring.
"Hello?"

"Is this the home of… Pietro Capoletti?" asked a voice she
didn't recognize.

The official tone was an icy spike, poking her awake.

"This is his daughter, Rosina. Who's speaking? What's the
matter?" Even before he replied, her body instinctively braced
itself for a shock. She had her feet planted firmly on the floor,
her arm against the wall.

"Miss Capoletti, your father is here in the emergency ward
of South County Hospital. I'm afraid there's been an accident…"

twenty-nine

The ensuing days melded into a blur. There was the rush to the hospital with Mrs. Fortenski, whom Rosa had to awaken by pounding at the door. Under the glaring, unkind lights of the emergency ward, the grim news was delivered to her alone. Her father, the victim of a hit-and-run, had suffered massive injuries including severe head trauma. He was in a coma.

She made frantic phone calls, summoning her brothers, informing family friends and phoning Mrs. Montgomery in the wee hours of the morning, asking to speak to Alex.

Mrs. Montgomery informed her tersely that she would relay the message when Alex awoke. Then she hung up on Rosa.

People arrived in a steady stream from church, the neighborhood, Mario's restaurant. It was an outpouring Rosa had not seen since her mother had taken ill. There were prayers and tears and whispered questions about why he had been out so late, but no one had an answer.

The next day, her brothers arrived and the consultations began. The doctors said Pop's condition was grave, but he might improve with intensive therapy. That meant a lengthy stay in a private care facility providing extensive, round-the-clock rehab. Sheffield House, a facility in Newport, was such a place.

Then someone from hospital administration sat down with Rosa and her brothers. An indefinite stay at Sheffield House was something only a heavily insured private patient could afford. And of course, with no insurance at all, their father wasn't likely to have that option. Lacking any means to pay for his long-term care, he would be moved to a public facility.

Rob put his fist through the wall of the consultation room. Sal stopped him from doing further damage and then went straight to the church to see what could be done.

There were more meetings, of course. Discussions with the church, with the bank, with friends. But the bottom line was, Pop's destiny was a state facility with little hope of recovery. Rosa was so terrified for her father and so confused by all the meetings that she had no time to stop and wonder where Alex was or why he hadn't called.

A few days later, Father Dominic had news. On behalf of an anonymous benefactor, a Newport law firm was going to pay every penny of Pop's medical bills, including his private care treatment.

People speculated about the identity of the benefactor, but Rosa and her brothers didn't dare question a miracle.

And Rosa didn't allow herself to wish for more than she'd already been granted. That fall, instead of going to Brown, she stayed alone in the house on Prospect Street and continued working for Mario. Her brothers both took extended leave, but once Pop was settled in Newport, Rosa assured them that she was fine, and they both shipped out again.

She had a hard time letting go of the dream. She contacted the professors of the classes she wanted to take. Without ex-

ception, each one gave her a course outline and reading list
and expressed the hope that she'd arrive the following semes-
ter. She kept herself from going insane from boredom by practicing Latin, studying invertebrate anatomy or reading opera
libretti. She fully intended to go her own way once Pop was
on his feet again.

But in the process of taking care of business, she made a
disturbing discovery. Her father had taken a high interest loan
and was about to default; he was on the brink of destitution.
How could she think of going to school when her father was
in such trouble?

That moment, plugging numbers into the cheap discount-
store calculator, had marked her transition from childhood to
adulthood. The change was invisible and no one witnessed it,
but that didn't matter. When she got up from the table, she
was a different person. She closed the door on being someone she'd always dreamed of being—a college girl, living in a
dorm, working toward a fabulous future. The door she forced
open that day led to long hours, hard labor, aching feet. And
a paycheck every Friday.

Adding to her heartache was the fact that Alex never called,
not once. Hurt and mystified by his silence, she phoned the college and got his number. Several times she dialed it but hung
up before anyone answered. Finally, late one night, her anger
fueled by loneliness, she called him. A strange voice answered.

"I'm looking for Alex Montgomery," she said.

"Hey, Montgomery! Some chick for you…"

When Alex came on the line, she coldly asked, "Were you
ever planning to call me?"

"No, I…no. I do want you to know how sorry I am about
your father's accident—"

"In order for me to know, you would have had to call."

"If there was something else I could do, I'd've done it, Rosa. It's complicated."

"What, speaking to me?"

He paused. "I don't really have anything to say for myself. I screwed up, okay, by not calling and then by making you think I…we… Listen, we had fun this summer, but everything's different now. We have separate lives. And anyway, I… I wish you all the best in the world," he said with a regretful finality. "But this—us—we're not going to happen. I hope you understand…"

"Actually, I don't. What made you change your mind? Did your mother finally convince you not to associate with a beach mongrel?"

"This was my decision," he said tonelessly.

Through a haze of shock, she managed to mumble, "Then there's nothing more to say," and hung up.

She still couldn't believe what was happening. The night of the accident had started out as the best of her life. With that phone call, it deteriorated to the worst. Worse even than losing Mamma, because she had faced Pop's ordeal alone. And now this—another blow, another loss. All the joy she'd found in Alex's arms was shattered by one phone call.

No one returned to the Montgomery place after that year, not Mrs. Montgomery and not Alex. Rosa considered this a small mercy. She didn't think she could stand it if he and his college pals showed up at Mario's Flying Pizza, to be waited on by Rosa Capoletti in an apron and hair net, a romance novel stashed under the counter.

She rationalized the loss in hopes of making it easier to bear. On one hand, she knew they were impossibly young and belonged in different worlds. But on the other hand, she had always felt a certain magic shimmering between them, invisible but very real. She'd believed in the power of that magic, so deeply that she couldn't let go.

As the weeks and months dragged on, she slept poorly, in short naps, and often forgot to eat. She worked full-time for Mario, and filled in as a sub every chance she got, willing to do anything to stay away from the empty house on Prospect Street and from memories of Alex.

Maybe he already understood what she was discovering for herself. It was easier to forget when you stayed miles apart.

thirty

Summer 1994

Rosa rubbed her aching back as she labored over a secret project. She was working on a business plan. Mario was talking about retiring. He wanted to hand the business over to his son, but Michael wanted nothing to do with it.

Rosa did, though. She was only twenty, but she had six years' experience in the business and she had a vision. Her plan would take years to complete, but at the end of it all, she would have something of her own. She wanted to turn Mario's into a fine restaurant. So far, she had only the germ of an idea, but she knew Mario would support and encourage her. With Pop laid up, Mario took it upon himself to look after her.

The phone rang, startling her out of her daydream. She grabbed it and answered.

"Rosa? Hi, it's Dr. Ainsley at Sheffield House."

Her heart dropped the way it did every time they called about Pop. "Is my father all right?"

"Better than all right," said the doctor with a smile in her voice. "He's coming home."

Immediately tears washed down Rosa's face. She shook all over. The staff had been promising her for weeks that once he reached certain benchmarks, he'd be discharged, finally.

She sobbed as she carefully took down all the information the doctor gave her. A social worker would come to the house and help her prepare for her father's return. Her brothers, currently stationed in Pensacola and Virginia Beach, would fly back for the homecoming.

Two years, she thought. What a long journey it had been. Pop was getting better, too. He would never hear again, but he'd regained the ability to walk and talk, to function just like anyone else. She had been praying for a long time that he'd be able to come home.

As he walked out of the hospital, his familiar flat cap in place, leaning on a cane, she saw that he was a different man, an old man, and it broke her heart to see how thin and weak he was. But his smile was filled with love for her.

She cooked for him and scolded him to eat like the most vigorous Strega Nona, and he grew stronger every day. Once assured her father was going to be well, she let down the invisible wall she'd built around her heart. She could breathe again. She could be young.

One of the first things Rosa did after Pop came home was to say yes to Sean Costello, a young sheriff's deputy she had met during the accident investigation. He'd worked longer and harder than anyone else, gathering clues from the vacant roadside field where a passing semi had spotted Pop and called in the accident. Sean had combed the scene inch by inch, seeking clues as to who had mowed her father down. Despite his best efforts, the hit-and-run incident was never solved. People speculated that it was someone passing through, a stranger who would never be apprehended.

As for Sean, he ordered pizza at least three times a week, trying to get Rosa to go out with him. He was steady and good-looking, reliable and gentle. And he had a large, affectionate Irish Catholic family. Even Mario approved of him. Now, with Pop at home and getting better, she had run out of excuses. It was time to join the living again.

All through that summer, she went to the movies with Sean, and sometimes he took her dancing in Newport. She saw him in church every Sunday and invited him to dinner at her house with Pop. Everything about the courtship proceeded as planned. It was perfect, right down to the roses he brought her at work every once in a while.

Except that no matter how hard she tried, she couldn't fall in love with him. And she did try. She wanted to feel that sweet burn in her chest. She wanted to float around thinking of him at all hours of the day. She wanted to picture herself in the future with him and their babies. However, the wish was a long stretch from reality. Love, like time, would not be forced, no matter how much she wanted it.

By summer's end, she came to grips with the truth and decided it was only right to tell him. Sean was a good man. He deserved a girl who would adore him because she couldn't help herself, not because she felt indebted to him. As they stood together on her front porch, she searched for a way to explain her heart to him. It was nothing he had done. The failure was hers. She had given everything in her heart to someone else, and she didn't know how to get it back.

It was late afternoon. Sean was on the night shift and impeccably dressed for work in his crisp khaki uniform and dimpled hat. His boots and gun holster shone so brightly she could see reflections in them. Rosa was torn between telling him now and waiting until morning, when he got off work.

Now, she thought. Afterward he could go to the station, be with the guys, unload on them if he needed to. "Sean," she said, reminding herself to maintain eye contact, not to chicken out. "I need to be honest with you. I'm not going to see you anymore."

"Come on, Rosa. What's this about?"

"It's about letting you find someone who deserves you," she said. "Someone who can love you. I can't be that person." She took his hands in hers, gripping hard. "I mean it, Sean. I'm so sorry I'm not the one."

"Damn, Rosa…" He kept hold of her hands, but his shoulders sagged a little. "All right, I wasn't feeling it from you, but I thought, in time…"

"I thought that, too. But it's not happening, and I can't force it. I'm sorry. I wish there was something else to say."

A late-model Mustang pulled up at the curb and a tall, broad-shouldered man stepped out. Rosa wasn't quite sure how she managed to stay standing, but she did. She even managed to send a look of icy disapproval to Alex Montgomery.

"Who the hell is that?" asked Sean.

"His name is Alex Montgomery." She let go of Sean. "Excuse me. I'll just be a minute." She stepped down to the curb and faced Alex. "You're not welcome here," she said. Her heart was nearly hammering its way out of her chest.

"I didn't think I would be." He looked different. Even taller, maybe, his hair longer. The all-American college man. "Rosa, could we talk?" He glanced at Sean. "In private?"

She laughed at his audacity. Two years of silence and now he wanted to talk. "Absolutely not."

At the hostility in her voice, Sean started to move toward Alex. She held him back, grabbing his hand again.

"I heard your father's better," Alex said. "I swear, I don't expect anything from you. I just want to explain why I left."

"I know why you left, Alex."

"You do?"

"Because you were a dumb kid. You couldn't handle anything more than a summer girlfriend. You didn't want to be in it for the long haul. Especially my long haul, given what I was going through. I understand. But I don't forgive you. I never will." She was appalled by his audacity and by the rage it inspired. She'd needed him when her father's life hung in the balance; where was he then? "You should go, Alex."

"You heard her," Sean said, posturing, his fingers brushing his holster. "Hit the road, pal."

Alex hesitated, but not for long. He looked at Rosa, then at Sean, then at their clasped hands. He yanked open the car door, got in and sped off.

"Sorry about that," Rosa said, trying hard not to shake. Her cheeks felt like they were on fire. "I can't believe he just showed up like that. He's nobody. Just some guy I used to know."

"He's the reason you're breaking up with me," Sean said. It wasn't a question.

part five

ENTRATA

Mamma never did approve of stealing, and she
never did explain why a perfectly good fish recipe
would be named for San Nicola. He's been the patron saint
of Bari, in Puglia, since Barese merchants stole his saintly
relics from Myra on the Aegean coast of Turkey in 1087.
Maybe he didn't care what they did with him after he was
dead, but that wouldn't be very Catholic of him.

Pesce alla San Nicola

Traditionally, individual fish are dressed inside and out with olive oil, garlic, herbs and lemon slices, then wrapped in parchment for roasting, which is a handsome thing to send to the table. But it all works fine with fish steaks or fillets in foil instead of parchment. Halibut, tuna steaks and cod are good choices, or if you live by the sea, try a small, perfectly fresh tinker mackerel (whole) or a small bluefish, sometimes called blue snapper, in season.

Preheat the oven to 400°F, or fire up the gas grill. For each portion, dress the fish with 2 teaspoons extra virgin olive oil, sea salt and freshly ground black pepper, 1 teaspoon minced flat-leaf parsley, 1 sprig oregano, 3 pitted black olives, 2 lemon slices, garlic slivers and 2 teaspoons fresh lemon juice.

Wrap each portion in foil or parchment. Place each packet on a baking sheet and slide into the oven or place on the grill and cover. Bake for 20 minutes, or until the fish just begins to flake.

thirty-one

While Andrea Bocelli crooned in the background, Rosa stared at Alex, who sat next to her on the couch. Her couch, in her home. Drinking her hazelnut coffee while his bruised jaw swelled visibly. The whole situation seemed completely surreal—except that it wasn't.

"Wait a minute," she said. "You have something to tell me about that night?"

"Yes," he said, "yes, I do."

"You had information about Pop's accident and you never told me?"

"Not the accident."

"Then what?"

He looked down at his hands, flexed and unflexed them.

Rosa was startled by his obvious discomfort. "What do you mean?" she persisted. Seeing the deep sadness in Alex's eyes, she felt an echo of that pain and confusion. A single moment had changed so many lives. Her father had struggled for two years to recover, and she completely changed the direction of her dreams. Alex followed the path that was expected of him, college and business school, a position in the family firm.

"When I heard your father was hurt," he said, "I didn't know how to comfort you."

"You knew where to find me. You could have picked up the phone, or, better yet, you could have gotten in your cute little MG and come to see me."

"No," he said quietly. "I couldn't."

She studied his face to see if he was pulling her leg. He regarded her with utter solemnity. She forced a small laugh. "What, were you held hostage by the Brown radical underground?"

"No. By a promise I made." He rested his lanky wrists on his knees and steepled his fingers. It was a gesture she recognized from long ago; he did it when he was thinking hard. "To my mother," he said at last, and looked up at her.

As she studied his troubled blue eyes, the deepening bruise on his jaw, she remembered something she had discovered early on in their friendship. Alex didn't lie. He never had.

"So let me recap this very strange conversation. You promised your mother you'd dump me."

"Yes."

Rosa got up from the sofa and went to the window, glimpsing her anguished face in the reflection. She composed herself and turned back to him. "Why, Alex?"

"I thought it was my only option. My mother and I made a deal."

"What kind of deal?"

"She took care of your father's medical bills."

Rosa went completely still. It took a moment to find her voice. "Come again?"

"She paid for his treatment, right up until the day he was discharged."

Rosa felt dizzy with wonderment. "When? How?"

"I went to the hospital as soon as I heard. You were with your family, but the priest, Father Dominic, explained what was happening. He was calling all your father's clients to let them know. The next day, my mother had everything arranged."

"I had no idea. None of us did, ever."

"That was the idea."

"My God, what was she thinking? It was wonderful of her." Rosa's thoughts were spinning. Finally the mysterious benefactor, the person who had given her father a second chance at life, was unmasked. "We tried and tried to find out," she said, "but the administrator at the law firm insisted we were never to know. I wish I'd known," she said. "She made a miracle happen. I wish I'd had a chance to thank her. And if we'd known, my family would have paid her back—"

"That's not what she wanted." His gaze tracked her as she paced back and forth. "She didn't want gratitude, either."

Rosa stopped and turned to him. Although she thought she knew the answer, she needed to hear him say it. "What did she want?"

"For me to stop seeing you."

So that was the deal. Rosa crossed her arms over her chest and shuddered. "What was she thinking? Did you ever ask her?"

"Of course I asked her. She always wanted me to have a certain kind of life," he said.

Like the life she'd had? Rosa wondered. A loveless marriage, suicide? Rosa felt furious, manipulated, nauseated. Yet the object of her frustration was gone forever. She'd never get the whole story. "I wonder if she believed it was worth everything she spent."

He steepled his fingers again. "That, I can't tell you. She was clearly unhappy about something. Maybe everything."

Rosa's heart lurched at the anguish in his voice. He almost never spoke of what had happened with his mother. He did such a good job hiding his feelings that she often forgot what he was dealing with.

He looked at a picture of a seascape leaning against the wall, one she'd never gotten around to hanging, as though searching for answers there.

"So you thought walking away rather than explaining this was the honorable thing to do."

"She didn't want it known. Then, after your father was better, I came back to explain everything to you." He turned to look at her for a moment. "I could tell it was too late. You were with someone else and everything had changed."

"I didn't want to hear any explanations from you."

"So I gathered. I drove straight to the airport that day. I went abroad to study at the London School of Economics. Then I finished my degree and went to business school and, after that, everything—all this—seemed so distant. Like it had happened to other people, in another life." He got up from the couch. "I told myself it was for the best, Rosa. I was a kid from a screwed-up family. I didn't know how to make a relationship work. And I sure as hell couldn't see how our lives could ever fit together. So I left you alone."

He crossed the room and took her hand. "Everything's different now." He smiled with the undamaged side of his face. "Now I see exactly how we can fit together."

She was dumbstruck as she pulled her hand away. "Why, because we were so successful last time?"

"Because we can get it right this time," he said.

She escaped him and sat down, absently massaging her bare

foot. She felt like crying, or flying into a rage. "You went to your mother for help. Why not your father?"

"That wasn't an option." He cut his eyes away. "There's nothing more to say."

His quick, evasive shift unsettled her. "There is, Alex. You're not a liar. You want to try again yet you start by keeping things from me. How is that going to work? I tell you everything, like before, and you hold back. I suppose that's always been our pattern, only I didn't see it then." She realized that she had revealed her heart. Not just to him, but to herself. She went to the sofa and sat down. "Finish the story, Alex. Or we don't have anything more to say to each other."

Moving like a man in pain, he sat down next to her. Then he turned and touched her cheek, gently, perhaps regretfully. "Our parents were screwing around," he said. "I nearly walked in on them the night of the Labor Day picnic."

Rosa's first reaction was utter confusion. It took her a moment to grasp whom he meant by "our parents." Then she wanted to laugh at the patent absurdity of the statement, but all that came out of her was a harsh sound of disgust and impatience. "You should have said something long ago. I would've assured you that you were wrong."

"I wish I was. I'm sorry, Rosa."

He sounded so sure of himself, but he couldn't be. Still, this was Alex. He didn't lie. He believed it was true. She folded her hands carefully in her lap. "What do you think you saw?"

"That night, after we...after I dropped you off, I came straight home. I was thinking about what you'd said, that I should apologize to my mother for fighting with her. I went looking for her. That's when I heard them...in my mother's bedroom."

Rosa's temples pounded. No. No. No. "But you didn't see them."

"Come on, Rosa. I was a dumb kid, but I wasn't that ignorant."

She felt hollowed out, a little queasy. Her father and Mrs.
Montgomery? Impossible. Although, she reflected, there had
always been a part of her father that was like an undiscovered
country, one she had no inclination to explore. Her mind didn't
go there, even though he was a widower. She'd been willfully
ignorant of his needs as a man. People could go on indefinitely
without sex. Lord knew, she was proof of that.

"I don't believe this," she said. "It's insane."

"I know what was going on, Rosa. I didn't tell you because
I figured you'd freak out, too. And you are."

"So now that your mother's gone, you can suddenly stand
the sight of me," she said, not bothering to temper her resentment.

"That was never the issue," he said.

"God, you're crazy, Alex."

She put together the events of that terrible night, adding
this new twist. That had always been an unanswered question
in the investigation. What was her father doing, out on his bicycle so late at night?

Weeks later, when he regained consciousness, he had no
memory of that night, but for the first time she wondered if
he might just be saying that.

And by wondering that, she was forced to entertain the idea
that her father had had a mistress. And not just any mistress,
but Emily Montgomery. Rosa was appalled at the idea, but
deep down a tiny part of her opened the door to listen. Emily
was an attractive, lonely woman trapped in a loveless marriage.
Rosa's father had been widowed terribly young. Perhaps...

She looked at Alex. "Does anyone else know?"

He hesitated, and she knew that by asking the question, she

was buying the story. "No," he said. "I don't think so. I sure as hell didn't say anything."

How it must have hurt Alex to carry the knowledge around, to see his parents together, knowing what he knew.

"Do you think your father…?"

Alex looked out the window. "If he had any suspicion, he was as silent about it as I was." He flexed his hands, studying them as though they belonged to someone else.

Chills skittered over her skin. "It's so…tawdry. They should have known nothing good could come of it. Didn't they read *Lady Chatterley's Lover*?" She looked at him. "What? Don't you dare laugh, Alex."

"I'm not. I swear." He reached behind her and gently massaged the back of her neck. She nearly groaned from the pleasure, but instead, shifted away from him on the couch.

"My dad's part of the package," she said. "You know that, right?"

"Why do you need to shape your life around your father?" he asked.

"Because that's who I am," she said. "It's what I do." She looked at him steadily. "My father's not going anywhere. I've even toyed with the idea of moving back to the house to help him now that he's getting older." She shifted her glance away. "For what it's worth, he doesn't seem to like you any more than you like him."

He dropped his hand from her neck. "I never did a damned thing to him except keep his sleazy secret and leave his daughter alone, just like he wanted."

"He didn't want—" Rosa stopped. He did. Pop had barely tolerated Alex. He used to take every opportunity to enumerate all the reasons they didn't belong together. Agitated, she got up and paced aimlessly. She felt like an accident victim herself, numb with shock, battered and dazed. "I think you should go, Alex."

"I'm not leaving."

"Why not? You're good at it."

He glared at her. "I suppose I deserved that."

"I deserve some peace and quiet. It's late, and I have some thinking to do. I mean it, Alex. Please."

He studied her face and she struggled to appear impassive. Finally he stood up. "I'll call you."

Alex was in his office in Providence, cleaning out his desk. Everything else had been transported to Newport. All that was left were the personal items in his sleek Danish maple desk: an antique wooden slide rule that had belonged to his grandfather, a framed photo of Madison with her kids. In the pencil tray of the top drawer lay the egg case of a skate, a treasure Rosa insisted was a mermaid's purse, a lucky charm. He picked it up. The small dark pod weighed nothing.

"Alexander?" His father stepped into the office. He was dressed as always in a tailored suit, every hair in place, every line of his face arranged to convey disapproval.

Alex slipped the object into his pocket. "I was just finishing up here."

"There's no rush, you know." His father picked up a box and moved it into the hallway.

"I've got this," said Alex.

"I don't mind giving you a hand." When his father picked up the next box, the bottom dropped out of it and its contents spilled on the floor. Both of them bent to retrieve the papers.

"What's all this?" his father asked, picking up letters, cards and notes in all different shapes and sizes, mostly handwritten, a few typed.

"Just some business correspondence." Alex grabbed a roll of

packing tape to reinforce the bottom of the box. He saw that he was too late; his father was already reading some of the notes.

"This is about the Access Fund," he said, then read aloud from one of the letters: "'Thank you for this opportunity...'" And from another in the tremulous writing of an elderly person. "'You've given me a future I never thought I'd have.'" Some of the notes included photographs of clients' homes, their children or grandchildren, young people holding college diplomas.

Alex watched his father's face as he sorted through the notes. Surprise gave way to a perplexed frown.

Alex was chagrined. This was something he needed but didn't flaunt. His Access Fund clients earned the firm next to nothing, but he considered them his most important investors. He braced himself, expecting sarcasm from his father, who had always been critical of the unproductive fund.

Yet unexpected sentiment showed on his face as he put the papers back in the box. "And all I get from my clients is a bottle of Glenfiddich at Christmas," he muttered, carefully sealing the box for transport.

Then, as quickly as it had come, the moment passed. "Are you acquainted with a Sean Costello?" asked Alex's father. "South County Sheriff?"

Alex's gut churned. "Not personally. Why do you ask?"

"I've had a message to call him. Wonder what he wants."

"It could be something to do with the storm damage on the property." Alex turned away and busied himself with the last of the packing. He had no opinion of Costello. At one time he'd wanted to believe the guy was a good match for Rosa. Alex had gone straight to the airport that day, driving too fast, the image of Rosa and Costello burned into his mind. He'd tried to be happy for them. She was young and beautiful and all alone in the world except for her scoundrel father. No way should Alex have expected her to wait around for him.

As he wrapped a framed photo of his mother, he was touched by a twinge of pain. Had that sadness always haunted her eyes, or did he notice it now because of what had happened? Before, he'd seen only coldness in her face and felt only anger at the lengths she'd gone to in order to keep him and Rosa apart.

He shoved the picture into a box. "Did you and Mother ever...?" He wasn't sure what he was asking. "Were you happy together?"

"We were married for thirty-six years."

"That doesn't answer the question," Alex pointed out.

"Of course it does."

thirty-two

On the day Rosa got up enough nerve to talk to her father about the things Alex had told her, he wasn't home. She let herself in and blinked the lights, but he didn't call out. There was no sign of him in the back. She noticed, though, that the side door of the garage was ajar.

"Hello," she called, stepping into the dim workshop adjacent to the garage. "Joey, are you in here?"

He started, dropping something on the floor. "Hey, Aunt Rosa."

"Hey, yourself." She eyed the objects laid out on the workbench. "What are you up to?"

"Fixing something on this telescope," he said. "Alex found the original booklet that goes with it." He held up a slim pamphlet of yellowed paper.

"You went to Alex's?"

He rolled his eyes. "Not the junior high stuff again. Jeez."

"He gave you those, too?" She jerked her head toward

two large banker's boxes, each labeled Montgomery Financial Group.

Joey's gaze flicked away. "It's just some stuff he was throwing out. He's fixing his house, and he has a whole Dumpster full of trash."

There was something furtive in Joey's manner. "Is everything all right?" she asked him. "You're not in any trouble, are you?"

He snorted. "Not hardly. There's nobody to get in trouble *with*."

She studied him for a moment. The Mohawk was gone; he'd probably tired of the daily ordeal with stiff gel. The pink color had faded somewhat, and the only piercing she could see was a stud in his right earlobe. He really was a good-looking kid, she reflected, when he wasn't trying so hard to look bad. "Haven't you met any kids at work?"

"Sure, but what am I going to do, take off my apron and go hang out with them?"

"I don't know. How about that cute girl who keeps coming in for Jamoca Almond Fudge?" Rosa asked, remembering a tidbit someone at the restaurant had passed on to her. "The one who looks like Keira Knightley. I doubt Jamoca Almond Fudge is her only reason for stopping by." She saw a flush rising in his cheeks. "Hazard of living in a small town," she said. "Everyone knows your business. Now, where's your grandfather?"

"He went to do someone's yard. The… Chiltons. Does that ring a bell?"

"Yep. I'll try to catch him there. Stay out of trouble, kiddo."

"Of course."

She drove a little too fast, eager to get this over with. Her father's truck was parked at the side of a New England saltbox–style house facing the sound. She found him in the back, raking clippings into a pile, and waved to get his attention.

He turned and waved back, then removed his gloves.

"Hiya, Pop." She kissed his cheek. "You got a minute?"

"Of course. I have an hour, if that's what you need."

She took a deep breath. What she was about to say would change their relationship. It might do irreparable damage. But she had to know.

"Are the Chiltons at home?" she asked.

"They come on weekends only. Rosa, what's the matter?"

She took another breath and stood in front of him, signing as she spoke. She didn't want him to miss anything. "Pop, after your accident, Mrs. Montgomery paid your hospital bills. Did you know that?"

His face registered a succession of reactions—shock, disbelief, suspicion and, finally, wonder. But no guilt. Nothing to indicate he'd known.

"It's true," she said. "She never wanted anyone to know, but Alex told me. He also told me the reason she did it."

"And why would this be?"

"You were with Emily Montgomery the night of the accident. In her bedroom."

Now she saw it—the guilt. The expression on his face confirmed her worst fears.

"It's awful, Pop. I mean, I know you must have been lonely, but a married woman?"

His face darkened a shade. "Alexander Montgomery told you that? Told you I seduced his mother?"

"He didn't say seduced."

He took a bandanna from his back pocket and wiped the sweat from his face. "How can you think I would do such a thing? That boy dishonors the memory of his mother."

"Does he? Are you denying this a hundred percent?"

"He sends you here with this terrible accusation. What kind of person is he, eh?"

"He's confused. If you can set the record straight for him, then I think you should."

He made a slashing motion with his hand. "No more, Rosina. Do not start up with him again. He is as bad for you now as he was as a boy, and this is proof."

She could tell he was trying to turn the subject away from him, but she could be stubborn, too. "Tell me about that night, Pop. I need to know."

"There was no love affair with Mrs. Montgomery." His gaze was unwavering as he spoke. "That is all you need to know."

"If it wasn't an affair, then what was it?"

He shoulders sloped downward. "A misunderstanding."

She refused to soften. "Tell me."

He nodded, steadying himself with his rake as he sat down on a rock wall. "When I came home that night, she called me. She was very upset about her son."

"Because of me."

He nodded. "She was…not well, Rosa. I went to see her because I was worried."

Not well. "She'd been drinking?"

Another nod. "She was all alone and quite ill. I took her to her room, tried to calm her down so she would go to sleep. She wouldn't listen, though. She carried on…for hours, it seemed. Whatever Alex thinks he heard… I was trying to help a hysterical woman. It was nearly midnight when I left her. And that, my Rosina, is what happened. I am sorry I said I didn't remember, but that was the only lie I told."

She wished she felt more satisfied with his assertion, more vindicated. But she didn't. "Maybe things would have turned out differently for us if you and Mrs. Montgomery had left us both alone. You wanted us apart as much as she did."

"You missed out on nothing but heartache. Alexander was a boy, not a man. He would have been careless with your heart, not because he's a bad person but because he wasn't ready. I don't think he will ever be ready."

"You took away any chance we might have had to find out."

"No, Rosina. Your chances were over when he walked away."

Rosa was at the restaurant at closing time, supervising the nightly wrap-up when her cell phone chirped with her father's ring. It was close to midnight; Pop was always asleep by ten. She was already worrying when she retrieved the text message: Joey missing.

Just that, and nothing more.

Her hands shook as she sent a message back. "I'm out of here," she called to Vince. "I need to go check on my father."

Vince straightened up from wheeling a canvas-sided laundry cart between tables. "Is he all right?"

"I think so." She tugged her purse strap up her shoulder, then dug inside for her keys. "Don't forget to clean the tap lines in the bar. And padlock the Dumpster, don't just latch it. The raccoons are bad this—"

"Hello? It's me, Vince," he reminded her, making a shooing motion with his hands. "I've got this, all right? Just go."

She bit her lip, nodded once and dashed for the door. As she drove through the summer night with the top down, she scarcely noticed the canopy of stars or the coolness of the air. She was speeding and thinking about Joey. Where in the world had he gone?

Kids tended to hang out at the drive-in theater on White Rock Road, which hadn't actually played a movie since 1989. The abandoned parking lot became the scene of impromptu parties, and the enormous screen a target for hurled stones, beer bottles, the occasional can of paint. It was not the most wholesome place for Joey, but he was unlikely to come to any harm there. Then there was the video store, the state park and other kids' houses. She racked her brain trying to decide where to begin, but she could think of nothing. She didn't know the kid, she thought with a pang of guilt. She needed to spend more time with him, but she was always busy at the restaurant.

She pulled into her father's driveway and parked. He was waiting for her by the front door, looking lost and quite possibly ten years older.

"I got up in the middle of the night," he said. "For the bathroom. I decided to check on Joey, you know, like I did when you and your brothers were small."

She nodded, remembering the secure feeling she used to get when Pop would open the door to her room, make a satisfied sound in his throat and shuffle off to bed.

"You looked everywhere?"

"All over the house. His jacket's gone. And the bike. I'm gonna call the sheriff."

"In a minute." She rushed upstairs to Joey's room. There was something absolutely chilling about the sight of a child's empty bed, the covers thrown back, in the middle of the night. Pop had obviously already gone through it, and she cursed her nephew under her breath.

"He didn't run away for good," she told her father, who had followed her upstairs. She gestured at the laptop computer, which sat open on the dresser, a Starship Enterprise screensaver drifting across the screen. "He'd never go anywhere without his—" She stopped as an idea hit her. "Is that old telescope he was working on still in the shop?"

Pop hurried for the stairs, hope shining in his eyes. "I checked the garage for the bike but I didn't think about the telescope." He led the way through the one-car garage that had always been too cluttered to actually house a car, flipped on a light and headed into the workshop. It smelled of ancient motor oil, lawn fertilizer and disuse, and held the detritus of years. There were old motor parts lying about, spools of fishing line, plant food and snail bait, bicycle chains hanging from nails on the walls.

"It's gone," said Pop. "The little *parte di merda* went out to look at the stars. Why would he sneak? Why wouldn't he tell me?"

Rosa tapped her foot. "Beats me. So what do you want to do? Wait for him to come home, or should I go out looking?"

"I don't feel like waiting up all night, worrying my heart out."

Rosa didn't blame Pop. He wouldn't rest until he knew Joey was safe. "So where do you suppose he went with that thing?" She drummed her fingers on the work bench. Somewhere within biking distance, she thought. Somewhere high and dark. She could think of a dozen places like that. It was going to be a long night. She and her father returned to the house.

"Wait here," she said, gesturing for emphasis. "If he gets home first, make him call me before you kill him."

"Yeah, okay. And you send me a text message if you find him first."

"I will. He's fine, I'm sure. But he won't be after I beat the snot out of him."

She went to her car and got in. Now what? Point Judith? The Singing Bluffs? It would take a genius to figure out the best place to see the stars.

She snatched her phone from her purse and punched in the number. "It's me," she said when he answered. "I hope I didn't wake you…"

thirty-three

"You have to understand," Joey said to the girl beside him, "it's my first time."

"Mine, too," whispered Whitney Brooks, even though they were completely alone at the top of Watch Hill and there was no need to whisper. "Just do the best you can."

"Yeah, all right." He smiled in the darkness. She was unlike any girl he'd ever known. Maybe she did look a bit like Keira Knightley. And there was a wildness about her. She liked extreme rock climbing and kiteboarding. She knew how to make kamikazes with Rosa's lime juice and vodka, and she had a fake ID, which she'd used to get a real tattoo of a phoenix at the small of her back. She was hot, but that wasn't even the best thing about her. She was also incredibly smart, and she wanted the same thing he wanted.

He couldn't see her face as he said, "Here goes nothing," and bent his head. *Work, please work,* he thought. Then the most incredible sensation came over him—blinding bright elation, a sense of triumph so powerful he thought he might burst. "Wow," he said in a raspy whisper.

She moved against him, her compact, sinewy body brushing his. "Here, let me—" she reached out for him "—it's my turn, after all."

"Be careful," he said, then cringed. What a dweeb, talking like a baby.

"Don't worry," she said. "I know what I'm doing."

"I thought you said this was your first time."

"Shows how much you know." She bent forward and emitted a long, slow sound of pleasure. "This is incredible, Joey. It's perfect. Just perfect."

Joey caught his breath and felt a soaring delight, sharing her pleasure.

Watching her look through the telescope, he beamed with pride. The transit of Mercury was so rare that, after tonight, the celestial event would not be seen for years. The telescopes of professionals and amateurs alike were trained on it tonight, but not here. He and Whitney were all alone. They took turns looking at the colorful, pulsing beauty of the planet transiting the moon.

"You're quiet. What are you thinking?" she asked him without looking up from the eyepiece.

"That I'm glad I met you." It was easy to be totally honest in the dark.

"I'm glad we met, too. If it hadn't been for my insatiable appetite for Jamoca Almond Fudge, we might still be strangers."

He grinned. "That's true." The minute she'd appeared in the ice-cream shop, he'd felt something special in the air. Maybe she had, too, because she'd lingered through two helpings of Jamoca Almond Fudge and three free glasses of water. After that, she came in every day, and by the end of the first week, he learned her name. By the third week, he learned that she went to a school called Marymount in New York and that her family had a summer house on Ocean Road. It was probably like Alex Montgomery's place, huge and fancy. She and Joey didn't seem to have much in common, but when he mentioned the telescope, she became his new best friend.

Before long, they were trading instant messages and email, and even though they didn't call tonight their first date, they both knew it was. And nature had cooperated by providing a rare celestial event and a crystal clear night.

She, too, loved the stars and the planets. Joey dreamed of being an astronaut while she had always been fascinated by astronomy. Between them, they had a virtual encyclopedia of knowledge.

"This is the best night ever," she said.

Maybe he was only imagining it, but she seemed to be leaning closer to him. He could smell the shampoo she'd used on her hair, could feel her warmth as she brushed up against him. Maybe if he leaned a little closer, it might seem almost like an accident when he put his arm around her. Joey wasn't usually shy around girls, but Whitney was different. Other girls he'd gone out with—all two of them—giggled at nothing and talked about their favorite boy bands. Whitney was quiet and patient, and even though she didn't say much, he knew there was plenty going on in her head.

Finally she spoke. "You should probably kiss me now."

Oh, man, thought Joey. "Why do you say that?"

"You want to, and I want you to, so we should do it."

He shook his head. "We'll feel all weird if we sit here and talk about it and plan every move."

She laughed and shifted closer to him. "That's what I've been doing ever since I met you—planning this."

He broke out in a sweat. She sure as hell was different, with her disarming frankness and direct gaze. With a jolt of panic, he realized he didn't know what to do. Where should he put his hands, his mouth?

Calm down, he told himself. Here was this girl he was crazy about, and she wanted to kiss him. Who was he to hold back?

He cupped his hands around her shoulders and she scooted even closer. He was glad Grandpop had made him lose the tongue stud and nose ring, refusing to feed him unless he took them out. This, he decided, was going to be the best kiss ever. Because he wasn't going to worry about doing it right. He was just going to kiss her and hope for the best.

He took a deep breath and went for it.

"Hold it right there." The blinding beam of a nightstick sliced between them like a light saber.

Whitney gave a little scream. Joey crab-walked backward, his heart hammering "Nearer My God to Thee."

"You must be Miss Brooks," said the sheriff. "Your parents are very worried about you, young lady." He flashed the beam toward the road below. "Come with me, please."

The sheriff. Jeez, didn't he have anything better to do?

"We weren't doing anything wrong," Joey said, finding his voice at last. "We came up here to look at the transit of Mercury."

"I don't care if you're looking at the man in the moon, kid. Mr. and Mrs. Brooks sent me to find their daughter who, it turns out, is absent without leave."

"How did you find me?" Whitney demanded in a superior, rich-girl voice Joey had never heard before.

"You left your IM box open, so they figured out where you'd gone as soon as they checked your computer."

Joey suppressed a groan. You'd think she'd have the smarts to shut down her messages before leaving the house. He exchanged a glance with her but could tell nothing by her grim expression. Nothing good, anyway. He picked up the telescope and tripod.

The sheriff went for his gun. "You," he barked. "Drop it."

"It's a telescope, okay?" Joey said. "It doesn't belong to me. I don't want to break it."

"I said, drop it."

"But—"

"Are you deaf?" the sheriff demanded.

That sparked Joey's temper. "No," he said, setting it down gently instead of dropping it. "No, I'm not." Maybe the deputy was, though. "All I want to do is put it in its case."

"Please," Whitney added.

"Yeah, please," Joey agreed.

The guy hesitated, then nodded once. Joey knelt down to lay the pieces in the antique velvet-lined case. Then they were led down the rocky path.

At least, Joey thought, he wasn't in trouble. He'd told Grandpop after dinner that he was going out, and Grandpop had offered a vague nod which Joey took as assent. And even if he didn't have permission, Grandpop slept like, well, like a guy who couldn't hear. All summer long, Joey had been coming and going as he pleased.

Tonight, he decided, he'd just make nice with Officer Friendly and sneak back home, no harm done.

The fantasy sustained him until he reached the bottom of the path. Next to the squad car sat a small, gleaming convertible. Two people stood next to it.

Aunt Rosa stepped forward. "You are in such trouble."

Joey swallowed with an audible gulp.

It was worse than he could imagine. His aunt text-messaged Grandpop that he was fine. Alex made him lock the bikes together; he'd have to come back for them in the morning.

"I'll take that," the sheriff said, reaching for the telescope.

"I've got it." Alex Montgomery stepped forward. "It was mine, and I gave it to the kid."

That's all Joey was in that moment. A kid. A punk. Just a few minutes before, he'd been on top of the world, with a view of the stars, about to kiss a girl.

Alex took the scope away and shut it in the trunk. Joey doubted he'd ever see it again.

But that wasn't the worst moment Joey would suffer. The worst was when they made him get in the back of the squad car with Whitney. Behind the cage. There were no handles or locks on the rear doors of the squad car. Joey had never realized that until tonight.

"Thanks, Sean," Aunt Rosa said.

Great, thought Joey. *She's on a first name basis with the law.*

"Not a problem. I still pull night duty sometimes. Keeps me in touch with the nonvoters."

It was decided that the sheriff would drive both Joey and Whitney to the Brooks' house, where he would apologize. From there, his aunt would drive him back to town.

"You're gonna behave, all right?"

"Yes, sir." Joey wanted to protest that they hadn't done anything, but he knew better. Being absent without leave made grown-ups freak. He'd seen it in his own household many a time. His parents went ape-shit when the twins went missing, which they did a lot. His sisters liked to party.

And he didn't. It was so unfair.

He turned to Whitney, who sat quietly, staring straight ahead. "You okay?" he asked softly.

"Don't say anything, kid."

"I was just asking if she's all right."

"What'd you do to her, kid?"

"*Nothing,* okay?" Whitney said with that superior tone. She pursed her lips and continued staring straight ahead. Joey prayed she wouldn't cry. He couldn't stand it when girls cried; he felt totally helpless. His sister Edie was a crier. The whole house shook when she sobbed about a bad grade, a boyfriend, a broken nail. But maybe crying helped, he reflected, counting the squares of the grid that imprisoned him. Not crying was actually painful, an ache of pressure in his chest. Maybe girls cried because it let off the pressure.

To his relief, Whitney didn't cry. She just sat there until they pulled through the gate of her parents' house. It was one of those summer places that got featured in magazines, a historic house with historic gardens and historic statues everywhere. Probably Roger-effing-Williams had taken a pee right on the grounds. Whitney had told him there was a gun emplacement somewhere that had figured in the Battle of Rhode Island a zillion years ago. Whitney's mother thought it made the Brooks family better than regular people. Whitney didn't, though; she tended to scoff at her mother's snobbery.

Waiting in front of the house, her parents looked as grim as the couple in that famous *American Gothic* painting, only they wore better clothes, even at one in the morning.

The squad car door opened and Whitney slid out. Joey followed, eager to escape.

Whitney's mother broke out of the frozen pose and hurried across the cobblestone drive. "Where in heaven's name have you been, young lady?" she said. Whitney looked over at Joey and mouthed along with her mother's next words: "We were worried sick about you."

Joey almost lost it, but he managed to stand up straight, shoulders back, chin tucked, eyes ahead, stiff as a new recruit. "Mrs. Brooks, ma'am, I'm sorry about tonight. It was my idea."

"I found them at Watch Hill," the sheriff reported. "They claimed they were looking at stars."

"We were," Joey asserted. "A planet, actually. The transit of Mercury was tonight and we both wanted to see it."

As he spoke, the Alfa pulled up beside the squad car. Whitney's mother flared her nostrils as Aunt Rosa got out of the car. She was still in her work clothes, a black dress and high heels.

Whitney's father spoke up for the first time. "And you are…?" He looked at Aunt Rosa's boobs, even though he pretended not to. Joey disliked him and his patronizing tone immediately.

He stepped forward. "Sir, my name is Joseph Capoletti, and this is my aunt, Rosa Capoletti."

Mr. Brooks gave him the once-over, taking in Joey's hair, the earrings, the clothes. "Wait inside, Whitney," he said, still glaring at Joey. "Go to your room."

"But—"

"Now, Whitney." As she marched toward the house, Mr. Brooks turned to the sheriff's deputy. "Thank you for bringing our daughter home. You've done a good night's work."

The cop didn't say anything. He was probably pissed at Brooks's attitude, patting him on the head like a birddog. He got back in his car and spoke into the radio, then pulled out of the driveway.

Meanwhile, Alex got out of the Alfa. The Brookses were glaring at Rosa as though trying to freeze her with their eyes. "We'd appreciate it, Miss Cappellini—"

"That's Capoletti," she corrected. Joey could see her getting ticked off. It wasn't anything physical, just a certain energy that seem to zap around her like an invisible force field.

"Yes, well, we'd appreciate it if you would support us in keeping Joseph away from Whitney."

"Oh, I'm sure you would," said Aunt Rosa.

Clearly they didn't hear the sarcasm in her voice.

"I'm glad we agree. Whitney is a very sheltered child. She's not accustomed to boys like your nephew."

Joey held in a snort of disbelief. Whitney was the go-to girl when you needed a fake ID or booze. And judging by the way she'd come on to him tonight, he figured she'd had plenty of practice. But her parents didn't want to hear that.

"Joey will be held accountable for his actions," said Aunt Rosa, her temper still seething just below the surface. "However, it's a free country, and unless you lock your daughter up, she might make friends with boys like Joey, so get used to it."

"Look, Ms. Cap..." Mr. Brooks cleared his throat. "We don't want to press charges—"

"Hey, maybe *I* want to," she said, snapping like a dry twig. "Did you ever think of that, *asino sporco?*"

Joey bit the inside of his cheek to keep from laughing when Alex stepped forward.

"Excuse me," he said, nodding at the Brookses. "Alex Montgomery," he explained. "I live down the road—"

"Alexander, of course." Mrs. Brooks shifted effortlessly into social mode as though she was at a cocktail party. "Our mothers went to Brown together. Mine was older, of course, so she was terribly shocked to hear of your loss."

"Oh, for heaven's sake," Rosa said under her breath. "Get in the car, Joey. I'm taking you home." She turned to Alex. "I assume you can find your own way home?" She didn't wait for an answer but got in the car and gunned the engine.

Joey kept holding in laughter as she peeled out, leaving Alex looking like a doofus while the Brookses fawned over him. "You shouldn't have ditched him," said Joey.

"He lives a quarter-mile down the road, and this car only seats two."

"What was he doing here tonight, anyway?"

She went screaming around the turnoff to Winslow. "He

was the one who figured out where you'd be." She clicked her red fingernails on the steering wheel. "I guess maybe I shouldn't have ditched him with those people. Me and my temper."

Joey tried to shrink down in the seat of the Alfa. Maybe she'd stay off track and forget to tear him a new one. "He probably doesn't mind," he suggested. "He might have needed a nightcap anyway."

Mistake. He should have kept his mouth shut. "What he needs," Rosa snapped, "is to be sound asleep in bed. That's what we all need. But you and your little girlfriend weren't thinking about that, were you?"

"She's not my girlfriend."

"And I'm not my mother's daughter. I wasn't born yesterday, Joey. I know a pair of revved-up teenagers when I see it. Look, this is for your own good. Don't give your heart to a girl like that."

"Like what?"

"Summer people."

"I'm summer people."

"You are not. You're just here for the summer. There's a difference."

"I have no idea what you're talking about. Anyway, nothing happened. Nobody gave anyone's heart away. That's your issue, not mine."

"What?"

Joey wished the car had an escape hatch. He should learn to keep his big mouth shut. Oh, well. In for a penny, in for a pound. "You know what. You and Alex, that's what."

"There is no me and Alex."

"And I'm not my father's son."

"You're not funny," she said, accelerating through the last

stoplight before home. "And quit trying to change the subject. You sneaked out, you were groping some girl—"

"Like I said." He exaggerated the enunciation of each word, figuring his best defense was to distract her with snottiness. "We just wanted to use the telescope."

"If it was so innocent, why didn't you get permission?"

"Grandpop said it was okay."

Rosa slowed the car a bit and glanced over at him. "He didn't tell me that."

"He probably forgot," Joey blurted out, "like he forgets everything else."

She slammed on the brakes right in the middle of a deserted street. "What the hell is that supposed to mean?"

In the yellowish glare of a street lamp, Joey could see something flickering in and out of her anger. He thought maybe it was fear. He would need to choose his words carefully, he realized a little late. It would freak him out if someone told him his own dad was losing it. He'd better remember that. This was Rosa's father.

"Joey?" she said over the burble of the engine.

He cleared his throat. "Grandpop forgets stuff," he said as gently as he could.

"So does everybody," she said. "I forgot your mother's birthday last month and I still haven't sent her a card."

He felt a little sorry for her; she was so desperate to believe this was nothing. He'd tried that, too, when he first moved in. Grandpop was a deaf guy. That made him more likely to forget to turn off the water in the sink, or to leave his electric razor on, or to ignore the mail when it dropped through the slot on the front door. He wondered how much of this Aunt Rosa knew.

"I'm not talking about that kind of forgetting," Joey said. "I'm talking about almost everything. Every day it's something.

He left the truck running until it ran out of gas. He left a pot of beans boiling on the stove. The house reeked for hours and now there's a huge black circle on the ceiling from the smoke. When I tell him anything, I usually have to repeat it about a zillion times. Half the time, he calls me Roberto, and when I correct him, he gets all mad."

Rosa blinked fast, like she was batting away tears. Oh, man, thought Joey. Not another one. Fortunately she didn't cry. "Have you...talked to Grandpop about this?"

"Constantly, but he blows me off. Alex said—"

"Whoa, Bubba." Any possibility of tears disappeared, probably boiled away by her temper. "You mentioned this to Alex?"

"Maybe," Joey said quietly. "I didn't think it was any big secret. Besides, the smell from the burned beans was all over me, so when I went to Alex's and he asked—"

"You went to Alex's?"

This was going from bad to worse. "He had some astronomy books to loan me, okay? It's a free country."

"So you said something to Alex, but not to me," Aunt Rosa observed. "Maybe you should just write a press release. Have you discussed this with your parents?"

"No. My dad would probably have the same reaction as you."

"What reaction? How am I reacting?"

"Loudly," Joey said.

Across the road, a light went on and curtains stirred in a window. Rosa shifted gears and drove on in complete silence to the house on Prospect Street.

thirty-four

Linda snapped on a pair of rubber gloves. "Okay, let's get started."

Rosa looked around her father's house and grimaced. "Now I know how Hercules felt when he saw the Augean stables."

"Aw, it's not that bad."

"It is. I can't believe you volunteered for this."

"Hey, what are friends for?" Linda grabbed a bottle of Windex.

"Probably not degreasing my father's kitchen ceiling, but I love you for being here."

"It's all right, Rosa," Linda assured her. "You've helped me out of many a jam. Were you able to get an appointment at the doctor for him?"

"They worked us in at eleven o'clock." To cover her unease, Rosa turned away and switched on an ancient radio that had sat on the same shelf for decades. After a rumble of static, she found a local station playing Belle and Sebastian, and then got to work.

Rosa went into the den and surveyed the area. She visited her father all the time. She'd stepped over piles of clutter, but it had never occurred to her that Pop was having serious problems. As time went by, his carelessness had increased, but Rosa hadn't thought anything of it. She wanted to cry but refused to allow herself the luxury. She didn't deserve to cry. She was a Bad Daughter.

In the past twenty-four hours, since Joey had declared the Emperor naked and forced her out of her cocoon of denial, she had faced facts. Her father was in trouble and she hadn't allowed herself to admit it. She'd been so wrapped up in the restaurant and her own life that she'd ignored what was going on right under her nose.

She hadn't said anything to him. Yet. This morning, she let herself into the house and announced that she was going to do some cleaning and sorting. He'd waved her in, completely indifferent. Linda insisted on joining her and tackling the more obvious things. Rosa knew she could have engaged the restaurant's cleaning service, but thought better of it; this was her penance.

She had arranged to take off an entire day and night from the restaurant, leaving Vince in charge. It was perhaps the third time she'd been absent from Celesta's. Joey was at work, and Pop was out puttering in his garden, where the tomato bushes were heavy with fruit starting to ripen and the dahlias were bursting into bloom. From time to time, Rosa would glance out the window. The sight of him, bent over a plant or snipping a flower to tuck into the brim of his hat, filled her heart. He was everything to her, and she was eaten alive by guilt.

She spent a solid hour putting things in the trash—junk mail, wrappers, used plastic bags he'd saved for no apparent purpose, rusty paper clips and thumb tacks, empty mason jars.

The desk was covered with papers—more circulars and junk mail, mostly, but she also found packets of unopened bank statements, personal correspondence and…bills. The power company, the gas company, subscription services. Some were stamped Final Notice.

Her first inclination was to sit down and pay the bills. That wouldn't solve the problem, though. The issue was deeper than that. She went out back, noticing as she passed through the kitchen that Linda had it gleaming already and was applying primer to the ring on the ceiling. Rosa caught her father's attention and showed him the envelopes. "Pop," she said, "you've been forgetting to pay your bills."

He glanced at one of them, postmarked six weeks before. "Put them on the desk. I'll take care of them tonight."

"They were on the desk. Pop, you're worrying me. You seem to be forgetting a lot of things."

"What, forgetting?" He waved a hand in annoyance. "I've been busy."

"But, Pop—" Rosa stopped herself and glanced at her watch. "There's no time to argue. We need to get to your appointment."

"What appointment? I don't have any appointment."

"Yes, you do. As of eleven o'clock this morning. Dr. Chandler says you haven't been in to see him in three years. Three years, Pop. That's nuts."

"He charges a hundred fifty for a lousy office visit. I feel fine. I don't need to see any doctor."

"But I need you to." She took his arm. "*Please.* For me. Just to shut me up."

He glared at her, and for a moment she was afraid he'd refuse. Then his gaze softened. "You worry too much." He smiled and placed a kiss on the top of her head. "I'll go, then. Just to shut you up."

★ ★ ★

Dr. Chandler's office was adjacent to South County Hospital, and Rosa perfectly understood her father's reluctance. This was where they'd brought Mamma for her treatments, and they would forever associate this place with gloomy, excruciating futility. Years later, Pop had been taken to the emergency ward here after his accident, and Rosa's memories of that time were streaked with the violent horror of nightmares.

Today's appointment took much longer than it should have. She read *Rhode Island* magazine, *Newsweek* and *Women's Day*. She was trying to decide between *Parents* and *Highlights for Children* when she realized she couldn't remember a single thing she'd read. The wait was too nerve-racking. She stood and went to the window, looking out across the tree-shaded hospital lawn, the busy parking lot.

Everything was such a mess. A few times, she took out her cell phone to call Sal or Rob, but resisted. No sense worrying them, too, until she knew exactly what they were dealing with. She didn't allow herself to call the restaurant, either. Vince always got ticked off when she tried to micromanage while he was supposed to be in charge.

There was always Alex, of course. She could call him. Since he'd told her his suspicions about their parents, she'd only seen him once, last night when she needed help finding Joey. Alex needed to know he was completely wrong about her father. Best to tell him in person, she decided, tucking the phone away.

By the time Pop came shuffling back to the waiting room, Rosa was frantic. "What?" she demanded.

"We're supposed to wait."

"Wait for what?"

"He sent samples to the hospital lab and put a rush on them. He wants us to wait here for the results."

Rosa's heart pounded with dread. Lab tests usually took a

few days. She wondered why there was such a rush. It couldn't mean anything good. The last thing Pop needed was to see her fall apart, though. She sat down and patted the seat beside her. "How do you feel?"

"Fine. I was fine when you dragged me here," he grumbled. "I swear, when you got nothing to worry about, you think of something." There was a twinkle in his eye as he patted her knee. "Your mother was always worrying. You're just like her."

She put her hand over his. "I hope so." Impulsively she asked him something others had asked him many times before, but for Rosa, it was a first. "Pop, why didn't you ever marry again?"

He didn't answer right away, but stared across the waiting room, out the window. A courier came in and dropped off a box with the receptionist.

"I was a good husband to your mother," Pop said. "I would not be a good husband to another woman. It would not be fair, because I gave everything I had to my first marriage. Love is like that for some people."

It was a lovely, mournful sentiment, Rosa thought. Maybe it was true for her, too. Maybe that was why she'd never really gotten over Alex.

Dr. Chandler came to the door, a file folder in hand. "Mr. Capoletti? Would you and your daughter step into my office, please?"

She nearly hyperventilated on the short walk down the hall. The office was contrived to look homey and warm, with mahogany shelves and plush chairs, but to Rosa, it felt like a prison cell. Dr. Chandler motioned for them to sit down.

"I'm glad you came in," he said. "The reason I rushed the lab was that I hoped we might be dealing with a fairly simple matter here." He leaned back in his chair and smiled. "Turns out we are. It's a pretty severe vitamin deficiency, completely treatable."

Rosa slumped with relief. "A vitamin deficiency?" She turned to her father. "Did you catch that?"

He nodded, his eyes bright with tears. For the first time, Rosa realized he'd been as petrified as she.

"Your neurological changes—the numbness and tingling in your hands and feet, difficulty maintaining balance, digestive upsets—are classic symptoms of vitamin B-12 deficiency. You've had some other symptoms, too, the fatigue, confusion and poor memory."

Rosa dug herself even deeper into guilt. How could she not have noticed all those symptoms? "My father doesn't have a poor diet," she said. Then she turned to him. "Do you, Pop?"

"My diet's fine," he stated.

"That could well be," said the doctor, "but you have a helicobacter infection. It blocks B-12 absorption. Fortunately the treatment's simple—a course of antibiotics. Once we eliminate the infection, the symptoms will go away."

Rosa looked at her father to make sure he understood. He nodded. "You'll write me a prescription, then."

"Right away. This infection can lead to ulcers, so you'll want to take the whole course. In ten days, you'll be good as new."

In the now-immaculate kitchen, Linda greeted them. "I got a huge shock changing a lightbulb upstairs," she said.

Rosa nudged her father. "I thought you were going to get the wiring checked. You promised."

"I'm gonna do that next week, all right?"

"Pop—" She heard a car in the driveway. "Someone's here."

She and Pop went around the side of the house to see a silver Miata and a white Explorer parked at the curb. Alex Montgomery and a strange woman with a small dog both arrived at the same time. She watched her father's face and caught the exact moment he spotted Alex.

"Son of a bitch," he said under his breath.

Given what Alex believed about her father, she couldn't figure out why he would come here. The short, heavyset woman looked vaguely familiar, but Rosa couldn't place her. The woman set the little dog down and it ran straight for Pop. It was a terrier mix, brown and white with a clownish face. Pop regarded it in confusion.

"Hello, Rosa," Alex said with a slightly formal air. "Mr. Capoletti," he said, nodding to her father. "This is Hollis Underwood and Jake. Hollis is with Paws for Ability."

Rosa got it right away. She looked at her father to see if he realized what Alex had brought. Pop was glaring at Alex with deep dislike. Hollis scooped up the prancing dog and stepped in front of Pop so he didn't miss what she was saying. "I'm a friend of the Montgomerys from way back," she said. "Alex thought you might want to see what an assistance dog can offer."

"I don't need any dog," Pop said stolidly, watching the squirming, exuberant terrier, which strained toward him, licking frantically.

"Jake is a rescue dog," Hollis said, then set him down again so she could sign as she spoke. "We found him when he was a puppy, and he's just completed his training as a signal dog. He's ready for adoption if we can find the right home for him." Without asking permission, she headed for the back door, then turned to address him. "Let's go inside and I'll show you some of the things he's trained to do."

To Rosa's amazement, Pop went along with her. She could hear Linda greeting them and exclaiming over the dog. Stunned, she turned to Alex at last. "What the hell is going on?"

"How about 'Hello, Alex'? Or 'How are you, Alex?' Or

'Thanks for helping me find Joey last night'? Or, here's a thought, 'Sorry I ditched you after dragging you out of bed'?"

"Are you finished?"

He laughed. "I'm just getting started."

"What are you doing here? What's up with the dog lady?"

"Joey said your dad might be able to use some help," he said simply.

Offended pride rose up inside her. Joey had a big mouth. "It wasn't his job to tell you."

"No. He decided to do that on his own."

"It's none of your damned business."

"Maybe not." He jerked his head in the direction of the house across the way, where Mrs. Fortinski just happened to be watering her plants in an open window. "Is it the neighbors'?"

Rosa lowered her voice. "You have a terrible opinion of my father. Why would you try to help him?"

"This is for you. If training with an assistance dog helps your father out, then it helps you out."

She hated that logic. She hated any logic that worked against her. "He won't go for it. He's never had a dog, or even a cat or goldfish. It's not his style." She realized they were talking around the real issue. "I told him what you said, Alex. He categorically denies what you said about him and your mother."

"Of course he does."

"He said she called him that night, and he went to see her because she seemed...upset."

"Drunk, you mean."

"I'm sorry, Alex."

"Sorry? Sorry for what?"

"The thing you should remember and hold on to is that she didn't do...what you've thought all these years. I'm sure she believed she was doing what's best for you. And if you want to change your mind and take that dog home, I'll understand."

"I won't change my mind. And thank you for...what you just said."

That night in her apartment, he'd told her plenty about the past. Yet now it occurred to Rosa that the biggest thing he was holding back was the way he felt about his mother's suicide.

Which was probably the most important thing for her to know. "Alex—"

"I need to go. I've got some papers to file at the courthouse." Then he did the unthinkable. He bent down, kissed her lightly on the cheek and said, "See you, sweetheart."

She felt like she was on fire as she followed him out to the truck. "Just a doggone minute."

He stopped on the front sidewalk, keys in hand. "Now what?"

"You kissed me and I wasn't ready."

"You are now." Without warning, he kissed her again, this time full on the mouth.

Across the way, there was a splat as Mrs. Fortenski misfired with her watering can.

"And that's just for starters," Alex said, releasing her. Then he strolled to his truck, waving as he pulled away from the curb.

"Well, well, well," said Linda, bringing a black plastic bag out to the curb for garbage day. "Alex the wonder boy strikes again."

"He kissed me," she said, wondering if the neighbor got a snapshot.

"You don't say. Should I dial 911?"

"Come on, Linda."

"Come where? The guy is crazy about you, Rosa. Why not relax and enjoy it?"

"Because I don't trust him," she blurted out.

"And you don't trust yourself with him."

Rosa bit her lip. "I simply don't see the point of getting involved with Alex Montgomery."

"Why does there have to be a point? Just be with him. See where it goes."

"I'm not letting it go anywhere."

"Then you're an idiot."

"No, I'm protecting myself."

"You've been doing that for years. Don't you think it's time to let him in?"

"For what?"

"Rosa, if nothing else, for the sex. You don't get laid nearly enough."

"How do you know how often I get laid?"

"Maybe you should lower your voice," Linda said, nodding toward the neighbors' window.

Rosa threw up her hands and headed for the house. She and Linda stepped inside just in time to see Jake sniffing the mail on the floor under the slot.

Linda frowned. "What the—"

"Hush," said Rosa. "Watch him."

The dog paused to look at them for a moment, then went back to the mail. He managed to pick up a mouthful of envelopes along with a grocery circular and a catalog; then he trotted off with them.

Rosa and Linda followed the dog to the den, where Pop sat in his easy chair. Hollis sat quietly observing. She said nothing when Rosa and Linda showed up, but motioned for them to wait and watch. The dog dropped the mail and went back for more, twice. After three trips, all the mail lay beside Pop's chair. The dog gently lifted up on his hind legs and brushed his front paws with gentle insistence against the cuff of Pop's pants.

He picked up his mail and said to Hollis, "He did good."

"Remember what I said—reward him."

Pop bent and patted the dog on the head. "Good boy," he murmured. "Good Jake."

Hollis nodded approvingly. "Well done, both of you."

"Now, how can I get him to pay the bills for me?"

She laughed. "That's not in his job description, but there's a lot more to learn. Jake knows forty commands. He can alert you to bells, alarms and timers, dropped objects. And if your computer makes a sound when you get mail, he can tell you about that, too."

"No kidding."

Rosa was amazed. Pop readily claimed he didn't like dogs. Too many of his clients had ill-behaved pets that ruined gardens and soiled yards. She stepped into the room. "So you like that dog, Pop?" she asked.

"Yeah. A dog's a big responsibility, though."

"You don't have to make a commitment right away," Hollis said. "We need to be sure you and Jake are compatible. There are forms to fill out, a visit from a social worker. Then the training begins." She paused, and Jake did, too. He tilted his head to one side, watching Pop with total absorption. "So what do you say, Mr. Capoletti? You up for it?"

He looked right back at Jake. "How else am I going to learn?"

"This is how it works?" Rosa asked Hollis.

"Yes," said Hollis, watching as Jake sprang into Pop's lap and settled into the crook of his arm. "That's how it works."

thirty-five

Alex awakened to the crunch of car tires on gravel. Damn, he thought. What time was it? According to the antique clock on the wall, 6:30 a.m.

Then he remembered with a groan of misery. Portia van Deusen had called to say she was on her way to the Newport Jazz Festival; she planned to drop off some of his stuff. But why would she do it herself rather than sending someone? And why at this hour?

Two things came to mind. She was best friends with Hollis Underwood, who had probably filled her in about Rosa. And Portia must still be mad at him about the broken engagement. Let her be, he thought. She'd brought it on herself, even though he'd agreed to let everyone believe she had dumped him and not the other way around. Only Gina Colombo, his assistant, knew what had really happened.

Yawning and scratching his chest, he went to the window, squinting at the white sunlight streaming in.

He paused in mid-yawn and mid-scratch when he recognized his visitor, and his scowl changed to a smile. Rosa was rummaging in the trunk of her car, and emerged with a large wicker basket covered with a red-and-white checkered cloth. She wore a red polka dot halter top, red clamdiggers, gold hoop earrings, big sunglasses and ruby-colored finger- and toenails. The adult-entertainment version of Red Riding Hood.

"Oh, man," he said and ducked into the bathroom. There, he stuck a toothbrush in his mouth and rolled it around while simultaneously splashing water on his face. No time to shave. Then he stepped into the nearest presentable clothes—a pair of swim trunks. He finished brushing, grabbed his Red Sox T-shirt from a hook behind the door and sniffed. Not too bad. He tugged it on over his head, then finger-combed his hair as he went downstairs to answer the door.

Rosa looked as fresh as a flower, standing there, smiling up at him. "I hope I didn't wake you," she said.

He stifled another yawn. "Not at all." He held open the door for her. "I make it a point to get up at 6:30 in the morning when I'm on vacation."

"Liar," she said, marching past him with the basket. Something inside it smelled incredible, and he followed the fragrance into the kitchen.

"Wow," she said, "you've been busy." She checked out the paint job on the wainscoting, the newly sanded and sealed floors, the painted cabinets.

"Until 1:00 a.m. every day," he said.

"I would have called first," she said, "but it was too early and I didn't want to wake you."

He didn't even try sorting out her logic. "Rosa, what's going on?"

"A picnic," she announced, putting a handful of napkins into the basket. "A breakfast picnic, to be exact. We used to do this when we were kids, remember?"

Hell, yes, he remembered.

In the basket, he spotted a thermos of coffee and some rolls that were still steaming hot. "Couldn't we just eat it here?"

"Then it wouldn't be a picnic."

"But it would be breakfast." He had worked like a dog yesterday, and now that he was awake, he was starving.

"That's not the point," she said and looked up at him brightly. "Ready?"

He was physically incapable of saying no to this woman, or to food on any terms. Besides, he wanted to know what she was up to. The presence of food was a good sign. Maybe this was a peace offering. He offered a sleepy smile and picked up the basket. "Yeah. Lead on, MacDuff."

They went out the back and across the yard, which over the years had lost its spectacular lushness. Alex couldn't help noticing the way Rosa's tight red pants, cropped off just below the knee, hugged the finest ass he'd ever seen. Jennifer Lopez only aspired to have a butt like this.

"You're awfully quiet," she remarked.

He cleared his throat. "Still waking up. Do you do this often?"

"Nearly every day. I get up early, I mean. If I don't, the day is shot by midmorning. That's when I head over to the restaurant."

His gaze lingered on her a moment longer. "Sleep deprivation agrees with you."

She slowed her pace and looked over her shoulder at him. "You think?"

"No question."

They walked along the ancient path, which was overgrown by brambles and beach roses. "No one ever comes here," she said. "No one ever has except—" She broke off and brushed a branch out of her way.

"Except us," he finished for her.

People flocked to the beaches that had parking and easy access. But he had always preferred this all but inaccessible piece of paradise. This was remote, a world apart, the dunes bordered by an ancient, half-collapsed wooden fence with sand blown up against its base. There was no gate but a gap where the fence was down, and Rosa stepped through and along the slope toward the beach. The newly risen sun spread a glow of benediction across the water.

Alex loved the feeling of privacy and privilege it gave him. He'd been a lot of places but none had ever quite matched the beach of his boyhood. There was a feeling of serenity here, of belonging. He wondered if Rosa understood how much she was a part of that, how important she'd been to the person he had become. He had never told her that, but he suspected he would one of these days, soon.

"How about here?" She indicated a spot on the sand.

"I've got a better idea," he said, walking past the spot and moving closer to the water's edge in the shadow of a huge rock. It was, he believed, the exact spot where they'd made love the first and only time. "How about here?"

She looked him straight in the eye. "Here is fine."

They spread out the checked tablecloth and he opened the basket. Rosa set out the feast she'd brought—mascarpone and hot rolls whose fragrance had been teasing him all during the walk, a wedge of melon and something in a plastic container.

"Coffee?" She held up the thermos.

"Bless you. I take it black."

"I know. That's how you ordered it at the restaurant."

He took a sip. "You have a good memory."

She smiled at him over the rim of her coffee cup. "Hungry?"

"Starved."

"You'll like this," she said, setting out two plates. She served a frittata, a savory egg dish with herbs and cheese.

Alex ate in silent ecstasy, plowing through two helpings of frittata, three rolls slathered with creamy mascarpone and half the melon. "You're incredible," he said.

"I know," she said, sitting back and admiring the sunrise. "It's a gift." She lifted her cup in his direction. "Aren't you going to ask me why I went to all this trouble?"

"Because you're trying to seduce me," he said with a grin. "And congratulations, it's working."

"Dream on."

"Believe me, I do. Actually, I was curious, but I didn't want you to change your mind and take it all away."

"I've never taken food away from a person in my life," she said. "It's to thank you for the dog." Her voice trembled with emotion. "You see, my father never will."

Nor did Alex want his thanks. Ever. But Rosa's gratitude he would take, any day of the week. "So it's working out?"

"Yes. Your friend Hollis is truly a miracle worker."

"She's pretty incredible."

"She was such a snot when she was younger," Rosa said.

"People change," he reminded her.

She pulled her knees up to her chest. "In just a few days, that dog changed his life. I feel guilty for not coming up with this on my own long ago."

"He probably wouldn't have agreed to it long ago."

"I was pretty upset when I found out Joey told you about my father's troubles."

"I wish someone would have spoken up about my mother's troubles," he blurted out before he could stop himself.

"Oh, Alex." Her hand trembled a little as she touched his face. Rosa had the unique power to coax emotion from him. He didn't know why he sought it out, except that it felt so real, unlike so many other things in his life.

She took off her sunglasses and watched his face. "In a horrible way," she said softly, "I was lucky to lose Mamma when I did. I'm sure she was a flawed human being, just like everyone else, but I was too little to see her flaws. Now when I remember her, she's a saint."

"Your point being, of course, that I had the misfortune to know my mother's flaws."

"Go ahead and get defensive. I'm not backing down. And that wasn't misfortune. It was life. I suppose, if I'd known my mother longer, I would have known a more realistic picture. God, what I wouldn't give to have her right here with me now, warts and all. You had thirty years with your mother. I envy that."

"And you had a mother you regard as a saint. I envy *that*."

She paused. He felt the tension straining between them.

"I wonder, Alex… Have you thought about seeing someone…a psychologist?"

"It's a waste of time. I know damned well what my issues are." He forced a smile. "This day started out so well."

"I didn't come here intending to bring up your mother, but she's always there. She always will be so long as you refuse to deal with what happened."

"Spare me the New Age homilies," he said, then added, "please. I'm desperate here, Rosa. We need to change the subject."

A smile flickered across her mouth and he felt the tension ease. "This is not turning out the way I'd planned," she said.

"How is it supposed to turn out?"

"I wanted to bring you a delicious breakfast and sincerely thank you for helping my father, not upset you."

"I'm not upset," he said. "I swear it." To prove his point, he ate a third helping of frittata and finished off the orange juice. "Honestly," he said, "this is the most pleasant breakfast I've ever had. Ever."

"Really?"

"A beautiful sunrise, a beautiful woman, a meal fit for the gods." If he could do this every day, he would never want another thing in life. And he hadn't even had sex with her. Yet.

He covered her hand with his. "Could you please pass the melon?"

She got a little skittish then and took her hand away. "Sure."

Though he wasn't really hungry anymore, he ate some and smiled at her. "When you feed me," he said, "it's like you're coming on to me."

"Oh, please. I feed a hundred forty seatings a night." But she blushed. He could see that immediately.

"Not like this," he said, leaning back on his elbows and crossing his legs at the ankles. He patted his now-supremely-satisfied belly.

"Alex," she said.

"Mmm?"

"What are you thinking about?"

He put his hand on her thigh. "Having sex with you."

She scooted away from him on the blanket. "That's asking for trouble."

"Come on, Rosa. It's asking for the next natural step. There's nothing standing in our way."

"Except ourselves. Oh, not to mention our friends, families and lives. It can't work out for the same reason it didn't work out the first time. The world won't go away and leave us alone, Alex."

He edged closer to her. "Fine with me. Then let's go away and leave the world behind."

"That's just it. I'm not a jet-setter. I don't want to be anywhere but here."

"You know, just because it isn't easy doesn't mean we shouldn't be in love."

"You need more coffee." She refilled his cup, her hand unsteady. "Now, run that by me again. It's too early in the morning to decipher triple negatives."

"I want a second chance with you, Rosa. That's all I'm saying." He set aside the cup, then touched her cheek and let his fingers wander into her hair.

"I thought you were saying something about sex."

"Well, that, too," he admitted. "That comes with the second chance."

She took a cube of melon, closing her lips around it provocatively before popping it in her mouth. "You're saying you want to have sex with me."

"Of course I do. Who wouldn't?"

"Alex!"

"Sorry. I mean that as a compliment. You're hot."

"And you want me because I'm hot?"

"Actually, I'd want you even if you looked like a ling cod," he said, then quickly backpedaled. "I mean, you don't, but even if you did—ah, shit." He abandoned talk, grabbed her and pulled her against him. Before she could push him away, he kissed her long and hard, the way he'd been wanting to ever since finding her again.

Kisses had been invented for moments like this, when words failed but there was still so much to say. Her mouth was cool and sweet from the watermelon, and she felt perfect in his arms.

When he pulled back, she looked a little dazed, her eyes unfocused and her mouth slightly puckered. Another good sign. "I guess," she whispered, "I'm on board with the idea."

"With what idea?"

"Sex. Isn't that what we're talking about?"

"Oh, yeah," he said, pressing her back on the blanket.

She twisted away from him. "I didn't mean here. It's broad daylight."

"I thought all that changed with Vatican II."

She glared at him. "Not funny, Alex."

"Well, I don't think it's funny to offer me sex and then change your mind."

"I didn't offer," she said. "You asked."

"And you said okay."

"Did I?"

"No, actually you said 'I'm on board with the idea,' which sounded like okay to me, until you started making it conditional—"

"Of course it's conditional," she said. "All sex is." She put the picnic things away in the basket. "Everything about this is complicated. After all that's happened, I just don't see how this can work."

"It's simple, Rosa, but maybe you're scared to try."

"We're from two different worlds. Our friends don't get along. Our families can't stand each other. They never have and never will."

"I don't want to have sex with them. Just you."

He was rewarded with an amused twitch of her mouth, which he probably wasn't supposed to see.

"Well?" he said.

"We're both adults now. We know how to set limits."

We know how to get past them, he thought.

"Whatever the lady wants," he said, and got up to help her fold the tablecloth.

It was a start, at least. She really believed she could keep her emotional distance, even now. Alex grinned as he led the way back to the house by the sea. In some ways, he knew her better than she knew herself.

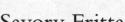

Savory Frittata

Always use naturally nested eggs laid by uncaged chickens. The eggs taste better, and the chickens will thank you.

4 medium potatoes, scrubbed and diced fine
6 large, fresh eggs
1/4 cup cream
3/4 cup chopped tomatoes
1 small zucchini, grated
1/4 sweet onion, chopped
1 Tablespoon minced herbs, including oregano, thyme, flat-leaf parsley, red pepper flakes, garlic
2 Tablespoons olive oil + 1 Tablespoon sweet butter
salt and pepper to taste
1 cup shredded cheese

In a wide ovenproof skillet, grill the potatoes in olive oil and butter until browned. Add zucchini and onions, then tomatoes and herbs. Season with salt and pepper. Whisk the eggs together with cream and pour the mixture over potatoes. Sprinkle on the cheese. Bake at 400°F degrees for 25 minutes or until top is firm. Serve in wedges warm, or at room temperature.

thirty-six

Alex had become a fast walker, Rosa reflected as she followed him back to his house, taking two steps for every one of his. He seemed to be in a particular hurry this morning.

In the kitchen, he set the basket on the counter. She went to the sink to start washing things but he stopped her, trapping her between him and the counter and turning her to face him.

"Alex, I—"

He interrupted her with a kiss, and it was like the one on the beach, the one that had melted her bones. When he came up for air, it was all she could do to keep her wits about her. "I'd better go," she said.

"Let's go upstairs," he whispered.

She pushed against his chest but it was like a warm, immovable wall. "I don't think so."

"You just said we were going to have sex."

Oh, God. She had, hadn't she?

"I meant…maybe at some unspecified point in the future… after we discuss it some more."

"I like this point." He smiled down at her.

He took her breath away—ocean-blue eyes, aristocratic features, lips she dreamed about, even though she'd never admit it. Everything inside her leaped up to say no, but when she was finally able to speak, what came out of her was "All right."

Upstairs in the big house, she stood face-to-face with him in an expansive, sun-flooded room with gleaming plank floors and a high antique bed, its linens looking deliciously rumpled, as though they still held his scent. She had the urge to dive headfirst into the bed. He kissed her again, backing her up against a bedpost and cupping her hips in both hands.

She turned her head to whisper, "This isn't what I came here for."

"Sometimes—" he touched her chin and brought her mouth back to his "—you just get a bonus."

His kisses made her lose track of time, of herself, of everything. He unhooked her top and undid the tie behind her neck. The look on his face made her feel like a goddess, and in that moment, she was a goner. And he was right. She *had* come here for this. With a sigh of surrender, she kissed him hard, hungrily, finally giving in to an urge that had been building all summer long. They left their clothes tangled together in a heap on the floor. He pressed her down on the bed and her hair fanned out on the pillow. She arched upward, reaching to pull him against her. She felt light-headed, barely able to think except for one thing that rang clear in her head. There were some things that simply didn't change and never would. And one of them was that each time Alex Montgomery held her in his arms and kissed her, it was like coming home.

Rosa didn't sleep or dream, but she drifted, there in his arms in the rumpled bed with the sun streaming over their entwined bodies. With her cheek pressed to his chest, she listened to the heavy thud of his heart. She didn't want to think or talk or plan anything, and that was so unlike her. Somewhere a vintage clock clicked quietly, but she lost track of time and didn't stir until she sensed a subtle twitching in his chest and raised her head to look at him.

"It's nothing," he said, leaning over to rifle in the drawer of the bedside table. He took out an inhaler and put it to his mouth. Three deep breaths and a smile.

"You're sure?" she said.

"Absolutely." He curled a lock of her hair around his finger. "Any more questions?"

"Mmm-mmm." She stretched like a cat, her gaze drifting lazily around the room at the beautiful wainscoting, richly detailed and dark with a patina of age. The windowpanes had the wavy, brittle quality of old glass. This was such a fine house. She couldn't believe he was getting rid of it. If this place was hers, she would stay here forever, filling the rooms with cut flowers, working in the kitchen with its view of the sea.

Rosa realized that they were already starting to relate to one another in silence, in the way of lovers, with their own non-verbal signals. They spoke without words, read each other's moods. Whether she admitted it aloud or not, they were acting like a couple. A very intimate couple.

A cell phone rang and Alex groaned. "Ignore it."

"It might be my father," she said, sitting up and grabbing her handbag.

Alex reached for the bedside table. "Or mine," he said and scowled into the display. "Hello, Dad."

Rosa tugged the sheet up under her armpits. Nothing like a call from a parent to dampen the mood.

"I understand," Alex said. His face was completely neutral. "Maybe another time, Dad."

Jerk, thought Rosa, wishing Alex's father could see the disappointment in his son's eyes.

"I haven't heard from Maddie, either," he said into the phone. "Last week, there was an email from Taipei. I'm sure she'll check in with you when they get to a place that has cell phone service... Yes, all right. Bye." He set down the phone and immediately slipped his arms around Rosa. "Sorry about that. Change of dinner plans tonight."

"Your sister's in Taipei?"

"Was. I think she might be in Mongolia now. She decided to show her kids the Far East. Her way of dealing with the tragedy," he explained, "in true Montgomery style. My father would probably do the same, except that the firm seems to be a more satisfactory distraction."

"I wish the two of you were closer," Rosa said.

"Yeah? Why?"

"There's such a... I don't quite know how to put it. A richness in being close, such a sense of security. That's how it's been for me, anyway."

"You're lucky, then. It's different between my father and me. I don't know how to explain our relationship, but 'sense of security' doesn't really fit the situation."

"It should."

"He always considered me a disappointment. When I was little, I was too sick for him to bother with, and when I got older, I distanced myself from him on purpose."

"Yet you went to work for his firm." She studied his eyes, troubled and hurting, and knew there was more to this relationship than mutual disregard. "You should fix things with him, Alex. I mean it. It's important. Things aren't as bad as you think. Have you ever asked him what he thinks of you, your relationship?"

He laughed. "It would never occur to either of us to talk about our relationship."

"And that's funny?"

"It's just not something we would ever do."

"Well, I bet what he truly thinks would surprise you."

"Then why is it such a secret?"

"Maybe because he doesn't really know how to show his feelings for you."

"It's never been hard for him to show disapproval. That's a feeling."

"I bet he thinks the world of you and just doesn't know how to express it."

He smiled and kissed her temple. "You're always ready to believe the best in people."

"You should, too, when it comes to your own father. You believed something terrible about your mother and it turned out not to be true." She studied his face but couldn't tell if he believed it or not. The distant clock chimed, and after the ninth ring, Rosa sat straight up, clutching the sheets against her chest. "Damn it!"

"What?" Alex propped himself on his elbows.

"I have to go." She jumped up and started getting dressed. "I scheduled a meeting fifteen minutes from now."

"Aw, come on. Skip it."

"Can't. We're doing the final menu for Linda's wedding. Her mother-in-law-to-be made a special trip just for this."

"God, what I wouldn't give to steal you away," he said, wrapping his arms around her. "Far, far away."

Rosa reveled in his embrace. She wondered if he knew she'd follow him anywhere. If he asked her to move to New York, to London, to Hong Kong or Taipei or Mongolia, she would do it. She would walk away from everything she knew and everything she loved, because she loved Alex more.

Frightened and exhilarated by the thought, she grabbed her purse and rummaged for a hairbrush, managing to dump her wallet, PDA, cell phone and sunglasses in the process. "Damn it," she said again.

"Hang on," Alex said with resignation. "I'll help you." He pulled on his shorts and took the brush from her hand. "The world won't come to an end just because you're late to a meeting." With slow, rhythmic strokes, he brushed her hair for her.

She shut her eyes and dropped her head back, reveling in the searing intimacy of his touch. "That feels good."

"This whole morning has felt good."

"Remember the time you cut off my hair?"

He finished brushing, then bent and kissed her neck. "I remember everything."

She wanted to linger, but she broke away and began stuffing things back into her purse. "I really have to go."

The sound of a car door slamming came from below. She frowned. "Are you expecting someone?"

He looked a bit sick. Maybe an asthma attack was coming on. "Actually..."

"You need to sit down," she said. "I'll go tell whoever it is you're not feeling well." She hurried down the stairs.

He followed, yanking on his T-shirt and saying, "I'm okay, Rosa, but there's something—"

The front door opened and a tall, slender woman walked in carrying a large cardboard box. "Alex," she yelled, "Alex, I need some help with—oh." She set down the box with a thud.

It was Portia van Deusen, Alex's ex-fiancée. She recognized her from photographs—imposing and self-confident, with patrician features and designer clothes.

Portia's cool gray-eyed glare locked on Rosa as Alex made hasty introductions. "Portia is dropping off some things of mine," he explained.

"He left them in my apartment," Portia said. "We were engaged."

"I know," Rosa managed to admit. She had never suffered such a hideously awkward moment.

"We're not anymore," Alex pointed out.

"The rest of the stuff is in the back of the Land Rover," Portia said.

Grumbling, he headed outside.

"I was just on my way out," said Rosa. "I've got a meeting at work." This was too weird. She went to the door, eager to get out of there.

"Did he tell you why?" Portia asked suddenly.

Rosa froze with her hand on the doorknob. "Pardon me?"

"Why we broke up. Did he tell you?"

"Actually he's never mentioned you at all." Rosa felt evil as soon as the words were out of her mouth. Portia didn't deserve that.

She flipped back her silky hair. "He'd probably lie anyway. The truth is, he dumped me when I was pregnant with his child, and I miscarried."

Rosa nearly lost her frittata. "Oh, God... I'm terribly sorry." She looked across the driveway at Alex, who was pulling cardboard boxes out of the Land Rover. Dear Lord, was he capable of that? "I don't know what else to say. Please, excuse me," she said to Portia, and all but ran to her car.

Alex put aside the box he was carrying. "Rosa, I'm sorry. I knew she was coming, but I didn't think she'd get here so early." He studied her face. "Damn it. What did she say to you?"

Rosa couldn't even find the words. "I'm late, Alex."

He held open her car door. "I'll call you later."

"I really need to go." She bit her lip, trying to think of what else to say, but there was no time to sort things out. Besides, she wasn't sure she wanted to. If she sorted things out with him, she might have to deal with the truth—that she was falling in love with him, all over again.

She turned the key in the ignition and took off.

thirty-seven

Alex watched the love of his life take off, the top down on her red sports car, a white scarf covering her dark hair. She *was* the love of his life, and if there had ever been any doubt about that, there was not now. He knew with perfect clarity that they were meant to be together.

He wished she'd stuck around so he could explain about Portia. He vowed not to let the sun go down on this issue.

Swearing under his breath, he picked up a cardboard box of odds and ends—a basketball, some paperback novels, old CDs. "You should have thrown this stuff away," he said to Portia, setting the box on the porch. "You didn't have to go to this trouble."

"I wanted to see you."

He spread his arms wide and echoed something Rosa had once said to him. "Look your fill." He retrieved the last box from her Land Rover. "Thanks for bringing my stuff. Now, I've got work to do."

"The least you could do is offer me a cup of coffee."

"No, the least I could do is tell you I'm busy and so long."

Her eyes glittered with tears. "I miss you, Alex. Can't we just talk about getting back together?"

He felt a twinge in his chest. She was a piece of work, but he didn't enjoy hurting her. "No. We can't. Drive carefully."

She wiped the tears away with the back of her hand. "You won't be happy with that woman," she snapped. "Yes, Hollis told me all about her."

Great, he thought. Portia was like a bad fairy come to put a curse on his new connection with Rosa.

"She's not for you, Alex, and you'll find that out for yourself soon enough."

Like I found out about you? He didn't let himself say it aloud. He wasn't blameless in their fiasco of a relationship. He'd drifted into it thoughtlessly and hadn't bothered to figure out whether or not they were right for each other. His mother had been ecstatic, of course; she adored the van Deusens and couldn't wait for the nuptials. Neither, it seemed, could Portia. Alex had escaped by the skin of his teeth.

She stalked to her car and peeled out, spraying up gravel and crushed shells in her wake.

Alex went inside and shut the door, feeling a distinct twitchiness in his lungs. He took another puff on his inhaler and ran a hot shower. His docs put no store in the effects of warm steam, but it made him feel better.

As he was drying off, his cell phone chirped. Except that it wasn't his phone; the sound came from somewhere else. He followed it to the bed and found Rosa's phone in the tangle of bedclothes. The incoming call was from *Costello, Sean.* Alex frowned. The guy she'd dated, now the sheriff of South County. He didn't answer. It was none of his business, but it pointed up the fact that in so many ways, he and Rosa were still strangers.

At least, he thought, pulling on a golf shirt and clean shorts, he had an excuse to pay her a visit. He needed to see Rosa, to explain about Portia, to tell her it was going to be all right. *They* were going to be all right.

He would make sure of it, he thought as he sent a text message to her father. *We need to talk. Coming right over. Alex M.*

He loaded his pockets, then grabbed his inhaler, hesitated and stuck that in his pocket, too. Eager as he was to get to her, he had a stop to make on the way. Things wouldn't be right with her until he dealt with her father, one on one. Pete and Rosa were a package deal, and Alex intended to find a way to be all right with that.

Outside, the contractor's crew was just arriving. Repair and restoration on the carriage house seemed to be going well. He greeted the foreman, who was drinking Pegasus Coffee from a paper cup. "Good news, Mr. M," said the foreman. "We're going to finish on schedule. Just a few more weeks and we're done."

"That's great," said Alex. He got in his truck and headed inland, toward Pete's house. He felt like an awkward kid, vying for his girlfriend's dad's approval. But it had to happen, or he and Rosa didn't stand a chance.

When he turned the corner onto Prospect Street, Alex sensed something was amiss. He couldn't place it immediately. Then he looked up and his blood froze. There was black smoke streaming from a second-story window of Pete's house.

Even before his truck screeched to a stop by the curb he was thumbing 9-1-1 into his phone. There was an older lady standing on the sidewalk in front of the house.

"I called the fire department already," she said. "They're on their way."

Alex repeated the call and was told the ETA was three minutes. And sure enough, in the distance, he heard sirens. "Is he at home?" he asked the neighbor. "Is anyone in there?"

"I don't know. I didn't want… I was afraid—"

He took the front steps two at a time, tried the door and found it unlocked. Smoke alarms shrilled and blinked uselessly into the dense gray air. A wave of heat and acrid smoke hit him.

"Pete!" he yelled. "Pete!" Pete couldn't hear him, of course, but the dog could; a distant barking sounded from somewhere upstairs.

Blinded, gagging on smoke, he checked the downstairs rooms and then made his way upstairs. The middle room, the one that had been Rosa's, was ablaze, blasting him with light and heat. Pete knelt in the hallway, beating the roaring flames with a towel. His face was red in the firelight, his eyes terrified.

"Jesus, Pete!" Alex grabbed the old man's sleeve. "I've got you," he yelled, holding on. "Where's Joey? Is he home? Joey," he repeated.

"At work," Pete yelled.

Alex gave him a tug. "Let's go."

"Jake," Pete protested, pulling back. "Still in there."

Oh, Jesus, thought Alex, hearing ominous pops and hisses as the fire gathered momentum. "Get out," he said. He grabbed Pete's face between his hands and added, "I'll get the dog."

"No—"

"Go!" Out of patience, Alex half shoved him down the stairs. He thought he heard the sound of sirens drawing close. Hurry up, he thought. Hurry the hell up.

The terrified dog had scampered to a corner of the burning room and was barking at the flames. His eyes streaming and his lungs convulsing, Alex plunged after him. "I've got you," he said. "Come to Papa." He grabbed the dog and held it like a football, whirling toward the exit. Flames surrounded the doorway now, and the hallway outside was a river of fire.

Alex couldn't remember the last time he'd taken a breath. He staggered toward the window. Through the curtain of flames, he saw Rosa's photographs, books, a shell collection on a shelf. The source of the fire was a ceiling fixture, now a flaming hole.

He couldn't open the window one-handed, and he refused to set down the squirming dog, so he stepped back and put his foot through the glass. Maybe the noise would alert the firefighters.

The infusion of fresh air fed the fire, and it roared like a dragon behind him. He kicked most of the glass from the frame. Just a few feet below the window was the porch roof. He ducked out the window and stood in the light, the graveled roof seeming to undulate beneath him, swaying as he fought for breath. Something trickled down his back; he'd probably cut himself getting out.

When he opened his eyes, he saw a ladder touching the eaves. A firefighter in full bunker gear appeared, his face masked, his hands gloved. Jake growled in fear.

"Boy, am I glad to see you," Alex gasped, moving toward the ladder. He was dizzy and wheezing. He felt himself sway and stumble on the slanted roof.

"Easy, fella," the firefighter said. "We'll get you down."

"Take the dog," Alex said, handing it to him. "I don't feel so good."

As soon as the dog was nestled securely in the firefighter's arms, Alex felt an invisible wave slam into him.

His eyes rolled up in his head, his bones collapsed and he felt himself falling.

thirty-eight

Somewhere in town, sirens and truck horns sounded, but Rosa barely noticed. All through the meeting, she had felt Linda's stare taking her apart, piece by piece. Vince seemed equally curious, but when she glared across the table at him, he rolled his eyes to the ceiling, all innocence. It was disconcerting to say the least, and she tried to ignore them during the meeting.

They were seated around a table in the bar, and the beautiful nautilus shell was directly in her line of vision. Morning sunlight caused its delicate inner whorls to glow as though lit from within, and the sight of it made her think of Alex and the way they had been together this morning...until Portia showed up.

Portia, she thought. Portia Schmortia.

Rosa could barely sit still. She was relieved at the conclusion when everyone seemed thrilled with the menu for the reception: tinker mackerel alla Santa Nicola, penne pasta with tomato, arugula and mozzarella, arancini, pizette, egg pasta with lobster and asparagus, Guinea hen stuffed with vegetables and a towering Italian cream cake. As the gathering broke up and people wandered toward the coffee, Rosa walked Mrs. Aspoll and Mrs. Lipschitz to the door.

"You don't know how much fun this is for me," Rosa told them, "being a part of Linda's wedding. It's just like we planned when we were kids."

Mrs. Lipschitz beamed at her. "I remember the two of you in my nightgowns, parading up and down the stairs with flowers from your father's garden. I hope you know Linda has instructions to toss the bouquet directly at you."

Rosa gave a nervous laugh. "Honestly, if I got engaged every time I caught a bouquet, I'd be J-Lo. It doesn't work on me."

"It will at Linda's wedding, and it's about time. I'm so happy for you, dear." Mrs. Lipschitz gave her a hug and left the restaurant.

Rosa was seriously ticked off as she went in search of Linda and found her with Vince, leaning in close as Linda spoke rapidly.

"What's going on?" Rosa demanded.

The conversation stopped. Gazes lowered and feet shuffled.

"What?" she asked.

Vince said, "We were just discussing your sex life."

Her cheeks began to burn. "I see. And what, may I ask, is the nature of this incredibly high-minded discussion of my... sex life?"

"Well, mainly that you finally have one again."

She swallowed hard. No wonder people tended to leave their home towns. If you stayed too long, privacy went out the window. "And how would you know that?"

"Hel*lo*," said Linda. "You practically rolled out of bed to get to this meeting. Even my mom could tell."

Unconsciously, Rosa touched her hair and wondered feverishly if Alex had somehow marked or branded her in some visible way. "How is this your business?"

"We love you, Rosa, and we want to be sure you're not making a mistake."

"Whether or not I'm making a mistake is…" Rosa hesitated while stinging tears welled in her eyes. "It's too late. I've already made it." She covered her face with her hands. They pressed close, a human cocoon, murmuring with sympathy.

"What is it, honey?" Vince asked. "You can tell us. Don't keep it in."

"I ran into his ex," she said miserably, accepting a Kleenex from Linda. "She wanted me to know that he dumped her when she got pregnant with his child."

Linda gasped. "There's a child?"

"She miscarried."

"She's lying," said Vince. "I can smell it."

"Did you ask him?" Linda handed her another Kleenex.

"Yes. Well, no, not yet. It's not just that. We have bigger issues. Our values are so different. People like Alex and Portia van Deusen, they're a breed apart. They try on relationships like trendy outfits and discard them when they don't seem to fit anymore."

"And people like us don't do stuff like that?"

"*I* don't," said Rosa. "You should see that woman, Portia van Deusen. She's…perfect. Absolutely perfect. Beautiful, educated, stylish. She's everything a man like Alex needs, and he lost interest in her completely. When she was pregnant, no less. It makes me wonder how long he'd keep someone like me around."

"You're not her," said Vince.

"No. I'm shorter. Louder."

Linda burst out laughing. "And that matters?"

"Come on, Linda, you know better than that."

"Listen, don't judge his relationship with you by his relationships in the past."

"According to the most basic principles of psychology, past behavior is the single best indicator of future behavior."

"Well, according to me and everyone else here, you're not asking the key question."

"And what's that?"

"Do you love him, Rosa?"

She crushed the Kleenex in her fist. "I've always loved him. I probably always will."

"Then—"

"That doesn't mean I can be with him. How can I trust him with my heart?"

Linda handed her another tissue. "You have to ask yourself what is the bigger fear, that you'll get hurt again or that you'll walk away before you ever find out what could have been."

"Thanks, Dr. Lipschitz, but I don't like either of those options. I like my life just the way it is. I wish you guys would understand that."

"Ah, Rosa." Linda's eyes were damp, too. "You've already started to change. You think you have it all, but you're missing the only thing that really matters."

She looked from Linda to Vince. "You never liked him. And now you're trying to push me into this?"

"You said the magic words," Vince pointed out with a smile. "You said you love him. And he's not so bad. He's ready, Rosa. He's finally good enough for you."

A cell phone rang, and several people checked theirs. Rosa looked in her purse and frowned. Odd. It wasn't there. Maybe she'd set it down in her office, or in her car. As it turned out, Teddy's phone was the culprit. He took the call, retreating to a corner of the bar and lowering his voice.

Rosa stared long and hard at the nautilus shell behind the

bar. She heaved a sigh. "Whatever happened to happily ever after?"

"It's still an option," Linda assured her. "But you'll never get there if you don't take a risk."

"You could say the same about disaster."

"That's why it's a risk."

"I just can't—"

"Rosa, we've got to go." Teddy crossed the room in two strides and yanked open the door. "There's a fire at your father's place."

She raced Teddy out to his Jeep. They jumped in, and he peeled out of the parking lot. The ride to Prospect Street was the longest in all eternity. She hardened her spine against the back of the seat so she wouldn't collapse. She used Teddy's phone to try her father's cell, but got no answer. That could mean anything, she realized with a shudder.

"You're sure he's okay?" she asked Teddy.

"That's what I heard from the dispatcher."

"What happened?" she demanded.

"I didn't get much information. Started upstairs, I think he said."

"Oh, God. *Joey*."

"The kid's at work. You know that."

"Maybe it was bad wiring. Damn. I warned him about that. I should have taken care of it myself. But Pop's all right. You're sure you heard right."

"That's what I heard."

Things didn't look okay as they turned on to Prospect Street. A ladder truck blocked the way and a crew swarmed over the house. Flames licked from the upstairs windows. Neighbors gathered on the sidewalk across the way.

The most chilling sight of all was a red and white EMS vehicle, its lights rotating ominously, its rear doors wide-open.

Rosa gasped. "He's hurt."

"They're probably just here as a precaution," Teddy said.

She spotted a white Ford Explorer parked in the driveway. "That's Alex's truck. What the hell...?" She jumped out before Teddy came to a complete stop and jostled her way through the crowd. "Pop!" she yelled, wishing he could hear her. "Pop."

Then she saw him next to the rig, haggard but standing on his own, holding Jake in his arms, a bag valve mask against his face.

Rosa gave a cry of relief and ran to him. "Thank God you're all right." She hugged him and kissed the dog on the head. "What happened?"

When she stepped back to sign the question, she saw that something was wrong. Pop didn't look hurt, but his eyes were filled with sadness.

"It's just a house," she told him, knowing it was so much more. "We'll replace everything—"

"Rosa, I don't worry about the house," he said. "It's not that. It's—"

"Make way," someone yelled. "Step aside, please."

"Rosina," said Pop. "I am so sorry..."

"I don't understand..." She looked at Alex's car. It couldn't be him on that stretcher, strapped to a backboard and cervical collar, buried in fireproof blankets. It couldn't be.

She must have swayed or staggered a little, because Pop took her hand and held on tightly. Through a fog of dawning comprehension, she watched the EMS crew navigating a path toward the open rear doors of the ambulance. An EMT ran alongside the stretcher holding an IV bag high in the air. Someone else barked coded language into a radio. Another worked an automatic external defibrillator similar to the one they had at the restaurant.

Screaming, Rosa wrenched away from her father and lunged toward the ambulance. They wouldn't let her near. Still, she managed to catch a glimpse of the victim. Just barely, but enough to confirm what she already knew in the pit of her stomach.

thirty-nine

They wouldn't let Rosa in to see Alex because she wasn't immediate family. However, lacking any other source of information, the EMTs relied on her. As she stumbled through details in a flat, incredulous voice—age, weight, allergies, medical conditions, insurance coverage—it struck her how little she knew about him, this man who had just saved her father's life, this man she was afraid to love.

She felt numb with terror as she entered the hospital. She'd made this trip before, after a midnight phone call. This time, her father walked in on his own, submitting to tests as a precaution.

"I'm looking for Alex Montgomery," Rosa said to a nurse. "He was just brought in."

"I'll send someone."

Another nurse, this one harried-looking and studying reports on a clipboard, approached her. "You're with Mr. Montgomery?" she asked.

"Yes, I…we… Is he all right?"

"The doctors are evaluating him right now, ma'am." She flipped a page of the chart. "What was he doing prior to the fire?"

A trap door of guilt gaped open, and Rosa teetered on the edge. Just a short time ago, he had held her in his arms. She leaned forward and told the nurse, "He ate…a normal breakfast, eggs and fruit and coffee." She refused to hold anything back, so she added, "We were together, you know?"

The nurse's expression conveyed that she did.

"He seemed perfectly fine, but he did use his inhaler at least once. He's a chronic asthmatic, and this morning his lungs were twitchy," she added. "I told the EMTs about it."

"What time?"

"Early. I left him around nine-fifteen. Can I see him? Please?"

"I'll keep you informed, ma'am." The nurse made a note and went through the heavy double doors to consult with the doctor.

Rosa's father sat on a bed in a curtained area, still holding Jake. Pop looked grim, his face ashen with regrets as he gave a statement to a man with a notebook. "It was an accident," he said, "but it shouldn't have happened. I knew the wiring was bad. I got a neighbor, Rudy, who's an electrician. I was supposed to have him check it out. It completely slipped my mind."

Rosa clutched at the curtain frame. She thought about the night Joey had told her about Pop's forgetfulness. Just getting him a dog wasn't enough; she should have known that.

"It didn't seem so bad at first," Pop went on. "I tried putting it out myself, didn't know it would spread so quick. When the curtains caught fire, I called 9-1-1. And Jake, he panicked and ran off. I could not leave the house without him. If Alexander had not arrived, both Jake and I might not have made it out."

Rosa shut her eyes as her father finished making his statement.

"There was a great cheer when we saw them both on the roof," he went on. "Alexander gave Jake to a firefighter and then…"

Rosa opened her eyes to see that her father was weeping again.

"Then something happened. He fell. It was like somebody shot him. He collapsed and went off the roof. I'm sorry. So sorry."

Her father wanted to stay and wait for word about Alex, but Rosa put Teddy in charge of him, sending them to pick up Joey from work. They'd have to salvage what they could from Pop's house. After that they'd be staying with her until they figured out what to do.

"And you?" asked Pop, watching her with a terrible worry in his eyes.

"I'm staying here."

He nodded. "Of course." With those two words, he indicated his changed opinion of Alex. Rosa could see it in his expression.

"I'll let you know when I hear something."

"Yes. And Rosina—" He hesitated, then said, "It is… We will talk about it later."

"About what?"

But he didn't hear her. He was already heading for the door.

No one would give her a report on Alex's condition.

The charge nurse flicked a glance at the closed door of the exam room, a resuscitation bay surrounded by wire mesh glass. The area was so crowded with doctors and technicians that

Alex couldn't be seen. "They're still working on him. I promise, they're doing the best they can."

Rosa wondered if the nurse had any idea how unsettling her words and manner were. "Can you tell me if you managed to get hold of his father?" she demanded. "Can you at least tell me that?"

"I understand someone's on the way."

Rosa paced. She got a drink of water and paced some more. Then she searched her handbag for her phone and remembered it was missing. The nurse had said someone was on the way. She could only assume that meant Alex's father. His sister, Madison, was somewhere in Asia, and he didn't have any other family. Portia? Maybe she should be contacted. An ex-fiancée might qualify as family if she kept quiet about the "ex" part.

He needed *someone*. If she were in his position, she knew she'd draw strength from the presence of friends. Friends and family, surrounding her, supporting her, willing her to get better. She wanted that for Alex but she didn't know how to give it to him. His whole world was an alien planet to her.

As the minutes crawled by, more people showed up. Slowly, in small groups, they all came to see her, much as they had the night her father was hurt. Shelly and the guys from the restaurant. Mario and his family. Linda and Jason. They came because they loved her, and they wanted to be there for the man who had walked through fire for her father. She realized with a deep gratitude that these people were her whole world. They had propped her up through the bad times and celebrated the good.

She found herself remembering her vow this morning, which seemed an eternity ago. Only this morning, she'd believed she would follow Alex to the ends of the earth. Now she wondered how she could even think of leaving. This was the only place where life made sense.

Vince came to sit with her. Although she was grateful for his presence, the whole situation felt ghoulish, like a death watch. She and Vince were clutching each other in terror when the automatic doors swished open and a tall, elegantly dressed man hurried across the foyer, followed by Gina Colombo, Alex's assistant. Neither of them seemed to notice Rosa as they were whisked into the exam room.

Through the glass wall, she could only see Alex's father from behind. He was broad-shouldered and athletic-looking. At first glance, he seemed to possess the graceful, emotionless demeanor of an android. She quickly realized it wasn't true. Those big shoulders were very expressive. As she watched, they drooped and then shook violently.

It took a minute for her to find her voice. "That's his father," she told Vince.

His arm slid around her. He didn't say anything, didn't try to assure her that everything would be all right. He knew she'd stood right here in the same waiting room twelve years before, not knowing if her father would live or die and then learning that he would exist in some shadowland between the two, perhaps forever. So Vince knew better than to offer reassurances before they had all the facts.

Mr. Montgomery was signing papers on a clipboard when Gina came out. In a business suit with a short skirt, she looked crisp and professional, but her face was ashen, her eyes troubled.

"They said you came in with him."

"Yes," said Rosa. "How is he?"

"Going up to ICU, that's how he is."

"Hey," said Vince.

Rosa waved her hand to settle him down. She could see the terror in Gina's eyes. Her anger was just a mask for an abject fear Rosa understood all too well. "Please, what's his condition?"

Gina seem to soften slightly. "The burns are minor but…
they need to do more tests for possible brain trauma. They're
worried about intracranial hemorrhage. He's been intubated
and hasn't been conscious since he was brought in."

Icy terror closed around Rosa. Her father had suffered brain
trauma. It had taken him two years to get better. "I want to
see him."

"You can't," said Gina.

Rosa walked away to peer through the glass. There was a
screen around the gurney so she couldn't see much. She stood
watching the team getting ready to move Alex. His father hov-
ered, looking helpless. Then someone pushed the screen out
of the way, and she could see Alex at last, but only a little. She
caught a glimpse of soot on his forehead, like an Ash Wednesday benediction. The top of the laryngoscope and the Ambu-
bag obscured the rest of his face. He was missing one tennis
shoe. There was a cut on his cheekbone right where she had
kissed him this morning.

Only this morning, but so long ago.

She leaned her head against the glass, tormented, feeling
Mr. Montgomery's eyes on her but physically unable to move.
Then he turned away from her and she saw him, that inat-
tentive husband, that cold unfeeling father, bend and press a
kiss on Alex's soot-smudged forehead, then squeeze his son's
hand. When he straightened up, his lips were moving rapidly
in what could only be a feverish, desperate prayer.

Behind her, Vince and Gina were conferring like thieves.

Rosa watched the room empty out as a pair of orderlies an-
gled the gurney through a wide door and down a gleaming
hallway. Nurses and technicians wheeled the accompanying
bags and monitors alongside the gurney. Speaking rapidly, a
doctor directed traffic. Mr. Montgomery followed, his head
bowed. The empty room looked ransacked, like a crime scene,

with tubes left hanging, blue and white packaging on the floor, trays of instruments everywhere.

Vince touched her on the shoulder. "Honey, Gina needs to tell you something."

Rosa nodded, resigned to whatever the snappy, defensive woman might have to say to her. It was clear that Gina was devoted to Alex. Rosa was glad he had people in his life who loved him. She found herself wishing he had more.

"There's something you should know about Alex and Portia van Deusen," Gina said without preamble.

That. It seemed like an eternity had passed since Portia had told her about the pregnancy. Rosa whipped a glance at Vince. The big mouth. But it was too late now; Gina obviously knew something. Rosa folded her hands and waited.

"Whatever happens with Alex," said Gina, "I don't want you believing what Portia told you."

Rosa flicked another glance at Vince. "You shouldn't have—"

"Yes, he should. Because Portia lied. I'm not supposed to know anything about this, but… What can I say? I'm his closest friend." She looked around the waiting area, which was deserted except for the three of them. "Portia was never pregnant. She lied and said she was so Alex would marry her."

Rosa took a moment to catch her breath. "That's the oldest trick in the book."

"It's old because it works," said Gina. "Especially on an honorable man who wants to believe the best of people. When they were dating, Alex didn't have the first thought about marrying her, but the minute she said she was carrying his child, he offered."

"It's diabolical, really," Vince said. "Once she gets a ring on her finger, there's a miscarriage, but she's still got her rich husband. I saw that once on *Dynasty*."

"When Alex figured out what Portia was up to," said Gina, "he ended the engagement. He let her act like she broke it off, you know, to save face."

"How did he figure out she was lying?"

"I figured it out. You could ask me how," Gina said, "but there's a gentleman present."

"I guess we saw the same episode of *Dynasty*," said Vince.

"Gina, why are you telling me this?" asked Rosa.

"Because he's the best man I know. I don't ever want his integrity questioned. If something happens to him...if he doesn't—" Gina's voice broke and she stared at the floor, pinching the bridge of her nose. "I just think he'd want you to know the truth about that situation, but he's too much of a gentleman to tell you himself."

Hours later, most people had left. That was when Rosa noticed Mr. Montgomery across the hall in the gift shop, staring unseeingly at the last remaining copy of *Investors Business Daily*. She squared her shoulders and went over to him.

"Mr. Montgomery?" She was surprised by the hesitation in her own voice.

He replaced the newspaper in the rack and turned to her stiffly. "Yes?"

"I'm Rosa—"

"I know who you are," he said.

She took a deep breath. In all the years she'd known Alex, she had never actually had a conversation with Mr. Montgomery. Now she knew why. He was formidable. "Sir, I want you to know how grateful my family is to Alex for what he did."

"I'm sure they're extremely grateful."

"And I've been waiting all day to find out how he is. I know I'm not his family, but I..." She took another breath, this one deeper than before. "I'm not leaving."

He studied her as though she was a lab specimen with an unusual growth. She could see Alex in his face, in the sharp cut of his jawbone, the blue eyes, the abundant sandy-colored hair, the broad shoulders. Yet the expression on his face was that of a stranger, a disapproving stranger. She found herself wishing she wasn't wearing the tight red pants, the polka dot halter top, the red high-heeled sandals.

Without taking his eyes off her, he reached down for his briefcase and stalked toward the main exit. "Come with me," he said.

He led the way outside, taking out a cigar in a yellow-and-red tube. She followed him past a sand-filled ashtray where a few people stood around, smoking cigarettes with a slightly shamefaced air. Mr. Montgomery was unapologetic as he lit his cigar.

"He had a severe asthma attack, probably induced by smoke inhalation. That caused him to lose consciousness while on the roof, and at that point, he fell and went into cardiac arrest. There are some broken ribs. What the doctors are most worried about is the intracranial hemorrhage. If he doesn't regain consciousness…"

The briefcase dropped from his fingers as though he'd suddenly gone weak. It popped open and manila file folders fanned across the walkway, but he didn't seem to notice. She squatted down to put all the spilled files back.

"I'll get that," he said quickly, and with the speed of a man half his age, he scooped up the strewn papers and photographs.

In those few seconds, Rosa had seen…something. A notice on letterhead from the South County Sheriff's Office. Some grainy eight-by-ten color photographs, close-ups. She burned with curiosity but there was no way to ask him anything without seeming hopelessly nosy.

He shut the case with a decisive snap. "They advised me to contact the rest of the family. That can't mean anything good."

He sank down on the heavy cedar bench and dropped his head into his hands. The cigar seemed forgotten between his fingers.

"What can I do?" Rosa asked, trying not to feel panicked by his despair. "Is Gina still here?"

"No. I told her I'd be in touch."

"Can I call your daughter for you?"

"She's overseas and her cell phone is useless. I left her a message and sent her email."

Rosa had a strange urge to reach out to him, maybe pat him on the shoulder. She didn't dare. Here was a man who was all alone, his wife gone, his daughter away, his son on life support, his friends weirdly absent.

She sat down on the bench, took the barely smoked cigar from him and stuck it in the sand ashtray. Then she drummed up her courage and put her hand on his arm. "I'm not leaving you. I'm going to stay here until Alex gets better."

"I certainly can't stop you."

Rosa gritted her teeth. "Listen, I don't need for you to like me, just to understand that I love him every bit as much as you do."

Mr. Montgomery hung his head. "I never should have let him come here after his mother—" His voice broke and he cleared his throat.

"He's a grown man," she reminded him. "It wasn't a question of you letting him do anything. It was his choice."

"I've never understood the appeal this place has for him, why it keeps drawing him back, again and again, even though he could go anywhere in the world."

"Don't you have a place like that?"

He lowered his hands and looked at her as though she'd

spoken in a foreign tongue. "I'm not a sentimental man, Miss Capoletti."

"This is not about being sentimental," she said. "It's about finding your home, the place where you belong."

"Alexander is a Montgomery. He doesn't belong in some backwater resort town. If he had stayed where he belongs, none of this would have happened." He gestured angrily at the looming facade of the hospital building.

Rosa sniffed. "If you stay in bed every morning and never get up, nothing will ever happen to you. But that's no way to live."

He glared at her. She braced herself, thinking he would lash out again. He didn't. His expression remained fierce as he said, "I can see why my son likes you."

She didn't know what to say to that; it sounded more like an accusation than a compliment.

forty

Pretty much everything Grandpop owned was in the back of the old pickup truck, lumbering toward the other side of town, where Aunt Rosa lived. Joey adjusted the passenger side mirror and looked at the depressingly small load, mainly from the garage, which had survived the fire and subsequent dousing with water and foam. Jake perched on the seat between them, checking out each car as it passed.

Joey had lost everything, too, but fortunately that didn't amount to much, though he'd miss his clothes and laptop computer. The telescope, which Alex had returned to him after the night at Watch Hill, had been in the garage. Still, it was the creepiest feeling in the world to come home for lunch and find the street blocked by emergency vehicles, the upper story of the house stark against the sky, like a black skeleton.

His cell phone rang and he looked at the display. He leaned forward so Grandpop, who was driving, could see him. "It's my folks," he said. "Again." Then he took the call. "Hello?"

"Is everything all right?" his dad asked.

"Same as it was five minutes ago when you called," said Joey. Since the fire, he'd talked to his parents at least five times.

"I won't apologize, sport," said his dad. "This is serious stuff. How does Grandpop seem to you?"

"He's still all right. I swear it, Dad. He's got his dog and his pipe to smoke, and we're taking some stuff over to Aunt Rosa's place. We're going to stop at the hospital to see how Alex is doing, and then we're having dinner at Celesta's." Sheesh, thought Joey. How many times did he have to go through this?

"I requested leave," said Dad. "Tell Grandpop I'll be there this weekend. And I just got through to Uncle Sal. He's going to be there too."

"Great. Have you seen Aunt Rosa's apartment?" Joey said. "It's got, like, four rooms, total."

"We'll work things out when we get there."

"Fine. I have to go, Dad. We just pulled into the hospital."

"Okay, sport. Listen, you tell Alex I said thank you a million times."

"Got it, Dad. You bet."

Grandpop parked and put Jake on his leash.

"If they let you in to see him," Joey said, "you should tell him thank you."

"He knows he has my gratitude."

Joey glared at him. Alex was a good guy, but Grandpop never wanted to see that. The old man's scowl deepened. Joey didn't flinch. Then Grandpop said, "You have *la vecchia anima*, Giuseppe. You are wise beyond your years."

"Well, somebody in this family has to be."

They found Aunt Rosa on the covered walkway in front of the hospital, talking to some tall guy in a business suit. She got all nervous when she saw them, and introduced the guy as Alexander Montgomery, Alex's father.

"I hope your son is well," Grandpop said.

"He's in intensive care," said Mr. Montgomery, who looked like a cold fish. "We're waiting to hear."

Like most people, Mr. Montgomery wasn't used to talking to a deaf guy, and Joey could tell Grandpop hadn't caught what he said. He nudged Grandpop and mouthed "waiting to hear."

"Well," Mr. Montgomery said in a clipped, sort of distracted way. He glanced down at the briefcase in his hand. "Well, I certainly don't know what to say at this point, but there is something else you should—"

"Mr. Montgomery?" A woman in pink scrubs hurried toward him.

"Yes?" He had the look of a man facing a firing squad.

"Could you come with me, please? You're needed in the ICU right away."

forty-one

Sirens and glaring lights. The hiss and roar of water rushing through hoses, the crackle of flames, blazing heat… Alex lay helpless under the bombardment. He felt strangely immobile, his limbs encased in concrete, his throat rigid.

"…hear me, Alexander? Squeeze my hand if you can hear me."

Why would I do that? He spoke but no sound came out. His whole throat was intensely sore. He tried to claw at it, but someone held both his hands.

"Open your eyes." The stranger's voice sounded painfully loud.

He tried to drag his eyes open, but when he did, a piercing glint of fiery white light drilled straight into his head, and he ducked for cover.

"Alexander, do you know where you are?"

Enough, already. With a supreme effort of will, he opened his eyes and glared at his tormentor. Actually, there were four of them, maybe more.

What the hell...

"You're at the hospital, Alexander," said the woman with the grating voice. "There's a tube in your throat to help you breathe. Now that you're awake, we want you to breathe on your own." She spread a plastic sheet like a dropcloth over him and placed an enameled basin on his chest. Someone's hands clamped around either side of his head. "When I say three, we'll get that tube out. One, two, three..."

Alex gagged, feeling something in his throat that shouldn't be there. The something moved, slowly and sickeningly at first, then was ripped from his throat with startling violence.

He gagged some more and then puked. The nurse seemed unperturbed as she took away the basin. She swabbed his face and removed the plastic sheeting. He lay back, gasping, and lifted his hand in supplication. There were strips of white Velcro on his fingers and a clear tube going into the top of his hand. *I feel like shit,* he wanted to say, but no words came out.

He took a deep breath and felt himself cracking in two. A moan of pain escaped him.

"I'm Dr. Turabian," said the woman. "We're glad you decided to join the party. You've got some cracked ribs. That's the pain you're feeling. You went into cardiac arrest and you've got a head injury, but you were pretty darned lucky. You won't be able to talk for a day or two."

I don't feel lucky. She was right; he had no voice at all.

She handed him a white marker board with a marker on a string and a cloth. "Now, there might be some short-term memory loss. After we get you cleaned up, we'll be asking you some questions."

She did something with a monitor while the nurse swabbed salve on his lips. "The EMTs said you were quite a hero. You were the only one hurt in the fire. The older gentleman and his dog are fine."

Thank God, thought Alex. Thank God. Pete was all right. The dog made it. Sweet relief poured through him.

The nurse finished cleaning up and they both left, leaving the door slightly ajar. Time passed. Alex didn't know how much. He studied the monitors, but for all their buzzing and humming, he couldn't find a clock on any of them. He wondered what day it was. The same day he had made love to Rosa?

"Alexander?" His father's bulk filled the doorway of the cramped white room. He approached the bed and loomed over Alex, obliterating the glare of the high-powered overhead lights. "Son, thank God you're all right."

Alex took a moment to assimilate everything. It felt surreal to have his father here, holding his hand, no less. Maybe Alex was on drugs. Hallucinogens.

Just in case it wasn't a weird vision, Alex scribbled "Thx 4 coming."

Then something even weirder happened. At first Alex thought his father was choking or gagging. Then he was stunned to realize he was crying. To Alex's knowledge, his father had never cried. Not even when they laid his wife to rest.

Are you... Alex grimaced in frustration at his inability to talk. He wrote "U OK?" and tapped the white board.

"Yes." His father took the ornamental silk handkerchief from his breast pocket and scrubbed his face with it. "You gave me a scare, son. I didn't think I'd lose it like that. This kind of took me back, you know, maybe that's it."

Alex sent him a questioning look.

"To when you were little. We were in and out of the emergency room so many times."

"Felt routine to me," Alex wrote.

"Not to your mother and me. Each time, we were terrified they wouldn't get you breathing again. And each time, it killed me a little. Just now, it all came back. The incredible fear of losing you."

Stunned, Alex thought he'd heard wrong. His dry lips cracked and stung with the effort to offer a reassuring smile. "Not going anywhere."

They sat together for a while. Alex could not remember such a comfortable silence between himself and his father. It was a strange finish to a strange day. Contrary to the doctor's warning, he had no trouble remembering every detail. Things had started out pretty damned great, he recalled, thinking of Rosa. After making love to her, he knew the day couldn't possibly get better. But it got worse in a hurry.

His father handed him a plastic water bottle with a straw. "Dr. Turabian says you're moving to a regular room in the morning if all your vitals check out. You can have visitors once you're moved. There are some people waiting to see you."

Alex frowned.

"Rosa Capoletti, for one. She's charming. I expect you've always known that. And there's a young man with pink hair and Gina's here, as well. And Pete Capoletti, of course. But they can't visit you in the ICU. Once you're moved to a private room, you can have visitors if you feel up to it."

"Of course I feel up 2 seeing Rosa," he scrawled.

"I hope you look better in the morning," his father said bluntly. "And you smell like an incinerator."

Now, that's the dad I know and love, Alex thought, his lips cracking as he smiled.

"I could bring you some things. Clean clothes, a razor and toothbrush."

Alex took a sip of water and nodded as much as he was able. Then he wrote, "Rosa?"

"I spoke to her at length. Delightful girl. I always thought so."

"BS," Alex wrote.

"I did." He seemed agitated and restless in the small room. "It was your mother who objected to her. And speaking of your mother, we have several things to discuss."

"M...? She has nothing to do with today."

"On the contrary, she has everything to do with it." Alex's father stopped and stared down at his hands, turning them palms up in his lap, looking bewildered.

Alex tapped on the word "Mother" again.

His expression grim, his father took a thick file folder from his attaché case.

forty-two

"Whoa, wait a minute, slow down," said Rosa, alone with Alex in his flower-filled private room. Sunshine flooded through the slats of the venetian blinds. No one but his father had been allowed to visit him the previous night; ICU visiting rules were strictly enforced. "You lost me after the storm damage."

Alex smiled at her from the bed. He was sitting up, wearing a pajama top printed, disconcertingly, with the Playboy bunny symbol. Furnished, he claimed, by his father. A singed right eyebrow gave him a perpetually quizzical look.

"When that tree fell on the shed on our property and took out a power line, they had to tow my mother's old car—the blue Ford that had been parked there forever." His voice was raspy and whisper-soft from a throat damaged by the breathing tube. "Your friend Sean Costello noticed something about the car."

He handed her a glossy photograph of a right front fender with a long yellow scratch. "Sheriff Costello has a good memory. He was a rookie deputy the night your father was hit, but he remembered Pete rode a yellow bicycle. The tire treads match the marks, too." He indicated a manila file folder. "Costello expects everything to be verified by the state crime lab, but it's not a priority case since it…since she…"

Finally, with a queasy sense of certainty, Rosa understood. "Oh, no. Sean thinks…?" She couldn't even finish the thought.

"It was a hunch. He paid a visit to my mother in Providence. She claimed she didn't know a thing. Then the next day, she took her own life."

"Oh, Alex. Oh, my God." Rosa sank down on the swivel chair beside the hospital bed. She shut her eyes as anguish welled up. Mrs. Montgomery had been drinking that night; Pop had been trying to help her. She must have followed him, though Rosa could not fathom why. She was hysterical, her father had said. Who knew what she was thinking? She'd hit him by accident, surely. Rosa couldn't help but wonder what Mrs. Montgomery had been feeling that night, knowing she was responsible for such a terrible thing. What was it like, Rosa wondered, to live with that kind of guilt for so many years?

Judging by the way Emily Montgomery had ended her life, it had been torture. "Alex," she said, "I had no idea."

"No one did. That was what she wanted. Appearances at any cost. Even if it meant living in hell for the rest of her life."

Rosa let out a soft gasp. "You can't let yourself be angry at her anymore, Alex. Everything she did was out of love for you. She made terrible choices, but she had the best of intentions."

"She ruined your father's life and destroyed herself, and you want me to forgive that?"

He was trying to put her off with his fury; Rosa could see that now. Along with the flash of rage in his eyes, she saw a glint of tears. That's good, she thought. Finally.

With slow deliberation, she took his hand between hers. "Yes," she said, "I do."

★ ★ ★

Alex felt her sympathy like blows from a hammer, and the pain took him by surprise. He wrenched his hand away, unable to bear her touch. Still, her words, uttered with calm deliberation, cracked straight through to his heart, and his grief burst wide-open. For the first time since that blood-freezing early-morning phone call at the beginning of the summer, Alex came apart. All the rage and devastation inside him welled up and erupted, and his body convulsed with shuddering sobs.

His mother was gone. She'd driven him crazy all his life, and the way she had died would torture him forever. He shook with a violent, angry grief, the harsh sobs clawing at his throat. He wept for his mother and all the ways he'd failed her. He wept for the happiness that had slipped through her fingers, and he wept because he'd never been able to change that.

He had the presence of mind to turn away. "Shit," he said when he could finally talk. "I didn't mean to do that. God, that's embarrassing."

Rosa sat quietly by, waiting. She didn't reach out to him, but she didn't leave either. "Are you all right?"

He used the bedsheet to wipe his face. "That's the first time I've cried for my mother," he said. "It's the only time."

"You should have done that long ago." She seemed completely unperturbed by his breakdown.

Alex lay back against the pillow. His head throbbed. He felt drained and exhausted, but for the first time since his mother's death, he felt a certain quiet in his heart.

"I'm so, so sorry." She put her hand over his again, and this time he didn't take it away.

"Yeah," he said. "Me, too. I need to talk to your father. I don't know what I'm going to say to him, though." His mother had left him and his father to deal with the broken pieces she had left behind. He had no idea how to begin doing that.

Knowing the true nature of the issue between his mother and her father hadn't put his guilt at ease. He felt weak and shaken as he put away the photographs and paperwork. "I need to tell your father I'm sorry. God, that's so inadequate. I was there that night. I heard them, and I thought the worst. Then I turned around and took off. If I'd stuck around, they never would have—"

"Don't, Alex. It's over. It's in the past and we can't change it."

He brought her hand up and pressed it briefly, fiercely, against his lips. "Then let's talk about something else. Let's talk about the future."

She tried to pull her hand away. "Not now," she said. "You need to get better. Alex—"

He kept hold of her hand. He had broken down and cried in front of her, and she had watched him with a sense of awe. And in that moment, he could see everything in her eyes— regret and pain and hope and…love.

"Just listen, okay?" he said. "I need to ask you something."

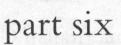

part six

DOLCI

Dolce is Italian for sweet, and it applies not just to music and food, but also to life itself. Just as every meal should end with something sweet, so should every life be filled with *il dolce*.

Torta Crema (Italian Cream Cake)

1 stick unsalted butter, softened
1/2 cup shortening
2 cups sugar
5 eggs, separated
2 cups flour
1 teaspoon soda
1 cup buttermilk
1 teaspoon vanilla
1 cup flaked coconut
1 cup chopped pecans

Cream the butter and shortening, add the sugar and beat some more. Add egg yolks and beat. Mix flour and baking soda, and add alternately with buttermilk. Stir in vanilla, coconut and pecans. Fold in stiffly beaten egg whites. Pour batter into three well-greased round cake pans or a 13 x 9 x 2-inch baking pan. Bake at 350°F for 40 to 45 minutes, until a stick of dry spaghetti inserted in the middle comes out clean. Cool before frosting.

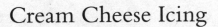

Cream Cheese Icing

1 package cream cheese, softened
1/2 cup pure unsalted butter, softened
1 box powdered sugar
1 teaspoon vanilla
Chopped pecans and coconut

Beat cream cheese until smooth. Add butter and sugar, then stir in vanilla and beat until smooth. Frost cooled cake in pan or in layers. Top with chopped pecans and coconut. Serve with good strong coffee, or espresso if you have the equipment.

forty-three

The groom was going to faint; Rosa was sure of it. As she gazed into his endearingly nervous face, she saw that he was sweating a little, and his eyes darted with barely suppressed trepidation. She could tell he wanted to get this right.

She knew he was wondering—*Should I smile as I say my vows? Say something original, or is that too hokey?*

Go for it, she wanted to urge him. Don't be afraid. Nothing's too hokey when it's true love.

Rosa held her breath while he struggled with a moment of panic. His hand shook a little as he took the ring from the satin pillow.

Silly man, thought Rosa. He had no reason to be nervous. Didn't he know their love would last forever and a day?

She sneaked a glance around, even though she was supposed to be paying attention. There was nothing, she thought, quite like the feeling of being with everyone you love on the most perfect day that had ever dawned. Rob and Gloria were present, both resplendent in full dress uniform. Pop and Joey summer by the sea

stood between them, beaming at her and then at Alex. Sal was officiating, his deep voice reverberating through the church.

Come on, she thought, her heart pounding with anticipation. Go for it. Just say the words. Just say it. *I do.*

Such a simple phrase, but so filled with mystery and magic, faith and uncertainty. For a second, a heartbeat, she was terrified that he'd chicken out. Then she saw his mouth form the words. *I do.* He spoke with all the depth of love she could see in his eyes. Wedding guests shifted in their chairs to look on fondly.

Beside Rosa, the bride's sister let out a loud sob.

"Rachel, for Pete's sake," Rosa whispered out of the side of her mouth. "Not so loud. We want to hear them—"

"...pronounce you husband and wife," said Sal in a triumphant voice. The music swelled and the happy couple turned to face the world as a married couple. Rosa saw the joyous love in their eyes and felt a flood of affection for them both. That and the sense that, finally, everything was as it should be.

At that point Rosa lost it, too, weeping with happiness for her best friend, Linda, and for Jason, who looked as though he'd just won the lottery. She mustered her courage, if not her dignity, and handed Linda the bridal bouquet for the recessional. Then Rosa took the proffered arm of Jason's brother to follow them down the aisle while the music swelled romantically. As she walked past Alex, she knew her whole heart was in her eyes.

Two weeks after the fire, he looked wonderful, the cut on his cheek nearly healed and his right eyebrow growing in nicely. She still couldn't believe what he'd asked her, right there in the hospital, only a day after he'd been brought back from the dead, literally. He'd asked her if her father's home had been insured, and when she told him it wasn't, he'd made an incredibly generous offer. He wanted Pop to live in the re-built quarters on his property.

"Isn't that a little ghoulish?" Rob had asked. "After all, it's where she left the car she was driving the night she creamed him."

Sal had a different take on it. He had listened to the story from Rosa, from Pop and even from Alex. "Let Pop decide," he'd said. "They've both got some mending to do."

Under the August sun, there was a glorious shower of bird seed, a lengthy pause for photos, then a limousine cavalcade to the reception. After the short ride, Rosa stepped out of the limo and felt a thrill of anticipation. The deck of Celesta's-by-the-Sea was festooned with white net bunting and satin rib-bons. The weathered sign by the entrance had a special notice: Closed For Private Event.

"This is our first, you know," she said to Alex. "Our first wedding reception."

"It's going to be perfect," Vince said with confidence. "The 'Best Place to Propose' is good for other things, too."

She felt Alex looking at her, and when she saw the pride in his eyes, she nearly wept again with happiness. This, she thought as she took his hand and led the way inside, this was what she'd been missing all her life. She used to believe she had it all, but that was just a smokescreen. She needed more. *Deserved* more.

She stopped in the foyer of the restaurant, which had been decorated with swags of white silk roses. The portrait of her mother by the podium had its own little garland over the top of the frame. *Hi, Mamma,* she thought. *It's a new day.*

Rosa turned to Alex. "I love you," she said. "You know that, right?"

"Yes," he said, "absolutely. And, Rosa—"

"There you are," said Leo, emerging from the kitchen, the

thick doors flapping behind him. "We just ran out of polenta, and none of the table candles have been lit. Butch is fit to be tied."

Rosa gritted her teeth in frustration, but held it in. If she freaked out, everyone would follow her lead. She let go of Alex's hand. "I'll just be a few minutes."

"Sure."

Arriving guests soon filled the deck, the bar and the dining room, and Rosa headed for the kitchen. Tying an apron over her bridesmaid's dress, she ordered someone to light the candles, then pitched in, finding a sack of cornmeal and setting it on to simmer herself. Within a relatively short time, things were under control, and she peeled off the apron.

The party was in full swing in the dining room, the ensemble playing, guests sitting down to a wedding feast they'd tell their grandchildren about. Rosa sat with the wedding party, but she scarcely ate as she scanned each table, making sure the salad was perfect, the entrée impeccable, the champagne flowing. People raised their glasses in toast after toast, and Linda and Jason looked ready to burst with joy.

Alex looked surprisingly at ease, seated with her father and brothers and Joey, whose hair was now back to its normal shade and length. Jake the dog slept under the table near Pop's feet. At Linda's insistence, Gina Colombo, Hollis Underwood and Mr. Montgomery had come to the reception. Only a few weeks ago, the combination of personalities at that table would have seemed bizarre, but now, everything was as it should be.

And then the simple truth dawned on her. She finally acknowledged that it didn't matter who you were or where you came from. Love and respect put everyone on equal footing.

After dinner and countless toasts, couples crowded the dance floor. The best man claimed Rosa for a dance, and she was swept into the festivities. The next hour was filled with laughter and dancing, with greeting people and making introductions. She caught a glimpse of Alex a time or two, but never quite managed to connect with him. Every time they started across the room toward each other, one of them would be waylaid en route. Finally, after another hour had passed, she felt a pair of strong, familiar arms around her.

"I haven't had this much trouble catching something since my father took me fly fishing in Vermont," said Alex, smiling down at her.

"You never told me your father took you fly fishing."

"I'll put it on the list. May I *finally* have this dance?"

She laughed. "My feet are killing me."

"I could always take you straight to bed."

The laughter stopped, but the smile remained. "That's tempting, but I'll tough it out. They're playing 'Fly Me to the Moon.' We can't miss out on that." She felt his hands skim over her bare shoulders and sighed with happiness as they moved onto the floor.

His arms tightened around her. "I feel like I need to make an appointment to talk to you."

"What would you like to talk about?" she asked, inhaling his scent, practically floating. Her feet didn't hurt at all anymore.

"Sweetheart, I think you know."

She hid a smile against his chest. Please, let her instincts be right this time. She sensed her whole life had been leading up to this moment, that everything that had happened to them had brought them here, finally. "You definitely don't need an appointment."

The piece ended, but before they could steal away somewhere, Ariel grabbed Rosa's arm. "It's time," she said, pulling her away from Alex.

"Time for what?"

Rosa didn't hear the answer as squeals went up from the female guests. The throwing of the bride's bouquet, of course. She aimed a helpless look over her shoulder at Alex as Ariel tugged her toward the stage. He grinned good-naturedly and stepped back to watch.

"I warn you, I have a wild pitch," Linda was saying to the women gathered around her. Then she beamed. "I wish for every one of you what Jason and I found today." She brought the beautiful pink and white bouquet to her face, then turned around and flung it up and over her back.

Rosa did not consider herself a superstitious person, but nothing—not one blessed thing—was going to get between her and those flowers. With a leap and a reach that nearly made her pop out of her bodice, she shot up in the air and snatched the bouquet. Amid hoots and whistles, she waved it in triumph.

Then she waved it again in the direction of Celesta's portrait. *How am I doing now, Mamma?*

Linda rushed down to give her a hug. "You did it, Rosa. Oh, I wanted it to be you. See?" she said to Vince and Teddy and anyone else who would listen. "Didn't I tell you?"

"We all told you," Vince added. "And we were right, weren't we?"

"Yes," said Rosa, holding the fragile bouquet against her heart. When she turned, she saw Alex coming toward her, weaving his way between the tables. In that moment, she didn't see anything but him. "Yes, absolutely."

★ ★ ★ ★ ★

Pasta with Garlic Scapes and Fresh Tomatoes

In Italy, you can find a garden anywhere there is a patch of soil, and in many areas, the growing season is nearly year round. It's common to find an abundant tomato vine twining up the wall near someone's front stoop, or a collection of herbs and greens adorning a window box. Other staples of an Italian kitchen garden include aubergine, summer squash varieties and peppers of all sorts. Perhaps that's why the best dishes are so very simple. Gather the fresh ingredients from your garden or local farmers' market, toss everything together with some hot pasta and serve.

In the early summer and mid-autumn, look for garlic scapes, prized for their mild flavor and slight sweetness. Scapes are the willowy green stems and unopened flower buds of hardneck garlic varieties. Roasting garlic scapes with tomatoes and red onion brings out their sweet, rich flavor for a delightful summer meal.

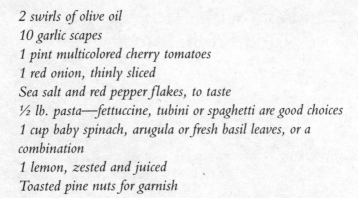

2 swirls of olive oil
10 garlic scapes
1 pint multicolored cherry tomatoes
1 red onion, thinly sliced
Sea salt and red pepper flakes, to taste
½ lb. pasta—fettuccine, tubini or spaghetti are good choices
1 cup baby spinach, arugula or fresh basil leaves, or a combination
1 lemon, zested and juiced
Toasted pine nuts for garnish

Heat oven to 400°F. Toss together olive oil, garlic scapes, tomatoes, onion, salt and pepper flakes and spread in an even layer on a parchment-lined baking sheet. Roast for 12–15 minutes, until tomatoes are just beginning to burst. If you have other garden vegetables, such as peppers, zucchini or aubergine, feel free to add that. Meanwhile, cook pasta according to package directions. Toss everything together with the greens, lemon zest and juice. Garnish with pine nuts. Serve immediately with a nice Barolo wine.

acknowledgments

As always, I'd like to acknowledge my ever-patient critique group: Rose Marie, Anjali, Kate, Lois, P.J., Susan, Krysteen and Sheila, for their talent, wisdom and courage to sample a number of culinary experiments. I'm deeply grateful to my agent, friend and champion Meg Ruley, and to Martha Keenan and Dianne Moggy of MIRA Books. *Molte grazie* to Mike Sharpe of Four Swallows Restaurant on Bainbridge Island, Washington, for patiently answering my many questions. And finally, a very special thank-you to my Uncle Tommy, who has no idea why I'm thanking him: you've never heard the sound of my voice, but you've always had my love, admiration and respect.

SUMMER
BY THE SEA

SUSAN WIGGS

Reader's Guide

mira

1. How do you think Rosa's life would have been different if she had been able to attend Brown University? What kind of career path do you imagine her following?

2. In a similar vein, do you believe that Rosa and Alex would have been able to sustain their relationship if she had joined him at Brown? Or do you believe that the various obstacles standing in their way (Alex's mother, different lifestyles and family values) would have eventually come between them?

3. The relationship between food and family plays a large role in the novel. Do you think that Rosa's memories of her mother cooking and taking care of her family were what truly inspired her to open her own restaurant?

4. In the novel, Mrs. Montgomery used the payment of Pete's medical bills as a means to keep Alex and Rosa apart. But after the discovery of her direct involvement in his accident, do you now have different thoughts about her motivations? And do you believe that Alex's childhood

illnesses and subsequent dependency on his mother made him more inclined to bow to her wishes?

5. Mrs. Montgomery and Mrs. Capoletti each took very different approaches to mothering. How do you think this shaped the people Alex and Rosa grew up to be?

6. Summer romances are part of growing up, particularly in summer tourism communities like Winslow. We see Alex and Rosa have a happy ending to what has essentially been a lifelong summer romance. How often do you think such romances blossom into something more? And do you see that possibility for Joey and Whitney?

7. Compare and contrast the roles that family relationships play in the lives of Alex and Rosa. How do you think their different experiences will influence their future as a couple and as potential parents?

8. Rosa and Alex are each forced to accept hard truths about their parents at several points in the novel. Discuss how growing up and learning to view your parents as "adult peers" changes family dynamics and interactions.

9. At the end of the novel, it's implied that the thought of her long-ago crime being brought to light was what compelled Mrs. Montgomery to take her own life. Do you think that, without that fear of discovery, events may have turned out differently for her? Or do you believe that there were other factors that prompted her actions?

10. Rosa and Alex have both led lives of privilege—she with a loving, supportive family to surround her, and he with more financial and social privilege. How does this affect the dynamics of their relationship and the way they relate to others?

11. What is the significance of the "souvenirs" (the nautilus shell and the mermaid's purse) that Rosa and Alex have held on to over the years?

12. Do you imagine Rosa and Alex staying in Winslow? What do you think their future together will be like?